D0009622
PINO

Hidden Passions

"Rob, I am no longer the girl you remember. I am just now realizing how much time has passed between us," Johanna said, her worry growing.

"Old, are you? Show me the gray that streaks your locks."

His teasing eased a tiny bit of her worry, and Johanna laughed. "Do you find any?" she asked, tilting her head toward him so he could view her braids.

"How can I tell when your hair is plaited so tightly?" he retorted.

Her smile grew as she loosened her hair until it flowed freely around her. "Now, do you find any?"

"Nay, not yet, but I am not finished searching." Rob brushed her hair over one shoulder, thus baring her nape.

"What are you doing?" she asked as he turned her head away from him.

He touched his lips to the sensitive skin of her nape. Johanna shivered against his caress, but heat soon returned to life throughout her body. "Do you find any?" she asked, almost breathless with what he was doing to her.

"Not yet," he replied as he kissed his way down to the collar of her white undergown. . . .

Denise Domning

A Love for All Seasons

A TOPAZ BOOK

To my nieces, Danielle, Melissa, and Katherine, who have been waiting impatiently to see their names in one of my books. Your Auntie Denise thanks you all for reminding her what it's like to be a little girl.

TOPAZ
Published by the Penguin Group
Penguin Books USA Inc., 375 Hudson Street,
New York, New York 10014, U.S.A.
Penguin Books Ltd, 27 Wrights Lane,
London W8 5TZ, England
Penguin Books Australia Ltd, Ringwood,
Victoria, Australia
Penguin Books Canada Ltd, 10 Alcorn Avenue,
Toronto, Ontario, Canada M4V 3B2
Penguin Books (N.Z.) Ltd, 182–190 Wairau Road,
Auckland 10, New Zealand

Penguin Books Ltd, Registered Offices:
Harmondsworth, Middlesex, England

First published by Topaz, an imprint of Dutton Signet,
a division of Penguin Books USA Inc.

First Printing, December, 1996
10 9 8 7 6 5 4 3 2 1

Printed in the United States of America

Author's Note

There was no standardization of date in the twelfth century. Clerks, depending on their affiliation, might name a day the first day in the first month of the first year of a particular monarch's reign. Or, a pope's. Or, an abbot's or bishop's rule. For common folk, it was the rotation of holy festivals that marked their days, e.g., the plow races on the first Monday after Epiphany or the first plowing done on Candlemas. A child was more likely to remember his or her saint day than his or her birthday.

It is for that reason that I chose to use saint days in delineating the events of this book. St. Agnes's Eve was an appropriate date to begin Rob and Johanna's reunion, for, by legend, this is the day when a woman divines her future husband. Of course, in Johanna's case, it is both a past and future husband.

For those who wish to know, the speaking of secret vows, as Rob and Johanna did, could actually be considered a legitimate marriage. There were cases where a charge of bigamy is used to separate a later marriage so the two who'd exchanged these sorts of vows could be reunited. The creativity of medieval couples in circumventing the patriarchal habit of arranging unions to suit the family, rather than the individual, never ceases to astound.

Now, as to the *horarium.* A monk's schedule was not necessarily fixed. Services flexed to fit the available daylight hours, longer in summer, shorter in winter. However, for the purposes of this book, I have given the hours a strict definition:

Matins	12:00	midnight
Lauds	3:00	A.M.
Prime	6:00	A.M.
Terce	9:00	A.M.
Sext	12:00	noon
None	3:00	P.M.
Vespers	6:00	P.M.
Compline	9:00	P.M.

Chapter One

Stanrudde
two hours past None,
The eve of Ste. Agnes's Day, 1197

Famine walked the land that winter. Folk thronged before the abbey's mossy arched gateway, waiting for bread not blessings. Children cried, women moaned. Men, their shoulders hunched against stinging sleet, jockeyed for better positions. There were so many, they packed the small field where the abbey held its yearly market, then spilled around the corner onto the coopers' lane, which followed the eastern edge of the holy house's walled compound. If some of the folk wore the ragged motley of the abbey's usual coterie of beggars, a far greater number dressed in the humble attire of the city's day laborers.

Johanna, wife to Katel le Espicer, yanked her plodding palfrey to a halt and stared in horror. "Mary, mother of God!"

From her pillion perch behind one of the five, following menservants, Johanna's maid freed a piteous, "Oh, mistress."

Shocked beyond response, Johanna could but stare at the crowded market field. If not as rich as London, Stanrudde was an affluent city, which should be able to take care of its own. "Theobald," she cried out to her husband's agent, who rode behind at the back of her husband's five menservants, "why are these folk not being fed from the town granaries?"

"Let me pass! Move, you witless oafs," Theobald of Peterborough snapped as he worked his horse from the back of this small troop. Like their servants, he wore the maroon and gray garments of Katel's house. When he came abreast of his mistress, he pushed back his sodden capuchin to reveal a delicate profile framed by a fringe of brown hair and a graying beard as he studied the crowd.

"There's naught left with which to feed them. Despite that, this thieving rabble persists in trying to take a share of what is not theirs by looting warehouses and breaking into the homes of decent tradesmen," Theobald spat out. His gaze swept over the rings gleaming atop Johanna's gloved fingers, then lowered boldly to what little was visible of her thick gold chain and her richest, if oft mended, blue-gray overgown between her cloak's edges. "Given the opportunity, they'd tear you apart for a chance at what you wear."

Turning in his saddle, Theobald looked at the servants behind them. "We ride on through. If any man reaches for you, kill him." Without so much as a by-your-leave, he leaned over and snatched Johanna's reins from her grasp, then spurred his horse into motion.

As her palfrey complacently followed where he led, Johanna turned her gaze downward to glare at the saddletree and indulged herself in hatred, for him, for his master, but mostly for this miserable life of hers from which there was no escape. Despite Katel's promise of the past summer, this morn he'd sent Theobald to force her from her convent retirement after she'd had only five months' peace.

They started into the crowd. No pathway opened for them. Theobald threw back his head. "Make way," he shouted, "make way for Katel le Espicer's wife!"

His call rebounded from the abbey's tall walls, then

dropped into the instant and unnatural silence that settled over the market field. Every eye turned on their well-fed betters. Of a sudden, Johanna could hear her palfrey breathe and the creak of saddle leather as the horses moved. Harness rings rattled; the icy rain hissed where it hit fabric and spat into the mud. Hostility rode the same damp breeze that brought her the stench of rotting meat from the shambles. A muted rumbling woke from the throng's far end, passing from mouth to mouth until it was a dark chant trapped between a dead and frigid earth and a leaden, uncaring heaven: the sound of her name.

Fear rose until it swallowed even her anger. She tugged her cloak more tightly around her and turned her betraying rings gem-inward to her palms. To die because of the pretentious finery Katel demanded she wear would be the most horrible of ironies. Only after the last of their troop rounded the corner of the abbey's stony perimeter and exited the coopers' lane for the chandlers' enclave did the crowd quiet.

Relief coursed through her. Never before had that small field seemed so broad or Stanrudde's folk so unfriendly. Someone yanked on her cloak's hem.

Johanna yelped in nervous reaction and turned in her saddle. At her palfrey's side stood Agnes, her former maidservant. Banished by Katel once his seed had taken root in her womb, the young woman's once lush dark hair now hung in damp, matted strings about her hollow-cheeked visage. Her shoes were naught but rags wrapped around her feet; only a threadbare blanket protected her and Katel's unwanted spawn from the rain.

The starving woman again caught her former employer's wife by the cloak him. "Mistress!" What remained of Agnes's life was invested in that single word.

At her cry, Theobald glanced behind him, his face twisting as he recognized his master's discarded leman.

He roweled around his mount and raised his hand to drive away the girl. "Get away, whore."

Trapped amid these horses and too worn by hunger to scream, Agnes could only turn her back to protect her child.

"Nay," Johanna cried, "you'll not strike one so hurt and helpless!" She spurred her palfrey until she stood between the starving woman and her husband's man.

Theobald, his hand yet held high in threat, glared at his mistress. "You know as well as I that whores like her are not allowed to approach household members. You'll move your horse and let me do as I must."

"Not this time." Johanna's words were as harsh as the wind whistling down the narrow lane. "I say you'll leave her be."

Theobald bared his teeth, his arm stiffening as if to strike her in Agnes's stead. "Do it," she goaded, straightening in her saddle until she glowered down at Katel's man from her superior height, "but think carefully over what you do. I am still your better. Strike me, and I will see you charged in court with assault, despite my husband."

Loosing a fiery breath of frustration, Theobald dropped his hand to his side. "I will tell the master what you have done."

"But, of course you must." Johanna lowered her wimpled head and retreated into the role of obedient wife that she'd played for all her marriage's sixteen years. "I would expect nothing less of you."

With a raging hiss, Katel's agent again turned his horse toward the city's center and the spice merchant's home. "Ride on," he shouted to the menservants.

Drawing her palfrey to one side, Johanna let the troop pass her. As they went, her maid and the menservants each shot her brief glances. She ignored them to wrench off one of her rings, then leaned down to press the bit of gold and stone into the starving woman's hand. "Take it with my blessing. I only pray it may be of some help to you. If any question the gift, send them to me."

Agnes clutched the treasure close to her heart, the thanks that filled her eyes making tears of shame sprout in Johanna's. "You were always kind, mistress, doing what you could. I know you would have aided me more if *he* allowed it." The searing emphasis in her voice left no doubt she meant Katel. With that, she darted away, clutching potential salvation close to her heart.

Johanna stared after her, guilt waking in her heart. But, she hadn't done more and not because Katel disallowed it. Indeed, she'd been grateful to leave her husband's bed to Agnes and all the other women Katel had used after the birth of her son in her second year of wedded bliss. Guilt grew. Ah, but if she'd been more of a wife to her husband, Agnes might not have needed her charity.

Johanna killed that bitter thought as she turned her palfrey's head toward the town's center and the house her father had built. It wasn't she who'd failed Katel, but he, her. If her husband had been a more forgiving man, theirs might have been a true marriage, instead of the mockery it was.

Not a soul stirred along the narrow lane, and the unusual quiet roused her from her bitter thoughts. Johanna glanced around her. Set wall to wall, the dwellings that lined the lane were so alike, what with their whitewashed walls framed by dark timbers and caps of thatch, that they gave the appearance of being one long building. Just now, every one of them glowered blindly down onto the street, lower-level workshops closed, second- and third-story windows tightly shuttered. The householders were besieged. That trade should be halted on a normal business day spoke to the desperation of Stanrudde's starving.

Once again, the fear she'd known in the market

field returned. Had not Theobald claimed that the hungry were attacking their betters in the hopes of finding wealth enough so they could afford to fill their bellies? Of a sudden, Johanna wished she hadn't let the menservants ride ahead of her. She drummed her heels into the palfrey's sides, urging the tired beast into something faster than a plod as they rounded the corner from the chandlers' enclave onto the ropemakers' street. They were barely on the lane when someone leapt out to grab her mount by the bridle. Johanna gasped in blind terror, yanking desperately on her reins in an effort at escape.

"Nay, Mama, it's me," her son cried.

Johanna breathed out her fear as she stared down at her only child. There wasn't much of Katel to be seen in Peter, save for his blessedly well-shaped nose. Instead, she and he shared the same curling reddish gold hair and bright blue eyes, even the same pattern of dappling freckles on their pale skin. Now ten and four, Peter had added at least a hand in height during the five months of her absence, for her son's head reached past her waist as he stood beside her horse. It wasn't his father's small frame that he'd inherited, but his grandsire's far larger form.

Their son was the only thing to come from their misbegotten union that both she and Katel cherished. As love for her only child washed over Johanna, she leaned down in the saddle and ran gloved fingers through his tousled hair. "Peter, you frightened me half unto death!"

The corners of her son's mouth lifted briefly, then the golden wisps that were his brows rose. "Mama, what are you doing here? I thought you were set on staying with the sisters."

All Johanna's anger and bitterness returned. So she had been. How easily Theobald had pried her from the quiet comfort of the convent simply by reminding the prioress that she was Katel's wife, and her husband wished her to return to him.

"Your father has called me home for some reason of his own," Johanna said, struggling to keep the harsh edge from her words. It was wrong to berate Peter's sire in front of him. In an attempt to hide her hatred for his sire, she turned the question around on her child. "I think I should be asking that of you. Why are you out and about when you should be in Master Alfred's shop, hard at your labors?"

Peter shrugged his newly broadened shoulders beneath his brown tunic and leather apron, the mark of his apprenticeship to Stanrudde's goldsmith. "He isn't in the shop this day, but at the market hall with the other councilmen. That's how I knew you'd come. Mistress Ann sent me to him with a message, and I met Theobald in the green. Since our shop is in this direction, I thought I'd wait to greet you."

He shifted to stand closer to the horse. "Mama, now that you have returned, will you stay?" There was the barest hint of hope in his voice.

Guilt again twisted in Johanna. However much her retreat into the convent had hurt Peter, watching his parents locked in their hidden and hateful war was by far the worse. Now that he no longer lived at home, Johanna had no reason to continue in the situation. Nor would she. She shook her head. "You know I cannot."

Pain flashed through Peter's blue eyes, then his face lost all expression. Johanna patted the yet childish roundness of his cheek. "It is better this way, my little love. Know you, I am counting the hours until Eastertide when you come to the priory and we have a true visit," she said softly. "Now, be off with you, while I go to see what it is your father requires of me."

As he stared up at her, Peter's mouth tightened, the sadness in his gaze growing. Of a sudden, he was a boy no longer. "Mama, you must have a care. Papa was acting strangely when I visited last week."

Johanna leaned back into her saddle to peer down at him as a quirk of worry took root in her. "Is it drink?" she asked, trying her best to gentle the question, as if in doing so she could avoid reminding Peter that his father was slowly losing himself to wine and ale.

Again, Peter lifted his shoulders, his eyes shifting uneasily from her to the row of houses that lined the lane. He released her palfrey's bridle and stepped back from the horse's side. "Nay, he drank only a little. Rather, he smiled often to himself, as if cherishing secrets. When he spoke of you, it was to call you whore. What is wrong with him, Mama? Why is he doing this?" His words were an aching cry.

Tears sparked in his eyes as he betrayed one parent to warn the other. The pain was more than he could bear. In the next moment he turned and raced down the lane.

Chapter Two

Stanrudde
two hours past None,
The eve of Ste. Agnes's Day, 1197

Johanna watched Peter go. No doubt he meant to find some place to hide where he could indulge himself in emotions no longer appropriate to a lad his age. Hatred for Katel reawoke. How dare he misuse his son by speaking ill of her before him. Damn Katel. Damn herself for believing he would ever let her leave him. What if he'd used her absence to create some new way to torment her? She turned her horse toward the market square and home.

It wasn't far to the city's center. Stanrudde's small green was where the unemployed came to be hired, goods were measured against the standard, trade infractions were judged, and merchants pilloried. The city's market hall stood at the wee square's far end. Although taller and wider than the houses on the square's other sides, it looked much the same with its wooden walls stretching upward into a thatched roof. This year's unending chill and persistent moisture, whether rain, snow, or today's sleet, had dulled the building's whitewash to the same gray as the clouds overhead.

As Johanna brought her palfrey to a halt next to Theobald and the menservants, Katel's agent shot her a scathing glance. She ignored him to look at the armed men gathered before the hall: the town guard. Save for their captain, who was a professional soldier, Stanrudde's policing force was drawn on a rotating basis from the city's young and fit. A motley group, some in padded cloth vests, others in leather hauberks, the only thing they had in common, beyond the swords fast buckled at their sides, were their bored expressions as they watched their betters argue. All twelve of the council members stood near the pillory, worrying among them the issue of the hungry. Just now, the crippled wool merchant was violently protesting the idea of driving the starving beyond the city walls, while the big smith insisted the crowd was too big to be controlled.

It was with ease that Johanna found her husband among them; Katel was the shortest and roundest of his peers. Once, long ago, her husband had been a comely man, slender of build, with golden hair, clear-cut features, and fine dark brown eyes. Now, at six and forty, some fifteen years her senior, years of over-indulging in drink had left his skin unnaturally red and his nose bulbous. His eyes and mouth were trapped in piggish folds of fat, while his hair had thinned and grown lighter still, making him appear full bald beneath his cap when he was not.

Held in place by a massive gold chain, Katel's gray cloak parted far enough to reveal the maroon samite tunic embroidered in precious metal threads he wore beneath it. Johanna sneered. It was a good thing he wore his thicker cloak, the one lined in squirrel fur. Only that garment was wide enough to conceal the patchwork at his gown's seams; it had been altered many times to accommodate its owner's ever widening girth as Katel could not afford to replace it.

Scorn died. Their gowns and jewels were all that now remained of the wealth Katel had once commanded. Over the last years, his drinking had caused his trade to suffer and prosperity to slip through his fingers. This year, what little profit he'd earned had been eaten in maintaining the sham of wealth or lost through poor investment. Had it not been for the income from the properties Johanna's sire had bound in trust for Peter, they might well have stood with the starving before the abbey.

"Master Katel, your wife has rejoined us," Theobald called when he deemed he'd waited long enough for his master's notice. "Shall I escort her home?"

Katel turned, a soft smile on his face. Johanna's hatred set to simmering all over again. It wasn't some plot Peter had seen, rather Katel gloating over how he could yet force his wife to his bidding when she'd vowed never again.

It was with a mummer's finesse that her husband's face took on an expression of deep hurt. "Why, there you are, Johanna. Wherever have you been these last months?" he called, his voice carrying in its tenor tones the sound of a docile and loving husband who nobly bore grave insult.

Stunned by these wholly unexpected words, Johanna's eyes flew wide. From all around the square, shutters squealed as they opened to let folk peer past the panels at her. So, too, did the guard and Stanrudde's most important men turn to look. They all stared at the woman they thought was Stanrudde's richest wife, waiting to hear what wrong it was she'd done.

Ah, but sixteen years of Katel made her almost as able a mummer as he. Johanna bowed her head in the perfect portrayal of a meek housewife. "Husband, how come you to ask so strange a question?" she cried with just the right note of feminine distress. "You know full well that I have lived within the walls of a convent for these past months."

"If that is so, then why did the lady prioress write to complain you'd left their house?" Katel asked, the quiet hurt in his voice ringing around the square. The unspoken implication of adultery weighed in his every syllable.

Johanna flinched. Never once in all the years of her marriage had she considered an adulterous liaison; she dared not. Were she to stray from her wedding vows and be discovered, the terms of her father's will gave Katel control of the properties entrusted for Peter. It was to guarantee her son had something to inherit when he came of age that kept Johanna faithful to her vows. That, and the pleasure of using her virtue to stand between Katel and the wealth he wanted. Now she carefully raised her head to look at him.

Katel watched her, deep satisfaction glowing in his eyes. Her husband was waiting for a protest of innocence. Ah, but as he'd not actually accused her, such a protest might seem a guilty outburst.

Her gaze strayed to those around him. Even though a prioress and all her nuns would swear that Johanna had held close within their walls for the past five months, Katel's broad hint had already dirtied her good name. Whether high or low, every man watched her in new suspicion, while eying her husband in pity as a man obviously too dense to add the sums and see his wife was cuckolding him.

"My pardon," Katel said to his fellow council members, "I would see my wife safely settled within mine own walls. You will excuse me?" The loving tones of his voice made him out to be the perfect cuckold: the husband who, for his heart's sake, could barely understand why his wife had left him in the first place, much less recognize how she now sinned against him. Johanna damned him again and again. Was he so far gone in his hatred for her that he no longer cared how such an accusation might hurt Peter?

Too heavy to mount with ease, the spice merchant turned to walk at the troop's head as they made their way down Market Lane. With the need to protect her child and herself burning in her heart, Johanna turned her horse to follow him. The moment they were private, she'd give him the sharp edge of her tongue over this game of his, whatever it was.

Taller than any of the buildings around it, the house built by Johanna's sire, Walter of Stanrudde, was now enclosed by a stone wall erected by Katel to keep the world from seeing into his private domain. Between corners squared by blocks of white stone, its walls were made up of layer upon layer of round, grayish stones, some whole, others split to reveal their glossy black hearts. Slate, not reed, lay upon its sharply peaked roof.

Once it had been a home, the source of happiness and pride for Johanna. Now the tall dwelling glowered down at her, all cold stone and bitter mortar. Her marriage to Katel had poisoned the place for her.

Her husband strode within the gate, but only Theobald and Johanna rode in behind him. As she brought her palfrey to a halt, Johanna's gaze shifted to the small kitchen shed that stood at the far end of the house. No smoke flowed from beneath the peaked vent that perched atop its thatched roof. Why would Wymar, their cook, and sometimes her only friend within these walls, have let the kitchen's fire die? Curiosity was brief against the larger matters presently at hand.

Katel retreated across the courtyard, seeking respite from the wind in the shelter of the forebuilding, the small square outthrust of stone that enclosed the house's external stairs. Theobald swung down from his saddle. Johanna stayed where she sat, not yet willing to give herself up to Katel's control. All three of them watched as four of the five menservants rode on, taking their worn mounts to the spice merchant's larger stable, located just outside the city walls. The one behind whom Johanna's maid rode paused just long enough to allow the young woman to dismount.

Leatrice stopped just inside the courtyard, her cloak

held tightly around her. Framed by thick hair that was so dark a brown it was almost black, her pretty face was solemn as she gazed upon her master, then glanced at her mistress. In her brown eyes was the reflection of Agnes and her misery.

Johanna shook her head, finding no triumph in the girl's forthcoming ruin. Despite Leatrice's arrogance, she rather liked her. This lass had a boldness all Katel's other women lacked.

"Why, here is my little sweetheart," the spice merchant called in friendly greeting to his paramour, who had accompanied her mistress to the convent. "I have missed you these five months. Come kiss me in welcome!"

The wind opened Leatrice's cloak as she started across the tiny courtyard, molding her maroon and gray gowns to the bulge Katel's babe made in her belly. Katel's brows rose in surprise, then ebbed into an expression of bland disinterest. "Oh, but I thought you more careful than this," he said to her. "Whose child is that you bear?"

"Master," Leatrice cried out in hopeless protest, "you know the child is yours."

"Now, Leatrice, do not add lying to the list of your sins," he replied in what was an almost gentle warning. "I daresay there've been more than a few who've tasted of you. Indeed, it appears you've shown a decided lack of virtue. Your immoral behavior now requires I dismiss you from my employ. Begone with you."

Katel did not even trouble himself to the pretense of outrage. In a world that believed only the words of men, a breeding and unmarried woman was especially suspect. He was well shielded from any accusation she might make.

Leatrice paled until her eyes were great, dark circles in her face. She dropped to her knees in the muck before her former lover and bowed her head. "I beg your pardon, master. You are right to chide me for trying to shift my sin onto your innocent shoulders. Can you forgive me?" she begged, her voice sweet and feminine.

Pleasure tinged Katel's cheeks a deeper pink. Johanna's eyes narrowed in disgust. This was how he liked his women, groveling. He lay a paternal hand upon the maid's shoulder. "But, of course. No harm has been done to me."

"You are too kind, Master Katel." Leatrice made it sound as if she truly believed this. She came to her feet, then retreated to the gate where she paused to look back upon her master. Anger lurked beneath her shock and hurt, the sort that comes when one trader discovers he had been cheated and seeks some avenue for revenge. "Since you have convinced me that I should speak only the truth, I have no choice but to tell all of Stanrudde that your good wife has lived as a nun for these past months." With that, Leatrice turned and hied herself beyond Katel's reach as quickly as one in her state could move. She was too bright to believe her attempt to strike at him would go unpunished.

Johanna choked back a grateful laugh. Now, here was a new twist. Not only was Katel being betrayed by a woman, but by the one he'd just destroyed.

Rage darted across Katel's face. "An empty threat," he snarled quietly. It wouldn't do for the neighbors to hear him shouting at a maidservant, lest they suspect he wasn't the kind master he seemed.

"Shall I fetch her back for you, master?" Theobald asked, his face dark with the desire to repay Leatrice for the damage she did his employer.

"Nay, she may say what she pleases. It cannot hurt me." Katel looked up at Johanna, vicious pleasure filling his expression. "Soon, all the world will know my wife is an adulteress, and I will have those properties."

Bolstered by Leatrice's unexpected support, Johanna leaned forward in her saddle. "Katel, to prove adultery, one must produce both a paramour and witnesses," she snapped in scorn. "I defy you to do so."

The confidence that bloomed in Katel's eyes sent a stake of fear through her heart. "Ah, but I can do both. When I tell the world you came not virgin to my bed, they'll believe you capable of repeating the same sin. As for who lays with you, who else would I name but the same man who deflowered you those many years ago. Only lust for you could have brought Robert the Bastard back to Stanrudde."

Shock stole Johanna's breath from her. Rob was *here*? Although it was sixteen years since she'd last seen him, her mind retrieved his image as if they'd parted only yesterday.

He'd been but seventeen then, not even fully bearded. Still, her fingers remembered the rough softness of the skin on his jaw. His dark brown hair was thick and heavy. When she toyed with it, she could make it curl along the raw-boned outline of his cheeks. His nose was narrow and just a shade too long; his fine gray eyes smiled at her from beneath gently curving brows.

With the memory of his smile came the sweet recall of his lips pressed to hers. There had been great joy in the melding of their bodies. Pleasure's ghost was followed by a sword's thrust of pain. Johanna's skin chilled to a deathly temperature as her fingers tightened around the palfrey's reins and her heart descended into seething blackness. She had loved and trusted him, but Rob had deserted her. His cruel betrayal had trapped her in this hell that was her marriage.

Turning her searing gaze on her husband, she hissed, "Fool! You picked the wrong man to name as my paramour, for where Robert of Blacklea is, I will never be."

With that, she turned her horse. Making vicious use of her goad, she sent the poor, tired beast hurtling out of her home's gate, then back down Stanrudde's lanes. All that mattered was that she put as much distance as she could between herself and the man she most despised.

Chapter Three

Stanrudde
two hours past None,
The eve of Ste. Agnes's Day, 1197

"Make way, make way for Johanna, wife to Katel le Espicer!"

The arrogant, impatient shout brought an instant quiet in those unfortunates waiting in the abbey's market field, then rode the wind over the compound's stone perimeter wall. It blew across the courtyard's short expanse, passed the stables, and finally tumbled into the open window of that holy house's small hospitium. Standing at the window of this inner guest house, the one reserved for only the most august of the monastery's visitors, Robert of Blacklea, now Grossier of Lynn, caught his breath.

To hear Johanna's name thus twined with Katel's was as if Katel reached across the years to once again attack him. The pain of what he'd forfeited welled up in him. Rob closed his eyes and leaned his head against the window's frame.

The memory of Johanna and the time of their first loving immediately filled his inner vision. It had been summer, the moss on that stretch of river bank they called their own had been greener than emeralds. The day's soft mist had just turned to rain, heaven's tears streaming through the willow branches until her gowns clung to her like a second skin.

As Johanna's image reappeared in his mind's eye, Rob drew a breath in appreciation. Mayhap only he might hail her a great beauty, still no man would deny that her face had a fine-boned elegance that would serve her long past the time when other women faded into crones. Her hair was a mix of gold and red. It curled enough that, when it was loosened, it flowed about her slender form in wanton waves.

Each time she looked on him, her eyes became all the bluer in her love for him. As if but an hour, not sixteen years, had passed since her last glance, his heart basked in the glory of her sweet affection. This time when Rob caught his breath, it was in despair.

If his heart persisted in believing she loved him still, logic said any affection she'd ever held for him was gone, destroyed beyond redemption. He opened his eyes to stare blankly at the abbey's wall, toying with the massive knot of gold that was his mantle pin. Johanna, and the wrong he'd been forced to do her, haunted him. To be so stricken at the mere sound of her name did not bode well for his high-flung hope that protecting her from Katel's wrongdoing would somehow free him of this burden.

The corners of his mouth lifted into a small and bitter smile. Free him, indeed. If he ever achieved the freedom he wasn't certain he wanted, his peers, nay, all of society, would see that it didn't last long.

By the time an independent tradesman reached his third decade, as Rob had done three years ago, he was expected to take a wife. This was especially so when a man was as wealthy as Rob had become. Nigh on all the trading households of England had paraded their daughters before him, as had at least half of the lower nobility, with no success.

Aye, but he wasn't foolish enough to think he could continue to refuse. Folk were already whispering about him and rumors were bad for trade. His obsession with Johanna had to end as did his lingering belief that the two of them were well and truly wed.

There was a touch on his elbow. Rob glanced down at William, his eleven-year-old apprentice. The lad's brows were raised in confusion as he studied his master through eyes as green as his sire's. Eye color was the only thing Will had from Arthur. All else, his slight frame, curling, tawny hair, and strong will came from the boy's far more forceful dam.

"Aye, lad?" Rob asked, knowing the boy's confusion had its roots in his master's strange behavior since their arrival at Stanrudde.

"It's the brother you wished to see. He's come at last."

"Ah," Rob said, a spark of pleasure breaking through the odd heaviness of spirit that had plagued him since discovering Katel's theft. He turned his back on the window and his troubles, then ran supple fingers through his hair to straighten it. "By all means, admit him."

As William crossed the room, descending the short stairway to ground level in order to assist the elderly monk up the steps, Rob glanced down at himself and freed a soft sound of annoyance. While he stood at the window, pining after the unattainable, the wind had pried open his thick, marten-lined mantle, allowing the sleet to spot his carefully crafted blue tunic. Although the moisture dribbling from the ledge had missed the soft leather belt with its golden studs and his tunic's ankle-length and heavily embroidered hem, his footwear had not been so fortunate. Never meant to see the out-of-doors, these fine leather shoes were ruined. Lifting a foot, Rob wiped one shoe's worth of spots on a leg of his more mundane, and concealed, chausses. The rough wool of this garment that covered him hip to toe grew damp.

A new, deep rumbling rose from those hungry folk awaiting the opening of the abbey's gate for their daily bite of bread. Startled, Rob half turned to listen. In the next instant, the sound sorted itself into the syllables of Johanna's name. Fear for her shot through him, and he turned all the way round, then willed his gaze to penetrate solid stone. The chant intensified until it reached a threatening tenor.

"Brother, we'd be honored if you used the chair," Will said as he reentered the room with the monk. "Here, let me move it nearer to the heat."

Wood scraped across the floor as the lad heaved the hospitium's only chair toward the room's center and their brazier. The monks heated this chamber with a brass pan filled with glowing coals, held off the floor on a tall tripod. It was a poor substitute for a hearth. The brazier required an open window for ventilation, which meant the majority of its warmth was lost to the chill air entering the room.

"Master Robert, Brother Herbalist is here," the lad called, making the formal announcement required of him.

Rob ignored him, his entire being yet focused on the sound of Johanna's name pulsing from the crowd. Only three days ago, a tradesman had been assaulted in his home, he and his wife beaten nigh unto death as what grain they had in store was plundered. He could not bear the thought of Johanna so injured.

"Will they do her any harm?" Rob called over his shoulder to their visitor.

"I doubt they'd try it," the monk replied calmly, "not as long as she rides with her husband's men as her escort."

This assurance did nothing to ease Rob's fear. This past autumn had taught him just what sort of man Katel employed. He glanced at his apprentice. "Lad, run you your fastest to the gate and watch that the goodwife's party passes unharmed. If the crowd should set upon her escort, send the porter to warn me while you rouse our men to aid her." His agent and his household guard had retreated to the abbey's stable to dice out of sight and earshot of the holy brothers.

Excitement washed all other emotion from Will's gaze, and his hand dropped in eager anticipation to the hilt of the dagger he'd been allowed to wear on this trip. The thrill of danger was another facet of character he had from his dam, for it was nothing his father had ever owned. "Aye, Master Robert," he replied, already racing toward the room's exit.

As Will blew out on the gust of wind that surged through the window when he threw open the door, Rob waited, taut and tense. Behind him, the monk rose and closed the door. As swiftly as it had begun, the muttering from the field died back into the low moan of hunger. Rob breathed in relief, then turned to welcome the man who'd nurtured the love for trade in his heart, only to catch his breath in a wholly new fear.

Death was closing its fist around Colin the Apothecary. The black habit of the Benedictines swallowed the former tradesman, while naught but onionskin stretched over his bones, his skull nigh on visible along his jutting cheekbones and outthrust brows. Deep hollows encircled eyes as black as his hair had once been; the stuff now wreathing the monk's face and head was that pure white given only to those whose hair had once been a true ebony. It was as if each one of Colin's three score years had taken a bit of him in passing, thinning and pruning him until, one day far too soon, he'd be no more.

"Come into the light," the former tradesman commanded, his strong voice belying his delicate state, "that I might better see you."

If Colin could speak so, he was not as frail as he appeared. Rob did as he bid, holding out his arms to give the man a better view. Years of sadness and care disappeared from the monk's thin face as he studied his dearest friend's former student. After a moment, he cocked his head to one side.

"You are the last man I expected to emulate the Lionheart," he said, referring to both the manner in which Rob wore his hair and beard and Walter of Stanrudde's protégé's dislike of the French-speaking aristocrats who ruled this land.

Rob shrugged, lowering his arms. "These days, many men choose to wear their hair almost to their shoulders and keep their beards trimmed close to their jaws. I do but keep fashion with a horde of others."

Colin raised a chiding brow. "What? No admission that you know how well it becomes you? Aye, and with that gown of yours," he pointed to the floor-length blue tunic embossed with embroidered lozenges, each oval containing a stalk of wheat done in golden thread, "were I a lass, faith, but I'd swoon."

As Rob laughed, the monk leaned into the low-backed chair. The look on Colin's face intensified as if he sought the man concealed beneath the finery. It surprised Rob to find after years of being heralded as the best and brightest of his trade, he now nervously awaited this single man's judgment. At last, approving creases cut into Colin's lean cheeks.

"Beanpole," the monk teased gently. "I think me you're even taller now than when you departed Stanrudde. You should have stopped growing a full head sooner."

Tension drained from Rob at this ancient and familiar complaint. "I know taller men," he retorted, giving what had always been his standard response. "Have you forgotten there was once a time when you and Master Walter found my height handy? While other lads could duck and hide in a crowd to escape their master's eye, I was instantly visible."

"So you were," Colin replied, his eyes gleaming at their old game. Jerking his head to the side in a general rightward direction, he said, "See that?"

"What?" Rob asked in confusion, glancing between the bed, the brazier, and the stack of pallets at the far wall that had been provided for his servants.

"The bed, you great twit," Colin said in fond irritation.

Rob looked. It was a nice enough piece, with a mattress long enough for him to lay comfortably upon it. Poles, onto which a spiraling line had been carved, were painted a pretty green. They thrust upward from the mattress frame to support a wooden roof and curtains of thick, warm wool dyed a rich red color. He shrugged. "Aye, what of it?"

Colin grinned. "It's our finest piece, usually reserved for the bishop's visit. You have no idea the agitation your stay has caused our esteemed abbot. I'll take that as a gauge of your success in the business of selling *koren*, guessing you've done right well for yourself."

Pleasure and humility warred within Rob. "What I've done was built upon the generosity of others, yours, Master Walter's, and Master Wymund's. Moreover, I had help at the onset. Not only was there Master Walter's bequest, but Master Wymund made Arthur and me his heirs when his second wife also left him childless."

"He made Arthur his heir as well?" The words leapt from Colin's mouth before he could restrain them. Rob smiled as he watched a man given to blunt speech seek the facade of polite disinterest that better society demanded of its members.

"Of course . . . what I mean to say is . . ." the monk tried again, his brow drawing down in frustration. ". . . that Wymund stated that intention before accepting you and Arthur as his apprentices. However, I must admit I never expected . . . bah!"

Colin's frustration vanished in the face of a curiosity that could not be denied. "Truly? His heir? Then, does Arthur remain with you in your trade? I never judged him the owner of the mental agility or social grace necessary for the level of trade you have achieved," he said, displaying his own lack of grace and far too forthright nature.

Rob laughed aloud, free of his cares and worries for this moment. "How could I ever have forgotten your penchant for blunt speech?"

"I have no idea," the former apothecary retorted with a healthy dose of scorn aimed at himself. He grinned. "Walter never ceased to point out how my refusal to play pretty games with words kept me trapped as his employee, working at street-level trade. It's a good thing that was all I ever wanted. Now, answer my question."

"He chose not to remain with me," Rob said with a swift lift of his brows. "Instead, he sold me his portion and married himself a cordwainer's fair widow. While she crafts shoes, he waits on her. My apprentice is their first born. I am godfather to two others."

"That lad is Arthur's get," Colin cried, now even more astonished. "Frankly, I always wondered if he had energy enough to set his seed into a woman's womb. Does she hold him down and force him?"

Again, Rob laughed. "Ach, but I have missed you, Master Colin." The title slipped from his tongue without thought, born as it was of long habit.

"*Brother* Colin," the churchman corrected without rancor.

Rob shook his head. "I fear I've known you too long as one to remember you are now the other."

Colin only waved him toward the bed. "Come and sit near me that I need not crane my neck so to see you."

Rob did as he was bid, shoving aside the bed curtains to settle himself on the mattress's edge. As he shifted to stretch his long legs out before him, Colin rose to heave his chair around to face the bed. When the monk was again seated, the two of them were eye-to-eye and less than arm's length apart.

In that instant the circumstances of their parting and their long separation rose between them, creating a chasm almost too vast to be spanned. Tongue-tied, Rob could but stare at the man who, with Master Walter, he had adored. As if similarly affected, Colin said nothing.

The quiet in the room stretched, the rushes on the floor rustling. The bed's draperies sighed as the wind eddied in them. Sleet spattered against window's ledge and shutters. The next gust caught one of those wooden panels, lifting it and sending it clattering back against the hospitium's wall.

Colin looked in the direction of the noise, his gaze lingering on the spot where Rob had stood. His expression grew distant as he lost himself in the past. "You care for her still." It was a breath of a comment.

Rob opened his mouth to reject any conversation over Johanna, then caught himself. To avoid his past was to destroy all hope of ever laying it to rest so he could move beyond it. With a sigh, he leaned forward and braced his forearms on his knees.

"How could I not? We were as close as brother and sister, she and I," he said, politely skirting the truth as much to protect his own emotions as Johanna.

His gaze still fixed on the window, Colin loosed an amused and scornful snort. "Best not say that, lad. Incest's an even greater sin than fornication."

Rob rocked back on the mattress as the monk's brutal honesty tore past his carefully tended veneer, exposing the raw emotion seething beneath it. "You've no right to mock me and what I feel for her," he hissed. "Especially not after you said you saw what happened between us, yet did naught to stop us. Damn you, but you aided Master Walter in seeing I carried her hatred with me for all my life's time."

When Colin turned his head to look at Rob, there

was only sadness in his expression. "You harangue when I but stated the truth you yet choose to avoid. As for blame, know you that my guilt over what happened between you two lays heavily upon my shoulders."

As pain and anger retreated to its own private corner of his soul, shame washed over Rob. Somewhere, deep in him, he'd hoped his Colin would return anger for anger. Then, could he have ranted over the unfairness of the way he'd been parted from Johanna and, in doing so, eased a little of what ached in him.

He bowed his head. "I beg your pardon, master. My words did no justice to the love and kindness you and Master Walter showed me, nor to the gratitude I yet bear you both. Know you that as a man full grown, I understand the whys of what you did." Lifting his head, Rob hazarded a small smile. "I fear you found a wound in me that not even one of your potions could heal."

Death crept back to settle comfortably into the lines around Colin's mouth and the creases on his brow. "So I expected," he replied. "Unlike Walter, I harbored no illusions you would either rise above the hurt we did you or forget what you felt for her. I think me the constancy of your heart is both gift and curse for you, lad."

Once again, Colin's words bolted through Rob. If this was true, he was tied to Johanna for all time, just as he'd promised her sixteen years ago. As Rob swallowed, then swallowed again, trying to force his heart back down into his chest, the monk sagged deeper into the chair as if his sadness weighed more than he could bear. If they didn't escape this subject, they'd both soon be sobbing.

"Master Robert, can you hear me?" Will's shout rose from beneath the window to shatter the gloom in the tiny chamber.

On any other day, Rob wouldn't have deigned respond to such a call. An apprentice did not shout to his master as if he were dog, an apprentice came into his master's presence and humbly begged his question be addressed. However, he was so grateful for Will's distraction that he rose and went to the window without hesitation. A half-story below, the boy was hopping from foot to foot on the slick grass, trying to keep warm while he awaited his reply.

"I hear you," Rob called. "What is it, lad?"

Will looked up in relief. "Brother Porter eats sooner than the others, and since we are both Williams he says it's only right that I should share his bean soup. May I?" On his face bloomed the hopeful look of a growing and ever hungry lad.

"As you will, but mind your manners," Rob said, his tone carefully modulated to remind the lad that even in sharing a cup of soup he represented the house of Robert the Grossier.

Will grinned. "I'll be very careful. My thanks, Master Robert." In the next instant, he was gone.

"You let him speak so to you?" Colin asked, his now hollow voice touched with quiet disapproval.

Rob only shook his head as he returned to seat himself on the bed. Leaning over, he gave the monk's knee a pat. "Enough of me and mine. Tell me of your life here. Although I suspected you meant to take your vows, I am astonished that a monk's life is so full. Days, I have waited on your visit," he said, giving more emphasis to the complaint than he felt. "Did you forget I was here, or do you brothers truly work so hard?"

Colin lifted his shoulders in helplessness. "Know you, I meant to come each and every one of the past days. Any more, time seems to slip through my fingers, with the hours ending too soon for the number of chores I wish to complete. But then, you know how I can be when I'm busy at my pots and stills." He tried to smile.

"Do they give you no aide to ease your burden?" Rob retorted, his voice deepening slightly. It'd not surprise him to find Colin, an Englishman, misused by the Norman abbot of this place.

Sharp amusement snapped in Colin's dark eyes. "Watch yourself, lad, it could be your own sire you denigrate with your dislike." Then, knowing full well the hive he'd just stirred, the monk leapt swiftly into explanation, denying Rob the chance to protest the bastardy he refused to accept.

"Nay, it's starvation's contingent of diseases that is my taskmaster now. Each day I strive to replenish our meager defenses against them, all the while knowing they cannot be vanquished until bellies are once again full." His gaze fell to his age-twisted fingers in his lap as if he couldn't believe them incapable of miracles. "Most of those who die are but children," he whispered.

"Master," Rob cried softly, recognizing now the source of Colin's sadness. Slipping from the bed, he knelt before the monk, taking his hands to offer comfort. "Do not torture yourself so. Death comes for us all, sooner for some than others. If many of those outside yon gates are meant to die, then there's naught we can do to forestall it."

"Ah, but you're wrong, there is much that can be done," Colin spat out, lifting his head to reveal the frustration and anger twisting his face. "Not one, Rob, not one of the merchants in this town has dug deep into his own purse to aid the hungry. Oh, I'm not saying they haven't given to the abbey, but where Abbot Eustace sees open-handed generosity, I know better. *I* know each of their houses and how much they would have in store."

The fire in him died, leaving him naught but an old, tired man sitting in a chair far richer than any he'd ever owned. "I tell you, lad, the world's changed, and I like it naught at all. Stanrudde has grown into a crowded, stinking place filled with uncaring folk and iniquities I never dreamed existed two score years ago. These days, the honest man must work twice as hard to buy the same loaf of bread I bought for you. This winter, he'll buy no bread at all, no matter how hard he works."

Although Colin caught himself before his plea tumbled past his lips, there was no way to keep the question from his eyes. No longer did the former tradesman look upon the lad who'd been his employer's apprentice. Instead, he watched Robert the Grossier, buyer and seller of grains, who did his business in Lynn, the city built on East Anglia's wealth in wheat.

Rob sat back on his heels and rubbed at the creases in his forehead. Of late, they'd been trying to make themselves permanent marks on his face. "Would that I had grain to offer you." The words came out too flat, too hard, and he hurried to explain.

"You, better than any other churchman, knew what my answer must be. This year's harvest was sold even as last year's shipped. What I could delay sending on my contracts, I did, although it meant taking a grave loss this year. All I have, save for what I need to keep my own house throughout the winter, I've either sold or given to the priory at Lynn. I've no wish to profit off another man's misery, and so vows every God-fearing grossier I know."

Ah, but not all men feared God as much as they coveted gold. All across this land, speculators held back their stores. As they dribbled it onto the marketplace, the price of grain rose to a king's ransom.

Of these men, there were two kinds: the first had nerves of iron and strong connections at the royal court; the other was an utter fool. If discovery for the first meant ruin through the confiscation of all their worldly goods, for the second sort it was ruin, followed by a quick trip to the gallows. Since Rob knew Katel was not of the first sort, this left the spice merchant in the second category.

Again, he scrubbed at his face, this time trying to tame his worry over Johanna. True, Katel had proved himself a clever thief. It had taken months to track the one who'd bought a small portion of Rob's grain out from beneath his contracts. But then, Katel had always been adept at claiming what belonged to others. When it came to selling anything, even his own spices, the man was not so adept. Rob was certain that if and when Katel tried to put his ill-gotten grain on the market, he would be discovered. Unless Rob could find a way to privately reclaim the seed before that time came, Johanna would either hang with her husband or be left shamed and impoverished by his demise.

Colin offered him a weak smile. "My pardon, since it was I and Walter who raised you, I should have known that of you," he started. The last of his words were drowned out as folk began to shout and scream outside the abbey's gate. A horse loosed a terrified cry.

"What now?" Colin said irritably, coming to his feet with a grunt. The monk crossed to the window.

Rob joined him, towering over his much shorter mentor as he peered in disinterested curiosity at the wall and gate. Judging by the ringing echoes, another of Stanrudde's wealthy personages had appeared. The folk without were haranguing the poor soul for the sin of eating when they did not.

Suddenly, the small wooden door in the gatehouse room that was the brother porter's domain flew open. Will dashed out and raced toward the stable, a wooden spoon yet in his hand. The brother porter flew out on the lad's heels, cowl falling back to reveal a pate as bald as a babe's. Panic brought the monk's habit high over his hairy knees. He started toward the guest house, then veered in indecision toward the abbot's lodging. After a few steps, he again aimed for the hospitium.

"Brother William," Colin called to him, "what is it?"

The monk stopped, yet dancing in place with anxiety as he glanced around for the source of the voice. His gaze found Colin, then leapt to their esteemed visitor. "Master Robert . . . Young Will . . . in the street . . . they're trying to get her off her horse . . ." he stuttered.

Beyond the wall, a woman screamed in terror. The sound of her voice raised the hair on the back of Rob's neck. Years or not, he knew his Johanna. Without a second's thought, he vaulted through the window. He was running for the gate almost before his feet hit the damp and springy earth.

Chapter Four

Blacklea Manor
Late May, 1173

Robert of Blacklea's parched throat tried on its own to swallow, while hunger gnawed at his belly. Although his home was no more than two hundred paces from him, he was too tired to crawl any farther. It had taken all of the night just to reach the garden's center.

Around him, beans rustled in the morn's fresh breeze, while the earth beneath him was yet clammy with dew. The coolness of the ground seeped past his shirt and tunic to temper his overheated skin. As he drew another shallow breath, he could nigh on taste the rich stench of manure. Only two weeks ago, he and Papa had spread the wealth of their byre and latrine on the newly tilled portion of their croft, which lay nearby.

But, two weeks ago life had been normal. Now, Mama was dead and Papa had lost his mind. Ten was too young to be left with no one to love him.

Slowly, because his legs and arms were tender where Papa had hit them, he pulled his knees into his chest. When he was the smallest ball possible, he buried his head against his legs. If things were ever to be normal again, he had to succeed at bringing Mama back to them. His brow creased as Mama's image formed before his inner eye.

Her face was round, her hair a pale gold, but not

as pale as Papa's. A fine web of wrinkles touched the corners of her eyes. Rob remembered how the brown of Mama's eyes always sparkled green when she smiled. "Come back," he whispered, the sound rasping from his dry throat. "Come back, Mama."

Day's light grew steadily brighter, and Rob clenched the eye that wasn't already swollen shut until his mind was again full dark. The mud that caked his face began to dry and draw, and his cheek twitched in irritation. Mama's image was consumed, just as the sun ate the morning mist. Rob let his head droop in frustration toward the garden floor. No matter how hard he conjured, something always intruded, destroying his attempt.

"Travelers!" Dickon, son to Harold the Miller, called. His voice was sharp with excitement, his words rising from just beyond this garden's enclosing wall. "Come everyone, come and see!"

As Dickon repeated his invitation all along the pathway to the far fields where the men were haying this week, loneliness filled Rob. Two weeks ago, he would have been equally as excited over such news.

The sound of snorting pack animals drifted to him on the breeze. Cart wheels squeaked as they turned, growing louder as they neared Blacklea's tiny green, only a few rods distant from where Rob lay. There was a brief instant of quiet, followed by a sharp crack. A man's shouted warning was drowned out by the resounding crash of the cart bed hitting the earth.

"Rob? Where are you? You must come and see."

Barely audible over the purr of the doves perched on the byre's rooftop, his three-year-old sister's call shredded Rob's concentration. He shut his ears to Gretta's voice, fighting back his ever-present urge to coddle and protect her. She no longer needed him. Since Mama's death, she'd dwelt with her godmother and namesake, Margretta the Platfoot.

"Rob, where are you lad?" There was no ignoring

this call: Margretta Platfoot's voice was as strong as her flat-footed gait has weak. "The bailiff's here with a spice merchant whose cart has broken its axle."

Margretta's voice grew in volume as she crossed the wee courtyard stretching between the toft's enclosing earthen wall and Ralph AtteGreen's cottage. "Rob, are you hiding from me, boy? Come now, your sister's wanting you."

The cottage door's leather hinges squealed in protest as that panel was thrown wide. "God damn you to hell, old woman! By what right do you trespass into my home?"

Margretta yelped; Rob cringed. Papa's words were still running into each other, just as they had done last even. Until last week, Rob hadn't known Papa could be so dangerous.

"Mother of God, but you frightened a year's life out of me, Ralph AtteGreen," the old woman cried out, her voice steadying as she continued. "What are you doing here when you should be haying with the other men? Why, you're drunk!"

"I'm a free man, old woman," Papa retorted, his tone dark and thick. "I do as and when I please."

"Where's Rob?" Margretta's voice was suddenly cautious.

"Gone," Papa grunted. "Drove the bastard from my toft last night, I did."

These hard, hurting words made tears fill Rob's eyes. He was no bastard. Bastards were fatherless children, the lowest of the low, conceived by fornication or adultery. Papa cursed such children, saying it was better to drown these brats than let them live in shame. Now, because of the terrible lie Mama told just before she died, Papa wished that death upon his own son.

"Tell me you did not!" Margretta's tone was shocked. "Why, Gilly's barely cold in her grave."

"Aye, but buried she is. If she'd wanted me to continue to pretend that dark-haired devil is mine, then she shouldn't have died." Papa's complaint was almost a sob.

"Why, you ungrateful wretch!" Margretta shouted. "I'll see you pay for this. Rob! Rob, where are you, lad?"

"Meddling bitch!" Papa roared. "Get out of my home!"

Margretta shrieked. Fabric rent. Flesh impacted with flesh. "Help me, neighbors," the old woman screamed. "Help, help!" Her last word disappeared into a gag.

"Nay, Papa, nay," Rob whispered against his father's madness. He covered his ears with his hands, then pressed his head hard against his knees and let hopelessness take him to a timeless place beyond hearing or seeing.

"I've found the lad!"

The call, bellowed from directly overhead, startled Rob from his dazed musing. His uninjured eye flew open. One row over the leafy beans was crushed beneath the heavy soles of two short-topped boots. Out of these shoes grew a pair of thick legs clad in bulky red chausses and cross-gartered in dark green.

Rob turned his head to follow the legs upward. The big man wore a rich green gown woven with golden threads beneath a fur-trimmed mantle. His golden mantle pin and the tiny brass medallions on his belt caught the sun with blinding impact. Dazed by the brightness, Rob shut his eye. When he opened it once more, the stranger was kneeling in the muck beside him.

Never before had Rob seen a man as red as this one. Two flaming, bushy brows crested over eyes as pale a blue as the mill pond in winter. Hair, the same bright red color curled in wild abandon around the big man's head, while his beard, a bare shade lighter, covered a broad jaw. What skin was exposed in all this hair was sunburnt to a painful hue, making his tawny freckles and dark moles stand out in sharp relief, while it peeled across the bridge of his great, arching nose.

With gentle fingertips, the stranger felt at the bruises and lumps on Rob's head and shoulders. "Ach, poor lad. You're fevered. I'll wager me you laid here all the night long." Where before the foreigner's voice had been a thundering roar, it was now a muted rumbling, but there was outrage in his quiet tone.

Before Rob could think to resist, he was lifted from the beans and cradled against the man's burly chest. The fabric beneath Rob's head was soft. He breathed deeply. The stranger's tunic carried with it a tangy-sweet scent he didn't recognize.

As his tall rescuer carried him from the garden and around the byre's far end, Rob could see over the toft's low, enclosing earthen wall to the green beyond it. A small, two-wheeled cart lay at the near side of that open expanse. Its axle had split in the middle, the splintered ends now resting on the ground. Guarding it and the string of pack animals laden with baskets that surrounded it was a group of men dressed in the same padded cloth vests and leather caps that Blacklea Manor's guards wore.

A flicker of interest rose within Rob at this exotic sight, then died against his greater need to lay beneath his own blanket within familiar walls. He waited for the man to turn right toward the neat cottage that had been home for all his life. Instead, the big man continued straight on, walking toward the gap in the toft's wall.

Panic choked Rob. As sure as he breathed, if he stepped one toe beyond the toft's wall, all hope of conjuring Mama back to life would be lost. With a hoarse croak, he struggled to lift himself upright in the man's arms. His attempt only made spots and stars swim before his eyes, even in the darkness behind his swollen eyelid. By the time his senses steadied, he and the man were in the green.

Too late! Rob sagged as his fragile hold on the world he knew shattered. Mama was beyond his reach for all time. Now, nothing would ever be the same.

The stranger stopped beside his cart. "Aleric, bring me yon skin," the big man called.

"Aye, Master Walter."

One of the men, long and lean, stepped forward with the water container. He set the skin's spout against Rob's lips. At the touch of cool liquid against his skin, Rob's mouth opened on its own. Water dribbled down his dry throat. Swallowing was so painful it was a moment before he realized this was water and something more. The strange taste of it made him turn his head aside before his thirst was quenched.

At his refusal, Master Walter shifted Rob in his arms and continued on toward the green's center. Rob turned his head far enough to see who was gathered here. The men had all come down from the fields. Their sweat-streaked chests were bare, the shirts and tunics tied around their waists wearing a coat of hayseed. The women were far neater in their bright gowns and homespun headcloths, but their hands were stained with the fruits of their kitchens. In rote habit, Rob counted them, his brain tallying and separating as he always did: two and forty men and boys, seven and fifty lasses and women. Of them, four and seventy were married, the remainder being either widowed or yet too young to wed.

Papa, wearing only his shirt and chausses, hung between Wilfred, Blacklea's bailiff, and Peter the Archer, sergeant of the manor's few protectors. The sun made Papa's pallid hair gleam almost white. His new madness, along with too much ale, made his jaw slack and kept his brown eyes closed halfway.

As the merchant moved into the crowd, old Margretta came to walk beside him. Pale-haired Gretta was cradled in her godmother's arms, sobbing softly against Margretta's shoulder. The old woman's face bore an angry red mark, and her sleeve was torn from her gown.

"You poor creature," Margretta crooned as she squinted shortsightedly down at Rob.

Master Walter stopped before Wilfred, the long-faced Norman who was Blacklea's master in lieu of its lord. "Bailiff, look upon what this man has done. The lad hangs onto life by his fingernails alone."

Wilfred raised a dark and unconcerned brow. "While his mistreatment is unfortunate, Master Walter, the boy yet lives. There's no law against a man beating his son."

"I am not his father!" Papa shouted. "His mother confessed it to me with her dying breath."

Rob shrank into the merchant's arms. Papa shouldn't speak this lie aloud before the entire village. Didn't he care that he hurt Mama by naming her a Norman's whore?

The merchant loosed a harsh laugh. "Convicted by his own words. Now, you've not only assaulted the goodwife here, but another man's child as well. And, that is against the law."

"Rob's your son and no other's," the bailiff sniffed, ignoring Master Walter's charge. "Gilemota raved in her last days, distraught by her babe's death and fevered from the delivery. Any claim she made against Lord Graistan was born of that delirium."

"How can you say so when that bastard," Papa said, again throwing the awful charge at his son as he jerked his head in Rob's direction, "was born just seven months after Gilly and I were wed? Jesus God, look at him as I have had to all these years. He's his sire's image with that dark thatch and those gray eyes. You dare not call me liar, not when every man here knows

Gilly laid with Lord Henry for the two months before she and I were joined."

"Too late, Ralph," Dickon's sire, Harold the Miller, shouted. "You cannot cry misuse now, not when you've raised the lad for ten years as your own without complaint. You knew full well what Gilly had done prior to your joining. If you were so concerned over what grew in her womb, you should have waited a few months before you wed her." His opinion was supported by a general, positive muttering among the crowd.

"Aye, we all remember how eager he was to wed Gilemota," Margretta said, raising her powerful voice. "He wanted to make certain no other man received the dowry her lord had settled on her in trade for what she'd given him."

Margretta scanned the crowd, finding the support she sought in their broad faces, then turned her gaze back on Papa. "Ralph AtteGreen, Gilly's bedplay made you both a free man and a landowner when she wed you. I say the price you pay for your freedom is to raise her child, despite his parentage."

"The priest placed no cloak over us at our wedding," Papa roared. "I did not accept him." He threw himself at Margretta, despite the bailiff and the bowman.

As Papa's captors struggled to subdue him once again, Blacklea's folk all raised their voices. Neighbor argued with neighbor over how Papa had changed and what should now be done with Gilemota's son. Tears pricked at Rob's eyelids. No one wanted him now that they all thought him a bastard.

"Have you no shame?" Master Walter's deep voice crashed through their arguments. "Would you send a child back to a man who has done such harm? I say if his father wants him no more, let his godparents see to his welfare as is only right."

"He has none," Margretta replied with a sorry

shake of her head. "His godfathers died years ago, and fire took his godmother and all her family this past winter, God rest their souls. There's no one else."

Rob turned his face into Master Walter's chest. He was alone, alone, alone. The merchant's arms around him tightened. Startled, Rob looked up at him. Master Walter's expression was grim as he stared at Blacklea's folk.

"If none of you will protect him, I will, charging every one of you to bend your knees before your priest for you sorely lack Christian charity." The merchant looked down at the child in his arms. "Why, this very morn I caught myself thinking on how I needed me a new scullery lad."

Despite the kindness that dwelt in Master Walter's pale blue eyes, terror made Rob shrink within himself. The merchant was a stranger who lived in a place that was not Blacklea. To leave Papa, Gretta, his home, and everything familiar would be worse than dying.

"Master Walter, what are you saying?" The complaint, made in a fine tenor voice, rose from the broken cart at the crowd's far edge.

Blacklea's folk parted to let a youth of barely more than a score of summers pass. Although the green gown beneath his brown mantle was fine, his pin was plain, and he wore no jewels upon his fingers. As short as Papa, the young man had golden hair and clear skin. A slender nose set high above a soft mouth lent him an almost girlish beauty. Just now, an expression of pained concern darkened his high brow.

"Master, you can do these backward folk no favor by taking on what should be their burden," the youth began as he stopped before the spice merchant. "Come, let us retire to the manor house as the bailiff has invited whilst they decide the issue among themselves." His gaze dropped to Rob. Apprehension flashed through his luminous brown eyes as his nose wrinkled. "Jesu, but he stinks. He's ruined your gown with his filth."

"Better a ruined gown than a broken boy, Katel," Master Walter replied in gentle chastisement.

This Katel stepped closer to lay a cajoling hand on the big man's arm. "Master," he said in a whisper, "I know you mean well, but there are times when you blind yourself to the obvious. Can you not see how these scheming folk plot against the weight of your purse? I say this whole matter was arranged for your benefit so they might foist this bit of offal onto you."

"Katel," Master Walter cried softly, his voice filled with surprise, "what eats at you this morn that makes you callous? To what corner of the world has your compassion flown?"

"But, master," this Katel persisted, his voice touched with fear, "he's a bastard. You should not sully your prominence and prestige by involving yourself with one so unworthy of your attention."

Master Walter studied the youth for a quiet moment, compassion touching his blue gaze. "Katel, you mistake me for your sire—this boy is nothing to me. You, on the other hand, will someday be the master spicer and I but your father by marriage."

Despite his master's reassuring words, the youth shot a worried glance at Rob, as if he still feared being usurped in his master's affection. He bowed his head. "I beg pardon for misjudging you, Master Walter."

"Given," the spice merchant said easily as Katel retreated to a spot beyond Rob's view.

Master Walter scanned Blacklea's folk. "Be you all my witnesses in this." To Papa, he said, "I'll give you ten pence for the lad, purchasing him as my servant. When he has earned back that sum by his efforts on my behalf, I will free him to do as he pleases in the world."

"He's yours on the condition he not call himself my son," Papa retorted.

A tiny whimper escaped Rob. He wasn't a bastard. Papa was his father, just as Dickon was Harold's son. This was too much to bear. Every muscle loosened, and he hung in the merchant's arms, too heartsore to protest.

"Rest assured that I will never name this lad your son," Master Walter replied, his words iron hard. With that, the merchant turned and strode back to his cart.

"Aleric, you'll transport our lad home. Use my horse as he's the stronger. We'll surely be back on the road by the morrow's dawn, so you should catch us there the day after." He glanced sourly at the broken wain. "We'd better be on the road by the morrow, else this is the last time I do favors for monks."

"I doubt that, master," Aleric said with a quiet smile.

As he slung the waterskin's strap over his shoulder, another man led forward a great white steed, its trappings as magnificent as its rider's attire. When Aleric had mounted, Master Walter lifted Rob into his man's arms. Rob moaned as he was jostled and shoved into the saddle before Master Walter's servant. His head fell back against the man's chest. Aleric's vest reeked of sweat and, despite its padding, had not even a hint of softness to it.

"I have me an idea," Master Walter said, still standing at his man's knee. "When you arrive home, tell my daughter I have decided to put her promises and pleadings to the test."

"He's giving way," someone near the group's rear muttered, and laughter rippled over the spice merchant's men.

"I am not," the merchant retorted, his voice rising slightly in self-defense. "Aleric, tell my daughter that the healing of this lad is to be her first chore as mistress of my house. If she succeeds in the task, I'll consider allowing her to forgo learning her letters to do as she claims the other lasses do and begin learning household management."

"Aye, master," Aleric said, setting heels to the horse.

With a call of "Fare-you-well," the man turned his borrowed mount and set it to trotting away from Blacklea's green. The jolting gait made stars again appear before Rob's vision. With naught but despair left in him, he let the blackness swallow him. His heart was broken, and he would die for certain now.

Chapter Five

Stanrudde
Late May, 1173

Seated on a stool at the center of the spice merchant's new hall, Walter of Stanrudde's only child looked down at the portable desk in her lap. From beneath the concealment of Johanna's blue skirts, a tiny paw emerged. New claws, sharp as pins, caught at her stockinged ankle. Choking back a giggle, Johanna stared at the parchment spread atop the desk's sloping surface.

It was her third lesson in reading. This time she tried, she truly did; she stared at that sheet until her eyes crossed. The parchment was worn, its edges smudged and finger-marked by the countless students who had used it before her. Where her tutor, Brother Mathias, swore there were words, she found nothing save swirling ink stains.

Frustration weighed heavily on Johanna's heart. It wasn't the lessons she minded so much, it was Brother Mathias; he liked teaching her no more than she liked being taught by him. But, someday she would marry Katel, Papa's oldest apprentice, and Katel wished her to learn to read and keep the accounts.

Johanna reminded herself she was fortunate to be betrothed to one as handsome as Katel, or so said the gaggle of lasses who labored in Papa's house and the apothecary shop. She should be trying to please him, since it was Katel who'd given her her new kitten; Puss was to serve as a reminder of their betrothal while Katel and Papa were traveling.

Ah, but they'd be gone all summer, and it would be years and years before she and Katel could marry. Vindicated in her reluctance, Johanna set to teasing the kitten hiding beneath her stool. This time, the youngling tom sank its claws past her stocking and into her skin. A squeak of pain slipped out from between her clamped lips.

Instantly, Johanna bowed her head over the parchment and formed deep creases on her brow. Only when she wore this expression did Brother Mathias believe she was trying. The silence in the room continued uninterrupted. When Johanna could bear it no longer, she peered up from her pose.

Hands cupped behind his back, Brother Mathias stood before the wide, arched opening in this chamber's western wall. The white surplice that lay atop his black habit gleamed in the late afternoon light. Beneath dark hair gone rusty with age, her tutor's face was heavy in the cheeks and weak at the chin. The monk's brown eyes, honed over years of tutoring the scion of Stanrudde's merchant class, narrowed in suspicion and reproach.

"Lower your gaze," he commanded, no affection in his tone.

Dutifully, Johanna turned her gaze back to the angled wooden box in her lap. Brother Mathias detested her habit of staring directly at him. He said such behavior made her lewd. Johanna wrinkled her nose in contempt. Even she knew eight was too young for that. Lewdness was something done by wild apprentices and maids with breasts.

"Are you finished?" Mathias bit out.

"I am still pondering this word," she answered, stabbing a finger toward the center of the skin.

"Hurry it. Vespers will soon be upon us." Once again, he put his back to her.

Good. It shouldn't be too hard to stall until Mathias had to leave for the priory. She held her meek pose for another moment, then raised her head to look at the whitewashed wall across from her. Instead of wood, Papa's new house was made up of layer atop layer of rounded stones set in a bed of thick mortar. Although the inner wall wore a coat of plaster, the plasterer had let the texture of the stones show through. Thus, what should have been a flat surface became a swirling maze to tease her eye.

Johanna followed one looping avenue over and around the stones until her gaze touched on the wooden dividing wall that cleaved this long room into two, hall and bedchamber. In the far corner stood three chests, one painted in shades of green, one brown detailed with blue, the third a rusty color bound with brass. The rusty-colored one held their linens, while the others contained what had been her mother's wealth in serving platters, their aquamanile, the ewers, and eating utensils. They were her dowry and would stay so, even if Papa married again and got himself a son.

She glanced impatiently back to the window and the monk. Brother Mathias hadn't moved. How much longer?

Just then, the kitten hiding beneath her skirts laid his head upon his mistress's foot and purred; Johanna's toes thrummed with his pleasure. The corners of her mouth quirked upward at the sensation. Unable to resist, she tilted her head to one side until the tail of one golden-red braid brushed the floor. Puss's purring stopped. Back and forth her plait's end swept, just outside the edge of her hems. A ball of gray fur erupted from beneath her skirt. The kitten sank his claws into the leather thong that bound her hair, flipped himself onto his back, and kicked joyously at this new toy. Johanna snickered as the kitten turned in frantic play, leaping, pouncing, and chasing at the thick layer of rushes that covered the floor around him.

"What is this?" Mathias roared. He leapt for the kitten, foot raised to smash the wee creature's head. "Begone, you servant of Satan!"

"Nay!" Johanna shrieked, launching herself off the stool. The desk smashed on the floor; the stool clattered onto its side. She caught the monk by his cord belt and shoved at him. "Katel gave him to me! You leave him alone!"

Startled by her attack, Mathias stumbled, missing his prey. All his fur on end, Puss hissed, the sound bigger than he. Still spitting, he fled the hall for the bedchamber.

The monk turned on Johanna, his eyes wild at such unbelievable boldness. "Foul bitch, not only do you dare to reprimand your better, you shoved me!" His words were a raging breath.

Johanna took a backward step. Mathias grabbed her arm and raised his hand. Concern turned into shock. It had never occurred to her the monk would strike her. Papa never hit her, no matter how angry she made him.

"Helewise!" she shrieked in fear.

The housekeeper must have been waiting just inside Papa's bedchamber door, for she swept into the room almost before Johanna's call left her mouth. Helewise's green overgown and brown undergown clung to her ample curves. Held to her head by a thin metal circlet, a fragile veil draped the housekeeper's unremarkable face, the fashionable loop of fabric beneath her jaw serving to support a second set of chins. As she stopped beside her charge, she lowered her head as did every demure female when facing a man, especially a churchman. But, behind Johanna's back where the monk couldn't see, the housekeeper caught a fistful of her charge's gown.

"Brother Mathias, what goes forward here?" Helewise's voice was soft, her tone filled with naught but feminine distress.

"Stand back, servant. This insufferable daughter of Eve has dared not only to speak rudely to me, but to lay hands upon my person. She will be chastised."

"Brother, I cannot oppose you, for if she did as you say, she richly deserves the lesson. However, might it not be better if Master Walter delivered it? Her attack on you has done her sire the greater damage as her behavior maligns both his house and reputation. He'll want to see the lesson truly learned, I think me."

Johanna stared at the rushes on the floor as she set to bargaining with God. Papa said Helewise could bend any man to her will using naught but her sweet demeanor and soft words. It was this skill, not cooking or cleaning, he urged his sulking, tantruming daughter to learn. Should Helewise succeed this day, Johanna vowed to do as her father requested.

Vesper's call began as an alto clanging at St. Stephen's, Stanrudde's northernmost church, then rolled from holy house to holy house, until the abbey's church bell added its thundering tones to the sweet cacophony. The faithful had best hurry; there was naught but a quarter hour before the start of the evening service.

With an irate breath, Mathias released his grip on Johanna's arm. "I stay my hand solely for her sire's sake," the monk hissed. "Never should I have allowed Master Walter to twist me into this. Tell him she is a terrible child and an even worse student. I'll not return to this task until she kneels before me, begging my forgiveness and displaying the welts he has raised upon her."

Johanna dared to peek up at Brother Mathias in surprise. He was refusing to teach her? The monk shot her another raging look then leaned down to fetch his parchment from the ruins of the desk. With skin in hand, he strode for the hall's exit. Still stunned, Johanna listened as he clattered into the stone forebuilding, which shielded the house's exterior stairway from the elements. The massive door at the forebuilding's base creaked as it opened.

"Good evening, Brother Mathias." Arthur, Papa's younger apprentice, called his greeting to his tutor from the yet open workshop window in next door's apothecary shop. Liking the twelve-year-old lad only a little better than he did Johanna, Mathias did not respond.

Johanna sagged against Helewise in amazement. She was free! Elation swiftly reached the end of its tether, and her spirits crashed back to earth. Papa would be furious when he returned from his tour of the summer fairs. And, Brother Mathias wanted to see welts. A start of fear went through her. She looked up at Helewise. "Will Papa beat me?"

Now that the crisis was passed, irritation clouded the housekeeper's face. "Well he ought, little mistress. I think it a shame your sire believes himself too big to use a reprimanding hand on any soul. Your strongheadedness dearly demands just such a punishment." She levered Johanna away from her, then aimed an accusing finger at her charge. "Were you my daughter, I'd have your hide. What sort of woman will you become if you behave this way? You are headed on the road to destruction, I tell you. Why, every woman in the world knows better than to lay hands on a churchman."

Outrage returned, tearing through all Johanna's new promises to behave. "But, Brother Mathias meant to hurt Puss!"

Helewise made an impatient sound. "And here's another instance where your father coddled you. He should never have allowed Katel to give you that cat. That creature has twice gotten into the milk this day."

"Aleric!" Once again, Arthur's voice rose from the street-side window a story below them and drifted through the open window. "What are you doing here, and who is that in your arms?" the apprentice shouted.

"Arthur, come you and help me with the master's horse," Papa's most important servant called to the apprentice, his deep voice ringing in the quieting air.

Helewise gasped, all color draining from her face. Johanna's heart lurched. Helewise said the road was dangerous for any man, but all the more so for a rich one. She made Johanna pray three times a day for her sire while Papa was journeying.

Johanna leapt for the hall's exit, her plaits flying. Helewise was close on her heels. Dashing into the forebuilding, she careened down the steps, her path lit by what bit of the dying day's light streamed in through the two tiny windows at the forebuilding's western roofline. At the base of the building, she dodged around the half-opened door, turning away from Market Lane as she headed back behind the house.

Their private courtyard was nothing more than the space caught between the house, outbuildings, and the wall that surrounded Herebert the Ropemaker's enclave. Just now, Aleric stood at its center, his back to her. Papa's big white horse snorted and huffed next to him. Sweat stained the steed's flanks, while the bright saddle trappings were fouled. As chubby Arthur claimed the horse's reins, Aleric turned.

Johanna stopped short. In the agent's arms lay a lad, dried blood and dark purpling covering every bit of his visible skin. The breeze lifted, flowing from Aleric to her. Johanna's stomach twisted. The lad smelled worse than the beggars who gathered around the priory.

"Aleric, what of the master?" Helewise cried out, nearly stumbling over Johanna in her haste to reach her brother.

"Worrier," Aleric chided with a brief smile. "I'd have said were aught wrong. I am but returning with Master Walter's newest servant."

Helewise laid a gentle hand on the boy's brow. "Holy Mother of God, what happened to him?"

"He was beaten by his sire as that man attempted to drive him from their home." There was deep affront in Aleric's low tones.

Johanna took a step back, her heart aching. This was what Brother Mathias wished Papa would do to her. She took another backward step, wanting only to escape looking on what might be her own fate.

Aleric's gaze caught hers. "Nay, you cannot leave, little mistress. You must tell me what I'm to do with the lad. Your father has made the healing of him your task."

"Mine?" she squeaked in surprise. She knew nothing of healing; that was Helewise's job.

"Aye. He says if you do well in it, he'll delay your reading lessons, honoring instead your request to manage his house."

She stared at the tall servant, shock giving way to relief, then gratitude to God. The Almighty had done better than answer her prayer. He had saved her. Squaring her shoulders, Johanna thrust out her chin and strode to Aleric's side. The tall man made an odd choking sound, but Johanna ignored him to squinch her eyes just as Helewise did when she looked at the sick. Oh, but he was so hurt. She was only eight. What if she couldn't heal him?

Chewing her lower lip, Johanna looked up at Helewise. The housekeeper's brows rose, inviting her charge to spill a treatment plan. Johanna racked her brain, seeking to remember what Helewise did for those ailing folk who crossed their threshold.

"He needs to be in the kitchen, lying on a pallet before the hearth where it's warm?" This was a fairly safe wager as the kitchen's hearth was where Helewise always laid the sick.

A touch of a smile appeared at the corners of the housekeeper's mouth. "And, what else?"

"His clothing should be removed, and the filth washed from his wounds?" That's what Helewise had done for the beggar who'd dropped at their doorstep last winter. Glancing at the years-old burn mark on the back of her hand, she added, "Then we must put salves on his bruises and cuts?"

"Aye, that's a well-thought plan, little mistress," Helewise said. "Who will you have me send to fetch a pallet from the hall?"

"Arthur?" Johanna asked.

Helewise's head bobbed once in approval, and she called the command into the stable. At Arthur's positive response, the housekeeper turned to her brother. "Aye, then, our little mistress says we're for the kitchen, Aleric."

Johanna breathed the worry from her lungs as she turned to run ahead of them to the wooden cooking shed. In Helewise's reaction was the offer of aid. The housekeeper would watch that no foot was put wrong, but say nothing to Papa about how she'd helped. Freedom from Brother Mathias was within reach.

Set in the small area between the rear wall of the house, the stable, and the apothecary shop's back yard, her father's kitchen was hexagonal in shape. Johanna blinked as she stepped inside, letting her eyes adjust to the dimness within the room. Smoke from the ever-burning fire on the kitchen's central hearth flowed upward, drawn out through a shielded vent at the apex of the shed's thatched roof. A great pot, its bottom blackened by constant use, hung over the flames on its ratcheted chain. Thick bunches of herbs dangled from the crisscrossing rafters overhead, while stoppered containers of hardened leather, some so big she could barely put her arms around them, stood on shelf and floor. Wedged between casks of oil and wine were sacks of shelled almonds, while the morrow's fish swam hopelessly in a broad, lined barrel at the far wall.

At his worktable with knife in hand, Old Philip looked up from the cubes he was making of yesterday's bread. Small and wiry, the cook's hair lay flat against his skull beneath his cap, his skin slick with a day's worth of sweat. "And who do you seek to heal at my hearth this day?" he called to Helewise as she and Aleric followed Johanna into the room.

"Not Helewise," Johanna responded before the housekeeper could speak, "me. Papa sent me a lad to heal." With her words came a strange sense of ownership. Papa had given this lad to her, trusting she would care for him as she ought.

"Is that so?" Philip replied, his grizzled brows lifting in tune to his question.

Philip's son, Tom the Lackwit, looked up from scouring the remains of lamb stew from a tureen. Although only a little younger than Katel, Tom's round face was yet childlike. His bottom lip hung slack as he watched Aleric bear the lad into the room. "Hurt," he said after a moment.

"Aye, Tom," Johanna replied. "I'll be needing one of your cleaning cloths and hot water to wash him."

Tom hesitated, pondering this unusual command coming from an even more unusual source, then nodded and trundled past the hearth to do her bidding. Pleasure shot through Johanna. Now, this was how life should be, she the mistress, while others did as she commanded.

When the makeshift bed was ready, Tom set the basin at its head, and Aleric lowered the unconscious boy to the pallet. The lad freed a muffled cry, then lay still. Kneeling at his side, Johanna began to wrestle his filthy, bloodstained tunic from him. It caught on his arms and would not move. The lad moaned as her efforts made his head joggle against his hard bed.

Helewise knelt beside her to cup the boy's skull in her hand. "Shall I bathe him for you?" she asked quietly as she lifted Johanna's patient a little so his tunic could be eased over his head.

"Nay," Johanna said, grunting against the effort it took to remove clothing from an unresponsive body. "Papa has made this boy mine, and I must do for him."

"Why, Johanna of Stanrudde, you surprise me. Even as I watch, the babe in you is being replaced by a sober woman."

The pride in Helewise's voice made Johanna's heart glow. Her lips tried to curve into a smile, but she kept her mouth tight in an expression appropriate to the mistress of the house. Aye, she would show Papa she was of more use to him as a housewife than a scholar.

Chapter Six

Stanrudde
Late May, 1173

There was a fire burning behind Rob. Although the hiss and crackle was comforting, he lay too close. Even nude with but a single blanket atop him, sweat trickled down his back. Ah, but if he moved, he'd loose the final tendrils of the dream he'd been having about Mama and Blacklea.

Something brushed against his face. Rob clenched his eyes shut, drawing a breath to keep from reacting to the tickle of it. The air around him smelled of day-old fish. There was an awful lump covered with prickly fabric beneath his cheek. Grimacing in discomfort, he shifted his head until it no longer troubled him.

Again, that something brushed his face. Raising a hand, he batted at it. With that, the ragged ends of his dream slithered into some hidden recess of his mind. Sighing in disappointment, Rob opened his eyes.

Although the fire behind him barely managed to keep night at bay, the shimmering golden light was strong enough to show him a thick table, legs like small tree trunks, just a few feet beyond his reach. From where he lay, he couldn't see the table's surface, but the floor beneath it was bare earth, long since beaten into rock hardness. Beyond the table, dancing shadows played along the wall, curling around large casks and finding glittering beads of sweat on the waxen surface of the great wheel of cheese. On the wall above these items hung six long knives, four rasps, three large ladles, and five sieves, all of them gleaming in the low light.

Rob frowned. Wherever he was, it wasn't the kitchen at Blacklea manor house where all the village women baked their bread. John the cook had only two long knives, two ladles, one rasp, and three sieves.

In dreadful realization, Rob closed his eyes. This was Master Walter's kitchen. Despair followed fear. His world was destroyed. No longer could he proudly call himself Robert the Counter, heir to Ralph Atte-Green, the richest man and only freeholder in all of Blacklea. Instead, he was disowned by his sire and sold like a slave to a merchant from someplace called Stanrudde.

A touch of outrage joined his despair. What if Master Walter forever after called him Robert the Bastard, instead of Robert, son of Ralph? It was neither right nor fair that he should be called so when he was no bastard.

"I know you are awake." It was a girl's voice. "Look at me, Robert of Blacklea!"

Rob clenched his eyes even more tightly shut. Was it not bad enough he'd lost everything important to him in life? Now some lass thought she could tell him what to do. She lifted his blanket, allowing cooler air to enter beneath it. With a gasp of shock, Rob shifted on the mattress to glare up at his tormentor.

The girl sat on a stool beside him. Her reddish gold hair was tangled and loose. Bare wisps of that same golden-red color rose to peaks above her blue eyes and freckles were strewn like golden seeds across her face. Her gowns were blue trimmed with a band of glittering stones, but they were rumpled as if she'd slept in them. In the same hand that she had clenched around his blanket's edge she held a long straw.

Anger flared into being at this indignity. "Drop my blanket," he croaked.

A superior smile blossomed on her face, as if daring him to make her do so. He reached up to take the blanket from her, but his arm trembled so badly, he couldn't jerk it from her grasp. It was she who released it to him, and she knew it.

"Don't do that again," he warned in an effort to save some shred of pride, once again gathering the woolen sheet around him.

His gaze lowered to the kitten writhing in the crook of her elbow. Mama disapproved of any attempt to hold a cat, especially scolding when he let it dangle so. Rob leapt on the girl's misdeed. "You're not supposed to hold a cat that way. Don't you know anything?"

Her eyes widened at his insult, then her jaw firmed and thrust ever so slightly forward. A quirk of appreciation shot through Rob. She wasn't one of those weak-willed lasses, but the other sort, the kind that punched first and cried after.

"Puss is mine, and I may hold him any way I like. *I* can do anything I like, because I am Johanna, daughter of Walter le Espicer," she announced in a grand and lofty voice. "You are my servant and cannot tell me what to do."

Her words tore through his already aching self-image. "I'm no girl's servant! Master Walter hired me as his scullery lad," he cried, then struck out again at her. "Once I have earned the value of the ten coins he gave my papa, I will be a free man, unlike you, who will always be a girl."

That tweaked Johanna the Spice Merchant's Daughter right prettily. She dropped Puss to the floor and set tight fists on her hips. As the kitten skittered away to chase after mice and shadows, Master Walter's daughter leaned toward him, her skin reddening until her freckles stood out as pale, cool spots. "I am the mistress here! You are not being respectful. Everyone must be respectful of me."

Merchant's daughter or no, she was younger than he. No babe in arms was going to lord over him. "Respectful! Hah!" He paused a beat, then threw out the comment that always destroyed the village lasses. "You are so nasty, I think no man will want to marry you."

This lass only lifted her chin, her lips again curving into that superior smile. "I will so wed. I am already betrothed to Katel."

Rob shrugged as if unaffected by her claim, all the while hiding his surprise. She was only a little girl. How could she know whom she would marry? In Blacklea no one thought of wedding until they were ready to start their own families. Stanrudde was, indeed, a strange place. Even more disturbing was the realization that her retort left him both weaponless and defenseless against her. Rob sorted desperately through his muddled thoughts for some way to put her in her place. When he'd found it, he smiled and raised a haughty brow.

"I am surprised he wants you. You are ugly, and your nose is too big."

Hurt far deeper than he'd intended flashed across her face. She set a hand atop the bridge of her nose, a much smaller version of the merchant's great, arching beak, as if to shield it from his eyes. "Papa says I have a nose of authority." Her voice was low and uncertain as if she'd been teased about this many times.

Regret destroyed Rob's moment of triumph. He'd only meant to bludgeon her into submission, not draw her heart's blood. He shrugged, then offered an olive branch. "It's not that big and, mayhap, I do remember you gave me water when I ailed."

Puss meowed, the frightened sound coming from the nearby tabletop. With a frantic cry, Johanna leapt from her stool. Rob lifted himself up on his elbows until he could see. The kitten dangled over the edge of a large bowl on the tabletop. Before Johanna could reach it, the bowl rolled over the table's edge, crockery shattering around the cat.

With a wordless cry of horror, the master's daughter snatched up the dripping creature and turned on Rob. Her expression twisted in fear. "That was curded cheese for the morrow. If Philip learns Puss did this, he'll tell Papa, and Papa will take Puss from me. You must say you did this," she demanded.

"What?" he croaked, surprise making him tumble back onto his mattress. He liked the cat, but not enough to be punished for what Puss had done.

Johanna crouched down next to him. "You have to help. I'll die without my cat, I love him so. Say you were rising and stumbled into the table, please?" This time, there was more pleading than command in her voice.

Rob frowned in consideration. Although he didn't much like to lie, Johanna was the master's daughter. Setting his jaw, Rob lowered his brows into the expression Papa had taught him to use when bargaining. "What do I get for taking your beating?"

"There'll be no beating. If you help me, I vow to share Puss with you."

He shook his head. True, she might not be beaten for a broken bowl, but there was no guarantee the same would apply to him, were he to claim responsibility. Sharing the cat wasn't enough reward for the risk involved, and she knew it.

Johanna's eyes filled with tears. "I'll never again say you are my servant," she offered, suddenly sounding as young and helpless as Gretta. A teardrop dribbled down her cheek, and her lips began to tremble. "You'll be my friend, this I swear."

Even as the thought of friendship with a girl made Rob grimace in disgust, his long habit of protecting his sister wouldn't let him refuse her. Ah well, what could it hurt to let her think on him as her friend? He caught himself. Except if some other lad knew of it.

He offered her a nod. "As long as you vow to tell no one of this night's work and there's no beating, I'll say I did it. In return, you must vow to grant me a favor when I ask it of you." He went on in explanation, since she was just a lass and might not know about giving her word. "Be careful how you swear, for an oath is a promise made before God. You'll be damned to hell if you break it. Place your hand upon your heart as you say the words."

Johanna of Stanrudde placed her hand upon her chest. "I will grant you a favor, this I vow." When she was done, she breathed in relief and smiled. "Thank you, Robert."

"Rob. My name is Rob." He yawned. "Just know that if anyone's truly angered over this, I'll spill the truth."

"No one will be," she assured him. "I won't let them be."

He snorted in disbelief. "You're barely more than a babe. What can you do to stop them?"

Johanna shot him an impatient look. "I told you, I am mistress here. Everyone must do as I say. I have been mistress for six years, ever since my mother died with my newborn brother, just as your mother did."

Stunned, Rob gaped at her. "How do you know it was a babe's coming that took my mother?"

Johanna laid a hand on his shoulder. Oddly enough, his skin didn't crawl at her touch. "Aleric told us your tale before he returned to Papa."

All the pain of Mama's death and Papa's betrayal poured over him, the wave of sadness dragging him down into despair once more. A shudder shot through Rob. If Master Walter's servant had said this much, it was certain everyone here also knew Papa had disowned him. He could never again return home. Tears stung at his eyes, and he buried his head into the folds of his blanket in shame.

"Rob?" Johanna's voice was hesitant. "Papa always says a good master is like unto a father to all those who dwell under his roof. If you like, I will share my papa with you."

Her words lit a fire in his heart. Rob wrenched himself around, not caring that she might see his tears. "I don't need your father, I have one of my own!" he shouted. "Go away, go away and leave me be."

He threw himself back down onto the mattress and pulled his blanket up over his head. To his horror, a sob escaped him, then another. Even the knowledge that Johanna listened did not stop them. Not only could he never go home, but there was no one left to love him.

Chapter Seven

Stanrudde
two and a half hours past None,
The eve of Ste. Agnes's Day, 1197

Rob reached the abbey's gateway only to find the tiny portal inset into the much larger gate doors barred. As he tore the wood from its braces, Johanna screamed once more. He yanked on the wee door's handle. It gave not an inch. He whirled. Brother William danced just behind him, near the entrance to the tiny room that was the porter's domain. The monk's eyes were wide in frantic worry for the woman beyond the walls.

"Open the damn door!" Rob roared at him.

Brother William squeaked. His hands fluttered in the air as if he had no idea how such a thing was done.

"Brother, your key," Colin called from the hospitium's window. The monk blinked, then ducked into his cubicle. Iron jangled as he wrenched the key ring from its peg.

His heart consumed by worry, Rob yanked open the tiny square window in the door to scan the market's field. Trapped by the boiling crowd at the center of that expanse was a lone and mounted woman. Even though her face was hidden by her cloak and wimple, Rob knew it was Johanna. His fiery girl kicked out at those around her, which was far better than her mount was doing; the stupid beast but turned in confusion.

Rob drew a calming breath. That Johanna fought so said she was yet unharmed.

With a cooler head, he assessed the folk seething around her. Their shouts, threats, and curses rebounded against the abbey's thick walls, then disappeared with the smoke that swirled up from the city's sea of thatched roofs and into the clouds. Despite the violence of their words, the horde seemed content to simply rebuke Johanna because she was wealthier and better fed than they. Then, from the corner of his eye Rob caught a snippet of stealthy movement amid so much honest fist shaking.

Again, he scanned the area, this time his gaze wandering to the far edges of the open expanse. Out of the darkened alleyways, brigand and ruffian alike slithered onto this field. The pustules on Stanrudde's underbelly were slowly working their way through the mob around Johanna, drawn to her by the lure of her rings and the gold encircling her throat.

This put a whole new urgency to the situation. Where the crowd was content to rage, these men would not hesitate to kill Johanna to make what was hers theirs. In the next instant, Brother William leapt from his room and iron grated on iron as he fitted it into its slot.

"Master Robert," Will's voice rose from the hospitium, where Rob's household guard now armed, "Hamalin says to tell you they'll be set in only a moment."

Rob relaxed. With his servants behind him, he could hold both laborer and thief at bay until the town guard arrived to clear the field. As the monk turned the key, Rob started to close the peephole's door, then froze. Johanna had ceased kicking in defense and was digging into her purse.

"Nay," he breathed in horror, realizing she hoped to distract the crowd and win her freedom by strewing coins. "That is nothing," he told her. "It's your rings and your chain you must throw. Give them what they want, and they'll leave you be."

His warning went unheard. Johanna lifted her fist and rained coins down upon the crowd. Folk roared. Neighbor turned on neighbor in a desperate grab for these crumbs. With the scrupulous thus occupied, the ruffians howled in triumph, their chances of winning far richer treasures having just trebled.

"Nay," Rob shouted as Brother William began to open the door.

Grabbing the handle from the monk, Rob threw wide the burly sheet of oak. As it opened, those on the opposite side surged within, seeking sanctuary in the abbey's courtyard. It was their hands and feet they wished to keep, the loss of any one appendage being a rioter's punishment.

Using elbows and shoulders, Rob thrust into their ranks, forcing his way onto the field. His household guard was not so fortunate. Although they shouted and harangued, there was no penetrating the ever-growing throng between them and the now jammed opening.

Rob dared not wait on them. Across the field, a man exploded from the tangle of folk around Johanna to grasp her horse's bridle. Fear made Rob's battle through the crowd all the more desperate. Johanna's attacker lifted his hand, a knife glinting dully in his fist. With a butcher's practiced stroke, he drew the blade across her mount's neck.

"Nay!" Rob bellowed as blood flowed.

The plump palfrey squealed and bucked in terror. Johanna flew from her saddle to disappear into the frenzied crowd as they closed on the dying beast. Rob forgot he wore a long dagger. Nothing but the distance between him and the spot where Johanna had fallen existed. With his fists, alone, he carved himself a path to the side of the woman he yet believed was his wife.

* * *

Johanna's heart nearly stopped as she left the saddle. Ah, but such a death would be too easy for a fool like herself. Dropping onto a man's broad back, she caromed off him to land on the marketplace's mucky ground. Stars came to life before her eyes, and she gasped as the breath left her lungs. What need had Katel of a plot to destroy her when she so obligingly destroyed herself for him? In her blind rage over something that had happened years ago, she'd ridden right into this attack.

Her vision cleared. Yet breathless from the impact, she braced trembling arms beneath and began to rise. A foot caught her in the shoulder. With a yelp, she tumbled backward and rolled onto her side. Another man stepped on her legs. Still more folk stumbled over her as they streamed toward her dying horse, intent only on claiming a bit of free meat for their pots.

It was the horse murderer who yanked her to her feet. Clamping a blood-befouled hand over her nose and mouth, he pressed her head against his shoulder as if he meant to slit her throat as well. "I'll have that chain, see if I won't," he shouted as he yanked at the gold chain that nestled between her overgown and her cloak.

The links held. He yanked again. Johanna clawed at his hand, her lungs crying for air.

Other men encircled them. Her hopes lifted, then plummeted. These newcomers cared only for what she wore.

They set on her captor, raining indiscriminate blows down upon both of them in an effort to claim her. Her assailant released her. Gagging and gasping, Johanna dropped to her knees. The butcher fell beside her, someone else's knife in his chest.

She was yanked to her feet by her cloak, then reeled from hand to hand like a child's poppet as the group battled over her. Her cloak left her shoulders and her wimple her head, her hair tumbling free from the sedate traveling roll Leatrice had made of it. Her hands were wrenched and twisted as her rings departed, her forefinger ring taking both glove and skin with it. A knife's point scored her abdomen as her pearl-studded belt was cut from her.

Two men snatched her chain at the same time, pawing at each other over it. The tussle intensified, each man grabbing a handful of her gowns to aid their cause. A broken doll, Johanna sagged between the two, half senseless from her battering. As the fronts of her gowns gave way, so did the gold. The winner sprinted for the nearest alleyway, leaving her in the loser's disgusted grasp.

It was the sound of a miracle when the bleat of the town guard's horn rose in the field's far end. Screaming in new panic, the mob churned in the cramped marketplace. Folk scattered every which way, intent on preserving life and limb.

Johanna breathed against the impossibility of having survived to this moment and waited for her captor to release her to flee. Instead, he lifted her to her feet, holding her before him as if to assure himself she owned nothing further of value. Stunned beyond tears or pleas, she could only stare into his face. A hollow shell of a big man, he wore a thief's "X" branded into his cheek.

His gaze dropped to the torn fronts of her gowns, then he fingered a tress of her hair. Without a word, he clamped an arm around her waist and turned. Johanna had no choice but to stumble along beside him as he pulled her across the field and onto the coopers' lane.

He moved down the rutted and muddy street until he reached a tight, dark space between two houses. Sliding into its narrow dimness, he dropped her onto the filth of the alley's floor and wrenched up her skirts. A terror even greater than that of death woke in Johanna.

"Nay," she breathed, trying to shove her gowns back over her legs as she rolled onto her side.

He slammed a foot into her chest. Air whooshed from her lungs. Fighting for breath, Johanna struck at his leg, but her arms felt disconnected at the elbows, her blows kittenish and soft. His chausses freed, the thief fell atop her, holding her in place with his body as he worked her skirts up over her thighs. His bare flesh was obscenely warm against her chilled skin.

Her stomach turned in horror and fear as she writhed beneath him. He pressed his mouth to hers. She raked her nails across his face. With a growl, he drew himself up far enough to deal her a heavy blow.

Again, stars swam in a hopeless sea before her eyes, making blackness swirl around her, paralyzing her limbs. As he once more fixed his mouth over hers, there was movement in the shadows overhead, then her attacker was lifted from atop her. With a bellow of furious ownership, the thief turned in midair and set upon this new challenge to what little value he'd snatched from the spice merchant's wife.

Breath returned to her lungs. Johanna's head steadied. The battle moved away from her, back toward the alley's entrance. Hope rose. As long as they were busy killing each other, they'd hardly notice she was leaving.

Struggling to her feet, she limped deeper into the alley's shadows. Every muscle ached. The need to sob filled her, but she fought it back, afraid she'd fall to pieces if she released even a single cry.

Behind her, one of the two screamed, the sound choked off with a suddenness that spoke of death. Johanna moved faster. Ahead of her, a wall rose up to stand between her and freedom. With the tiniest of cries, she clenched her fist and hit the blind alley's end.

The winner's footsteps echoed in the dimness as he came to claim his prize. Johanna turned, pressing her back to the wall. A man, taller and broader than her previous attacker, appeared out of the dimness. She would die.

Anger at this filled her. Why should she have survived the attack in the field, only to perish even more horribly in this filthy place? It was the injustice of this that turned her fingers into talons.

Loosing a bold shout to hide her terror, she threw herself at this new threat. The man caught her hands, then pulled her close into his embrace. Her head was pressed against his shoulder. "Nay, love," he said to her, his tone warm and low. "You're safe. I have you now."

Johanna went still at the sound of his voice. Her fists opened, her fingers digging into the soft fur of his mantle. Beneath her cheek she felt the steady beat of his heart. She moved her head to the spot where it had always been most comfortable.

"Rob?" she mewled, a piteous sound.

"Aye, love."

Her heart, so long denied affection, sighed at this endearment. "He was going to . . ." she began to tell him, only to fall silent as a terrible trembling started in the pit of her stomach. In the space of a breath her quaking spread to every inch of her body, until even her toes shook. The horror of what had and had not happened washed over her, again and again. A single dry sob left her, then a tear trickled down her cheek, the harbinger of a bursting dam.

"You're safe, love," he crooned, his arms tightening around her. "You're safe now."

It was Rob; she was safe. Johanna buried her face into his shoulder and let the terror pour from her with her tears.

When at last her sobs subsided, she lay spent against him, beyond thought or care in her relief. He let her stay so, but rocking her gently in his embrace. It was a long while before she had strength enough to lean back in his arms and look at him.

Now that her vision was accustomed to the dimness, she could see the blood seeping from a set of scratches on his brow. His collar was torn. Light from the alley's opening gleamed against the familiar high thrust of his cheekbones, the gentle curve of his brow, and the narrow length of his nose.

She frowned. It was Rob, but he was so changed. Fine lines touched the corners of his gray eyes, while a beard covered his strong jaw and outlined the curve of his lips. He'd let his hair grow longer than she liked it on a man.

Without thought, she raised a hand and pressed one dark brown strand into a curl against his cheek. Thick and soft, his hair did as she bid, just as it always had. He smiled at this familiar game of hers. His amusement set deep creases in his lean cheeks and brought warm lights to life in the cool gray of his eyes.

In that instant, the boy who'd loved her reappeared. Time shifted, and the years melted away. It was the girl who loved him in return who raised herself to her toes and touched her lips to his.

The meeting of their mouths was nothing more than a gentle press of flesh to flesh. Yet, it was so warm, so familiar, so right, she wanted nothing more than to stand so forever. That was, until a spark of sensation shot through her, infinitely short, but oh so pleasurable.

Catching her breath against it, Johanna moved her lips on his as she fed her starving heart. Her caress made his kiss deepen, but just a little. This time, the spark returned, lasting long enough to wake years of banked hunger from its uneasy slumber.

Long suppressed carnal need stretched itself to life, demanding that she feed it. Johanna laced her hands behind Rob's neck, pulling herself closer in a plea for more. He groaned in soft compliance, the sound rumbling in his chest. His kiss deepened, until his mouth slashed across hers.

She gasped, aware of every inch of him. There was the brush of his hair against her wrists, the movement of his beard against her cheek. A pulsing warmth shot through her as the smell of him filled her, the taste of him left her craving more. Trembling, she shifted against him, letting her body flow into his. Just as had always happened, their bodies melded as though they'd been created one for the other.

Chapter Eight

Stanrudde
Mid-June, 1173

From his stool in the kitchen's darkest corner, Rob watched in misery as the midday meal was prepared. He hated Master Walter's house, or rather his kitchen, that being the only part of the house he'd seen since his awakening. There was nothing familiar or normal about this place.

Not the folk. He watched Tom lift a cauldron from the flames and begin ladling thick mutton stew into a tureen. Although the lackwit was a man full grown, he acted almost as young as Gretta. Nor the smells or tastes. Beside his son, Philip put the finishing touches on a fruit and marrow pie for the midday meal: a stranger creating an equally strange dish. Moreover, it was never quiet here. No amount of counting or imagining was strong enough to escape the endless noise. Hammers pounded on anvils from dawn to dusk, bells clanged, and, worst of all, folk shouted and called to one another, even deep in the night when all decent beings should be at their rest.

Of a sudden, homesickness churned in Rob. He longed for the comforting routines, the gentle woodland quiet spiced by the call of the lark and the song of the wind through a field of barley. He no longer cared that Papa didn't want him. As soon as he'd earned the value of those coins, he'd leave this awful place and go home. As if to punctuate his misery, the kitchen door flew open with an annoying squeak.

It was Johanna who danced into the room, her bouncing plaits glinting in a shaft of golden midday light, a jumble of green and brown fabric in her arms. Excitement filled her face. On her heels came Helewise. Rob glanced at the housekeeper. As always, Helewise's pale brown eyes were as cool as the metal band that held her veil in place. And, as always, her gaze pierced his soul.

Rob turned his attention to his blanket-clad lap as guilt twisted in his stomach. He should never have agreed to help Johanna. Although Philip had accepted his contrived tale over the broken bowl, Rob was certain Helewise knew he lied. He was equally certain the housekeeper now hated him for his sin.

"Rob, look!" Johanna cried, stopping before him to thrust her burden into his lap. "I begged and begged until Helewise said you may dress and eat in the hall this day."

From the bottom of the pile, she pulled out a green tunic and tossed it down on the ground before her. Crouching at its hem, she pointed to the large, ungainly stitches that puckered over a rent there. "I mended it for you myself." Her smile was broad in pride.

Rob stared in confusion at the wholly foreign garment, then looked at the brown chausses, green garters, and worn linen shirt yet lying in his lap. Only his shoes were his own. He shook his head in refusal. "You've given me someone else's clothing."

Johanna rolled her eyes as if he were as dense as the lackwit. "We have not, you goose. Everyone in this house wears green and brown, except for me," she said in sweet arrogance as she glanced up at the housekeeper. "I don't have to, do I, Helewise?"

Rob closed his fist around the voluminous linen shirt that lay uppermost on the pile. It felt fine and smooth against his palm. At last year's fair he and Papa had traded a yearling ram to the old clothes seller for a gown for Mama. That was one sheep for one garment. There were three garments here. He'd be years repaying the debt. Panic roared to life in him. They meant to trap him, he knew it. He shoved the clothing off his lap. "I'd rather keep my own garments."

"I'm afraid they are gone, lad," Helewise said. "They were ruined from blood and manure. The best I could do was make rags out of them."

Rob jerked around on his stool to stare in shock, forgetting for the moment he was afraid of her. "You can't have made rags of my clothing!"

The merest hint of confusion woke in the housekeeper's cool gaze. "Lad, you now serve in the household of Walter le Espicer. As a sign of our service, we all wear his colors." She held out the skirts of her green overgown and brown undergown in example.

Rob's pulse lifted to an anxious pace. So, if he had no choice but to take these garments, how much more did he now owe Master Walter? "Where are the tally sticks that show my debt, and how much does each day I labor count against what I owe?" he demanded of the housekeeper.

Astonishment briefly crossed Helewise's bland face, only to be swallowed by the coolness she ever aimed at him. "Oh my heavens, lad, who has taught you to think like that?"

Her question confused him. In Blacklea every villager knew the value of his labor against what he owed his lord. Were things so different here? "No one taught me."

Her lips almost curved into a smile. "Well now, yours is a reasonable request, but one only Master Walter can address. You must ask your question of him when he returns in September."

"September!" The word exploded from Rob, high-pitched and desperate. He wouldn't survive if he had to stay here so long. What if he began today and worked harder than he ever before had? They'd have to acknowledge his labor's value. Aye, he would surely be quit of his debt before August's end.

Dropping the blanket from his shoulders, he yanked on the overly large shirt. It was too long and bunched in his lap. He shoved his feet into the legs of his chausses, the one-piece garment that combined both stockings and an undergarment, and hauled it up over his hips. Coming to his feet to knot the waist string, he snatched up his garters from the floor, then thrust his feet into his shoes.

As he sat to swiftly crisscross the green garters around his calves, he glanced up at Helewise. Philip had come to stand beside her. Both adults were watching him as if he'd gone mad.

Rob tied his shoe lacings, then grabbed up the green tunic and stood to don it. The garment was huge, the sleeves extending beyond his fingertips, the skirt reaching well below his knees. Without a belt, it slid on his shoulders. He straightened as best he could, then turned to face the housekeeper.

"I will begin my work as Master Walter's scullery lad this very day."

Tom gave a sharp gasp, then moaned, "Nay, Papa."

"Scullery lad?" Philip's voice overrode his son's complaint. The creases on the cook's brow shot backward onto his balding pate as he shook his head and looked at Helewise. "Master Walter cannot do this. You know as well as I that, with nigh on all the household's gone to the fairs with the master, there's naught for him to do here."

Panic bounded higher in Rob. Not only would they add additional weight to his debt, but now Philip was going to deny him the right to labor. His gaze shifted to Helewise in the vain hope she would aid him. Instead, she lay a restraining hand on his shoulder.

"Sit, Rob." Her voice was cold and emotionless. "You are yet too ill for this."

"Nay!" he cried, tearing free of her hold. Desperation made his voice rise to a shout. "I will begin this day! Master Walter told all of Blacklea he needed a new scullery lad. I am that lad!"

Fear flashed through Tom's eyes as the lackwit looked to the housekeeper. "Nay, not for lads," he wailed, then turned and grabbed the wooden tray on which sat the marrow pie. "Tom's! Tom's!"

"Nay, Tom!" Philip cried, lunging toward his son.

He was too slow. The untouched dish splattered on the floor as the lackwit tucked the serving tray beneath his arm. "Tom's to do!" Tom shouted and reached for the tureen.

"Help me, Helewise," Philip begged, closing his hands over the dish's edge as he sought to save the day's stew. As Helewise leapt to add her weight to the tureen, Philip crooned, "Son, son, be at ease. Rob will not take your chores."

What Tom lacked in wit, he made up for in strength. The tureen tipped toward Helewise. Hot stew cascaded down her front. As the housekeeper yelped and released the dish, Philip lurched forward with a cry, stumbling into his son. Tom toppled backward, the tureen still clutched to his chest. His head hit the floor with a resounding smack. The child-man pressed his hands to his head and rolled from side to side, sobbing in piercing, high-pitched cries.

Rob looked at the mess Tom made. As he waited for the scolding to begin, he bit back a smile. It wasn't Christian to gloat.

Still dripping stew, Helewise squatted at the lackwit's side. "Be easy, Tom," the housekeeper offered sweetly. She cupped the lackwit's head in her palms. "Come now, let me see what you've done. Johanna," she called over her shoulder, "take Rob outside. It'd be best if he was no longer in the kitchen."

Shock slashed through Rob. How could she value the lackwit over a normal lad? "Nay," he shouted in righteous indignation. "I'll not go! Master Walter, himself, said I was to be a scullery lad." At his words, Tom's wailing rose to an impossible pitch.

Helewise shifted in her squat to fix him with a furious stare. "For Mary's sake, can you not see the damage you do? Now, hold your tongue and do as I say."

Tears sprang to Rob's eyes. The damage *he'd* done! Resentment followed hurt. So, this was how she meant to punish him for his lie. No doubt she'd add the cost of the spilled food to what he already owed. If that was the way of things here, then it was better to be a beggar than to stay.

Rob turned and sprinted out the kitchen door, only to be nearly blinded by the brightness of the midday sun. Through his tears, he caught a glimpse of movement in the gap between the two tall buildings at the yard's far end. He hied himself toward those constantly changing colors and shadows. If that was a lane, there'd be someone on it who'd know the way to Stanrudde's exit. If not, there'd surely be somewhere to hide until he could decide how to escape.

"Wait!" Johanna cried after him. Her call only goaded Rob into reckless haste. He exploded through the gap.

And tumbled over a handcart.

Wood cracked as both he and the cart fell onto their sides. Onions bounced onto the lane around him. "Why you stupid little fool," the handcart's owner shouted. "I'll teach you to watch where you run."

The onion seller caught Rob by the arm and hauled him to his feet, drawing back his open hand to deal a sharp, correcting blow. The passersby, who'd congealed into a knot of folk around this unexpected show, all shouted their approval.

Rob almost sighed with relief. If the man beat him,

he'd not call for the sheriff. Once it was deemed Rob had been punished enough, they'd be releasing him.

"Nay!" Johanna's piping voice rose from within the ranks of the onlookers. There was a flash of blue as she pushed her way through the crowd. When she reached its forefront, she planted her feet in the dusty lane and set her hands on her hips. Throwing back her head, she glared up at Rob's captor. "You'll let him go, churl."

Rob groaned in disbelief as every adult within hearing gasped at her insult. Speaking rudely to an adult was but a guarantee they'd give you worse than you deserved.

"Why you little vixen, I'll tan your hide for such disrespect!" Angry color bloomed in Rob's captor's broad cheeks.

Rob squeaked in an entirely new fear as he writhed helplessly against the man's hold. If Helewise held him responsible for what Tom had done, would Master Walter not hold him accountable for what this man meant to do to his daughter? Were that so, there'd be no corner of the world distant enough to escape the rich man's wrath. He had to save her.

The onion seller snatched her arm. Johanna lashed out with her foot, landing a bruising kick on his shin. Her victim yelped and released her.

"Helewise!" she screamed, trying to back into the crowd.

Roaring in rage and humiliation, the onion seller shifted his grip from Rob's arm to the back of his oversized tunic so he could lunge for her. Rob lifted his arms. Without a belt to hold him in his tunic, he slithered out of the garment. His captor fell sideways in surprise.

Twisting, kicking, and punching, Rob barreled through the crowd, dragging a shrieking Johanna behind him. They burst free and tore off down the lane. She snatched up her skirts and kept pace.

"Neighbors, neighbors," the onion seller cried after them at the top of his lungs, "stop those two children! The vandals have broken my cart."

All those who'd viewed the destruction of his cart took up his call. The hue and cry echoed against the tall walls of the houses lining the lane, bringing folk out of workshops and houses. Rob's heart lifted into his throat. He was done for. If they caught him within the city walls, he'd be arrested, then returned to Master Walter's house, burdened by even more debt in the shape of fines for vandalism.

He rounded a corner, then nearly smiled. Not a furlong ahead lay the city's gate, the massive wooden doors open between two half-built stone towers. Ahead of them, merchants and their lads dashed out of their shops, blocking Rob's path out of Stanrudde. All hope of freedom died. He slowed in defeat.

"This way," Johanna yelled, racing up from behind him to take the lead. "We'll go to my special place. No one will find you there."

She bolted onto an intersecting lane, then to an even narrower street. Here, the buildings fell away into a stretch of grass. A tall mound stood at its end. Atop the mound was a stone tower, flanked by a small wooden hall, much like Blacklea's manor house. The whole was encircled by a wooden wall.

"You must go faster," she demanded, releasing him to run ahead once again.

If he'd had any breath left, he'd have told her he was trying to do just that. As it was, his lungs felt as if they were tearing, his heart beating as if to burst. With her skirts held high over her knees, Johanna raced ahead of him around the mound.

"Stop, you!"

He shot a swift look behind him. The onion seller and another man burst out into the open area. From the tower's roof came a piercing whistle. Rob glanced up. Two armed men stood there. "They are going for the river," one of the guards called down.

It was only as he rounded the mound that Rob saw the river flowing through a gate in the city wall. On the far side sat a mill, the waterwheel turning with a steady clank and groan; on the near side were a line of what seemed to be large barns, each with a broad doorway set at water level. Willows grew between these odd dwellings and the river, their whip-thin branches trailing in the gentle current.

Johanna was barely panting as she tore around the last barn's corner, then thrust into the trailing branches and disappeared. Rob burrowed in after her. The trees' inner reaches had been thinned, leaving only an outer waterfall of green leaves and golden branches. Sunlight filtered through the mass to show Rob a long, narrow shelf of riverbank, carpeted with moss. The ground sloped gently downward from the tree trunks to the river's edge, its length completely empty; Johanna was gone.

"Where are you?" Rob gasped out, looking frantically around him for her.

"Here," came her whispered reply.

Johanna's head appeared out of the thick foliage from between two horny trunks. Barely visible through the dense branches behind her was the building's wall. Rob squeezed into the gap between the trunks and nigh on fell into a hole dug between the building and the trees. As Johanna yanked him down onto his seat, Rob's head disappeared beneath the surface of the earth. Overhead, the willow branches sifted back into place, concealing this odd hidey-hole.

He stared at the hole's moist, earthen floor to distract himself from his discomfort. Near the edge of Johanna's skirt lay a wooden poppet; scraps of fabric and a broken wooden spoon were strewn at his feet.

"They're behind this one." The onion seller's winded call came from just around the corner. Willow branches rustled as their pursuers trotted along the water's edge.

"They must be here. We saw them round the corner," his accomplice gasped.

Their footsteps thudded on the earth above and behind Rob's head as they moved on down the bank without stopping. He caught back the desire to sigh in relief. He wasn't safe yet. Branches rustled and snapped ever more faintly as the men searched along the river's edge, then a ferocious hiss filled the air, followed by the threatening flap of wings.

"Jesu! Swans!" one man cried. "Run!"

Rob's eyes flew wide in horror. An angry swan could kill a man, much less a lad. It was better to be arrested than to die.

"The swans," he managed to get out in warning to Johanna.

She shook her head. "Papa made this place just for me, so I could be busy whilst he's working in the warehouse," she whispered, pointing to the wall before them. "He told the swans they mustn't disturb me while I'm here."

Behind them, the men scrambled toward the warehouse's end. Hissing and flapping, the vicious waterfowl passed Johanna's hidey-hole without stopping. The birds followed the intruders to the building's corner, then offered another round of honking avian threats. A moment's silence followed this.

"We must look again," the onion seller said at last from the building's edge. "I'm wagering they're hiding in one of these warehouses."

"I'm not going back there again," his companion replied, decisive in his terror. To hide his cowardice, he added, "Besides, there's no point to it. They're either so well hidden we'll never find them, or they've already swum beyond Stanrudde's walls by way of the watergate."

The onion seller's response was a relieved string of

curses aimed at both Rob and Johanna's parentage. His voice grew fainter with each foul word. In another moment, there was nothing to hear save the chirp of birds as they darted from branch to branch overhead.

Rob's astonishment grew. This was a miracle, indeed. Not only had he escaped being arrested, but he now knew how to exit the city without being seen. He was free! As soon as he caught his breath, he'd be done with Stanrudde for all time. Aye, but without Johanna he'd never have managed it. Mayhap having a girl for a friend wasn't so bad a thing.

He turned to thank her. She had her poppet in hand. Humming tunelessly, she danced the plaything up the hole's wall. Grimacing in disgust, Rob leaned his head back against the rooty wall of this odd place and stared up into the branches.

From the warehouse roof a pigeon gurgled. Reeds rustled as the river chuckled along its banks, singing a merry song to the steady creak of the mill's machinery. The breeze lifted, tangling and sighing in the willow branches as it offered him the warm scent of moldering leaves.

Tension drained from him, replaced by an odd sort of peace. It sounded like home here. Soothed, he closed his eyes to drink in every bit of it and drifted into sleep.

The clanging of bells teased Rob from his rest. He opened his eyes to find thick, shadowy stripes on the wall before him. What sunlight yet trickled through the willow branches was tinged with rose.

He stretched. Although every muscle ached, he felt strong enough to swim a bit. He turned to bid Johanna farewell, only to discover he was already alone.

Coming to his feet, he peered through the curtain of branches for her. Someone sat on the river's edge; he could hear the splash of feet in the water. Rob frowned in irritation. Even his sister, as young as she was, knew better than to sit so near the river.

Clambering out of the hidey-hole, he shoved through the gap in the tree trunks. "Come back from there before the swans have at you or you drown," he cried, using the same stern tone he saved for his sister.

The person on the bank turned and pushed aside the branches. It was Helewise, not Johanna, who looked at him from the river's edge. Rob froze in horror, waiting for her to call the guard to come fetch him. Instead, she smiled at him.

"Why, thank you for your warning, Rob, but the swans nest a goodly distance downstream. They let us be up here." Her voice was alive with warm affection.

Rob's horror died into confusion. Helewise didn't look at all like herself. Her gowns were orange and gold, their fineness and color saying they must be her best attire. As if she were some wee lass, not Master Walter's exalted housekeeper, she'd pulled her skirts high over her knees so she could dandle her bare feet in the water without staining them. So, too, had she discarded her veil and band, laying them atop her shoes and stockings. With her head bared, the setting sun found reddish lights in her dark hair.

She patted at the ground beside her on the river's bank. "Hey now, it's a fine June even, this one. Come sit with me whilst I savor it."

It was the sweetness of her invitation that pricked Rob into taking a step toward her. He caught himself. This was no friend, but Master Walter's housekeeper who hated him. Aye, so she was. Did that not mean she might only hate him all the more if he refused her? Choosing a dry spot not too close to her, he sat, then drew his legs up to his chest. "I am sitting," he said.

She tilted her head to one side and studied him for a long moment. "Why did you run?"

However gently asked, hers was a serious question

demanding an honest answer. Rob turned his gaze toward his shoes. He could hardly tell her it was she who'd driven him to it by being unfair and unjust. He tried a dodge. "I am now an outlaw. If I return to Master Walter's home, I'll be arrested as a vandal."

Helewise's laugh was soft and low. "A simple misunderstanding, that, already remedied. At no cost to you, I might mention."

Rob's head popped up from his knees. He stared at her. How did she know he was worried over the cost?

Helewise only raised her brows. "By the by, I am not distracted. Why did you run?"

There was no help for it; he had to answer. Perhaps if he didn't tell the whole truth, it wouldn't be so grave a sin. "I hate it here."

"You haven't been here so long," Helewise replied, moving her feet in the water. Droplets spewed into the air, turning to pink and gold before they returned to the river's gleaming silver surface. "Perhaps, once you get to know us better, you'll come to like it."

Rob pressed his forehead against his knees so she couldn't see his face. "What choice have I but to stay? Master Walter bought me from Papa for ten coins. Now, I owe even more because I must pay for my clothing and a ruined meal."

Once again, Helewise's warm laugh startled him. He looked up at her. The lilt of her mouth was so gay it was hard not to smile in return.

"Oh, but I think me the master is going to find you an interesting sort of lad." She grabbed him by the arm and dragged him nearer until they sat hip to hip. Although he didn't fight her, neither did he relax against her. "Buy your clothing, indeed. And, why would you think you must pay the master for a meal Tom spilled?"

He looked up at her, his confusion growing until words burst past his lips before he knew he meant to free them. "Why are you being so kind now, when you hate me?"

Her eyes opened wide in true surprise. "Hate you? Why ever do you think I hate you?"

Guilt again twisted in his stomach. He stared down at his shoes. "Because I lied for Johanna when her cat spilled the cheese."

Helewise laughed. She crooked a finger beneath his chin to raise his head, forcing him to meet her gaze. There was nothing in her face save amusement. "So, it *has* been guilt eating at you. I thought I saw it in your eyes. Best you no longer lie for our little mistress if you cannot bear the weight of your sin, lad. Now, come. It's time we were for home."

Home. Despair washed over Rob. Would that he could go home.

As his eyes teared, Helewise's gaze softened. She freed his chin to finger-comb his hair back from his brow. Her touch was so much like Mama's that Rob's lips quivered.

"Tell me." It was a soft command.

"Blacklea is home," he whispered, the corners of his mouth drooping.

"And, you are sick with longing for it." She sighed, her voice as low as his. "So was it for me when I first came to Stanrudde. Lad, let us chaffer a bit here. You give me your vow to stay, swearing that you'll run no more until the master has returned. In turn, I will vow to beg Master Walter to release you from his service, should your sickness not have abated by that time."

She paused to point a warning finger at him. "However, you must vow to try your best to like it here, until that time."

Rob's pain abated somewhat as the possibility of escape opened up before him. September was only two and a half months distant. More important to his heart was the discovery that Helewise did not hate him at all. He nodded his assent.

"Good," she said in brisk acceptance, then levered herself to her feet. "Now we must be going, else we'll be out and about after all honest folk should be within their own walls."

Stepping from the water, she shook the moisture from her legs and thrust her bare feet into her shoes. After she'd stuffed her stockings into her belt, she caught up her veil and band. Tilting her head upward to a sky now streaked with mauve and orange, she fastened on the head covering. When the veil once again shrouded her soft cheeks, she looked down at him.

Rob's heart quirked in fear's return. Gone was warm and laughing Helewise, leaving only the cold housekeeper in her place. She held out a hand to him. It was a friendly enough invitation. He looked up at her again, squinting against the dying light to study her. Behind the cool expression glimmers of the other Helewise remained.

"Why do you make your face blank like this?" he asked as he rose to his feet.

Helewise's brows peaked in surprise, her face warming back into its previous softness. "Do I? I didn't know."

Rob nodded in new understanding. So it had been with Mama. When his dam was busy at her work, her face lost the special expression she saved for him.

His heart at peace, he took her hand and let Helewise lead him around the warehouse's corner. As they passed the now quiet mill, then started across the short grassy stretch before the tower's mound, he asked, "Will I be punished for running?"

"Nay, you did not know what you did was wrong," Helewise replied, leading him down a lane. Folk hurried past them, intent on finishing their last chore of the day before retreating to their homes and suppers.

"Is Johanna being punished?" Rob shot her a worried look. It would be unfair if Johanna was punished and he was not.

"She is, but not for aiding you. She should never have spoken so to a merchant, even if he is no more than a regrater."

"What will happen to her?"

The corners of the housekeeper's mouth lifted. "A terrible thing, indeed. It's the chamber pots she must empty on the morrow. A rude and filthy job given to a rude lass with a filthy mouth."

Rob shuddered in pity for Johanna, but his easiness grew. If Helewise treated the master's daughter so, she would only ever be fair with him. Then, a new worry woke in him. Even Johanna had aught to do on the morrow, while he had no job to his name. "What will I do for Master Walter if Tom is to be the scullery lad?"

Helewise glanced down at him. "Do you know, I think the master will be glad of Tom's suggestion that you work with Master Colin in the apothecary's shop. It is a great honor, this. You will be the youngest servant ever within those walls."

Although Rob wasn't certain what an apothecary's shop was, he very much liked the sound of being someone special. Pride teased at his lips, trying to make them lift into a smile, but he remembered the courtesy Mama had taught him to use. "My thanks," he said, borrowing Wilfred's solemn tones as he continued. "I will endeavor to serve Master Walter and Master Colin well."

"I'm certain you will," Helewise replied graciously. After a moment's silence, she added, "By the by, Rob, there are no tally sticks in our household. Instead, we figure the worth of our accounts by beads strung on wires and scribe those amounts onto parchment. Do you think you might like to learn how to do this?"

Beads on a wire? He frowned up at her. What sort of counting was this? Mayhap it was the way Wilfred did his accounts. Rob had watched the bailiff use dried pea pods on a string to calculate amounts. If so, then it was no different than how Rob used a twig to mark lines in the dirt as he counted the bushels of grain Papa took from their fields. There were many different methods of counting, but the counting, itself, was always the same. No matter how it was done, there was great joy for Rob in counting.

"I would like that very much," he replied, savoring his first happy moment at Stanrudde.

Chapter Nine

Stanrudde
two and a half hours past None,
The eve of Ste. Agnes's Day, 1197

Rob caught his breath as Johanna fitted herself to him, but it was more than this suggestive movement that sent him all the way to passion's edge. With every touch and kiss, she told him she loved him still. It was the need of his heart that rose to meet, then match, his body's lust. She was his wife, his to touch and love at his will.

Thrusting his fingers into her hair, he kissed her cheek, her ear, then nuzzled at her throat. Pleasure deepened into driving need. He dropped a hand to her hip, drawing her nearer still. Even with so much fabric between them, he could feel her thighs pressed to his.

She made a sound that was half sigh, half moan, then lifted herself in delicious parody of what he longed to do with her. It was a patent reminder that the whores he'd used these many years had offered him naught but the pretense of satisfaction. Only Johanna had ever made him ache in pleasure. He quaked, indulging himself in the full depth of his desire for her.

"Master Robert, where are you?" Will's frightened call pierced the quiet in the alley, shattering his master's lust.

Rob tore his mouth from Johanna's and stared at her in shock. "My God, my God, what am I doing?" he breathed. The answer came from deep within him: adultery in the eyes of the world.

Instantly, he released her and stepped back. Johanna murmured in complaint, extending a hand as she invited him to once again cradle himself against her womanly curves. Her body's heat flowed across the short distance between them, twining around him, a siren's song. His heart begged him to answer her. How could it be adultery to love his own wife? But, logic laughed that even if their secret exchange of vows had made a true marriage, no one would believe that now, not after so many years.

Swallowing, Rob took two more backward steps to assure temptation's death. She was safe now. It was time for him to go. He could send the guard to see her home. Even as he commanded himself to move, his feet rooted themselves to this spot. He stared at her, drinking in her image.

With her wimple gone, Johanna's hair hung loose and tangled around her. Time's passage had darkened its color to more red than gold, but it yet retained its willful wave. She was taller than he remembered, but just as slender, or so said her sodden and filthy gowns as they clung to her every curve. That was, save for where they hung agape, revealing the shadowy valley between her breasts. He forced his gaze to the safety of her face.

Her neck was scratched. Blood smeared her cheek, but it was not hers. Her passion for him set her fair skin afire beneath what would be the morrow's bruises. Under the graceful line of the nose she so despised, her lips were yet soft and warm with his kisses. Her eyes were just as blue as ever. In their depths, his heart swore it saw the reflection of his love for her.

As his mind-dimming passion ebbed, logic strengthened and sneered at such a fantasy. If there was anything to read in her face or her behavior of the last moments, it was but shock. He was misinterpreting the stunned outcome of a horrible experience as love.

Rob looked away from her to stare out the alley's end. In the field, folk cried for mercy from the town's guard. They had more hope of pity than did he. Even if Johanna loved him still, she was and would always be Katel's wife in the eyes of the world. To challenge that was to place her in harm's way, as her father intended.

Only as Katel's name crossed his thoughts did Rob recall his reason for coming to Stanrudde. With it was the realization of the opportunity standing before him. Here, in the privacy and concealment of this alley, he would warn Johanna and, in doing so, resolve some of the debt he owed her. Turning back to the woman he dared not love, he said, "Johanna, I must leave you now, but before I go, heed me in this. Your husband has done something that places you in grave danger."

Her brows lowered as confusion flashed across her face. Rob watched her struggle with her thoughts as if she could not recall who or where she was. His heart fell; logic crowed in triumph. She was yet so stunned by her experience, she hadn't heard a word he'd said.

Confusion passed to be replaced by horror, and she stared at him as if only now recognizing who he was. Following this came blazing rage. Her mouth tightened, and she crossed her arms as every shred of softness in her disappeared.

"You!" she hissed, her eyes narrowing. "I cannot bear your presence. Move aside and let me pass!"

Rob flinched as her hatred stabbed at him. Rather than drive him away, it only made his need to be free of her memory all the more urgent. "Johanna, you cannot leave until you listen to what I have to say."

"Nay!" she shouted, trying to push past him.

He shifted to block her path, not daring to touch her. "You must," he insisted, "else I fear for your life and safety. I would not see you hurt."

Johanna went utterly still, her face whitening to a hue so pale he feared she would faint. In the next moment, bright spots of rage flamed to life on her cheeks. Ever so slowly, she raised her head to stare at him.

"*You* would not see me hurt?" These disbelieving and sarcastic words left her in quiet, furious gusts.

Rob stared at her. What sort of question was this? Of course, he did not wish to see her hurt. Had he not just shown her this by coming to her aid in these past minutes?

"*You would not see me hurt!*" she repeated, this time her words a quiet shriek.

Again, she made as if to move past him and, again, he blocked her way. She freed a squeal of frustration and whirled to show him her back. "You'll say nothing to me," she shouted to the alley's end. "Never again will I listen to your lies!"

Anger shot through Rob, tangling with the guilt and pain that already lived in him. Stung, his pride raised its pompous head. How dare she accuse him of lies, when he sought only to protect her. "I have never lied to you," he snapped.

"Have you not?" she challenged, her gaze yet focused on the wall before her. "Are you not the same Robert of Blacklea who traded secret marriage vows with me, swearing to love me forever, but when my father offered coins, filled his purse and left me to my fate without a single word?"

It was not Master Walter's false tale that struck at Rob, but hearing it fall from Johanna's lips as if it were true. No matter that his mind had long been convinced she had believed it, his heart had clung to the hope that she would not be so easily misled. This drove him back from her, step by step, until he stumbled over the thief's prostrate form and nearly fell. As he steadied himself, anger roared in to replace the pain. Why hadn't she trusted in his love for her? She should have known the only way he could have been separated from her was by force.

Although he wanted to scream at her for doubting him, he sought calm and reason. "Johanna, I did not leave you by choice, this I vow to you."

"Nay!" she shouted, hunching her shoulders in a stubborn refusal to listen. "Say no more to me! You cannot think I will accept this vow when your last one was so false."

This time her words dug past all his ability to control. Pride screamed in agony; anger flared to an even brighter life. Despite that he had just proved his care for her, she dared to spurn him and his concern on her behalf. Rob glared at her back. Jesus God, there wasn't a merchant in all the known world who questioned his word or his vow. If she chose to reject where her betters trusted, then whatever debt he thought he owed her was no more.

"I have done my best," he returned in cold fury. "If you choose not to heed me, so be it. I will trouble you no longer."

Whirling on his heel, he stormed out onto the coopers' lane. May God damn her for her blind arrogance. She deserved to hang with her husband, for no other reason than the insult she dealt him.

In the abbey's field a guardsman thought to challenge him, only to reconsider when Rob speared him with his gaze. By the time he thrust into the abbey's gate, he could not wait to be done with Stanrudde and all things connected to Johanna. Ignoring Brother William's cry regarding his well-being, Rob bulled his way through the crowd that now packed the courtyard, seeking his own servants. They were nowhere to be seen.

"Hamalin!" he bellowed. As his agent and his men

were no doubt beyond the walls, still searching for him, there was no response.

This only sent his anger spiraling. With each breath he took, Johanna's slur and lack of faith drove deeper into him. As rage's heat grew, so did the need to slam his fists into a wall until either his hands or the wall were destroyed. Someone clamped a hand around his elbow. Rob whirled in wicked glee, ready to attack the one who dared maul Robert, Grossier of Lynn.

Colin looked up at him, his gaze taking in the jut of his former apprentice's jaw and what brewed in his stormy eyes. "You look somewhat the worse for wear," the monk said mildly. "Come, I have the abbot's release from services to entertain you as I will this night. We'll share a cup of plum wine. It'll help to ease what boils in you."

Rob had no desire to ease what ached in him. Instead, he wanted to cherish it until it grew to consume him. From the distant corner where it had taken refuge, logic's voice rose, faint, but clear. It was better to go with Colin, who knew him of old, than to make himself a horse's ass before those who'd never before seen him beyond control.

It was a moment before Rob could force himself to nod in agreement and another before he could unclamp his jaw to speak. "I leave. Within the hour. Tell my men."

"I can see that done for you," Colin replied, as if accustomed to being addressed in this sort of harsh, abbreviated language. Without releasing Rob's arm, he grabbed a passing brother and saw the message transferred.

"Come then," Colin went on in his soothing tone. "If you're leaving, then I'd have you see my workroom while we spend our last hour in privacy."

He clenched Master Walter's former apprentice's arm close to his side, as if Rob were blind and needed his aid to walk. It wasn't until they were striding alongside the frater's length that Colin murmured, "Did you find Johanna?"

Mention of her name loosened Rob's stiff jaw and trapped tongue. "I do not wish to discuss her or anything she said to me, old man."

Colin stopped abruptly. "She spoke to you?" he asked in astonishment.

"She did, may God damn the nasty bitch," Rob growled, happily venting some of his aching and injured pride. This was a mistake. As hurt eased, it made room for the memory of Johanna's mouth on his, of her body pressed to him. Heat and hate tangled. Damn her to hell.

Colin's brows rose as he studied Rob, his gaze delving past skin and bone to peer into the thoughts that lay beneath them. Whatever it was he saw there seemed oddly to please him, for he smiled. Once again, he pulled Rob's arm tight into his grasp.

"You should feel honored. Our Johanna is quite forthright about whom and how she hates. She hasn't spoken to me in years. Come," he said, leading him on toward the abbey's gardens at the compound's back where he kept his stills. "Come. My brew will ease what aches in you."

Chapter Ten

Stanrudde
Mid-September, 1173

"Wake up!"

Rob started, his eyes flying open. On the pallet beside him, Arthur loosed a mournful snort; even in his sleep Master Walter's younger apprentice cried for his home and his mama. Arthur rolled to his side and yanked his blanket over his head, still deep in his own sad dreams. If not Arthur, then who?

Blinking, Rob rolled onto his back and stared into the predawn dimness of the apothecary shop. Johanna appeared out of the gray. She knelt beside his pallet, her unplaited hair hanging around her face. As his vision cleared, he saw her overgown was on backward, which meant she'd dressed herself in the dark.

"I know something you want to know," she whispered.

Rob stared at her in confusion. It was his nightly duty to bar the door and, unlike Arthur, who sometimes forgot what was his to do, Rob was never remiss with his chores. He clearly remembered placing the bar into the braces as he, Arthur, and Rob's master and mistress retired for the night.

"How come you to be in here?" he demanded.

Johanna sat back on her heels and crossed her arms to show she was upset he hadn't responded to her tease. "The door was open." She was careful to keep her voice low, knowing she'd have worse than the chamber pots to do if she was found here.

Rob shook his head, positive he'd barred it. "It is not," he whispered. He'd be in as much trouble as she, were she discovered.

"It is so," she shot back. "If it had been barred, I couldn't have come in."

At this inescapable point of logic, bitter disappointment flowed over Rob. He hated making errors. Each mistake was a failure, when he'd vowed never to fail Master Colin. Disappointment deepened. Where his few, earlier mistakes had been of little consequence, this one was beyond all tolerance. Not only had he left the shop open, but Johanna had entered without waking him.

The wall behind Rob was covered with shelves sectioned into tiny squares. Within each of these wee cubicles sat a container of some sort: boiled leather flasks stoppered with wood, wooden bowls topped with chalk, pottery jars closed with wax. And, within each of these containers was a different potion, posset, unguent, tincture, or cure, some of them containing fabulously expensive spices. It was for their sake that he and Arthur slept on the workshop floor; in case of thieves, they were to raise the alarm.

"No matter the door, you aren't supposed to be here," Rob told her, his voice harsh with his own failure. "Go home."

Even in the semidarkness he could see her eyes narrow and her jaw jut out in stubborn anger. "You aren't being nice to me. Now, I shall never tell you what I know."

He shrugged to hide his frustration. When Johanna said "never," what she meant was she had every intention of pestering him until he had to know what she knew. Once he finally asked after it, she'd withhold the information until he apologized to her when he'd done no wrong.

Outside, the ropemaker's cock stuttered quietly, three times. The noise came from the distillery's roof, only a few feet lower and a cloth yard distant from Master Colin's bedchamber window. Both impatience and disappointment dimmed with the sound. Grinning, Rob sat up and jabbed Arthur in the back.

The apprentice groaned. "Leave me be; it's not yet morn."

"Nay, wake up," Rob hissed, being even more careful to keep his voice low. It would be a terrible shame to wake Master Colin before the cock crowed. He pulled off Arthur's blanket. "Rise now and quietly so," he commanded

Despite that Arthur was the apprentice and Rob a mere servant, the lad muttered and sat up, only to yelp softly when he saw Master Walter's daughter. "What's she doing here!" he breathed, scrambling to pull the blanket up over his bare and protruding belly.

"Hush," Rob told him as the cock once again stuttered quietly, but warming his throat for his performance.

Arthur grinned. "Do you think he's on the distillery roof?" he breathed.

Rob nodded, then tensed in delicious anticipation. He aimed his gaze upward to the ceiling above them. Arthur did the same. Johanna glanced between them, then at the ceiling, which was also the floor of Master Colin's bedchamber. "It's only a cock," she whispered, her pique over Rob's refusal to take her bait forgotten.

"Hush," both Rob and Arthur told her as one, their gazes never leaving the floor of their master's bedchamber.

Accompanied by the flap of its wings, the arrogant bird loosed a fierce and ear-piercing salute to a new day's start. Master Colin roared in response. His feet hit the floorboards directly overhead with a booming thud. Every jar and flask in the shop rattled, dust filtering down on Rob through the gaps in between the planks. The upstairs shutter nigh on splintered against the outer wall. Something hard slammed onto the distillery's roof. With a startled squawk, the bird's serenade ended.

"God in His heaven, how could I have missed?! Aye, fly, coward! If I ever get my hands on you, you're stew!" Master Colin shouted hoarsely after the departing fowl. "And, don't think I won't eat every last bite of you, myself!"

Rob and Arthur fell back onto their pallets, careful to spill their laughter only into their palms. Still round-eyed in surprise, Johanna giggled quietly.

"Colin," protested Mistress Katherine, the apothecary's young wife. Her voice was languid with sleep despite her rude awakening.

Rob glanced at Arthur, and they shared a moment of mutual disgust. Master Colin was ensorcelled by his wife. More often than not, his eyes glazed over when he looked upon her. Together, they'd vowed that when it was time for them to marry, they wouldn't let their wives make such fools of them.

"I hate that damn bird," Master Colin told Mistress Katherine in what was still a near shout. The bed ropes creaked as he settled back onto their mattress. "The only reason Herebert hasn't already wrung its neck is because he knows how much the creature annoys me."

"It's not that," Mistress Katherine said, laughter lilting in her tone. "You threw your shoe. Did you plan to make your appearance this morn with but one shoe on?"

Anticipating his master's coming request, Rob leapt to his feet and brushed the wrinkles from his shirt before straightening his chausses. He wasn't supposed to sleep in his clothing, as it caused excessive wear to the fabric when these garments were but loaned to him; once he grew out of them, they'd be stored for the next boy to use. However, this was the only one of Master Colin's edicts he felt comfortable disobeying. Having to dress each morn took too long when he was impatient to begin his day.

"May the devil take that bird! Now look what he's made me do!" the apothecary roared. A brief silence ensued. "Stop laughing."

"What makes you think I'm laughing?" his wife replied. This was followed by muffled laughter.

Still smiling, Johanna handed Rob his tunic from the pallet's end. As he tugged it on, Arthur shoved him his shoes. Rob stepped into them, leaving the laces undone.

"Rob, are you awake?" Master Colin didn't need to raise his voice to ask the question. Sound traveled easily through the gaps in the boards that separated the shop from the living quarters above it.

Again, Rob and Arthur shared a look, this time in amusement. As if anyone could sleep through what was becoming Master Colin's daily waking routine. "Aye, master. Shall I fetch you your shoe?"

"If you would be so kind." As always, the master asked, rather than commanded.

This was why Rob so loved Master Colin. The apothecary was steady in temperament and patient in the extreme. He never struck out in chastisement; there was no need for it. With but a single look, Master Colin could make Arthur and Rob feel smaller than worms.

"There's no haste," Master Colin added. "Stir the ashes before you bring it up, lad."

"Aye, master," Rob replied, cinching his belt around his waist and setting his cap upon his uncombed hair.

Johanna followed him to the workshop's narrow rear door. Rob paused before it. The bar was, indeed, out of its braces, standing in the spot it occupied during the day.

"See, I told you it was open," she said softly. "Mayhap, you forgot to bar it last night?"

"Mayhap," he said, his disappointment in himself returning.

Opening the door, he and Johanna stepped outside into the brisk and pinkening air. Trapped within the city's thick walls, the smell of gardens wet with dew mingled with that of wood smoke as fires came back to life in hundreds of homes and kitchens. In their own compound, Philip was the earliest riser; the yeasty aroma of baking bread wafted to them from the kitchen's vent.

Every winged creature in Stanrudde, cocks, geese, pigeons, doves, crows, even sparrows, lifted its voice to herald the new day until the air was alive with their joyous noise. Then, the first hammer rang against an anvil, followed by another and another, until the sound of iron mongering banished the morning's peace. Rob gave thanks he wasn't attached to a smith's household. Here, at the city's more civilized center, workshops didn't open until the ninth hour of the day.

Their distillery was no more than a waist-high stone hearth jammed lengthwise between the shop's rear wall and the back of Philip's kitchen. Held above the hearth on a network of rope stretched between four poles was a layer of thatching. Its purpose had been to shield the condensing concoctions from the elements, but it would serve that end no more. Master Colin had thrown his missile so hard it had punched a hole right through the bundled reeds. The shoe now lay on the hearth, leather sole upward, between the tiny, bulbous oven and their two simmering pots.

Lifting it from the ashes, Rob slapped off what he could of its gray coating, then tucked it into his belt. Beside him, Johanna shifted from foot to foot in impatience. "Why don't you want to know what I know?"

she asked when she could tolerate his silence no longer.

Rob shrugged to hide his growing interest in her news. If he was to get it from her, he'd have to be clever about it. Removing the two pottery *covre-feux* that had kept yesterday's coals warm throughout the night, he stirred the embers until they revealed their red hearts. "If it's for me to know, someone will tell me. I don't expect that someone will be you, since you've already said you'll never tell."

Johanna thrust herself between him and the hearth, her face filled with the torture of keeping a secret she longed to share. "Mayhap, I've changed my mind."

Rob caught back his triumphant grin. Generous in victory, he pointed to the coals. "Would you like to start the fires?" Helewise never let her do this, fearing she'd set herself ablaze.

"Might I?" Johanna asked in breathless excitement.

At his nod, she reached beneath the hearthstone's overhanging edge, finding the dried moss and twiglets they kept on the shelf there. As Rob tied his shoes, she fed the moss to the coals with the utmost care, watching until it began to spark and smolder. Atop this, she lay her twiglets. Flames appeared.

Rob handed her an armful of small pieces of wood, all of equal size and weight. When these were stacked just so, the fire that resulted owned an even temperature. Although she tried to arrange them as she knew she must, they kept slipping and tumbling from their pattern.

"So, what is it you have to tell me?" he asked casually as he reached out to help her.

Johanna glanced at him, her blue eyes yet alive with the joy of doing this forbidden task. "Papa returned by himself, very late last night. Everyone else comes this morn. Even though it was so late, Master Colin came to talk with him. I know because I listened at the bedchamber door, while Helewise tended to them."

Rob almost sighed as the weight of his error fell from his shoulders. It hadn't been he who'd left the door open, but Master Colin, who had forgotten to bar it upon his late return. For all his skill, Master Colin wasn't careful about remembering mundane details.

"What did they talk about?" he asked, his voice filled with his relief.

Johanna glanced up from once again restacking the wood, her lips quirking upward into a smug smile. "You."

Rob stared at her in shock. "Me?"

"You." She turned her back to him, directing her full attention on the sticks.

Rob stared at the front of her gown in horror. What if Helewise had spoken to Master Walter about returning him to Blacklea? He'd forgotten to ask her not to do so. Panic started through him. If Master Walter sent him home, who would see to Master Colin? The apothecary needed him. Each day, Master Colin told Rob he'd never had a lad as talented. Each day, the master asked what he would do without such a lad as Rob in his shop. Rob's eyes narrowed in refusal. He wouldn't go home; no one could force him to leave Stanrudde. Clamping a hand on Johanna's shoulder, he turned her toward him.

"What did they say about me?" It was a harsh and ungracious command.

"Mayhap I'll tell and mayhap I won't," she said with a haughty lift of her chin. "You weren't nice to me." Pulling free of his grasp, she turned her back to him once more to fuss with the sticks over the second set of coals. Once again, she knocked them into a messy knot of wood.

"Until you tell me, you'll do this no more," he snapped, shoving her to the side as he angrily reclaimed what was his own to do.

Johanna stepped back, seeming almost as relieved

to return his chore as she was to spill her news. "Master Colin told Papa about how you already know more than any lad he's ever met. Papa talked about priests and the abbey, but Master Colin talked about the apothecary scale." The wisps of gold that were her eyebrows rose in curiosity as she looked at him. "Do you wish to use the scale, Rob?"

Rob froze. His hand clenched around the stick he held. Flamelets licked at his knuckles.

With a swift breath, he snatched back his hand and sucked at his burned skin. Not even Arthur, who was his dearest friend, knew how deeply he desired to use that precious piece of equipment. How the scale balanced was more mysterious than how a juggler kept three balls aloft at the same time. Rob longed to place a bit of crushed leaf into the apparatus's attached dish, then hang a tiny lead weight off the loop in the gleaming wood of its free arm and watch as the bar evened. Longing shattered against a wall of reality, and Rob's shoulders slumped in hopelessness.

No matter how many years he stayed with Master Colin, he would never use that scale. Labor in any tradesman's shop was divided into two types: the things done by masters and those apprentices learning from them, and things done by the servants. As a servant, Rob might tally and sort the supplies entering either the apothecary's shop or the spice merchant's warehouses. Most certainly, he would clean and prepare the flowers, leaves, twigs, and roots for processing into medicines or flavorings. But, because he was no apprentice and would never have the money necessary to make himself one, he would never use that scale, or take lessons as Arthur did or know the pride of being called "master."

"Little mistress?" Helewise's worried call floated out of Master Walter's bedchamber window.

An answering flash of worry woke in Johanna's bright blue gaze. Rob could nigh on see her thoughts spinning as she sought some reason for not being abed as she should. Without so much as a fare-thee-well, she turned and squeezed through the gap between distillery's hearth and kitchen wall, then disappeared around the kitchen's corner. In the next moment, her voice rose from the center of Master Walter's tiny courtyard. "I come. I was but in the privy!" Johanna's soul was less troubled by lies than was Rob's.

When the fires were properly set, Rob reentered the apothecary's shop. The stairs to the upper story, more ladder than stairway, were just inside the doorway. Using both hands and feet, he clambered up the narrow steps. When his head breached the hole cut in the ceiling, he set his elbows on the floor and hoisted himself into the shop's upper chamber.

This house had once belonged to Master Griggo, father to Master Walter and teacher of Master Colin. When Master Walter had inherited both the apothecary trade and this house, Master Colin had stayed on, lacking the funds to set himself up into trade. The spice merchant needed someone to work his father's apothecary shop, which both utilized and sold locally many of the spices he purchased as it allowed him to concentrate on nurturing his own growing trade. When Master Walter moved to his new house, Master Colin had remained here, giving the apothecary his own household for the first time.

Judged against Master Walter's new home, this dwelling was hopelessly old and impoverished. Unlike Johanna's mother, whose dowry had included household goods, Master Colin wed a woman who brought with her apothecary jars, simmering pots, and what she'd learned of herbs at her own father's knee. Thus, their tiny hall held but a wee trestle table, a single chest, a bench, and two stools. But then, as their household dined with Master Walter, there was no need for hearth, cooking equipment, or service goods.

Rob turned to the woolen sheet that made two

rooms of this one wee chamber. "Master, I have your shoe," he called.

"Enter," Master Colin replied, and Rob ducked around the blanket's edge.

His master's bed was the only one Rob had ever seen. Poles like smooth tree trunks stood at all four corners of the piece. Spanning them near their tops were smaller branches, polished and straight, which held aloft the woolen bedcurtains. Thick boards made a frame within which the mattress nestled. Even after more than two months of familiarity, Rob loved to look upon it. Each time he did, the certainty that he'd one day own one just like this firmed in his heart.

Master Colin sat upright on the mattress, his nightcap yet on his head and a long, round bolster between his back and the headboard. Warm blankets were gathered around his waist, so only his chest and arms were bare. Dark hollows clung beneath the master's eyes, still his gaze was alert and filled with quiet pleasure. "My thanks, lad," he said, his voice warm as always. "Once again, you do me a boon when I do not deserve it."

The master's words set a glow in a place deep within Rob. "It was a pleasure to be able to aid you, master," he replied, placing the shoe next to its mate.

As he straightened, he glanced at plump Mistress Katherine, who sat between her husband and the wall. Only a little more than half her husband's six and thirty years, she clutched the bed linens to her chest. Her bare shoulders were cloaked in her free-flowing honey-colored hair. Although her eyes were brown, they sparked green, as Mama's had, but unlike Mama or Helewise, there was always too much laughter in her gaze, and this made Rob uncomfortable.

To escape her silent amusement, he turned his attention back on Master Colin. Why had his employer spoken to Johanna's father over him last even? It wasn't until Master Colin crossed his arms and cocked his head to the side that Rob realized he was staring.

"My, but you've got questions in your eyes this morn, lad," his employer said. "What is it that has you pondering so?"

Rob instantly swallowed his need to know. Johanna had spied to learn what she had. To speak of it was to betray her. Afraid to open his mouth against a wayward tongue, he but shook his head in a tiny, negative motion.

Master Colin's expression tautened in consideration, and he raised a hand to scratch at his bearded chin. "Rob, a man who lacks the courage to ask after what is his heart's desire is a man doomed to a lifetime of disappointment and missed opportunities." Here, he paused as if waiting for Rob to ask for the thing his heart most desired.

Rob's breath came faster. The plea to be apprenticed to Master Walter as Arthur was pounded at his teeth in its need to be uttered. Then, common sense warned him against daring to release it. Master Colin was speaking of attainable dreams, when what he wanted was beyond impossible. Everyone knew it took coins to be apprenticed, even in the humblest of trades. Besides, it was better to silently cherish the hope of *someday* in his heart than to ask, be refused, and live the rest of his life knowing that day would never arrive. Rob buried his hopeless wish, just as he knew he must.

"I shall take your words to heart, master," he replied, his voice sounding forlorn to his own ears.

"See that you do so this very day," his master chided, strange emphasis in his voice. "Moreover, know you that second chances are rare things in this world. Should one appear, never, never refuse it."

As Rob nodded to show he'd heard and understood, the bells of Stanrudde began to ring. Master Colin glanced toward the open window. When he again looked at Rob, his face had relaxed back into its normal, amiable expression.

"I'll not be attending mass this morn," he said. "You and Arthur hie yourselves next door to go with Helewise. See to it you do not make her late for the service."

"Aye, master," Rob said, turning to push past the curtain once again. The woolen sheet fell back into place, and he started for the stairs.

"And, Rob," Master Colin called after him, his voice rumbling down into tones of pained irritation, "stop sleeping in your clothing. Heed me in this, or I may be forced to reconsider keeping you as my servant."

Rob grimaced. "Aye, master," he replied in defeat, knowing he could no longer ignore the edict. Indeed, it was a morning for disappointment. As he turned to clamber down the stairs, Mistress Katherine took up where her husband left off.

"Wash before you leave," she called, "scrubbing not just your face, but your teeth, as well. And, I do mean scrub, not simply spewing a few droplets at your skin. Arthur, too. I swear you two are the filthiest lads in all of Stanrudde. Do you hear me, Arthur?"

"Aye, mistress," Arthur called morosely from the lower level workshop.

Disappointment grew and grew as Rob climbed backward down into the workshop until he had to stop and lean his head against a riser. Mayhap, he should have risked all and asked. Miracles happened. Hadn't it been a miracle that Master Walter found him in Blacklea? What if, just what if, he'd dared to ask and the answer had been yes? What if the opportunity would now be withdrawn, never to be offered again? As Master Colin said, second chances were few and far between. But, how was he to know which choice was the right one?

Rob sighed, his worries weighing like lead on his shoulders. In the workshop, Arthur was pouring water into their basin. Rob leapt from the stairs and went to join him in his ablutions, finding no pleasure at all in this day's start.

Chapter Eleven

Stanrudde
Mid-September, 1173

Rob's questions and worries hadn't lightened any by the time mass ended. Nonetheless, he and Arthur departed the church at a trot, just as they'd done every morn for the past months. Although Arthur was nigh on two years Rob's senior, they were of a height and matched each other, stride for stride. The apprentice looked at him, his golden hair gleaming in the early morning sun, his clear-cut features and green eyes alive in excitement. Arthur loved to run. Despite his weight, he could keep a steady pace, one of the few things at which he was consistent.

Cutting around blue-gowned, white-veiled housewives and scarlet-robed, bearded tradesmen, they dashed onto Market Lane toward Master Walter's house, which sat on the corner of that lane and the ropemakers' street. A line of pack animals now stood along one side of the woven willow wall that enclosed Master Walter's home. The sturdy beasts were yet burdened with baskets and sacks as they snorted in impatience, wanting either their pasture or their stable.

"They're back!" Arthur crowed, then grabbed Rob and stopped so suddenly that Master Herebert nigh on stumbled over them.

Touching a finger to his lips, the apprentice leapt

to the gate and pressed his back to the flimsy wall. He leaned into the gateway, taking care to expose no more of his face than the distance from the crown of his head to his eyes. Wondering what he was about, Rob joined him, rising on his toes to peer over Arthur's shoulder into the compound.

More pack animals filled the courtyard's tiny space. Men Rob did not know laughed and talked as they emptied the beasts' baskets and backs. Some of these goods made their way toward the house, while others were set aside to be later carted to the river warehouse. Rob let his gaze linger for a moment on Master Walter's dwelling. The house towered over the courtyard, taller than any of the buildings around it. Caught between the outlining blocks of white, the black hearts of the split grayish stones gleamed like polished metal in the morning sun. The slate roof shone like pewter, the silvery glow reflecting naught but importance back to Rob.

Pride glowed in his heart. To be attached to Master Walter's household was a grand thing, indeed. Theirs was the richest establishment in all of Stanrudde.

"Look at him." There was an impatient sneer in Arthur's voice as he pointed to the slender young man standing before the house's small square forebuilding.

Rob studied the object of Arthur's scorn. Dressed in the green tunic and brown chausses of Master Walter's house, the youth was short of stature and almost girlishly fair, his hair as pale as Papa's. The young man was toying with a short dagger, the jewels in the slim knife's hilt catching the light. Rob stared in appreciation. To own such a piece meant this was a person of consequence.

"Who is he?" he whispered.

"That's Master Walter's other apprentice." Dislike lay heavily in Arthur's tone. "Last year, the master made Katel his heir by betrothing Johanna to him. Even though all the town knows Master Walter did this only because Katel's sire is one of the richest merchants in London, Katel now thinks he can lord over everyone when he's yet just an apprentice, like me."

A flash of memory came to Rob with the name, waking a nubbin of dislike in him. This was the one who'd urged Master Walter not to take him from Blacklea. Katel had called him offal.

"What are you doing?" Johanna asked, her soprano voice slicing through the air behind them.

Arthur gasped and Rob yelped, both boys leaping back from the gate and their spying. "Nothing," they replied as one.

Helewise strolled past them and into the compound. "Enough dallying, my lads," she said. "There's work to be done. Rob, hie yourself back to the shop. You'll not be eating for another hour."

"But, why?" he cried in hurt and hungry surprise as he entered the courtyard on her heels. For all of the summer, he'd eaten with Arthur, the two of them using the same bench, trencher, and cup.

She glanced back at him, offering him that special smile she saved just for him. "This is not punishment, mannikin. Now that the household is full once more, we cannot all eat at once. The masters, along with their apprentices and the higher servants dine first, the remainder eating after."

Arthur dodged around Rob to plod alongside Helewise. "Please, might Rob still eat with me? He's but one small lad," he offered, although it wasn't exactly true.

"How now, Arthur," Katel cried out with all the flare of a mummer. As he sheathed his dagger, he shot Rob a frigid glance. "I'm struck to the core that you no longer wish to share your meal with me."

"Katel!" Johanna shouted in happy greeting as she threw herself against the young man. Wrapping her arms around his waist, she looked up at him. "Puss and I missed you. Come with me and I'll show you the bed I made for him." As always, Johanna did not ask, she demanded.

Master Walter's elder apprentice smiled as he leaned down to give his betrothed a brief embrace. "In a moment, my little wife. Why do you not go within and find Puss so you may show him to me? I'd see how much he's grown in my absence."

"Aye, Katel."

As Johanna whirled away from him, eager to do as he bid, Katel straightened and stared at Arthur. "Now, as for you, lad," he said, his voice cold, "I can only pray my eyes deceive me. Tut, but if you've been keeping company with him"—a jerk of his head indicated Rob—"you'll need to bathe every day for the next month just to rinse a bastard's stench from your skin."

Even though Arthur sidled closer to him at Katel's insult, Rob's fists clenched. Anger roiled in his belly. How could he have forgotten Master Walter's promise to Papa? It wasn't fair that folk would call him bastard when he was not. "I am no bastard," he retorted. "My father and mother were well and truly wed."

"Stop, Katel," Johanna shouted at the youth, then leapt to the housekeeper's side. "Make him stop, Helewise. Rob is my friend, and I don't want Katel to call him a bastard."

"Enough, little mistress," the housekeeper said, her voice tight.

"What is this?" Katel's voice cracked in outrage as he whirled on the housekeeper and his betrothed. "By God, but you know she's mine. Tell me you haven't allowed her to form affections with that bit of garbage!" Rob drew a startled breath at this and stared at Helewise. So did Arthur and Johanna. By tradition it was the housekeeper's right to punish apprentices for wayward or rude behavior, even those as old as Katel. Instead of rebuke, Helewise bowed her head until she disappeared into the meek folds of her headdress.

"I've done only what the master commanded," she said in humble reply.

Rob frowned at Helewise's strange reaction, for it made it seem as though she'd done wrong when she hadn't. The only time he and Johanna saw each other was at meals and church. Of course, there were the times they met behind the warehouse, when Johanna wished to speak with him, or he with her, but no one knew about these. Or, this morning.

Katel fixed the housekeeper with a raging glare. "I will deal with you later. Take her within this moment," he shouted. At his command, Helewise grabbed Johanna's arm and dragged the twisting, fighting girl toward the forebuilding's door. Johanna's determination to remain in the courtyard was strong enough to slow their progress to a snail's pace.

Master Walter's elder apprentice turned his fiery gaze on Rob. "If you've told folk you are a legitimate son, then you lie. Ralph of Blacklea disclaimed you before the whole of your village, saying his wife cuckolded him into accepting you when you're nothing but some nobleman's unacknowledged by-blow."

Once again, the pain of Papa's hurting words tore through Rob. Tears filled his eyes. "That's not true! You'll not call my mother a Norman's whore!"

Katel's dark eyes narrowed, and he leaned toward Rob as if to keep his words private between them. "As backward as this place is, what you see here will someday be mine. If you think because Master Walter showed you a moment's kindness you now have some hope of making this place your home, think again. I'll allow no rude farm wife's bastard to worm his way into any part of what is mine."

With that, the youth straightened and threw back his head. "Hear ye, hear ye," he shouted at the top of his lungs, spreading his arms in dramatic display.

His words rang against the stones of Master Walter's house. Every man within the courtyard stilled at his chores to look at the young man. They rebounded into the lane and street traffic gathered at the gate to see what went forward within the spice merchant's courtyard.

Certain he had their full attention, Katel shouted, "At the behest of the man his mother cuckolded, this lad is to be known as Robert the Bastard from this day forward."

Fed by shame and the hurt Katel's words did his mother, blind fury exploded in Rob. Its heat devoured all sense. No matter that Katel was older, taller, and two, mayhap three, stones heavier than he; all that existed in Rob was the need to hurt as he was being hurt. He launched himself at the youth.

Katel yelped, stumbling against the unexpected attack. Just as Papa had taught him, Rob set a blow deep into the youth's midsection. Gagging, the youth toppled back to sit on the courtyard's hard-packed earth. Rob fell on him. With his startled and yet unresisting victim beneath him, he used every ounce of his childish strength to pummel him.

Someone grabbed him by the back of his tunic. Rob was lifted to dangle in midair. Still sobbing in frustration, he swung wildly into the empty space in front of him. "I am not a bastard!" he screeched.

"Enough, Rob," Master Colin said quietly. The apothecary gave him a gentle shake, then lowered him to his feet.

Rob rubbed his streaming eyes to clear his vision. Katel sprawled on the hard-packed earth of the courtyard's floor. Yet gasping in his struggle to regain the breath Rob had knocked from him, the youth's face was white. This lack of color made the blood flowing from his nose and the marks Rob had laid on him seem all the redder.

Arthur touched Rob on the back in quiet congratulation for so surprising a success. From the spice merchant's gateway, folk laughed. Here, within the courtyard, Master Walter's household guard offered Rob quiet cheers and words of praise for his victory in so mismatched a battle. A second scuffle was going on at the door to Master Walter's house as Johanna continued in her struggle to escape Helewise's desire that she enter the forebuilding.

Wiping the blood from his face, Katel sat up. His skin darkened in humiliation. Rage followed shame, and he leapt to his feet. "I'll see you flayed for daring to attack your better," he shouted, yanking his garments back into order. Anger disappeared beneath a rush of triumph. "Nay, I'll do better than that. I'll bring my charges before the sheriff and see you driven not only from this house, but from Stanrudde's walls!"

Already trembling in fury's aftermath, this threat set Rob's knees to knocking. There was no hope for mercy from the sheriff. A servant dared not attack his employer. He'd be left homeless for certain now.

"Cease, Katel. It is not your place to demand punishment for Rob," Master Colin chided, his voice filled with irritated confusion. "What did you do to Rob to make him attack you?"

The elder apprentice's pale skin flushed ruddy at this. "It matters naught what I said to him. He is but a servant who will be dismissed for his actions."

Master Colin's chin jutted out at this pronouncement. "While that might be how your father runs his house, you know full well it is not Master Walter's way."

Katel turned on his mentor's employee, rage dimming into arrogance as his face twisted. "I'll not be chastised by one too poor to buy himself his own trade," he snapped, his tone condescending. "Stand between me and my right to justice, and I'll see you gone, as well." In the apprentice's face lived the certainty that what he commanded would not be usurped.

Rob leaned against Master Colin as the enormity of what he'd done sank into his soul. Katel was Master Walter's heir through Johanna, making him like unto a son. No doubt Master Walter would heed anything Katel said. In a single moment of blind rage, he'd not only brought shame down upon Colin the Apothecary and cost himself everything he cherished, he'd placed his beloved master in jeopardy. Tears started to his eyes, and he wiped his nose on his sleeve.

"Master, I beg pardon," he managed. Master Colin smiled at him, his hand moving across Rob's back as if to both reassure and comfort.

"What is all this ruckus?" Master Walter called as he exited the forebuilding's door. The spice merchant struggled to pull a too small blue brocade bedrobe over his hastily donned shirt. Bright red hair spiked this way and that from beneath his nightcap. His legs were bare, while on his feet were a pair of sabots, also too small for him.

"Papa!" Johanna shrieked in joy, breaking free of Helewise to throw herself at him.

With a laugh of equal pleasure, Master Walter grabbed up his daughter. "Poppet! I missed you."

"You were still sleeping when we left this morn," Johanna told him, nestling her head into his shoulder, "and Helewise wouldn't let me wake you. Papa, Rob is my friend. Do not let Katel hurt him and send him away," she pleaded into the collar of his robe, her arms tight around his neck.

"Hurt him? Send him away?" Master Walter glanced at her, then to the bruised and bloody Katel. With a growing frown, he clip-clopped across the courtyard to join his daughter's betrothed, juggling Johanna as he tried to draw the bedrobe closed against the morn's crisp air. "What goes forward here, Katel?"

What remained of anger departed from the youth's face, leaving only the distressed confusion of an innocent victim. "Master Walter, this lad attacked me. As he is but a servant here, I told him he is discharged, as would happen to any other had he raised his hand against his better."

"Do not let him," Johanna begged again.

Her papa gently set her down, then motioned Helewise to his side. "Take her within," he told his housekeeper. When Johanna opened her mouth to argue, Master Walter shook his head. "Do as I say, or I'll not give you what I've brought for you."

Excitement over a gift tangled with disappointment in Johanna's gaze. Avarice won. His daughter let Helewise lead her into the forebuilding.

"Go with them, Arthur," Master Walter told his younger apprentice. As Arthur complied with foot-dragging slowness, the spice merchant scanned the watching men. He raised a brow. "Have you nothing to occupy you this morn?"

There was a sudden flurry of activity as the servants turned back to their chores. Once he was assured a modicum of privacy, Master Walter looked at the one he'd chosen to be his daughter's mate. "Katel, what reason had the lad for his attack?" It was an oddly pointed question.

His apprentice sighed as if in deep regret. "Mayhap the fault lies on me, master. I found he'd been passing himself off as legitimately born when he is a bastard. No doubt it was thoughtless of me, but I insisted he speak the truth about his birth." This said, he bowed his head, as if taking to heart the sin to which he had just confessed and absolved himself.

Rob's mouth opened in astonishment. Katel was twisting his attack into something it was not. He drew himself up in honest outrage, ready to launch a defense, but Master Colin squeezed his shoulder. When Rob glanced up at him, the apothecary shook his head, warning him to silence. Despite his need to protect himself from slander, Rob did as he was bid and held his tongue.

"But thoughtless, was it?" Master Walter laid a big hand on Katel's shoulder. His tone said he knew his apprentice was not the innocent he pretended. "You said nothing to provoke him?"

"I did nothing wrong." Katel threw back his head in righteous outrage in protest of his master's subtle accusation. "It was he who attacked me."

"So he did." The spice merchant eyed the crusting blood and the now purpling spots on the youth's face. "From the looks of it, he gave you good return for the slur he felt you did him. Fit punishment for the one who was taunting him over his parentage." Master Walter's brows rose in condemnation. "The bedchamber window is open, Katel. I heard you."

With a raging glance toward Rob, Katel bowed his head. "He is but a servant, master. No matter what I did, he should not have attacked me," he said sullenly, yet trying to shield himself from his attempt to bend the truth. "If he had cause to mislike what I said, then he should have taken his grievance to you, as is meet."

"In that you are right, Katel, but I'll be asking you to have patience with him, forgiving him for my sake. He's not been in the house long enough to know what is what," his master replied, then said as he turned his attention on the lad he'd rescued, "Well now, Robert of Blacklea, I think me you look a sight better than when I last saw you."

Rob cleared his throat and launched into the pretty words he'd spent weeks practicing for the master's return. "My thanks, Master Walter, for taking me into your household—" This was all he managed to spew before the words dried up and blew away. He stared at the big man, tongue-tied and shy.

"You are most well come, Robert," the master replied, politely accepting these few words as full thanks. "Do you find the apothecary's shop to your liking?"

Katel's head bobbed up from his pose. "He was to be in the scullery! What is he doing in the apothecary's shop?"

Master Walter waved the youth to silence as he awaited Rob's reply. Joy flowed through Rob as he thought of his time spent under Master Colin's tutelage. "I do, master. There is so much to learn. Although I must wait for your say so to begin counting in the books, already I keep inventory here." He touched his forefinger to his head to indicate his mental tally of the bags and barrels they had in store.

"So, too, have I memorized the names and places of each cure in our shop, so I might put all where they belong. Arthur has helped me to recognize that each name is made of letters and that the letters are all arranged differently. This is so I cannot mistake the jars that resemble each other."

Across the courtyard, Arthur darted out the forebuilding, where he'd been hiding to spy on his master, and waved his hands in frantic warning at Rob. There was a horrified look on his face. Rob dropped into instant silence; how could he have forgotten that such sharing of knowledge between an apprentice and a servant was strictly forbidden?

"Is that so?" Master Walter asked, seeming not at all disconcerted by this break with tradition. "More and more, you interest me, Robert. What think you of life among the clergy?" Even as he asked his question, he frowned, as if the thought of making a churchman out of Rob did not sit well with him.

Katel straightened to stare at his mentor, new outrage coloring his expression. "Master Walter, what sort of lesson do you give this lad when you reward his violent behavior with the promise of yet more boons? Is it not enough that he already owes you his life, itself?"

Master Colin squeezed Rob's shoulder once again. Rob glanced up at him. The shadow of this morn's speech lived in the apothecary's eyes. Rob caught his breath in terrified understanding. Master Colin wanted him to ask Master Walter about apprenticeship. He shook his head. In this, Katel was right; he already owed Master Walter his life. How could he possibly ask for more? Master Colin's brows rose, both to chastise and to encourage. His master's expression warned that this was his second chance; there'd be no other.

Fear filled Rob's chest, nigh on squeezing his heart into stopping, but his longing for apprenticeship was the stronger. He closed his eyes, not wanting to see the reaction his words might wring from Master Walter, then opened his mouth to let his heart's desire spill from him. "Master, I do not wish to be a churchman; I wish to be apprenticed to you."

"Why, you ungrateful piece of ox dung!" Katel shouted with such violence Rob ducked, expecting a blow. "How dare you ask this of the master, when he has already dug deep into his heart and purse on your behalf!"

"Katel, you overstep yourself," Master Walter snapped. Katel froze, but his was the stillness of deep rage, not compliance.

"So you wish to be apprenticed, do you?" the spice merchant asked, as if he truly meant to consider the request.

Rob's spirits dared to soar in hope. "I do, master, more than anything. I would be a good apprentice. In time, when I have become a master, then will I repay you every pence I have cost you."

"Walter, I am willing to pay his fee as well as bear the cost of his upkeep," Master Colin offered. "You can take it out of my portion of the shop's profits, the part I've been putting toward its purchase."

"Nay, you will not!" Katel howled. His shoulders squared, his fists closed as if he but restrained himself from attacking either Rob or Master Colin by the barest margin.

He whirled on Master Walter. "In considering this farce, you not only mock me and my honor, you besmirch the name of your house. Mark my words, should you agree to this ludicrous proposal, every righteous apprentice within Stanrudde's walls will rise to tear both the bastard and Master Colin limb from limb!"

The spice merchant stared down on his protégé from his superior height, his gaze taking in his apprentice's menacing stance. The moment stretched, the courtyard's quiet broken only by the steadily growing calls from the regraters pacing the streets. So far this morn, there were onions, garlic, fresh apples, pears, and cheese. When Katel did not relax, the merchant's expression grew as icy as the cool color of his eyes.

"This is the second time you harangue me over him, when what I do with him is mine to me. Disapprove if you wish, Katel, such is your right as a man. But it is not within your rights to attempt to bend me to your will. Continue, and, despite my contract with your father, I will know I erred in entrusting my daughter to you."

Katel gasped, then paled against the hurt done him. His shoulders slumped, and his hands opened. "How can you favor him over me?" It was an aching plea.

Master Walter's expression softened in new understanding. "Ah, here is the crux of the matter. Katel, open your eyes. Whether or not I apprentice him, know you this lad is no more to me than Arthur. Look at me. I am not your sire, nor is Robert your half brother. Remember, it is you I have named as my daughter's husband, no other."

"Nay, I will not speak of this," Katel cried, his voice choked and hoarse as if he were close to sobbing. He turned his back on his master. "I would go now and seek counsel from my confessor."

"That would be proper," Master Walter replied, nodding at so appropriate a course of action.

As Katel nigh on raced from the courtyard, Johanna's sire turned his attention back to Rob. "You will have to pardon him, lad. He is the youngest son of his sire, who placed his bastard ahead of Katel in his heart, his shop, and his will. I fear Katel sees his half brother's face atop your features."

Then, shaking off the upset of the past moments, the spice merchant dropped a huge paw onto Master Colin's more delicate shoulder. "I think me you are right, Colin," he said, "this lad is not only bright, but bold and brave as well. Look on how he attacks a man three and ten years his senior and carries the day! If he owns the fire in his belly for trade as you contend, I'd say we've a lion on our hands and I, a third apprentice."

"Master!" Rob breathed in joy, looking from one master to the other. He gasped, clutching at his chest as his heart expanded until it pressed against his ribs. His mouth moved in words of thanks, but no sound exited; his throat had closed in ecstasy. For an instant, he feared he'd swoon.

"Once again, Robert, you are well come to this, having earned it by your own efforts." Master Walter grinned, revealing the gaps where he had lost his teeth. He turned Master Colin toward the house. "Colin, think you no more on the cost of his upkeep. After this year's profit, I can bear them well enough without asking your aid, old friend. If you wish to repay me, walk before me to shield me from those rude enough to stare. I feel like a damn dancing bear in this." He laughed as he plucked at the robe.

As the two merchants started toward the house, joy washed in a new wave over Rob. This time, it demanded he share his happiness. He looked for Arthur—not Arthur, his better, but Arthur, his friend and fellow apprentice.

Master Walter's second apprentice yet peered around the forebuilding's far end. The lad's face was dour, his mouth downcast. This set Rob's feet firmly back upon the earth. Mayhap Arthur also believed Rob shouldn't have been made apprentice. It hurt to think Arthur would no longer be his friend.

Rob worked his way to the forebuilding's end through the throng of adults who were either entering the house or returning to their labors. "Are you angry that I am 'prenticed to the master?" It was a hesitant question.

"Angry?" Arthur looked at him as if such a thing never occurred to him, then surprise died into deep gloom. "Nay, I am only sad. You're going to die, and I will miss you so."

"I am not going to die," Rob cried, shocked and more than a little concerned at this sort of talk.

"Aye, but you are," Arthur sniffed. "I pray you, Rob, watch yourself," he continued, his voice solemn as he turned his mournful gaze on his dearest friend. "No matter how long it takes, Katel will see you dead for what happened this day. This I vow."

Chapter Twelve

Stanrudde
the hour of Vespers,
The eve of Ste. Agnes's Day, 1197

Johanna didn't dare move her gaze from the wall before her as Rob once more walked out of her life. Just as his last departure had shattered her, this leave-taking was doing the same. How could she drive him away when she needed him so?

"Nay, he betrayed me once, I will not let him hurt me again," she commanded herself, too late. Her heart was already broken.

Closing her eyes, as if such a thing might stave off pain, she sought desperately for hate's shield. It was no more. Rob's claim of caring had torn open the ancient wound on her heart, allowing what festered for so long to flood forth.

Johanna buried her face in her hands. What sort of fool persisted in loving the man who had so cruelly used, then discarded her? Her sort, it seemed.

"Nay!" she cried into her palms, "I will not love him! He abandoned me."

The same accusation that had once generated seething rancor now rang hollowly in her ears. She sighed as she realized Rob's rescue made it a lie. The Rob who risked his own life for her was not the sort of man who would have deserted her for coins. That was something of which Katel was capable, but not Rob, never her Rob. He loved her.

Once again, the sweetness of his embrace filled her. This was followed by the glory of his mouth on hers, each kiss speaking of his love for her. Joy died, slaughtered by her own hard and hateful words. Rob loved her no more, she had seen to that.

Only then did Johanna understand how clever her father had been in forcing his daughter to wed where she would not. Had Rob been killed or castrated, either fate his due for having bedded his master's daughter, she might have made a martyr of him and loved him still. Instead, Papa must have placed Rob with a new master, she knew not whom, then bequeathed his former apprentice a substantial amount of money to make it seem his daughter had been betrayed. Even then, her sire had not been convinced of his success in destroying their love. It had been against the possibility of their reunion that Papa had bound her children's inheritance to the requirement she never commit adultery.

That reminder set Katel's threat ringing again in her ears. Johanna started in fear. Mary save her, but Katel hated Rob even more than he despised his wife. It wasn't just her pain or those properties he meant to gain with his false tale of adultery, it was Rob's destruction. She had to warn him!

Clutching her torn gowns closed, she hobbled to the alley's entrance and peered out into the muddy lane. Too late. The narrow street was deserted, brigands gone to ground, the poor retreating to their barren corners and rooms.

Johanna shuddered, helplessness washing over her. Every gruesome tale she'd heard of mutilation or murder done to those caught committing adultery came to vivid life within her. This was how Katel meant for them to die. Panic for them both set her heart to rattling in her chest.

"Mistress!" The call rang against the houses lining this narrow street from where the coopers' lane entered the chandlers' enclave.

She whirled and panic leapt to even greater heights. Theobald, along with one of their menservants, hurried toward her. No doubt alerted by the town guard, Katel meant to fetch her home, where he'd hold her tight until she suffered the fate he wanted for her.

Once again, she sought for hate's shield, only to find herself vulnerable and unprotected. The urge to run rose, then died. She was sore hurt and filthy, her clothing was in tatters, her hair uncovered and unbound. Where could she go?

Theobald came to a halt before her, boldly eyeing the damage done her attire. Johanna's stomach turned at his leer, and she slid her hand upward along the tear until she was certain none of her was revealed to him. This protective motion stirred wicked pleasure to life in his eyes.

"I see some man finally dealt you the lesson you so deserved. I've heard bold bitches like you enjoy a forceful coupling. Am I right?"

As his cruel words brought back the thief's attack in horrible detail, despair set its fist around her, dragging her down into hopelessness. This was a nightmare that would not end. Not only did her husband wish her dead; she'd been attacked and nearly raped. Worst of all, she'd destroyed the affection of the only man she ever loved. Somehow, to live beyond this day was more than she could imagine.

With a jerk of his head, Theobald beckoned forward the man who followed him. "Watt, take her to the master," he snarled as he turned and started toward the abbey's field. "I've got business to tend to."

In silence Johanna and Watt watched him until they could see him no longer. Only then did the servant remove his mantle and set that sturdy garment over his mistress's shoulders. Startled by this unexpected kindness, Johanna looked up at him as she concealed her ruined attire within its thick folds. There was nothing to see in Watt's plain face save the blank disinterest of a servant doing his duty.

He offered her his elbow, the continuing icy drizzle spotting his tunic's gray sleeve. She caught hold of his arm and took a step forward; he did not follow. Again, she looked up at him.

"I could turn my back, leaving you to go where you would, then say you had escaped me." His words were barely louder than a whisper.

Johanna eyed him in surprise. What he offered meant a beating and dismissal for himself, guaranteeing naught but starvation to look forward to after as he joined the ranks of the jobless. "What reason have you for aiding me?"

He shrugged, the motion anything but nonchalant. "It's in repayment of what you did for Aggie, mistress. She wasn't like Leatrice, who went seeking her own downfall with both eyes opened. The master had no right to use Agnes, then discard her like yestermorn's garbage." His voice rose with the depth of his feeling. "There comes a time in a man's life when he sees his honor is more important than employment. I tell you, there's more than me who'll be thanking you for what you did this day."

As kind as his offer was, Johanna shook her head. There was no escaping either Katel or the fate he planned for her. Not even her convent was beyond his reach. Despite her protests against leaving this morn, Theobald had pried her from its walls as easily as scooping soft butter from a dish simply by reminding the prioress that Johanna was his master's wife.

"I have nowhere else to go," she replied, her voice flat in hopelessness.

Watt gave a single nod in understanding, then strode forward. By the time they entered the spice merchant's courtyard, Johanna was leaning heavily on his arm. She ached from head to toe, her weariness bone-deep.

They and the gatekeeper were halfway across the tiny space when Katel charged out of the forebuilding. "May God damn you as a slackard, what took you so long?" was the thanks Watt received for completing his chore. "Best you be grateful I am in a generous mood, else you'd not remain in my employ another day. Now, hie yourself inside."

As he and the other man swiftly and silently complied, Katel glanced at his wife, then breathed sharply in dread. He snatched for her mantle's opening. Lifting one side of the garment, he hissed at her missing chain and what remained of her expensive gowns. He grabbed one of her hands, seeking the rings he demanded she wear in the pretense of the wealth he no longer owned. There was nothing for him to see, but tattered leather and scraped fingers.

Katel dropped her hand. This loss of wealth was so devastating, he was rendered momentarily beyond speech or movement. In the long moment of silence that followed, the wind howled around him, tearing fine strands of pale hair out from beneath his cap, flattening them against the brim with its ferocious breath.

Slowly, bright red color stained his neck. It seeped steadily upward, until his bloated face was suffused. Catching his wife by her arm, he dragged her toward the kitchen shed at the back of the courtyard, craving privacy in which to scream at her. As Johanna stumbled along beside him, a touch of gallows humor woke beneath her paralyzing depression. It would hardly do for the neighbors to overhear Stanrudde's most loving husband abasing his wife.

The kitchen door slammed against the wall behind it as he shoved her into the usually crowded room. Johanna caught herself against the thick worktable.

The chill gust of wind that accompanied her entry barely teased a forlorn crackle from the fire.

She stared in shock at the hearth. The flames were dying, choked by the day's ashes. Impossible! The kitchen's fire was never allowed to die. Johanna turned. Walls stripped of the foodstuffs and tools that usually cluttered their lengths stared blankly back at her.

Where was Wymar, their cook, and his scullery lads? She caught her breath in understanding. Were the hungry really so great a threat that the cook and his supplies had to take refuge in the house?

Katel slammed the door. With the tiny windows shuttered, the room plunged into smoky dimness. A single step brought them nose to nose. "You stupid cow," he shouted. "Do you realize what you've cost me?"

Exhaustion tightened its grip on Johanna as she prepared herself for what would surely be a long session of belittling. The only thing of which she was certain was that he would not strike her. Just as her father's will forced Johanna to remain virtuous, Papa had found a way to restrain Katel's native violence against her. Upon her complaint of abuse, those properties he so coveted, whose rents now supported him, instantly ceded to Stanrudde's abbey.

"Thank God I will soon be rid of you! You cannot know how that prospect fills me with joy," he went on, his voice vicious and dark. "Only when I see you on your knees, pleading for your life, will I know the cosmos has righted itself. It will be justice come at last when all that was stolen from me is restored."

Johanna bowed her head. Her eyes closed as she sought to shield herself from his venom. In the depths of her weariness, she forgot that she wore no wimple to hide her face from his view. Katel drew a sharp, startled breath.

His slap was so hard it spun her around as it

knocked her feet out from under her. Ears ringing, Johanna hit the beaten earth of the room's floor. Her mouth filled with the coppery taste of blood as she bit her lip. Shifting onto her side, she braced her forearm beneath her. As she lifted herself just a little, she shook her head, not so much to clear her thoughts, but in dazed disbelief at what he'd done.

Her husband leaned over her, his face nigh on purple with rage. "May God damn you to hell for the arrogant woman you are! You will heed me when I speak to you!"

Johanna looked up at him from where she lay. "You hit me," she said, yet too stunned by his attack to own any other emotion.

Katel stiffened. Frantic worry leapt to life behind his rage, as he only now realized what he'd done. His gaze shot to the reddened spot on her cheek as if to gauge the possibility of a mark. Worry disappeared, eased by the scratches and ripening bruises that already covered her face.

"Why not," he murmured. "The whole town will soon know you were mauled. There's no one to say who laid which bruises."

Shielded behind the damage already done her, a new and wicked eagerness came to life in his eyes. His fists closed. Fear shot through Johanna. Once he started, years of hatred would goad him to continue until she was no more. When she was gone, he'd cry to the world it was injuries suffered in the rioters' attack that had killed her.

In her exhaustion and hopelessness, a strange calm took possession of her. Trapped in its unearthly grip, her soul opened, and she looked in disappointment upon the woman she had been.

What a selfish child she was. Only once had Walter of Stanrudde denied his daughter her will: when he took Rob from her and forced her to marry Katel in his stead. Rather than accept this fate and find what happiness she could in it, she had chosen to tantrum, setting herself to hating everyone and everything connected with the life her father had given her. She sighed. The only one she hadn't hurt by this was the sire she'd childishly sought to punish.

"Beg," her husband demanded, ready to play out the last act of this black farce. "I would hear you beg for mercy."

At the sound of his voice, she looked up at him, her revelation so shattering that she was stirred to speech. "Do you know what I am thinking, Katel?" In her strange state, her voice was quiet and considering. Stark surprise filled her husband's gaze. Of all the responses he'd expected his threat to generate, this was not one of them.

"I am thinking our son deserved better than a dam more intent on hating and hurting all those around her than seeing to his needs. I find myself regretting my selfishness. In my determination to repay the world for the wrongs I perceived done me, I cheated myself of what was good in my life. I cheated Peter. And"—she shook her head in regret—"I cheated you of what any good wife owes her marriage."

Katel blinked rapidly. His fists relaxed, and he took a step back from her. There might have been a softening in his eyes, but it was gone in the next instant, indeed, if it had ever existed. Katel tensed and she could nigh on see his thoughts spin as he sought for the traps that must surely be hidden in her words.

In that moment the bell at their gate clanged in anxious call. Not content with a single announcement, the ringer continued yanking upon the string until the jangling grew to an urgent clamor. "Master Katel, Master Katel! The council calls you to come with all haste. There is new trouble afoot!"

His call brought triumph's glow to Katel's eyes, banishing both the desire to hurt her and his worry over his wife's strange words. "Nay, you will not get the better of me," he hissed at her, "not now, only days before my vengeance is complete. In fact, I must thank you for distracting me. I want you whole and well, so you might cry to the world of your innocence as you die. I think it will be that I most enjoy." He started to leave, then paused to turn to her again. "How I will laugh as I watch you and that bastard die for what you have not done."

Still, the bell jangled. "Can anyone hear me?" the desperate messenger shouted.

With a snarl, Katel turned and threw the kitchen's door wide. "Someone answer his call!" he shouted toward the house. As he stormed out into the courtyard, he spilled his troubled emotions on those beneath him. "What is wrong with you witless idiots, or do you expect the master to open the gate like some lackey? I vow I'll flay you all and feed your flesh to the pigs. Now, come and bar the gate behind me."

Johanna yet lay where she had fallen. Although she commanded her body to rise, not a muscle responded. Instead, she relaxed, tucking her elbow beneath her head to cushion her face against the cold, hard floor. Her eyes closed.

She would rest for just a moment. Aye, and after she had regained her strength, she'd call someone to stoke the fire and heat water for a bath. But not just now. As she drifted into sleep, a quirk of amusement woke in her, no doubt brought on by hysteria. All in all, death might well be worth that absurd look on Katel's face.

Chapter Thirteen

Stanrudde
Late April, 1174

"Well now, don't they look fine, indeed," Philip said as he lifted the browned and baked meat pasties from the kitchen's oven with his flat-bladed, long-handled wooden shovel.

Johanna awaited the arrival of the small, steaming pies in pride. She'd done it all, from chopping and cooking the filling to the mixing and rolling of the crust to crimping them shut. Well, most all of it. Philip wasn't as strict as Helewise about making her do everything herself. It was a shame Papa had already departed on his summer travels, this year leaving Katel behind to tend to their local affairs. He was missing her first moment of triumph as the mistress of his house.

Learning the household arts was now hers to do. Papa had been furious over the Brother Mathias's attempt to beat her, vowing she needed no more than what Helewise could teach her. Despite this edict, Katel continued to pressure Papa about her schooling, now talking about a nearby convent and how the nuns were willing to educate merchants' daughters the same way that noblewomen were tutored.

Philip turned and let the pies slip off the shovel onto the thick table. Johanna's heart sank. They didn't look fine at all. Only two of them looked like pasties, the others being any shape but half-moon.

Papa's cook raised a brow and set a hand on his hip at her downcast expression. "Come now, you cannot expect perfection on your first try. The next time you make them, they will be better."

Johanna looked up at him in despairing frustration. The next time! She had to do this again? Being the mistress was entirely too much work, and she was tired of being expected to do the same task over and over again.

Her spirits fell even further. Now that the cooking lesson was done, she no longer had a reason to avoid Helewise and the pile of mending she had waiting for her. The rest of this day would be spent stitching, with Helewise making her remove what had been sloppily done.

"Here now," Philip continued, his tone consoling as he turned all the pies face up, "look is not all that is important in the kitchen. There's flavor, as well. Give one to Tom and see if he doesn't think them as tasty as mine."

At the sound of his name, the lackwit raised his head from the chickens he was plucking. "You must taste one of these and tell our little mistress the sort of job she's done, Tom," his father told him. Tom frowned at so important a task as sampling his mistress's handiwork, but gave a single, short nod to show he was up to the rigors of it.

Juggling a hot pie, Johanna crossed to the hearth and offered it to him. Tom bit into it, the bite moving from side to side in his mouth as he waited for it to cool enough to taste. At last, he swallowed. "Good," he said with a single nod and set into the remainder of crust and meat.

A triumphant glow took hold of Johanna's heart, and she loosed a tiny squeal of pleasure. She could cook! Dancing back to the table, she tried the ugliest of them. It was not just savory, it was delicious.

"Philip, can I take these two to Helewise?" Since the bite in her mouth blurred her speech, she pointed out the perfect two in case he hadn't understood which ones.

"I will give them all to you," the cook said, tucking the pies into a cloth. "When you've finished admiring them, you can give them to Arthur and Rob."

"Nay!" Johanna cried in instant refusal. Although Philip didn't seem to think misshapen pasties any great matter, both Arthur and Rob would tease her over them.

"Come now, little mistress. You cannot keep them all to yourself. Besides, it'd be a boon if you fed those lads. Our meal is late enough already."

When she looked at him in confusion, Philip smiled. "Arthur will be here any moment to pester me for a bite to eat, since he is always hungry upon his return from the abbey. No doubt he'll bring Rob with him when he comes, as they went off to lessons together this morn. If you feed them for me, I can finish our meal."

Pride grew in her with his words. A swift smile touched Johanna's mouth. Philip thought her work good enough to feed those who labored for Papa. Better still, as long as she did this for Philip, she could delay her return to the house and the mending. That, alone, was worth any tease.

"I will do as you ask, Philip," she said, offering him what she hoped was a mistressly nod.

"My thanks," the cook said, waiting until she donned her mantle before handing her the knot of cloth. "Off with you, then."

The day's off-and-on shower had finally died into a gentle mist, leaving the whole world well and truly soaked. Johanna crossed the courtyard, carefully picking her way to prevent her hems from getting mucky, her thoughts on Rob and schooling. In the same fit of pique that ended her education, Papa had decided to send Arthur to the Benedictines, whose abbey school educated the majority of Stanrudde's apprentices. Rob had wanted to go as well, but Papa had insisted he wait until he'd passed his saint's day and entered his eleventh year. That had been yesterday; this morn, Rob had left for the abbey with Arthur, his very own wax tablet and stylus in his scrip.

At the gate, Johanna picked a dry spot just inside the opening and nibbled on her pie as she watched the passing traffic. Pack horses and carts were churning the lane into a sea of mud, while the foot-bound slogged through the thick stuff in wooden sabots, their cloaks dampened to dark hues. A regrater passed, calling to all about the extraordinary flavor of his cheese.

The minutes passed like hours and still the lads didn't come. As her impatience grew, holding herself within the gate grew very difficult. Although Helewise said lasses who strolled beyond their fathers' walls gained a name for being too forward, it wasn't fear for her reputation that kept Johanna clinging to the woven fencing, but the threat of another round of chamber pots. Only when she was absolutely certain they'd been too long did she dare step into the lane.

Her hands on her hips, Johanna peered in the direction of the abbey. Just then, Arthur rounded the corner as if the hounds of hell were after him. As he ran, he kept his arms wrapped around his middle, holding himself together. His hair was filthy with mud. Deathly pale, blood streamed from his nose and dribbled from a cut in his forehead. His tunic was torn and one shoe was missing.

"Helewise!" Johanna shrieked, darting back into her father's compound.

Arthur flew into the gate, then stopped in front of her, panting. "When they let me go, they were still holding Rob down. Someone must save him," he gasped out.

A burst of heat exploded in Johanna, too hot for just anger. Rob was hers to care for. She'd not stand for anyone hurting him. "Where!" she demanded, her fists tightening in preparation for battle.

"They've got Rob in the abbey's market field," he cried to Helewise, who'd appeared at the forebuilding's door. Then he began to sob.

Forgetting about chamber pots and reputations, Johanna hurtled through the gate. Down the ropemakers' lane she flew, past the chandlers' enclave, then through an alley to the coopers' lane. She burst out onto the small expanse that served as a marketplace for the abbey's once-a-year fair and stopped, her sack of precious pasties yet grasped tightly in her hand.

Beneath the sky's gray curtain, the field was mud in places and dotted with daffodils in others, the blooms vibrant against the bright green of spring grass. Rob was nowhere to be seen. Four of the town's apprentices stood in one corner of the expanse. All of them were near to Arthur's age, two attached to fullers, one to a butcher, and the last to Herebert the ropemaker. They were gathered close to each other as if sharing secrets.

Her heart seethed. She'd beat them to a pulp for hurting her Rob. Sprinting toward them, she barely slowed before striking her first blow. The elder fuller's lad yelped as the hardened leather of her sole caught him full on his shin.

She whirled to set on the butcher's boy, but he grabbed her by the arms and held her away from him. "Cease, I say!"

"You hurt Rob!" she screamed at them, kicking and swinging at her captor

"He hit me first!" the younger fuller's lad lisped in protest. Blood dripped from his swollen and cut lips.

He rubbed it off with his sleeve. "He nigh on tore off my face."

"It was a fair fight," Herebert's boy cried out. His brown tunic was torn, revealing a stained and patched shirt beneath it.

"Aye, one of him against four of us," the older fuller's lad said, a touch of shame in his voice. There was mud befouling his hair and tunic. A swath of red glowed angrily down the side of his face.

"There were two of them," the butcher's boy exclaimed in protest.

"You would count that puling infant, Arthur?" another retorted in scorn.

"What have you done with him!" Johanna shouted, her anger growing mostly because the butcher's boy was keeping her from landing a blow.

"Who? The bastard or Arthur?" he asked.

"Rob is not a bastard," Johanna retorted. Although she was uncertain of the mechanics, bastards were babes born from women who had no husbands. Rob had both a mother and a father.

"Be damned to hell if I know," the older of the fuller's apprentices said, daring to use a forbidden curse in an attempt at swaggering bravado. "Arthur went one way and he, the other."

Instantly, Johanna knew Rob was at their private place. He went there to think whenever he was troubled. Wanting only to join him and see that he was safe, she tried to pull free of the butcher's boy. "Leave go!" she commanded him, when he yet held her tight.

"Vow not to hit me and I will," her captor replied.

Rob had warned her again and again that oaths were sacred, and she should make them only when she meant to keep her word. Since she meant to do so this time, Johanna lay her hand over her heart. The cloth filled with pasties bounced against her chest. She raised her other hand to steady it; the bag's bottom was soggy and warm. "I so vow," she said, going still to prove her words were true.

He released her. She turned toward the Watergate and Papa's warehouse. Behind her, Edwin, the younger fuller's lad, sniffed. "I know naught what you others plan, but I'll never call him bastard again, no matter what Katel offers."

At the mention of her betrothed, Johanna stopped with a jerk and whirled on the lads. Katel had done this to Rob? She frowned. How could it be? Katel was only ever patient and friendly with her. He even played her games with her, although he drew the line at toying with her poppet. But then, so did Rob.

Everyone thought her fortunate to be betrothed to a man as handsome and amiable as Katel. That was, all save Emmalina, one of the lasses who labored in the apothecary's shop. Johanna's lip curled at this. Emmalina was only jealous, pining after Katel when he already belonged to her.

Herebert's apprentice struck the younger lad's shoulder a sharp blow. "You fool! She's to wed Katel. What if she tells him what you said? He'll have our skins, that's what."

"I'll vow not to tell," she offered.

As one, they glared at her. "Everyone knows a woman's word is worth nothing," the butcher's lad hissed, despite that he'd taken a vow from her the moment before. "What shall we do to ensure she holds her tongue, my lads?"

Stung by this betrayal and suddenly concerned for her safety, Johanna lifted her heels and sprinted in the direction of the Watergate. At halfway 'cross the field, she glanced behind her. Her heart leapt into her throat. They were after her!

Past the keep's mound she went, trampling clutches of daffodils in her haste. She slid around the corner of Papa's building and plowed into the willows, their branches golden-green with newborn leaves. Forcing herself between the two trees, she tried to drop into her hiding spot beside Rob. Having grown some over the winter, he nigh on filled the wee hole.

"Hie, move aside, they're after me," she hissed.

In silence, he made room for her. Johanna eased into the space, yet panting against the thrill of being chased. She went still as a mouse until she was certain the lads hadn't come this far in their pursuit. Only when she was content that she wasn't being followed did she look at Rob.

He was trying to wipe the mud from his face with his tunic's hem. One eye was already darkening to purple, while there was a swelling on his jaw. The knees of his chausses were now but gaping holes, and his knuckles were red and scraped.

"Does it hurt?" she whispered in awe.

"What do you think," he snapped, trying to turn his face to the side so she wouldn't see the tracks his tears had made in the filth.

"That it hurts," she replied, undaunted. Rob was touchy about his emotions. It made him short tempered to have someone see him cry. In an effort to grant him a moment's privacy, she stared into her lap.

The cloth bag containing her pasties had survived her race intact. All that running made her hungry. With her stomach grumbling, she opened the cloth's knot. The smell of fresh baked crust filled their tiny hidey-hole.

Tears forgotten, Rob breathed deeply, then leaned over to peer at what she had. She offered him one of the two better pies. The misery in his expression dimmed slightly as he took it from her.

"Where did you get these?" he asked, most of the pie already stuffed in his mouth.

"I made them myself." Pride filled her once again, then grew when he grunted to tell her he was enjoying it. Johanna took the other pretty one for herself, handing him one of the ugly ones when he finished his first.

As she ate, she looked across the hole toward Papa's warehouse. Rob's wax-coated tablet lay against its wall as if thrown there. What had started the day as whole was now in two pieces. Leaning forward to pick it up, she held the pieces together as if she could force them to rejoin.

Rob's scrawling attempts at letters now filled its soft surface. Johanna lifted a finger to trace a few of the marks. Of a sudden, she was certain she'd made a mistake in wishing to escape schooling for Helewise's tutelage. Scratching shapes into wax was definitely easier than mending.

"Did you break the tablet?" she asked, setting the pieces back onto the hole's opposite side.

"Nay," Rob hiccoughed in agony as he started on a third pie, "the other lads did. Or, maybe Arthur stepped on it as he made his escape. No matter how it broke, it is ruined. What if because of this, Master Colin will keep me from the abbey? What if I must wait until your father returns?"

Johanna frowned in thought for a moment. "I could tell him that Edwin, the fuller's lad, said he'd not fight with you again." Aye, that was what she needed to do. "Edwin should be punished, not only for attacking you, but because he lied and said Katel had offered him something to do so," she said.

Beside her, Rob choked. When he'd finally swallowed the bite trapped in his throat, he turned on her, his eyes alight in angry certainty. "I thought it must be Katel who had arranged this," he cried, "else how would lads who knew nothing of me think to call me bastard?"

Shaking her head in denial, Johanna stared at Rob. This could not be. "Katel didn't do this. He is good and kind. All the lasses say so."

Rob's eyes narrowed in scorn. "What do girls like them know of men and their issues? Katel hates me simply because Master Walter cares for me. Katel wishes me dead. Twice now, he's set traps for me in the shop, trying to twist things so it seems I've made an error, when I haven't."

Johanna's stomach moved to her toes as she struggled to make sense of all this. When Rob reached for another pie, she handed him the bag. In her confusion, her thoughts tumbled from her lips.

"Helewise says a mistress's most important function is to protect those who live within her house. If I am the mistress, then I must protect you," she told him. "I will tell Papa when he returns."

"Nay!" Rob breathed in panicked horror. "You'll say nothing of this to anyone. If you do, Master Colin might be hurt."

Johanna's shoulders squared as she added Master Colin to those she, as mistress, must protect. A quiet moment passed, then she frowned. "How can Katel hurt Master Colin, when he is a man full grown and Papa's friend?"

"You don't understand. Katel is your betrothed and, therefore, your father's heir. As such, he has Master Walter's ear. What if he told your father to be rid of Master Colin?" Conviction beamed from him. "He'd have to leave Stanrudde, that's what."

Although Johanna didn't think Papa would send away his friend, there was no doubt Rob believed this would happen. As she'd been wrong about Katel, thinking him kind when he was not, might she not also be wrong about this? Johanna opted for caution's course. "Then I vow to say nothing to Papa."

Rob nodded in relief, eagerly accepting her promise where the other lads had scorned her word. Johanna smiled at him, liking him all the more for doing so. Rob always treated her as if she was special, even more special to him than was Arthur.

A girl's laugh wafted around the warehouse's corner on the day's damp breeze, the sound of her amusement gay. This was followed by a man's muted voice.

Both Rob and Johanna shifted to peer through the willow branches in interest.

Johanna hoped it wasn't the apprentice and maid from last week returning. They'd come while Papa had been working in the warehouse just before his departure and Johanna had come back here to occupy herself. The two had tussled and rolled on the ground for what seemed the longest time. The lass's skirts had ended up bunched at her waist, then the apprentice had pulled his chausses down to his knees. Johanna had seen his shaft thrusting out before him, all swollen and red. He'd fallen on the maid once more, making her cry out as he squirmed atop her, his bare buttocks gleaming in the day's light. All in all, it had been a disquieting experience, leaving her with worrisome dreams.

The girl's long, dark plaits swung as she danced into the clearing. Johanna caught her breath. Emmalina! After her, came . . . Katel!

"Do not fret so," Katel was saying. "There'll be no one in the warehouse. It's empty until Master Walter sends back his first purchases."

"I hope you're right." Emmalina didn't sound worried at all. Instead, she giggled and leaned against Johanna's betrothed, her head tilted up to him. Johanna narrowly eyed the maid. Katel was hers, and Emmalina had no right to trespass.

Katel leaned his head down to touch his mouth to the girl's lips. Johanna's stomach turned. She could tell by the way Emmalina grabbed at Katel that they were going to do that awful wrestling. Beside her, Rob shuddered as if he was thinking the same thing.

She started to turn her back to them, hoping she'd never have to touch mouths with Katel, when yet another set of voices echoed around the warehouse's edge. Emmalina and Katel sprang apart. Johanna edged forward, drawn by the possibility of two couples battling over this stretch of riverbank.

It was Master Colin and Helewise who strode around the corner. Horror woke in Johanna at the thought that they might ever tussle, then died in understanding. They'd not come to kiss and tug, but to find her and Rob.

Although Helewise stopped at the tiny clearing's edge the moment she caught sight of Katel and Emmalina, Master Colin's face darkened. The apothecary lengthened his stride to cross the riverbank, then he grabbed Katel by the tunic front. "You worthless piece of ass dung," he roared, his voice thundering against the warehouse wall. "Arthur has returned, beaten and bloody, while Rob has not come home at all!"

Johanna again looked at Rob. He was shaking his head at the apothecary as if to warn him, fear written in every line of his face. Johanna's heart quaked in worry for Master Colin. She liked him. He let her play in his workshop while the lads worked.

Her betrothed held himself still in the apothecary's grip as he glanced from Emmalina to Helewise. "Take the maid and yourself home where you belong," he commanded.

As she always did when being addressed by a man, Helewise bowed her head. However, beneath the meek pose Johanna yet struggled to learn, the housekeeper hid full blown outrage. Again, Johanna's spirits sank. Helewise disliked Katel. Every line of her tense form said as much. Why had she not seen this before now?

"I cannot return until I have found Mistress Johanna," Helewise replied, her quiet tones masking the fact that she'd just blatantly refused to obey Katel's command.

"Helewise, do as he says," Master Colin said, his voice strained and tight. "Johanna is seeking Rob. As soon as she finds him, she'll bring him home with her. She'll be safe enough while she's at it."

Katel's breath hissed from him at the apothecary's words, his face tensing in hatred. "She's mine! I'll not have her spending time with that bastard!" he snarled.

Beside her, Rob stiffened at the slur. Johanna lay her hand on his arm, to show him she didn't believe it. He smiled at her, gratitude in his gaze.

Johanna looked back at Helewise. Somehow, Katel's rage pleased the housekeeper; Johanna could almost feel Helewise's smile behind the shield of her headdress. As the tension left the housekeeper's shoulders, she folded her hands demurely before her.

"Aye, Master Colin," she said, holding herself still long enough to show Katel she accepted the apothecary's command where she had refused his. Raising her head only slightly, she glanced at the maid. "Emmalina, come."

This time there was an awful edge to her words. Johanna cringed for Emmalina. The maid was in terrible trouble, worse even than chamber pots. The maid knew it, too, for she was awash in tears before she passed the men. Together, the two women rounded the warehouse's edge. There was the sound of a slap. Emmalina sobbed harder, then the sound of her cries faded.

Of a sudden, Johanna was certain she didn't want to hear what Master Colin was going to say to Katel. She looked at Rob in a plea to leave. Rob only shrugged in helplessness. There was no escape for them without revealing their presence.

"You'll let me go," Katel said with icy calm.

Master Colin gave the younger and more slender man a sharp shake. "You arranged to have Arthur and Rob beaten!"

His words not only thundered against the warehouse walls, they echoed into Johanna's heart. Edwin had not lied; even Master Colin knew Katel meant Rob harm.

"If Arthur says I set out to hurt them, he lies," Katel said, an undercurrent of scorn in his voice.

"I do not need a child to tell me what I can see for myself," Master Colin retorted, a new note of sadness in his voice. "Jesu, Katel, what has become of you? Your soul blackens before my eyes! Did you not come to Walter heartsore, much as Rob did? Yet, instead of reflecting the compassion your master has shown you, you set yourself to hating and hurting."

"You'll not chide me for what you believe lies in mine own heart," Katel snarled, a frantic edge to his voice. He shoved at the apothecary. "What do you know of how it feels to see your father give his affection to another, leaving you no crumb after? Because I was not adept enough at his trade, my sire threw me away, condemning me without a second thought to a life far less than what even his apprentices will own. Now you would ask compassion of me as I daily see that bastard steal from me what little I have left?"

"Ah, so you did plan Rob's beating," Master Colin said in bitter triumph.

Johanna watched as her betrothed went utterly still in the older man's grasp. In the next moment, Katel raised a cool brow. "You have incontrovertible proof of this?" Scorn lay heavy in his voice. "Without it, all you do is speculate." This time, when he thrust away from the apothecary, Master Colin released him. Silence lay as heavy and soft along the riverbank as the clouds in the sky. As Katel yanked his tunic back in place and straightened his hair, Master Colin stepped back and crossed his arms over his chest.

"Mayhap I cannot prove it outright," the apothecary said, "but, trust me, boy, I'll make certain Walter knows of this."

"Say what you like. You cannot hurt me," Katel replied, his voice now as smooth as silk. "For months I have praised the lad to my master, congratulating him for finding a lad so gifted." Katel paused to smile at Master Colin. "Who do you think Master Walter will believe, the one who is his heir and sings the lad's praises or the man who is jealous of me, because he remains too poor to buy himself his own trade?"

"You dance a clever dance, lad," Master Colin snapped, looking not the least bit frightened by the threat. "Best you beware. One day, you will tangle yourself in the webs you spin, bringing your own downfall upon you. I only pray I am there to witness it when you do." The apothecary whirled on his heel and stalked from the bank.

Katel waited until he was sure Master Colin was out of earshot. "Think so, old man?" he said to the empty space before him. "I think me you're wrong, and it won't be long before I prove it to you. Once I have the spice merchant's wealth behind me, you'll swiftly find yourself without trade or home." With that, he stormed from the riverbank and around the warehouse.

Johanna watched him go. Rob was right. Katel meant not only to hurt him, but Master Colin, as well. When Papa returned from the fairs, she'd tell him she wanted to wed Katel no longer.

Above them, the sky released a fine veil of mist. She looked at Rob. Tears touched his eyes, shed for Master Colin's sake. This time, he didn't turn away from her. Instead, as if he both begged her aid and sought to share his pain with her, he lay his arm around her shoulders. Once again, her need to protect him rose. But what could she do, when even Master Colin could not control Katel?

Trapped in mutual worry and depression, they clutched together in the hidey-hole. Only when the pasties were gone and the mist had turned to rain did they emerge from the bank and return in silence to her father's home.

* * *

Johanna woke with a start, yet breathing in panic against her dream. Although she knew it was only her fancy, it had seemed oh so real. Lying still upon her cot, she let the images coalesce until she found the tale in it. Katel had attacked her, not the kind and caring man he'd been, but the new man she'd seen on the riverbank.

She breathed out the remains of what had frightened her. There was no need to fear Katel, at least not just now. Most likely, he wasn't even in the house. When he hadn't appeared for their evening meal, Johanna asked after him to Helewise. The housekeeper told her Katel had gone to soak his pride, whatever that meant. At any rate, Helewise thought Katel would be at it all night.

Now fully awake, Johanna let her gaze travel the room, finding comfort in its familiar nightly landscape. At the far wall, a thick night candle set on its tall iron stand flickered a friendly yellow greeting to her. Its meager light made Papa's nearby trunks, the ones containing his and her clothing, seem to shift into their corner like huge, shadowy cats, curled one into the other. This made Johanna reach down to touch Puss, who was curled between her legs. The cat offered her a brief purr, then shifted to avoid her hand.

Johanna looked at the gaping emptiness where Papa's bed usually sat. Helewise always dismantled and stored the piece for safekeeping while he traveled. Of a sudden, she longed for her father. Were he here, she could have told him all, despite her vow to Rob. She could trust Papa to both keep her secret and advise her.

Her gaze moved to Helewise's cot near the door. The housekeeper was but a slight mound atop its surface. Johanna considered confiding in her, then rejected it. If Master Colin could do nothing to save Rob, neither could Helewise, who was less powerful than he. Nay, only Papa could manage Katel.

From their pallets on the floor all around her, the maids murmured in their sleep. The lasses were distraught over Emmalina's abrupt departure from their midst, none of them certain of the reason for her dismissal. Johanna rolled onto her side to look over her cot's edge at them. Caught two to a pallet, they cuddled and snuggled as they slumbered.

It had been very hard not to tell them what she knew, thus making herself the center of their attention, but today had changed her. No longer was she a babe, blindly trusting all she saw. She was the mistress of this house, the one who sought to protect those in her charge. Besides, if she spilled what she knew, one of them would surely tell Helewise. Not only could this threaten both Rob and Master Colin, but she could be punished for spying.

Only then did the answer to this puzzle come to Johanna. There was one person to whom she could spill her troubles. Once she'd told Katel what she knew, she could barter with him to secure the safety of those she loved.

Before she could reconsider, Johanna slipped from her cot and dragged on her undergown. Tiptoeing carefully over the maids, she crept to the bedchamber door. Puss rose to follow her.

Helewise rolled onto her back. "Where are you going, little mistress?" Her voice was sleepy.

"To the privy," she lied.

"Use the chamber pot."

"Nay," Johanna moaned quietly. "I don't like it. It stinks."

Helewise gave a tired groan, then pulled the blankets over her shoulders. "Do not wake the house by dropping the bar this time and come immediately back, do you hear?" she murmured.

"Aye. My thanks, Helewise." The housekeeper only sighed in reply.

Johanna stopped a step into the hall. Puss stood at

her ankles, waiting to see where it was his mistress went at so late an hour. Appreciating his company upon this strange quest of hers, she glanced around the hall.

As Papa took most of the male servants with him when he left, the big room seemed eerie in its emptiness, what with so few sleeping on its floor. She glanced to the side at where her dowry chests sat, seeking ease in the familiar presence. It was too dark in here to see them, there being not even enough light to make the brass gleam on the rusty-colored one. Still, she knew them as she knew herself, the brass-bound one sitting nearest to the bedchamber door with the green sitting between it and the brown-and-blue one.

Her courage fed, she turned toward the fireplace where Katel slept as befitted his rank. Since their hearth was hooded, the embers contained behind an edged stone, there was no need to cover it at night. Glowing coals, all that was left of the day's merry blaze, gilded Katel's blanketed outline. He was here.

She drew a breath in trepidation, but her need to protect Rob set her to sidling along the wall. When she reached her betrothed's pallet, she knelt beside him and wrinkled her nose. He smelled as if he'd bathed in ale. Was this what Helewise meant by soaking his pride?

Puss, who had trailed along behind her, seated himself on the floor beside her. With his tail wrapped neatly around his forepaws, he waited to see what would happen next.

A thick shock of pale hair fell across Katel's face. Johanna gently brushed the strands back onto his forehead to look at him. Katel's nose twitched, and he sighed, but did not awaken. He looked very different in sleep, all sweet-featured and as young as Rob. It was hard to be afraid of him.

"Wake up, Katel," she whispered, gently prodding

him. It wouldn't do for Philip or the other men in the room to waken. Betrothal or not, if Helewise learned she'd come here to speak with Katel, there'd be worse than chamber pots to do. Helewise said that a woman who comported with men at night, even if she did not lay with them, deserved the title whore.

Katel's eyes blinked open, but it was another moment before he actually saw it was she who'd awakened him. "Well now, if it isn't my little wife." His words were quiet and slurred, his tone harsh. "The same wife who travels unescorted about Stanrudde, keeping company with a bastard."

At this insult to Rob, Johanna's eyes narrowed. "Rob's no bastard."

Katel's brows jerked upward, his mouth twisting in anger. "It befouls you to form his name with such familiarity," he snarled, but his words tangled one into the other until she wasn't quite certain this was what he'd said. He stopped to clear his throat and gain control of his tongue. "Speak that name to me again, and I guarantee I'll see the brat beaten for trespassing with you."

Johanna huffed in outrage, but his threat worried her. She should never have come here. Bracing her knuckles on the floor, she started to rise.

As if her motion only now brought him to full awareness, Katel's gaze cleared. "Wait, Johanna." He reached out to catch her arm and hold her in place. "I beg pardon. I am not myself this night," he said, once more sounding like last year's gentle man.

These familiar tones made Johanna relax back onto the floor. Doubt crept into her thoughts. Mayhap, his behavior at the warehouse had been but a momentary aberration. She smiled at him in relief.

Katel returned her smile, then patted her cheek. "First lesson in husbands, my little wife. Never speak another man's name in their presence. Now, what are you doing here in the depths of the night? Where is

Helewise? Has she not warned you that it's improper for you to come unescorted into the places where men sleep? Doing so is almost more unseemly than speaking to me about the bastard. Well, if she hasn't, I vow I'll demand your father send you to the nuns."

Anger woke in her as Katel set to yet another attempt at manipulating her life. It spurred her into following through with her plan. "I came to tell you that I know the truth. You told those lads to hurt Rob."

Katel sat up so swiftly Johanna pushed herself back from him in a start of fear. He swayed unsteadily for a moment, then braced himself on his arms. "Best you keep your lies to yourself." It was a quiet, but vicious, warning, banishing the old gentleness, leaving behind only the Katel of the riverbank.

"I do not lie, Katel. I heard the boys talking in the abbey's marketplace. They said you'd put them to hurting Rob." There was a moment's guilt as she realized she'd broken her oath to the lads, then her jaw stiffened. They'd not believed she'd keep her word anyway.

Katel belched. His eyes gleamed in the dimness as he stared at her. The sight of an empty and warm lap was more than Puss could bear. He strode delicately across Katel's blanketed legs to curl himself atop the young man's legs. In absent reaction, Katel lowered his hand to stroke the cat's head, rubbing gently at Puss's ears. His reward was a loud purr.

At last, Katel said, "If you're so sure of yourself, why haven't you spilled what you think you know to Helewise?"

Johanna almost smiled as she recognized bartering's beginning. "Because I wish to make you an offer. I will keep what I know to myself for a price."

"What price?"

"You must vow to never again try to hurt Rob or Master Colin."

"Idiot babe," he retorted. "Spill what you think you

know to whomever you please. There's none who'll believe you. Now, go back to your bed, but know I will complain to Helewise in the morn that you have come and disturbed me at my rest."

Even though he put a sharp edge to his voice, Johanna recognized the next step in their trade. This was just how Papa said it would be: you name your price knowing the buyer will refuse and disparage your wares, then you call him back to you with a better offer.

"If Helewise beats me, I'll have to tell her what I know," she said in quiet triumph, "and she'll have to tell Papa."

Yet stroking the cat, Katel eyed her a moment as if trying to read her thoughts, then his brows lifted. "Mayhap we can come to some agreement. To set your heart at ease, I will give you my vow never to hurt the bastard or Master Colin, but you must give me what I want in return."

"What?" she asked, now certain of triumph.

"You must enter the convent school by week's end."

Johanna gasped, shocked and ready to refuse his counteroffer. Then, deep within her, a glow took life. That she should sacrifice herself to save Rob and Master Colin was right and just as it should be. Indeed, since she no longer wished to wed with Katel, it was the only answer.

In that moment, Johanna recognized her destiny. She was fated to be a martyr, or mayhap even a saint. Saints and holy women almost always refused to give up their maidenheads, sometimes even to their husbands. Of course, this usually often cost them their lives, often in the most hideous of ways, but that was a worry for later. Just now, she could almost feel the glow of godliness ringing her head.

Best of all, if she was mistaken about this calling or found she truly hated the convent, she need only wait until Papa returned. When she complained he'd bring her home.

Johanna nodded. "Aye, I'll do it, but only if you vow to me. Put your hand upon your heart as you do so to make it right."

Lifting his hand from Puss's head, Katel lay it against his chest. "Before God and all His saints I vow never to harm either the bastard—"

"Say Robert of Blacklea," she interrupted.

"Robert of Blacklea," Katel said in a choked voice, "or Master Colin on pain of my own death. How's that, little wife?" he asked, harsh amusement lingering at the edges of his words.

"I accept your oath," she replied solemnly.

He laughed at her. It was not a pleasant sound. "Good. Now, return to bed, remembering I will hold you to this agreement." He settled himself back down upon his pallet, careful not to dislodge the cat as he pulled the blankets over his head.

Johanna drifted back to the bedchamber, yet buoyed by impending sainthood. Rob would be safe. Master Colin would be safe. And she'd have no more mending to do.

Chapter Fourteen

Stanrudde
an hour past Terce
Ste. Agnes's Day, 1197

The bedcurtain rings squealed against their wooden pole as the draperies were pushed aside, then foot-steps retreated from the bedside toward the room's far edge. This startled Rob as he had no recall of returning to the hospitium or of going to bed. Opening his eyes, he squinted as the sun's cheerful brightness stabbed into his yet wine-sodden brain.

As he shifted on the soft mattress, seeking to escape the light, a wholly different sort of pain stabbed through him. "Jesu," he whispered as his head nigh on split in twain. This was the price he paid for at-tempting to wash Johanna from his system with wine.

Colin's brew had done more than ease his aches; it had filled the emptiness made when he'd left Johan-na's arms. By the time Hamalin announced that their party was prepared to leave, Rob was no longer sober enough to sit a horse. He remembered little after that, save that with each cup, there was less of Johanna left within him.

Rolling onto his back, he waited until the throbbing eased, then probed his heart to see just how successful he'd been. Bits and pieces of her remained, memories, warm and sweet, but the aching guilt he'd carried for so long was gone. His heart was at peace.

Despite his discomfort, Rob nearly smiled. Now could he ride for Lynn, and, when he was again within his own walls, let the world know he was ready to wed. Giving free rein to his imagination, he tried to concoct the image of his perfect mate. She formed slowly in his inner eye: time had darkened her hair to a color more red than gold, her eyes were as blue as a summer's sky, her lips, reddened from his kiss.

With a frustrated groan, he tried to yank the blankets over his head. They were too short. "You cannot be my wife when the world believes you married to another," he told Johanna.

"What's that you say, my good master?" Hamalin's voice matched the sun for its cheeriness. "Speaking to your friend, the flask?"

Taking care as to how he moved his head, Rob eased to the side until he could see his agent. Fair hair and reddish beard gleaming in the light, Hamalin sat in the room's chair. He wore his taunting grin as easily as he did his traveling attire: knee-length brown tunic, warm boots cross-gartered over thick chausses, and heavy cloak atop it all.

"What? Are you not wanting to leap from your mattress and gallop home?" this cocky servant asked.

"Mercy, Hamalin," Rob begged softly. "My head is already telling me how great a fool I am. There's no need for redundancy."

"Mercy, is it?" Bracing one ankle atop the opposite knee, Hamalin leaned back into the chair. Every line of his comely face said he was enjoying the outcome of his master's previous evening. "I am the one who should be crying for mercy. I had to sit and listen to the two of you sing."

"Tell me I didn't sing," Rob groaned in embarrassment.

"Aye, that you did and the monk along with you," Hamalin replied with a sad shake of his head. "I've heard better cats."

"Where is everyone?" Rob asked in an effort to rid himself of his agent's teasing. He kept his voice to a murmur in deference to his delicate condition.

"They have retreated to the stables, wanting nothing to do with a madman. I tell you, between that dash into yesterday's riot and the amount of wine you consumed last even, I'm astonished you live at all, much less retain the powers of speech."

Here, Hamalin paused, amusement ebbing from his pale eyes as his brows rose slowly in invitation. "I can listen if you care to spill the tale." In his calm gaze lay the promise of both a ready ear and a still tongue, should Rob wish to confide what it was that had turned a cautious and sober man into an intemperate fool.

Rob sighed. All Hamalin knew of this trip to Stanrudde was that his master's grain had been stolen and Rob steadfastly refused to involve the sheriff as any sane merchant would have done. Pride, yet aching from the wounds Johanna had laid on it, reared its head. How hard he had labored to protect a woman who but threw his efforts back into his face. It was against the chance of being judged a fool that Rob held tight to his tale, not willing to spill it even to one as closemouthed as Hamalin. If fortune smiled on him, he'd be returning to Lynn this day, leaving Stanrudde and Johanna's rejection forever behind him.

"Perhaps, another time," he murmured.

"As you will," his agent replied. If he wasn't hurt by Rob's refusal, there was no doubting his confusion. "If we're to be on the road before nightfall and you are to keep your appointment with the abbot, it is time you rose."

Rob loosed another quiet groan and buried his face into the bedclothes. He'd completely forgotten the abbot's invitation to dine this midday. The very thought of eating set his stomach to turning in protest. This only fed his head's pounding. "Tell Abbot Eustace I have died, then leave me to suffer in peace. We can depart on the morrow."

"I think that would not be wise," Hamalin replied without a trace of humor.

This brought Rob to instant alertness, and he dropped the blanket to eye his agent. "Tell me why."

"Yesterday afternoon's disturbance was but a precursor to greater civil unrest. Last even, whilst you sang, a crowd swept through town, forcing our fellow grossiers, the bakers, and food shop owners to open and distribute what they had in store. When all was said and done, their bellies were still not full. This brought them and those whose property they'd destroyed to the abbey's gate where they cursed you. Only when the abbot threatened to call his knights did they depart." Hamalin came to his feet.

"Cursed me?" Rob looked up at him, stunned. "Who knows me here well enough to curse me?" he asked, more to himself than in any expectation of an answer.

Hamalin shrugged. "Who knows, who cares, except to say I think it past time we returned home."

By strength of will alone did Rob begin to subdue the outcome of his indulgence. Pushing back his bedclothes, he eased his legs over to the side of the bed. Hamalin rose and stepped nearer, offering his hand as an aid in rising. When Rob took it, his agent pulled him into a sitting position.

Steadying himself on the bed's edge, Rob groaned, then put his hands at either side of his head to hold it together. "Jesu, Jesu," he cursed again, "and me in no shape to travel." Inwardly, he damned himself for indulging his anger and hurt. In doing so, he'd placed himself and his whole household in danger.

Hamalin laughed, but his amusement was friendly and mild. "You will be soon enough. I know you."

From a small basin resting on the coals in the brazier, Rob's man pulled a dripping linen cloth. Steam rose from it. As he squeezed the excess water from it into the brass pan, the coals sputtered, sending a cloud into the chill air.

He offered Rob the cloth. "Here, wrap this round your head. Mayhap, it will begin to draw some of the poison from your brain. Meanwhile, I'll go fetch Adelbert to tend to the washing and dressing of our grand and glorious master."

"A moment," Rob said, his words holding Hamalin in the room as he gratefully pressed his face into steaming linen. As the warmth seeped into his head, the pounding began to ease. With a bit of comfort, his thoughts started to organize themselves.

"I'd leave what *koren* we brought with us as a donation to the abbey." Rob spoke without removing his face from the depths of the cloth. As he'd not known what to expect in Stanrudde and had not wished to eat at the expense of the poor, they'd brought enough unmilled seed to feed themselves for three weeks.

"So I have already done," Hamalin replied, proving once again how well he knew his master. "I also had your gown repaired, so that your prominence might again shine forth to all who behold you. There was nothing to be done with your shoes. Your traveling boots will have to take their place."

Surprised, Rob lifted his head from the cloth's comfort to look toward the clothes pole on the wall. His gilded gown was folded over it, looking barely worse for wear. His mantle was beside it, freshened and free of stains. The corner of Rob's mouth lifted in wry acknowledgment of how much more he must add to the cost of indulging his heart's fantasy over Johanna. The abbey's laundresses must be blessing him this morn as they cooed over such swiftly earned riches.

The smile he sent Hamalin was more grimace than grin. "You are worth every pence I pay you."

"Best you remember that, for my contract renews next month," his man taunted gently, both of them knowing he'd go to no other house despite his employer's strange behavior of late. "If you've nothing else for me, I'll fetch Adelbert, not to see you again until after you've filled your belly and spun your yarns at the abbot's fine table."

Rob made a quiet, rude sound at this. "After your tale of last night's violence, I expect to get naught from the abbot but an interrogation as to whether I commit illegal acts whilst staying in his house."

"I doubt that," his agent retorted. "He was your defender last even. Had he believed the crowd, he'd have given you to them."

That the abbot, a Norman, believed Rob trustworthy enough to defend him did much to ease the hurt Johanna had done his pride. "I suppose in gratitude I must let him put his fingers into my purse." There was no rancor in Rob's voice, despite the thought of yet more coins leaving him.

A new disappointment woke beneath the throbbing in his head. To meet a man as well-lettered as Abbot Eustace in his present muzzy-brained condition did no honor to the monks whose learning had once filled him with great joy. Eons ago, or so it seemed, he'd been the abbey school's star pupil.

Hamalin laughed at that. "A small price to pay to avoid dining in the hospitium's frater with us lowly folk. While you sup on delicate dishes, we'll be choking down salt fish and bread made from bean flour, our cups empty and us unable to raise our voices to ask that they be refilled. While you exchange pleasantries, we listen to some monk droning out a sermon in Latin, which we cannot understand. All in all, it will be a long, dry meal." Touching two fingers to his brow in mocking salute, Hamalin left the room.

It was but an hour before Rob's personal servant had completed his careful ministrations. Rob held up the piece of polished metal to review the finished effect. His gown, collar again intact, gleamed back at him nigh as brightly as his clean skin. Once more his beard had been tamed back to a narrow line of hair clinging to his strong jaw.

He frowned at the purpled bruise that marked his forehead, then brushed down his hair a bit to cover it. There was nothing that could be done with the scratches that scored his face from cheekbone to beard, or with the dark marks that clung beneath his gray eyes, a testimony to his excess. At least, the aftereffects of too much drink had receded into the range of bearable. That it had done so in so short a time gave rise to the hope that he'd do better than simply endure the jogging of a horse later this afternoon.

It was with a touch of hunger coming to life in his belly that he set aside his mirror and left the hospitium for the abbot's lodging. That two-story house, with plastered wooden walls rising from a tall stone cellar, stood in front of what had once been the corner where the chapter house and the frater met. Rob looked around him, holding in his heart the disappointment of one who had hoped to find a favorite place unchanged.

Like many of the buildings that now filled this compound, the abbot's house was new. At every turn, familiar wooden buildings were being replaced by cold stone. Even the abbey's narrow church was being widened. A tiny smile twisted Rob's lips. Such expansion and in so expensive a material as stone was possible only because the times favored trade. Therein lay an interesting conundrum.

Everywhere, churchmen thundered in their pulpits against tradesmen who dared turn a lively profit and live well, saying such an activity went against God's plan. In turn, tradesmen, fearing themselves damned for pursuing wealth rather than contemplating God's holiness, gave freely and richly to those who cursed them. That the gold had its roots in base trade did not stop these same churchmen from using it to build finer and finer edifices to the greater glory of God. It was the way of life; one could not exist without the other.

Rob knocked quietly at the arched lower-level door in the abbot's lodging. There was no response. Frowning, he knocked again. Yet another long moment passed before a servant finally opened the door. Dressed in the sober colors of the abbot's household, the youth who greeted him took a stance upon the threshold that suggested he did not intend for Rob to enter.

The new bruises on Rob's pride flinched in pain. Mayhap the abbot had thought the better of his previous night's defense. He waited for some word of either invitation or refusal from the youth, but the servant said nothing, only stood on the threshold and blocked the way. The moment dragged.

"Did I mistake that the abbot invites me to share his table this day?" he asked at last, the cool comment being more statement than question.

The servant's shoulders sagged in what almost seemed disappointment. "Nay, Master Robert, you did not," he sighed. "Please, enter."

Stepping back from the doorway, the man allowed the abbot's visitor to step inside, then pointed toward the stairs leading to the second-story hall. "The abbot and the others await you."

Others? Rob's confusion grew as he started up the stairs. What others? This was to have been a private meal. When he stepped out into the hall, he stopped in astonishment. This small chamber was not just full, it was jammed with folk, every one of them watching him.

On the raised dais at room's end, Abbot Eustace sat in his massive chair, gilded crook in hand. The black cowl he and all his monks wore was thrown back so his miter might be perched atop his head. That peaked cap was alive with light as metallic threads sparked around the cooler glow of the fine gems that trimmed it. There was naught of the ascetic saint to this churchman's form; instead, the narrow-faced Norman showed his roots lay in the knighthood. His rich black cassock, trimmed in ermine, draped massive shoulders and bound around a great barrel chest while concealing an avid horseman's lean hips.

Clinging to their father abbot's chair like children to their mother's skirts were a number of the abbot's obedientaries, all wearing the black habit of their order. Among them, Rob recognized the sub-abbot, cellarer, sacrist, and the chamberlain. Standing before the abbot was a single solider. Helmed, he wore a metal-sewn leather hauberk under his cloak. His scabbard was empty, as church law demanded.

Rob raised a brow, his stomach tightening in concern as he again wondered if the abbot had thought the better of last night's defense. Dealing with Norman nobles, whether church or lay, thus subjecting himself to their sometimes changeable whims, always brought with it its own risk. Experience taught that to grovel or meet strength with strength could lead to catastrophic results. It was the appearance of calm and control that ever carried the day.

Drawing a cloak of composure around him as his shield, Rob shed his native English for the French Master Walter had insisted he learn. "Is something amiss, my lord abbot?"

It wasn't the churchman who answered him, but the soldier. "Master Robert, I am Otto, son of Otfried, captain of the town's guard. I have come to take you into my custody," he said in English.

No one saw the start of shock that went through Rob. The abbot was having him arrested?! Why? Simply because the crowd had cursed him? His pride writhed as new injury lay upon the old.

"I beg pardon, my lord abbot," Rob said to the churchman, forcing his neck to bend until his head achieved the posture appropriate to such a plea. "Have I done something to disparage you or this house that would cause you to relieve yourself of me in this manner?"

"Master Robert, you have no need to beg my pardon as you've done no wrong," Abbot Eustace said, rising slowly from the chair that symbolized his authority over this holy house.

The churchman took a step forward, his dark gaze alight with unholy fire as he held his crook before him like a sword. "Rather, I think that we shall both soon be demanding apologies from the town council. Not only does the council seek to force from me one who is under my protection, they do so without showing their faces!" His voice rose to a thundering roar so none might mistake the depths of the wound done to him.

Otto, son of Otfried, dropped to his knees, his empty scabbard clattering against the wooden floor. He bowed his head. "My lord abbot, the council does, indeed, most humbly beg your pardon. They feared to come here, thinking that by doing so, they might bring the wrath of the populace down upon your holy house. Know you that the guild hall was burnt to the ground last even. It is to protect the abbey they hold dear that they stay away."

The abbot struggled with this, trying to maintain outrage against the sop being offered to him. A sharp, upward jerk of his crook commanded the solider to rise. Otto returned to his feet with the squeak of leather and scrape of metal. With a glance toward Rob, the soldier finished his explanation.

"My lord abbot, further civil unrest must be avoided. Although the council has sent to the sheriff, we cannot know when he might arrive to enforce martial law. It is in the hopes of preventing further damage to either property or trade that the council begs you release Master Robert to them."

"What reason has the council to think that arresting me will prevent further violence?" Rob snapped, yet clinging to his French.

"Master," the captain said, "you mistake me. I have not come to arrest you. The council prays only that you will stand before them to answer their questions."

The muscles in Rob's neck relaxed a mite at the news that this was no arrest, but confusion lingered. "Questions? What sort of questions?"

"The council wishes to determine if it was your grain that was released onto the marketplace evening last, against both custom and law."

The blunt words stripped away all of Rob's control. "The council does not dare accuse me of grain mongering!" he roared in English. It took every ounce of his will to keep from attacking the one who spewed such a foul accusation before these witnesses.

Otto blinked at this unexpectedly violent reaction and took a step back in caution. On his face appeared the blank look of one who but did his duty and took responsibility for no more. "Master, that is an issue best addressed to the council."

Sucking cool air into his steaming lungs, Rob won back his calm. "My lord abbot," he said, slipping back into French as he again faced the churchman, "this charge is as ludicrous as it is foul. You know I have no wheat to release. All my party brought is in your abbey's cellars."

The cellarer stepped forward, his bony hands concealed in his habit's wide sleeves, his long nose nigh on quivering in outrage. "Aye, and so I have said to this man, Master Robert, telling him I can account for every *koren*. However, he pays me no heed, continuing to stubbornly insist upon your release into his custody."

Because his thoughts were yet slow from last night's overindulgence, it was only now that Rob dissected exactly what the soldier had said. As he understood, he drew another swift breath. Last night, the name of Robert the Grossier had been on the rioters' lips. So, too, according to the soldier, had grain been made available in the marketplace.

With that, all the pieces of Katel's puzzle fell into place and Rob damned himself for not seeing the trap laid for him. It was not the seed in the cellarer's storerooms that had prompted the council's interest in him; it was the stolen grain that had been released, and it had been done in Rob's name. Katel had not taken the grain to enrich himself at Rob's expense, but with every intention of using it to destroy the man he yet hated. Aye, and he'd very nearly succeeded. If the abbot had not been his defender last even, the crowd might well have strung him up.

Cold fury filled Rob. Katel was a conniving coward. Worse, he was an unethical tradesman. Did such a little man think he could threaten Robert, Grossier of Lynn?

In that moment he thanked Johanna for her rejection. In refusing his aid, she freed him from worrying over how a charge of theft against her husband would hurt her. Now, when he stood before the council, he'd do better than prove his innocence, he'd expose Katel's guilt.

Rob turned on the soldier. Once again, Otto, son of Otfried, stepped back, this time reaching for the sword he did not wear. Without moving his eyes from the town guardsman, Rob said, "My lord abbot, with your permission I will forgo our meal and submit myself to the council's questions."

Chapter Fifteen

Stanrudde
two hours past Terce
Ste. Agnes's Day, 1197

Leaving Hamalin and Rob's household guard complaining and shouting in the abbey courtyard, the captain of the guard, alone, escorted Rob out onto the market field. Once they were in that unguarded space, Otto looked at him in warning. "Master Robert, draw your mantle tight shut over that gown. If they cannot see who it is that comes, they will not attack us. Although I expect no trouble, should you be identified, retreat directly to the abbey. There are more than a few folk who'd like to see your body dangling in the town's square this day. These sorts have no care as to guilt or innocence; they only wish to repay the hurt done them in your name."

Rob gave the hapless soldier no sign he'd heard. Instead, all energy and thought were turned inward. Before he faced the council, he must be the master of himself; there was no room for muzzy thinking or aching pride.

It wasn't until they passed the chandlers' enclave that Rob lifted himself from his inward reaches and glanced around him. As he did, the preternatural quiet in the empty lanes set his nerves to jangling. Even the day's frigid breeze cried in lonely protest, prying around corners and into alleys as if seeking a single, beating human heart.

He stared at the cookshop ahead of him. A hole gaped, wattle and daub having been battered away to create a new entrance. What lay within had been smashed without regard for its value in the sheer joy of destruction. Next door, in an alemaker's house, a splintered wheel from a broken cart had been used to pry open the workroom shutters, where similar damage had been done to its contents.

On the next street, ravens' hoarse caws echoed eerily against house walls as the carrion eaters rose from a dog's carcass. Rob stepped over it. The beast had been only half butchered, the remainder left to rot.

He stopped in horror at the next corner. Between two lanes, where once had stood houses and workshops, all that remained were charred timbers and ashy walls. Wisps of smoke yet twisted and curled upward into the day's cold, still air. It brought with it the acrid smell of scorched thatching and the even more horrible stench of burnt flesh, all that remained of the folk who'd been trapped in the blaze.

"God have mercy," he breathed, sending his prayer heavenward for those poor souls.

Otto stopped beside him. "The fire started in a warehouse. The crowd had pulled open its doors, seeking grain and, when they found none, they set the place ablaze in their outrage. By the grace of God did only twenty-three perish."

It was with reason that the guardsman blessed himself. Cities were naught but a jumble of wooden-walled and reed-roofed structures set one against another. A fire beginning in one corner of a town could and often did decimate the whole place.

The captain of the guard sighed, his breath clouding before him. "Do you see why I fear for your safety? With your name on their lips, those who were hurt by the rioters have found a scapegoat on whom to rest their troubles."

Rob's hard won control strained as a new anger joined it. He had forgotten to what depths Katel's cruelty could descend. The spice merchant cared not a whit that innocents were hurt while he wreaked his revenge on Rob. It would be as much for the sakes of those who died as Rob's own that he made certain Katel was held accountable for this.

After they passed the wreckage, they turned away from the city's center and entered a section of town that had not existed when Rob left Stanrudde. Here, Stanrudde's walls had been extended to capture more land, the new area parceled out to the richer of its denizens. Tall houses stood secure behind strong walls with sturdy gates, the riches within them protected by servants like his own who were trained at arms. Because of this, there was far less sign of rioting in this district.

It was at one of these gateways that Otto halted. Bits of fleece clung to the mortar and stones in the outer wall and along the eaves of the house, proclaiming this the home of a wool merchant. The soldier pulled the string on the bell hanging above the arched, wooden gate. That merry cup of brass swung, clanging happily. So joyous a sound felt wrong against the depths of tragedy Rob had just witnessed.

"Who comes?" a man called, his voice deep and threatening.

"Otto, son of Otfried," the captain replied.

"What is your sign?" Undertones of suspicion remained.

"I come to the drawer of the short straw," Otto said, as if so strange a question with as odd an answer were an everyday occurrence in Stanrudde.

Behind the thick doors came the sounds of the bar being wrestled from its braces, then wood thudded hollowly to the ground and the gate creaked open.

The one who guarded the portal stepped out into the lane. Before he moved aside to allow Rob's entrance, he glanced both up and down the empty street, as if to assure himself no one witnessed the Grossier of Lynn's arrival.

Otto waved Rob within the wool merchant's walls. "Go, Master Robert. I must fetch the others, else they'll not know where to come."

Rob shot him a confused glance. Not know where to come? What sort of council did Stanrudde have? As the captain of the town's soldiery slipped away, the gate slammed shut behind Rob, and the bar dropped back into its braces.

The courtyard within the walls was a small square caught between a three-story house, a stable, and two warehouses. Except for the stray bits of wool, it was a well-kept place. Even the cobbles on the courtyard's floor had been swept, as there was no trace of yesterday's mud left upon its face.

The house's rear door opened, and a man no older than Rob appeared. Bearded, dark of hair and eye, on his forehead he wore an odd starlike scar, as if his flesh had once been badly torn. His tunic was a deep scarlet, his belt a length of leather studded with tiny golden knobs. Atop his fleece-lined mantle, he wore a braided golden chain. Leaning upon a single crutch, he stepped out into the courtyard.

"So I am the one, am I?" the cripple called as he limped toward Rob. "We drew straws, showing what we'd chosen only to Otto, not even looking to see for ourselves. This was so no one save he would know where this meeting was to take place. The council wanted no chance slip of the tongue revealing where we took you. Should those who rioted discover your whereabouts, I fear none of us can vouch for your safety or our own. Once we are all within these walls, he'll be back with this week's troop to guard my gate."

He halted before Rob and thrust out a hand. "Well

come to my home, Master Robert. I am Jehan, son of Peter the Wool Merchant. You may not remember me, but I recall you from the abbey's school. I fear you were too old and too advanced in your studies to notice a wee lad just beginning his own."

Rob did not extend his arm. He came to defeat his foe, not to befriend those who so foully and unjustly sullied his name and repute. Master Jehan did not notice. Instead, he stared in confusion at Rob's face, his hand dropping back to his side. "Odd," he said, "but you remind me of someone, but for the life of me I cannot recall who."

"Do not struggle overly much with it," Rob replied coolly. "When I have satisfied your council's questions"—he gave the word a sarcastic twist—"with my answers, I will be leaving Stanrudde, with no plans of returning."

"Ah," Master Jehan murmured, startled back into the role of warden. He briefly bowed his head, acknowledging as equal to equal the insult being done to Rob. "For that I can only beg your pardon. In all honesty, the majority of the council finds it difficult to believe you are at the root of this unrest; however, our town is naught but a bit of dry tinder. Were we to ignore what all of Stanrudde believes it knows, it would seem we protected you because you are a successful merchant, like ourselves. This would be just the spark needed to set our town to burning once more, mayhap with more devastating results this time."

It was as much explanation as any man needed. Were he put into the same position, Rob doubted he'd have done differently. He nodded in understanding. "Well said, but I cannot pretend I am pleased over it."

The wool merchant offered him a small smile. "Nor would I be, were I you. Since there is naught either of us can do to change the way matters lie in this present moment, why not come into the house and take your ease while the guard gathers the others?"

"My thanks," Rob said, returning the man's smile with true gratitude for his offer. "I have yet to dine this day. Might I prevail upon you for a bite to eat?"

"You can," Master Jehan said, turning toward the house. "Come, my wife has made the most wonderful cheese pie."

Rob strode alongside the hobbling man, surprised that the wool merchant so easily kept pace with him. As Master Jehan pushed open the house's door, Rob glanced into the first-floor workroom. Beyond tools used in processing fleece and sheepskin, it was much the same as his, complete with counting board and richly decorated coffers for contracts, account books, and coin.

Up a set of steep stairs they went, Master Jehan managing with an ease that spoke of a long familiarity with his infirmity. The wool merchant lifted himself into the second-story hall. Rob followed him, glancing about with an eye to comparing this dwelling to his own.

Light dimly penetrated the thin oiled skins covering the three slitted windows on the street-side wall. This bit of brightness showed him the painted linen panels that decorated the walls. There were also wooden cupboards, their shelves painted red and yellow, upon which was displayed a goodly number of horn and silver cups. A silver tureen sat in a place of honor amid them. Rob's estimation of his host leapt upward. Jehan the Wool Merchant did well for himself.

Four high-backed chairs were clutched near the hearth in the hall's corner. Rob glanced from them to the hooded fireplace. The hearth's angle suggested that its twin sat on the opposite side of the inner wall and used the same chimney. A kitchen within the house? If so, this was an unusual feature, as most kitchens were separate from the houses they fed.

At the room's back, two women were in the process of lifting the table boards onto their braces. One was young, the other moving into her middle years. Both wore the plain, sturdy attire given to those who served.

An old woman watched them, clean table linen folded in her arms. The grandam's green gown was fine wool, trimmed with glittering braid. An embroidered belt encircled her age-softened waist, held in place with a jeweled clasp, and a silken wimple covered her grayed hair, hair that had once been as dark as her son's, for the similarity of their faces claimed such a relationship.

"Mama, come greet Master Robert, Grossier of Lynn," the wool merchant called, confirming Rob's supposition.

The old woman turned toward him, a smile starting to form on her mouth, then she shrieked. The linen in her arms tumbled to the ground. Rob watched in astonishment as she turned her back on her guest, muttering Aves and furiously blessing herself.

"Mama!" Master Jehan cried, moving to his mother's side. "Clarice, come quickly!"

At his call, the door in the inner wall flew open, releasing the smells and sounds of cooking food into the hall. A young woman with pretty eyes and golden brown hair rushed into this room. She was a match for her husband, with her scarlet gown, gold-trimmed belt, and fleece-lined mantle. Putting her arms around the old woman, she cried, "Mother Alwyna, what is it?"

"A ghost," the old woman said, her words broken by frightened gasps, "I have just seen a ghost."

With that, Rob moved to stand at the windows, his back to the room. It was a polite effort to grant the family a moment of privacy in which to sort out the old woman's strange behavior. Behind him, Master Jehan said, "Mama, gather your wits. The councilmen will begin arriving at any moment." There was enough concern in his voice to suggest that flights of fancy were not his dam's way.

The sense of being watched made Rob glance over his shoulder. The wool merchant's mother was staring at him. Again, when her gaze met his, she started, the pink draining from her cheeks.

Fed by the danger Katel's plot had already put in his path, a chill shot up Rob's spine. It was said there were folk who could see the shade of coming death in a man's eyes. Was her reaction an omen, foretelling Katel's success?

This time the old woman lifted her chin and conquered whatever it was about him that frightened her. Without a word, she started toward him. He turned to face her. She stopped before him, still intently studying his features.

"What is it you see in my face, good wife?" he asked, keeping his voice soft and private as he struggled to tame his worry over her answer.

"I see the image of a man I once knew," she replied with an equal quiet. A frown of confusion formed on her brow. "This cannot be. I know all his sons, and you are not one of them. Surely, I am mistaken . . ." Her voice trailed off into a question, saying she was not at all certain of this.

In the courtyard below the bell again chimed merrily. The wool merchant's mother started at the sound and whirled away from him. "They come!" she cried, hurrying across the room to snatch up the linen she'd dropped. "Hie, hie, they come! Marta, fetch a fresh cloth for the table. Els, prepare a cup of spiced wine for Master Robert. Clarice—" the rest of her words cut off in the closing of the kitchen's door as all of the distaff side of the household disappeared.

So sudden was their departure, the air whirled and danced in their wakes. Master Jehan stared after them in the helpless confusion that affected all men when dealing with Eve's daughters and their emotions. At last, he turned to his prisoner-cum-guest.

"Women! I apologize, Master Robert. I know naught what came over my dam. She is usually most sensible." He shrugged away his confusion and patted the back of one of the chairs. "Come, take your ease. I'll see to it you get your bite to eat."

Chapter Sixteen

Stanrudde
the hour of Sext
Ste. Agnes's Day, 1197

While Rob dined on a full tray of cheese pie and cold meat slices, washing it all down with a cup of barley water instead of the spiced wine, the council arrived, one by one. As each man came, he stated his position on the matter at hand by either greeting Rob with an apology or passing him by to clutch in the corner nearest the windows. Since a position on the council required certain fiscal responsibilities for their districts, only the richest of Stanrudde's merchants were represented. Those who supported Rob's innocence included Master Edward, the grossier whose warehouse had burned, and a man Rob knew by his good reputation, a draper, two fullers, and Master Jehan and his father by marriage and fellow wool merchant, Master Gerard. At the window stood another draper, a goldsmith, two iron mongerers, and a miller. The last to arrive was the spice merchant.

Startled, Rob watched Katel enter. Why was he surprised to find the spice merchant was a council member? In order to carry off so outrageous a plot, he needed to be beyond suspicion and reproach as only a city father would be.

In that instant, Rob deeply regretted leaving his personal book in Lynn. Recorded on its leaves was his step-by-step documentation of the original thefts and the investigation that led him from those far-flung fields to Katel's doorstep. As his original purpose had been to quietly resolve the issue without exposing Katel's deeds, he'd left it behind. Now he saw that without this proof in hand, his accusation would not be believed.

Well, it was an easy enough thing to retrieve. Lynn was but a half day's ride if a man owned a hardened seat and a strong horse. Hamalin had both. He could be there and back in but a day and a night's time. With that comforting thought in mind, he studied Katel.

The change was startling. Gone was the comeliness, taken by the years and concealed beneath his excess weight. The maroon color of Katel's tunic only enhanced the sickly undertone that lurked beneath his now florid coloring. No doubt it was the rottenness that had ever lived in him finally eating its way to the surface.

Katel glanced at Rob as he greeted Master Jehan. Pleasure and disappointment tangled in his gaze. It said that, although the spice merchant had hoped Rob would have already hung, Katel retained complete confidence that Rob would not escape this fate.

With all assembled, Master Jehan invited the council to seat themselves. Resembling Christ's disciples in their number if not their wisdom, the twelve filed behind the table to find a place on the benches behind it. As they did so, the kitchen's door opened and the wool merchant's mother slipped quietly into the room to sit in one of the chairs near the hearth. Offering Rob a glance that might have been meant to reassure, she disappeared into the shadowy depths of the seat's high back.

Once again, Rob shielded himself in his cloak of calm and stepped forward to scan the assembled merchants. When he had their full attention, he said,

"Masters, you have called me here to inquire of me and my doings. Ask and I will answer you in all honesty. On this you have my word."

The miller leaned forward to look down the table at the others. "If we are to keep up the form, must he swear upon the relics?"

Rob's pride screamed, but there was no need to defend himself this time. Master Edward, the grossier, slammed a clenched fist down upon the tabletop. Anger at the insult done to one of his fellows was written clearly on his face.

"This is Robert of Lynn," he shouted, "not some regrater selling onions today and ribbons tomorrow. You do not ask if his word is good. All the world knows it is."

Katel straightened on his bench. "I would confirm what Master Edward says. When Master Robert served with me in Master Walter's household, he was never anything but truthful and honest. I cannot think that time has done aught to change that about him. We can accept his word without question."

Anger surged through Rob. Katel intended to support him, thereby making his own accusation impossible, at least one uncorroborated by evidence. Rob damned himself all over again. How could he have forgotten Katel never fought in the open as honest men should, but forever cloaked himself in appearances?

"Thank you, Master Katel," Master Edward said, then looked at Rob. "Know you, Master Robert, I have protested your innocence to them from the first. If I can do so despite that the mob destroyed my properties, then these men should accept my word as true! Once again, I beg pardon for the insults they lay upon you."

"You'll not beg his pardon on my behalf," one of the smiths bellowed, his voice as big as the arms straining beneath his sleeves. "I see no reason to doubt that it was he who did this. What other reason would the starving have to cry against him, save that it was his grain they could not afford to buy? He is not a local man!"

"All the more reason to ask yourself if it could have been him at all, Master Harold," Master Jehan protested. "We can all agree that Master Robert is no fool. Only a fool would come into a strange town and openly release illegal grain in his own name."

"Aye, and mayhap this is what he expects us to believe," Master Harold stubbornly insisted. "I say we have our culprit. We have no greater responsibility than to hold him for the sheriff as we would any other man accused of lawbreaking. And, in holding him, we not only satisfy those who call for his destruction because of the damage done to their properties, we also free ourselves of any connection to him." The smith brushed his hands, one against the other, as if removing from his gloved fingers any trace of Rob.

"Nay, we cannot!" a draper cried. "I tell you all, if we think to wait for the sheriff's arrival, there will be more upheaval. This time, they'll destroy our homes and livelihoods! We must hang him today. Only in this way will all truly be satisfied and we be free of threat."

"I will not see a fellow tradesman hanged simply because a crowd calls for it, despite that I am threatened," Master Gerard retorted in angry scorn. Even the outspoken smith nodded his head in agreement to this.

Gratified that the council would not bend in this direction, Rob took a step toward the table to reclaim their attention. "Masters, please. It would greatly aid me if you told me last night's tale." Aye, he needed to look at what Katel had done so he might know how to block the next twist.

Master Harold, the smith, turned on him. "You ask for what you already know! Yesterday, did your agent skulk about our town, calling in secret and underhanded ways to those brave or foolish enough to deal in outmarket grain. To these regraters did he sell what he had, promising them more on the morrow. These idiots took their illegal goods onto the streets and all too swiftly sold what they had at great profit to themselves. This left others yet clamoring for what was already gone, while still others cried for what they needed and could not afford. That's when those regraters let slip that there was supposedly more in store. A mob formed, the rabble going off in search for what your agent had promised for the morrow. It was you who set our town ablaze!" His outrage filled this room with its volume.

Rob waited until the ringing echoes died before speaking. "Who says it was my agent?"

"The regraters." This came from the goldsmith. He leaned forward as he spoke, bracing his elbow on the table. His handiwork, a chain with links shaped like arrowheads, glittered as he moved. "Some in the crowd were not content with seeking out grain; instead, they sought to punish those who would make a profit on their misery. They beat the regraters, trying to steal what coins they'd earned. When the guard rescued them, they most gratefully spilled their tale."

"This you believe?" Rob asked in surprise. "I've never known those who participated in illegal acts to be honest about their crimes. But, that is neither here nor there. It could not have been my agent, as he was within the abbey walls all of yesterday and last even. So will every monk who saw him swear."

"It was his man," Master Harold insisted, looking up and down the table's length at his fellow council members. "Did not the regraters describe the one from whom they'd bought their grain as young, comely, and fair of hair with red in his beard? Many have seen such a man in the grossier's company. Aye, and this fellow spoke with a strange dialect, just as Lynnsman would be wont to do."

"There are hundreds of men who answer to that description," Rob's fellow grossier replied with a snort, "and dialects can be affected. I tell you, masters, this is Robert of Lynn. If he vows it was not his agent or his wheat, that is enough for me. We must look elsewhere."

"Look elsewhere?" At the table's end, Katel shifted as if struck by this comment. "While I also doubt Master Robert is at fault for what happened last night, I must remind the council it is not our duty to look anywhere at all. I agree with Master Harold. All that the law requires of us is that we hold for the sheriff those against whom the hue and cry is raised, as has been done in this instance. It is not for us to decide whether Robert the Bastard is guilty or innocent of the charges."

If Rob refused Katel the reaction he no doubt thought to dig from him with that name, Mistress Alwyna had not his control. The old woman nigh on leapt out of her chair, then turned in the seat to stare at him. Her gaze begged him to confirm that he was, indeed, bastard born. Pride made Rob lift his shoulder until he could not see her.

"Ach," Katel said, his brows drawing down, his face the picture of regret. "Pardon, Rob, but I forget me that you've no fondness for that name. I apologize to you and the council for the habits of my youth."

Rob looked away from him, forcing down hatred as he pondered over why Katel might desire the sheriff's involvement. It could only mean there was some sort of trail connecting Rob to the grain. Ah, but if the council dared to insist he remain in Stanrudde for the sheriff's arrival, Rob would see to it there was more than one trail for the shire's lawman to follow. But already, the majority of the council swung in the direction of releasing him. A smile of triumph formed in Rob's heart, if not on his face, as he prepared to deal the blow that would free him from Katel's trap.

"Master Katel is right," Rob said as he again scanned the assemblage, "your council must keep to the law. Since my oath alone does not convince you that I speak the truth, I will stay in Stanrudde's abbey while I await the sheriff's arrival. To him will I spill my evidence and my vows."

"Nay," cried Master John, the cowardly draper. "The crowd will tear us apart!"

"Enough," the goldsmith said, his disgust cutting through the man's complaint. "You did not hear what Master Robert just said to us. If the sheriff proves him innocent as he vows he is, then each day we hold Master Robert here under false arrest, might he not be calculating the sort of damage we do his repute? I fear he even now considers suing us for defamation."

The room went silent. All eyes, save Katel's, turned on Rob. Rob but lifted his brows at this very real possibility.

Air left the smith in a great gust, and his shoulders sagged. "Were I an innocent man whose name is being sullied by a false charge, I, too, would consider a suit."

The goldsmith turned flinty eyes on his fellow councilmen. "Masters, if we are not certain he is our culprit, then I vote we release him, telling the townsmen he is proved innocent. So, too, will we inform them that the sheriff has been called to find the true evildoer. God knows it will cost us dearly to house and feed his men, but that will be less than the damage Master Robert's suit might do us."

Something hard hit the outside of the house, the sound of stone ringing against stone echoing into the hall. Another stone hit the wall. The third rock struck the window's covering with such force the skin tore from its mount. Stone and skin tangled as it bounced across the table, then rattled off its edge and came to a stop near Mistress Alwyna's foot.

In the lane men shouted. Iron thudded dully against wood as the town guard banged swords against shields.

Downstairs, the door flew open and someone roared up the stairs.

"They gather," the gatekeeper panted out as he thrust into the hall, "more with every moment. The guard is trying to drive them away, but there will soon be more than they can handle."

The shouting grew in volume, testifying to his claim. Yet another stone hit the house as the random calls sorted itself into a new cadence. Brutally and simply, the gathering mob began to call for the head of Robert the Grossier and death to all the councilmen.

Chaos erupted around Rob. Master Jehan and Master Gerard nigh on flew out of the room, no doubt to set the household to defending their walls. The smith bellowed, ready to charge out the gate and decimate those who dared to threaten him. Master John sobbed in fear, while the goldsmith suggested they give Rob to the mob and make good their own escape. Amid all this, Katel remained an island of calm. Too calm. It said he'd known this attack would come.

Rob drew a sharp breath. Katel had not trusted the council to go where he led. To make certain he achieved his goal, the spice merchant would keep the town aflame until the council had no choice but to hang Rob to preserve their own lives. Jesu, but there was no escape from him. Once again, the old woman's reaction to his face shot through Rob. It had been an omen; he would die.

He started as Mistress Alwyna touched his sleeve. It took all Rob's will to force himself to look at her, fearing he would see his death in her brown eyes. Instead, her gaze was filled with the need to aid him.

"Come and quickly so," she said softly. "My son has arranged to see you safely away."

That Katel watched without complaint as Rob followed the old woman into the kitchen was a testimony to his certainty of success. Rob crossed the small chamber to squeeze himself down the narrow winding stairs that led to the cellar that lay beneath it. Out the cellar doors they went, across the courtyard to pass between the house and stable. Behind the stable was a narrow strip of kitchen garden, now slumbering for the winter under a frosty blanket of straw. At the garden's end was a stream, the water standing still and solid within its banks.

Here Master Jehan and Master Gerard waited with six men armed with swords. At their master's sign, these men surrounded Rob. Their blades all pointed inward, rather than outward in defense.

"What sort of rescue is this?" Rob bellowed, turning this way and that within the circle of his captors. Even as the thought of escape filled him, he knew it was impossible. Should he manage to cross Stanrudde's lanes with his life intact to reach any of its gates, those exits were already closed to him. He was well and truly trapped.

"God forgive us, Master Robert, but the only sort we dare offer," the young wool merchant replied. "To keep Stanrudde whole, my servants must take you to our keep where you will be held as if arrested. Only there can we guarantee both your safety and our own. I ask you now, for your own safety, remove your gown to avoid identification."

"You have my word that I will return to the abbey and wait for the sheriff's arrival," Rob said through his clenched teeth. Within him grew the conviction that once he was in that moldy tower, the only way he'd leave was at the end of a hangman's rope.

Master Gerard only shook his head. "Nay, Master Robert, not even the abbot can protect you now. Only separating you body from soul will ease the crowd's blood lust. If you wish to live, you'll retreat to the tower until the sheriff comes."

Not even pride reacted any more, so deep was Rob's defeat. Who knew how long it would be before the sheriff came? With Rob caught, Katel would not be content to wait for the lawman's arrival against the possibility his victim might slip from his grasp. Using the crowd as his tool, Katel would pry open the keep's door, then laugh while Rob dangled.

"I will do as you bid without complaint only if you agree to send this message to my agent at the abbey," Rob said in the forlorn hope that he could yet save himself. After he opened his mantle pin, Mistress Alwyna took his mantle so Rob could loosen his tunic. "Hamalin must go at all speed to my home in Lynn. Once there, he should open my coffer, the one to which only he and I have the key, taking from it my personal book. This he must bring to me, as it both names and proves the guilt of the one at the root of this evil."

"By God, man," Master Jehan cried, his brown eyes taking life in anger, "if you know who has done this, spill his name and let us arrest him. We'll give him to the crowd in your stead, just as he deserves!"

Although Rob was yet certain he'd not be believed, he'd be damned before he died carrying the truth only in his soul. "If you will hear his name, then I accuse Katel le Espicer of seeking to destroy me by stealing my grain and releasing it onto the marketplace in my name."

Both tradesmen stared at him as if he spoke in a language they did not understand. "Master Katel? But he is such a harmless man," Master Jehan stuttered. "Nay, you must be wrong. He is your supporter. What reason could he have for harming you?"

"Jehan," the man's mother cried, "if Master Robert says it is so and that he can prove it, then it is. Was not Master Katel the last to arrive, and did not the crowd come upon his tail?"

As Rob handed the wool merchant's mother his tunic, her son shucked his own mantle and threw it across Rob's shoulders. Mistress Alwyna turned to Rob's guards. "Hie, off with you! Go and quickly so, knowing that if the crowd takes him and leaves you alive after, I'll see you all dead for your failure." It was a heartfelt threat.

Two of Master Jehan's men grabbed Rob by the arms and guided him down the ice-bound stream's bank. Every step took him nearer to what would surely be his last resting place. Rob glanced over his shoulder at the two merchants and Mistress Alwyna.

"Go," the old woman called to him. "Place your trust in me. Know that for the love I once bore your sire I will see your man protected and your proof safely transported."

Mistress Alwyna's jaw was firm, her gaze resolute. That she meant to aid him, he did not doubt. New bile rose behind his fear for his life. Rob choked on it as he understood that the old woman was once again and oh-so-subtly confirming that he was bastard-born. It was not for the sake of Ralph AtteGreen that she wished to aid him.

Chapter Seventeen

Stanrudde
October, 1179

"Oh, Rob, I cannot believe she is gone!" Johanna cried, with all the substantial emotion a heart of ten and four could muster. She kicked at the distillery's hearth as if to show him how deep her desire to disbelieve was. The silken skirts of her orange and green gowns flew wide, scooping up crackling autumn leaves with her movement.

"Why, I remember how at Eastertide she fair glowed with pride at finally conceiving a child. Something that makes a person so happy shouldn't kill them."

Standing at her side, Rob could only nod in sad agreement. Mistress Katherine's death was neither fair nor right. As if she could call the apothecary's wife back from the grave by will alone, Johanna lifted her head to stare at the closed shutters of Master Colin's bedchamber window. Rob joined her in perusal of those plain lengths of wood.

Only a week ago, when Mistress Katherine had begun her labor, she'd been full of life, buoyed against her pains by the excitement of producing the child both she and the master so desired. The hours passed, but the babe moved not at all. Using every potion and concoction they knew, the midwife and Master Colin battled to bring it forth. One day became two, then three. It had almost been a relief when the mistress at last gave way to death, for at least her torment ended. When she was gone, the midwife cut open her womb, only to find the babe within her dead as well. Since then, the apothecary had said no word, passing through the last four days like the wraith his wife now was.

It was Rob's helplessness in the face of Master Colin's grief that had driven him from the mourning feast yet going on in Master Walter's hall. In this familiar corner of the yard he sought to console himself, since he could not console his master. As if she sensed his distress, Johanna appeared only moments later.

Had it been any other lass, Rob would have driven her away, wanting privacy in which to struggle with his emotions. Johanna was different, being more friend than lass. Moreover, although she never said or did anything that remotely resembled an attempt at comfort, there was something about her presence that ever soothed him.

He sighed. Oblivious to the tragedy of Mistress Katherine's demise, the world beyond the apothecary's shop went on. In the lane a regrater was calling out the quality of his walnuts. Cart wheels groaned, goads flicked, and muleteers shouted to their pack animals. Warmed by the afternoon sun, the day's breeze brought with it the stench of the shambles. From two lanes over, a fuller, his apprentices, and his servants raised their voices in song as they fused newly woven cloth into finished goods to the tune's rhythmic beat.

When her stare failed to conjure up the apothecary's wife, Johanna turned her gaze downward to the distillery's hearthstone. "I am glad Papa called me home so I might bid her and her son farewell."

This almost made Rob smile, and he shot her a sidelong glance. "You make it sound as if your father keeps you trapped at that precious convent of yours when it's you that stays away from Stanrudde. I think me if that place were any nearer, Master Walter would bring you home every night."

Still staring at the hearth, Johanna pulled her face into an expression of disgust. "If you were going to be forced to marry Katel, you'd stay away, too."

Rob opened his mouth to tease that rich heiresses deserved no pity, when she lifted her head and smiled at him. His taunt faded as he stared at her, startled all over again by how she'd changed. Gone was the gawky girl whose nose had been too large for her face and whose wayward elbows had cost her dearly in his and Arthur's teasing last year. In that child's place was this new . . . woman.

Johanna had grown, her crown now reaching almost to his own newly elevated sixteen year old jawline. So, too, had her face rearranged itself, shedding babyish roundness to reveal a high clear brow and strong cheekbones. Her lips seemed fuller, her eyes wider and bluer. Even her nose now suited her.

Nay, it more than suited her; it gave her face a sort of elegance that took away his breath. Rob's gaze dropped to the slender line of her throat, then descended to where her sleek green and orange gowns clung to a new form complete with utterly beguiling curves. With startling swiftness, the desire to feel the roundness of Johanna's breasts cupped in his hands exploded in him.

Rob jerked his gaze back to the hearthstone, fighting this completely inappropriate reaction to his beloved master's daughter. To even think such a thing about Johanna was to betray the man who had saved his life, then given him both trade and happiness. Despite his will, however, the sensations lingered, filling every corner of Rob's being.

This was all the fault of Alice, the ropemaker's maid. A year ago, Alice had decided she loved Rob instead of the draper's lad. As often as she could, she met with him in Master Walter's stable. What began as a mere kiss or two rapidly became caressing, which led to the wondrous sin of fornication.

After almost a month of loving him, fickle Alice decided the smith's son was more interesting. Her rejection had broken Rob's heart, the pain far worse than all the pleasure she'd given him. Once he'd recovered and paid the penance his confessor set on him, Rob vowed to never again let a woman hurt him the way Alice had.

Not too long after that he discovered that with a few of the precious coins he earned by laboring outside his regular duties, he could buy himself the same sort of pleasure from one of Stanrudde's contingent of whores. If there was still penance to be done for fornicating, his heart was safe; both he and Arthur agreed that no sensible man pined over a whore. Better still, one of the tarts had taken an interest in him, teaching Rob's body to feel in ways he never dreamed possible.

From the corner of his eye, Rob saw Johanna draw a deep, sad breath. Her breasts moved seductively beneath her gowns as she did so. Once again, that wayward desire to touch her rose. Although he set to stamping it out, it evaded his attempts.

"His heart is broken," Johanna said of Master Colin.

Rob gratefully let himself be drawn away from his sinful preoccupation with her body. "Aye, I think so," he replied. Here was but another proof that no good could come of caring so deeply for a woman. If they did not throw you over for another, they died, as had his mother, Johanna's mother, and, now, Mistress Katherine.

"He truly loved her, I think me." The sadness in Johanna's voice was mingled with an awed respect. Her tone grew soft and distant. "He is so noble, just like the knights in the tales the nuns tell. I think if Master Colin were a knight, he'd have done great deeds against all odds in order to win Mistress Katherine's heart."

This ridiculous comment lifted Rob from both lust and grief. For reasons beyond his ken, Johanna adored those fantastic tales of knights who spent their hearts in unrequited love for an unattainable lady. More to the point, she hated to be teased about her obsession with these tales.

The corners of Rob's mouth tried to rise. Ach, but there was great joy in teasing her. If he went at it long enough, he'd get her to strike at him.

"Dear God in heaven," he said, laying a heavy coat of scorn atop his words, "why would you wish such a fate as knighthood on Master Colin? Better to be a pigherd than to be one of those noble thieves who tax honest tradesmen like ourselves in order to support their violent habits."

Johanna frowned at him, a storm gathering in her eyes. "Knights do not tax us, the king does. You only hate them because your father claimed you were sired by one. You know nothing of them or their way of life."

Rob looked down his nose at her. "And, you do? You said yourself once the convent began to take in merchants' daughters, the high and mighty found another place to send their own precious lasses, not wanting them contaminated by the stink of trade."

She stomped her foot in impatience, not wanting to admit her ignorance to him. "I know how they act by those tales," she cried.

"Only a lass would find anything the least bit admirable about those stories," Rob said, relieved and pleased that under her alluring exterior the real Johanna yet existed. "How is it you manage to ignore that the women whose hearts those knights seek to win are already married? Just like the whoresons they are, those noblemen are trying to tempt honest women into dishonoring their husbands and bringing ruin down upon themselves."

Johanna turned on him, the blue of her eyes brighter at the dispersion he was throwing on her fancy. "How would an apprentice like you know anything about these men and their motives? All you know is how to do is call, 'Come mistress, come goodwife, see my fine pepper! A pence will buy you a whole corn.' " It was an apt mimickry of the patter her father taught his apprentices to use.

"I can do better than that," he sniffed as if she'd hurt his feelings, "or have you forgotten that I now travel the fairs with your father? You should hear me at our booth calling to fine merchants and lords, alike. 'Come you, men of rich tastes. See my cumin and my coriander, smell this *caneel.* Is it not enough to make your senses reel? And, this my good lord, is our richest blend, made especially for those with the most discriminating of tastes. Can you smell the ginger? Do you like it hot or mild?' " The chant flowed from him in a fluid, easy stream. " 'Hotter, is it? Then, watch as I mix in a pinch of the finest red pepper'." He made the appropriate stirring motion with his hands, as if the special trough they used to mix and measure this concoction were before him. "Watch now as the red mingles with the green of the herbs and gold of our spices. Does that not just speak of sumptuous flavor? More, is it? More it is, watch, watch now.' "

Johanna was trying to frown, but laughter bubbled from her. "Stop that!" she commanded him, slapping at his upper arm.

Rob hunched his shoulder as if she'd hurt him. "Hey now. Just because I think your *lais* foolish is no call to leave bruises."

"They aren't foolish," she protested, then stopped to stare up at him, a frown of confusion on her brow. "How do you know they are called *lais?*"

"Do I look like an uncouth peasant to you?" Rob

retorted, lifting his nose in mock arrogance as he shifted into French. "Abbot William is so pleased with my proficiency in his native tongue that he regales me with those idiotic things."

Johanna squealed in pleasure, crying, "I forgot," in English, then joined him in the language of those who ruled their land. "If you've heard the tales, then you know it's no base love these men hold in their hearts. They are content to adore from afar, living for a single glance from their lady love." A new earnestness came to life in her expression.

"And twenty years worth of messages delivered by a swan," Rob sneered. Supported by his new education in bedding, he retreated to his native tongue and offered the death blow to her argument. "I tell you, no man is content with mere glances. If he cannot tumble with that woman, he'll swiftly find himself another to take her place."

"What do you know of men," Johanna huffed and crossed her arms, her own eyes narrowing in a scorn to match his. "You are only a lad."

"I am a man, full grown," he retorted, stung by her slur. "Do I not stand as tall as your father? Has my voice not deepened?" He let it fall to its lowest tone as he spoke. "Does not a beard grow upon my face?"

"Where?" she asked, skepticism heavy in the word. The wisps of gold that were her brows rose as she awaited proof of his claim.

"I shave it off as it is not yet thick and only makes my face look dirty." He ran his fingers over his upper lip, then along his jaw to indicate where the coarse, dark hair had been. It was already growing back. The stubble made his skin feel rough.

Johanna leaned toward him to squint at his face. "I see nothing. You are a lad, still." Her eyes gleamed in victory.

"It is there," he protested. Not willing to let her trample his pride by pretending blindness, he grabbed her wrist and lifted her hand to his jaw. Moving her palm against his skin, he said, "See? Feel where it returns."

A tiny crease appeared between her brows as she moved her fingers across his upper lip. "You did not lie," she said in surprise.

Rob caught his breath. Sensation pulsed from where Johanna's fingertips brushed against his skin. When she moved her palm against his jawline, a wondrous thrill shot down his spine. The desire he'd failed to kill earlier leapt from a mere spark to a full-blown fire in his belly.

When she drew her palm away from his face, he couldn't bear it. He caught her hand in his, lacing his fingers between hers, then drew their joined hands against his chest. As he did so, she took a step nearer to him. This sent a languid warmth oozing into every corner of his body.

Johanna tilted her head to look into his face. Her cheeks glowed with the same heat that filled him, making her freckles stand out like precious drops of gold. Wonder and pleasure tangled in her gaze. She took another tiny step toward him. The heat of her body embraced him. Her nearness was as intoxicating as wine. She sighed, her lips parting.

Something in Rob melted. Needing her closer still, he wrapped his arm around Johanna's waist, then waited for the awkwardness that usually plagued him when he held a woman. It did not come. Instead, Johanna felt as if she belonged in his embrace. The sensation was so right it set every inch of Rob into aching awareness of her nearness.

With another sigh, Johanna melded her body to his, pulling herself so close he could feel her heartbeat against his own. Rob gasped. Where her breasts touched his chest, he swore his tunic took fire.

Caught in this incredible web of pure sensation, Rob freed her hand to cup her chin in his palm. Tilting her head to his, he lowered his mouth to hers. Her eyes closed. So did his. Holding his lips still against hers, he released her chin to wrap his other arm around her, until she was cradled in his embrace.

A bonfire ignited between them. His mouth moved atop hers, his kiss growing in urgency. She responded by lacing her hands behind his neck so she might draw herself closer still. Her body slid up against his until the curve of her abdomen pressed against his already stiffening shaft. He groaned quietly against her mouth. She shivered. Rob freed an arm to slide his hand between them, cupping the amazing fullness of her breast in his hand.

"Mistress Johanna?" Helewise's call slashed between them.

They tore apart, both panting in their passion.

Shock and horror destroyed every bit of Rob's previous pleasure. He took a step back from her. How could he have let lust tease him into so dishonoring Master Walter? His heart continued its downward spiral into shame. He'd done worse than dishonor his master. Johanna was betrothed to Katel. By touching her, he'd committed adultery. Jesus God, had they been discovered, they could both have been killed for this!

Johanna stared up at him. Instead of either dismay or worry, her gaze was filled with wonder and surprise. She pressed her fingers to her lips as if by doing so she could recapture the sensation of their kiss. Her eyes glowed bright blue in remembered passion.

"I come," she called to Helewise as she whirled and squeezed through the space between the distillery and the kitchen. "I was looking for Rob, thinking he'd gone to the apothecary's shop, but I cannot find him."

Rob breathed out his horror as he realized Johanna sought to shield their sin with her lie. Driven by guilt and the need to protect her false tale, he turned and raced around the house's corner, pushing through the bushes to burst out onto Market Lane. Turning away from Master Walter's house and the wide window that overlooked the street, he made his way by a circuitous route to the warehouse on the river. There, he slipped around its corner and took refuge on the stretch of riverbank he and Johanna yet called their own.

Shielded by the willow branches, he dropped to sit, his back braced against the horny trunks. His emotions boiled, leaping from self-loathing to fear to the wonderful sensation of holding Johanna in his arms. And there they clung despite all his efforts to dislodge them.

If there was no awkwardness in holding her, would there also be none while laying with her? Even though his mind screamed he must not do so, his body filled with the imagined pleasure that would come from making Johanna one with him. Wanting filled him, followed by some deeper emotion he could not name.

It was in the wake of this unnamed feeling that a whole new image woke in him. Last month, when Katel returned from his own, now separate, circuit of fairs, he learned that the maid who'd served his needs before his departure had been unfaithful to him. Rob had seen the girl after Katel was finished. Her nose was broken, her skin split on both brow and cheek.

As it had then, outrage filled him at such cruelty. Katel cared nothing for the maid or what she'd done; it was his pride the girl damaged by her betrayal. If this was what Katel did to one for whom he cared nothing, would he not do far worse to Johanna if he learned she'd touched another man?

Rage, so sharp and strong it made Rob's stomach clench, drove through him. Johanna deserved better than that cruel, scheming little whoreson. Why did Master Walter insist that his only child wed Katel, when he must know what sort of man his eldest apprentice was?

Rob's eyes narrowed. Well, if his master wouldn't

protect his daughter, he would. Every muscle tensed as he tested the strength that resided in this new and powerful body of his. In that moment, he swore to himself upon his mother's grave that he'd never allow Katel to hurt Johanna. Never.

Night had long since wrapped its dark arms about the spice merchant's house, gathering all those within its walls into slumber's gentle embrace. That was, all save Johanna. Her body was too alive with sensation to rest.

Never in all her life had she dreamed that kissing could be such a . . . heated experience. She closed her eyes, remembering the strength of Rob's arms around her, the gentleness of his mouth against hers and the incredible sensation of his body pressed to hers.

Even recalling his touch made her most private parts grow soft and warm all over again. The intensity of that warmth grew until it was almost uncomfortable. Johanna rolled onto her back in an attempt to escape it.

Staring into the blackness overhead, she worked at sorting her thoughts. Why had Rob kissed her? Her heart swelled. Because Rob loved her! No doubt, he'd loved her from the moment of their first meeting.

The excitement of being adored in secret made Johanna smile. This was just like the *lais,* for she was betrothed to Katel. Rob dared say no word to her of his true emotion. Surely, knowing Rob loved her would make it easier to wed Katel when the time came.

Johanna's brows drew down, and she tossed onto her side. Where once she'd loved and admired Katel, she now hated him. He was an oath breaker. While she'd kept her word, entering the convent school as she'd vowed, he hadn't kept up his end of the bargain. Although Rob said nothing to her of it, she knew Katel still tried to trick him into making mistakes.

Katel was also trying to poison others against Rob. This very day, at Mistress Katherine's farewell feast no less, she'd overheard Katel speaking to several merchants. He had been slyly casting aspersions on Rob's accomplishments, the same ones her father had just finished praising. It made Rob look inept and her father a fool for believing his youngest apprentice gifted.

She shifted on her cot, once again jostling Puss. Disgruntled by all this motion, the cat gave an irate huff and rose. Gone heavy through a rich diet of Philip's scraps, the gray tom took his time stretching, as if to demonstrate how she'd hurt him after he'd so graciously agreed to sleep with her. He leapt off the cot to curl up on a pallet with a set of maids.

Johanna sighed at his departure, feeling strangely sad and lonely all at once. Across the room in his curtained bed, Papa grumbled in his sleep, then loosed a loud snort. She stared at the closed curtains in fond amusement.

At least Papa wasn't in a hurry to see her wed. Tonight, as he did every time Johanna visited, Katel asked Papa to set their wedding day. And, as he did every time Katel asked, Papa refused him. This time, no doubt because she'd reached the marriageable age of ten and four, Papa had given as his excuse the fact that her education was not yet complete.

Unlike most tradesmen's daughters who learned their father's skills at his knee, Johanna was learning to read, scribe, and keep accounts. As Papa's wealth had grown, he'd invested his coins into properties, using the rents and other profits he earned from these to buy yet more warehouses and buildings. It was the skills of a steward she needed, were she to manage what her father built, while her husband concentrated on selling spices.

Still, her reprieve wouldn't last forever; the day would come when she and Katel wed, whether she wished it or not. Years ago, she'd asked her sire to free her from their betrothal. Papa refused, telling her she'd best accustom herself to wedding Katel for the contracts were signed and the vows given. He'd gone on to say that even if he could break the betrothal, which he couldn't, he wouldn't do so. It was in joining his house to that of Katel's sire that Papa had gained access into the highest circles of trade. To break their agreement now would be bad business, indeed.

Johanna's jaw firmed in refusal. No matter what Papa said, he wouldn't wed her to Katel. He loved Rob, too. Somehow, she'd make him see that wedding her to Rob was far better than forcing her to marry Katel.

She closed her eyes with a happy sigh. Once again, her heart swelled with the wondrous torment of forbidden love. Oh, but the lasses at the convent would be positively green over this.

Chapter Eighteen

Stanrudde
an hour past Sext
Ste. Agnes's Day, 1197

Never had Johanna heard Stanrudde so quiet. Closing her eyes, she leaned back against the tub's wall and listened. From their nests in the kitchen's thatched roof, mice rustled and squeaked. Water lapped gently against the sides of her wooden tub. The fire hissed and spat.

Although it was the midst of the day, not a single crier called out the fineness of the ale he'd tasted. Not one regrater trod the streets, trying to rid himself of the remaindered goods he'd bought from some greater merchant. She opened her eyes.

The silence was unnerving, as if she were the only soul left alive in all the town. Even as she thought that she chided herself as a fool. A little over an hour ago, their gate bell had clanged. Twice in quick succession, she'd heard the gate open, then close, the bar again being dropped into place.

It had been the bell's clamor that had finally stirred her from her exhausted slumber. Johanna shook her head in amazement. Never in her life had she slept so long. Or, so deeply. So sound had her slumber been, she'd heard nothing at all of those who she knew had come into the kitchen. Wymar?

Whether or not it had been the cook, she owed

whoever it was a huge debt of gratitude. On the kitchen's thick worktable there stood a basket. If her eagerness to bathe kept her from looking into it, she didn't doubt it was filled with food. Beside it lay a comb and a fold of linen toweling. Even her bath had been prepared, the cold water standing in the tub needing only the addition of hot to make it bearable. That Johanna had found simmering in the single pot that now hung over the restored kitchen fire.

She smiled as she glanced at the hearth. Just as yesterday's dying kitchen blaze had reclaimed its life from the ashes, so, it seemed, had she. Her eyes narrowed in determination. Now that she owned it, she was loathe to let it go, even if in keeping it she remained married to Katel for the rest of her days.

For the first time since her return to Stanrudde, Johanna pondered her husband's threat against her. The probability of his success seemed so unbelievable. No matter what lies Katel told, a whole convent full of nuns would testify there had been no adultery.

Rather than inspire confidence, confusion and worry tangled in her. She knew her husband. He made no threats he did not expect to fulfill. Moreover, Katel would not have revealed even what little he had of his plot if he believed she could stop him. The very fact that she was in this kitchen, alone and unguarded, said he thought her no threat.

Johanna caught her breath in understanding. While that might be true, it was not the only reason she remained unwatched. Katel was encouraging her to run, just as she had done yesterday. He dared her to seek refuge elsewhere. As he had told her, he wanted her to scream aloud her innocence.

Understanding grew. Once again, she saw the reaction of the townsmen to her husband's broad hint of her adultery. In their eyes, Katel was a doting, but duped husband. It had not been to make her his prisoner that he'd sent Theobald to fetch her back to him after her attack. Of course he had upbraided Watt for being too slow in finding her. A caring husband did not drag his feet when the wife he adored was foully attacked by a savage crowd.

Johanna's shoulders sagged. Would that she might someday learn to control her impulsiveness. Yesterday's rage-driven race now seemed only to confirm Katel's implication of adultery, a guilty dash to avoid the husband she had misused.

Mary save her, but Katel was cunning. To be cuckolded was a terrible thing for a man, so terrible that the world forgave horrible murders and terrible mutilation done in its name. There wasn't a soul in all the town who'd believe Katel sought the humiliation of that title, all the while knowing his wife had done no sin against him.

Still, how could he imagine to succeed when she had so many witnesses to her innocence? Frowning, she worried the issue, tugging it one way, then the other in her mind, until she saw the answer. Their oaths would only serve her were she actually called into church court. If Katel did not care about them, then he did not expect her to have the opportunity to call them.

Why not? Katel was too clever to kill her himself as though driven to it by her betrayal. Were her innocence posthumously exposed, he'd face the charge of murder.

As consternation grew, so, too, did the need to turn their house upside down until she found some clue as to his plot. Days, Katel had said. There was still time.

Ach, but how could she begin to search if she did not understand what it was she sought? Even if she found something, Johanna wasn't certain she'd recognize it for what it was. It was with frustration churning in her stomach that she once more leaned back into the tub.

The worst of all this was the threat against Rob. If

she accepted she'd earned her fate by seeking to repay Katel's every slight with one of her own, until their war escalated to its ultimate conclusion, Rob was truly innocent. A wave of sadness flowed over her. Would that she had made this change in herself before she'd met with him. Yesterday's selfish child had not only hurt him, accusing him of a betrayal he had not committed, but had cheated her of the opportunity to warn him against Katel. Were she to now seek him out and be discovered, she would surely be damned as an adulteress the moment Katel's accusation came.

From the recesses of her memory woke the echoes of Rob's voice. Johanna came upright in the tub, hearing now what she'd been too angry to hear then. Rob knew! He had tried to warn her against Katel.

She breathed in new relief. If Rob knew, he'd have found a way to shield himself from Katel, just as he'd done so many times in the past. Excitement grew apace. If Rob knew, he could tell her what sort of proof she needed to stop Katel. True, she could not go to him on her own, but she could send Watt.

Confidence soared, then crashed back to earth. How? No longer was Rob Robert of Blacklea or Robert of Stanrudde. It was certain he wasn't Robert the Bastard, as Katel had named him. Not only did she not know where Rob was or what he called himself, she didn't even know what trade he now practiced.

That he was likely the only foreign Robert in town only made the task more difficult. If Watt went about asking every man upon the street about a Robert who was not from Stanrudde, Katel would soon learn of it, thus exposing Watt to his wrath, leading, most likely, to Watt's dismissal. Worse than that, Katel would swiftly see that the whole town knew his wife was seeking out this foreigner. Once again, this would but serve to convict her when Katel's charges came.

The water had gone from chill to icy. Johanna glanced in disgust at the corner in which she'd thrown her ruined gowns. If her anonymous benefactor had been unable to provide clothing, it was because her garments were yet at the convent. In her anger over how easily Katel had torn her from the retirement she'd believed would be permanent, she'd purposefully left them behind her. The Johanna of yesterday, with her spoiled, hate-filled thinking, had seen the time and energy it would cost her husband to retrieve them as suitable vengeance for how he'd forced her to go where she did not wish to go.

Once again, what she'd meant as a blow against others swung round to hit her. Since Katel only hired women shorter than he, none of the maid's attire would fit her. Johanna again glanced at her tattered clothing. However unwearable, they'd have to do.

Rising from the water, she leaned across to the table and grabbed the towel. It slid heavily off the edge, then unfolded, spilling a jumble of brown and green fabric onto the floor. Johanna cried in wordless wonder as she stared at the humble gowns dating from the days when her father ruled this house.

It was as if two beloved and long forgotten friends had come to call. Leaping out of the tub, she wrapped the towel around herself, then knelt down to gather the garments close. As she did, she looked at them again. The weave was all wrong for the gowns her father's servants had worn. So, too, were the colors amiss, the green being too light, the brown too strong. However old and worn, they weren't gowns from her father's time.

Who cared! No matter where they'd come from or that they were well darned and patched, they would do. They would more than do.

With these garments, faith took root in her. Too long had she been in the habit of concentrating on all that was bad in her life. Aye, so deep had her belief in the negative been, she'd nearly died. This morn she saw how much of what had happened yesterday was good. Aye, Katel threatened her, but had not both Leatrice and Watt offered their support? True, she'd been horribly attacked, but she had not been raped or killed. Rather, the Lord God had seen fit to send Rob to protect her.

She sighed. Would that she had not destroyed Rob's love, but even in that there was good. Only through her confrontation with him could this change in her have taken place.

When she was dry, she drew on the gowns and smiled. They were only a little short. There was a bit of cord to bind them to her waist, but no purse. Donning her own shoes and stockings, she once again draped Watt's mantle over her shoulders to keep the cold at bay. Then, taking up the comb, she smoothed her wet and tangled hair.

The scratch at the door was so faint, Johanna thought she misheard, until it came again. Startled, she turned to stare. For privacy's sake, she'd set the bar before stepping into the tub. If this was one of the household servants, they'd have tried the latch, then boldly knocked when the door didn't open. The tap was repeated, this time, followed by a woman's quiet sob.

"Please Wymar, I know you're there. I can see the smoke coming from the vent. Please let me in. I am so cold and hungry."

"Leatrice?" Johanna breathed in surprise.

Throwing aside the bar, she opened the door. Her former maid tumbled into the room on a shaft of piercing winter's light so bright Johanna squinted against it. Leatrice glanced around the barren walls and empty corners, then turned with a sharp breath of fright, only to gasp in deeper surprise. "Mistress, what are you doing here? Where is everything?"

Her eyes flew wide as she took in Johanna's bruised face. "May God have mercy! What has happened to you?"

"It is a story longer than I care to tell," Johanna replied, unwilling to discuss any of her personal situation with her former maid. "What are you doing here?"

"Wymar always has a crust of bread and a cup of broth for those unfortunates who cross his path." Leatrice hurried to the hearth and spread her cloak to capture the heat. "I never thought I'd be the one needing it," she added with a tiny sob.

Although not surprised that their cook would dare to defy Katel's edict that all charity be done outside these walls, Johanna shot her a stern look. "If either Katel or Theobald find you, they'll beat you senseless."

"No one saw me come. The apothecary's new wife took pity and let me through their shop. There is a wee space between their back hearth and the kitchen wall, just enough to let me pass."

"Ah," Johanna murmured.

As she once again barred the door to conceal from her husband and his lickspittle what they did not know, her many memories of using that same passage filled her. The last time had been the night before Rob disappeared. Master Colin had seen her, or so her father had told her.

She leaned against the closed door as the thought of the apothecary's betrayal tried to stir the embers of her anger and hatred. It was without reluctance that Johanna released her hold on the two emotions. If not Master Colin, it would have been someone or something else. Dear God, but she could have found herself in Leatrice's position.

"Please, mistress," Leatrice cried softly. "The babe within me cries for food. Might I have a bite to eat?"

"Let me see what I have to give you," Johanna replied, moving to the table and pulling back the cloth that covered the basket.

A goodly wedge of cheese lay alongside a thick slice

of ham. There was also several slices of bread, not the lighter, wheaten stuff, but heavy, dark slices made from some combination of oats and rye. Taking the basket, she joined her former maid at the hearth. Once Leatrice had grabbed a slice of the bread with a soft cry of thanks, Johanna set it aside to plait her hair.

"You know you cannot stay here," she said, her fingers working wet strands into one long braid. There was no thong to tie at its end, but her hair had curl enough that it stayed as she left it.

Leatrice freed a worried sob around the food in her mouth. "Oh, mistress, you cannot send me away. When my father saw my state and learned that I had lost my place with you, he sent me out onto the streets. Neither the monks at the priory or the abbey will let me in, as they already overflow with the starving. I have nowhere left to go."

"You cannot stay here," Johanna repeated with a shake of her head. Reclaiming the basket, she took a piece of cheese to break her own fast, then handed Leatrice another slice of bread. "If either Theobald or Katel find you, you'll not only be homeless, but bloody and bruised as well."

This time Leatrice gave a terrified moan. "But I cannot go back out on the streets! All the night long, I moved from one hiding spot to another, trying to avoid the bands that roamed the lanes." This time when she paused, it was to wipe away the tears that dribbled down her face.

"What bands?" Johanna asked, before she remembered that Theobald had spoken yesterday of what violence the starving did to the town.

The maid stared at her in disbelief. "Do you not know? Last even, Stanrudde was torn apart as men destroyed shops and set homes afire. It was terrible, mistress. I thought for certain I would be killed when a mob came to the abbey at the same time I knocked upon their gate. They were raging, screaming for the abbot to give them the one on whom they blamed all their ills."

"It is no one man's fault that the crops failed," Johanna retorted. It was an absent comment, made as she explored the tickle of a thought at the back of her brain. Afternoon last, this kitchen had already been stripped of supplies, emptied as if against potential attack. How could Katel have known what had yet to occur?

"Nay, mistress," Leatrice said, shaking her head at this misunderstanding, "they do not blame him for their hunger, but because what he did caused the hungry to rampage and destroy the town."

This brought Johanna out of her musing. "What sort of man can set a whole town aflame? Who is he?"

"Some foreign grossier. The folk around me said he had promised to sell grain, then took back his product because those who wanted it wouldn't pay enough money for it. When he did so, the hungry went searching for what he had hidden in store, tearing apart warehouses and shops to find it. Or something like that."

As she finished, Leatrice's eyes came to life with outrage. "Can you believe that the abbot protected him? I think me he should hang. How can a man let others starve when he has product to sell?"

Johanna raised her brows at this impossible story, one no doubt twisted many times over in its retelling. No tradesman would be so foolish. It was like calling the hangman to come and fetch him as that sort of price gouging and underhanded trade was punishable by death. "The abbot must have thought him innocent, else he would have given him to the crowd."

"Aye, so the churchman shouted to those in the marketplace." Leatrice retrieved her eating knife from her purse and cut the slice of ham in two. She offered half of it to her mistress. "I say the reason the grossier was protected is that he's rich. The rich take care of their own," she snarled, forgetting that Johanna was one of the class she condemned. "It's no different than what *he*"—the jerk of her head indicated the house and Katel—"did to me. He thinks because I am nothing and have no power against him, I can do him no harm. He is wrong. I will find a way to repay him for his betrayal, this I vow!"

Johanna smiled. "What heart you have," she said. If this slip of a girl, now without friend or family, believed she could wreak vengeance on a man many stations above her, Johanna would find a way to locate Rob and learn what it was she needed to expose Katel.

Outside in the lane, one man called to another, his voice loud, although his words were indistinct. Another shout followed. In the next instant, the lane was alive with voices. While Leatrice clung to the shadows in the kitchen, Johanna opened the door. Leaning outside, she peered toward the gate and the lane.

"What is it?" Leatrice asked, careful to keep her voice low. No matter her boldness, she was no fool.

Johanna frowned as she listened. "I'm not certain. They are yelling about going to the tower and seeing justice done."

"Mayhap the abbot has changed his mind about protecting that man. I'll wager it's the Grossier of Lynn they're going to hang." There was a touch of vindictive triumph in Leatrice's voice, as if seeing one rich man's life ended eased her own need for vengeance against Katel.

"Hmm," Johanna replied in disinterest. Unlike most folk she knew, she didn't much care to watch executions. However, the mention of Lynn brought with it the recall that her father had once had a friend from that town. Master Wymund, he was, also a grossier. She remembered she had liked him, mostly because he never visited that he didn't bring her a length of ribbon. The last time she'd seen him was the month before her father's death.

"From Lynn did you say?"

"Aye, Master Robert by name."

Johanna's heart stopped. Her fingernails dug into the wood of the door frame. She closed her eyes, summoning up the image of Rob in the alleyway. His gown had been embroidered into blue lozenges. Within each oval there had been a stalk of wheat done in gold. In that moment, she knew where her father had sent Rob all those years ago and who it was the crowd meant to kill. The need to protect her Rob exploded within her, driving her out of the kitchen.

"Mistress, wait," Leatrice hissed quietly after her as Johanna squeezed around the back of the tiny building. "Where do you go? Your hair is uncovered. Stop, I say! Don't leave me here alone!" The last was a low wail.

Johanna worked her way between the kitchen shed and the distillery's hearth. Rather than turn toward the shop's back door to pass through the workroom as Leatrice had done, she went instead to the side of the house. There, as she had done one time too many in the past, Johanna thrust her way through the tangled bushes. Without thought or plan for what she might accomplish, she raced down Market Lane toward Stanrudde's keep tower and Rob.

Chapter Nineteen

Stanrudde
Late June, 1180

Johanna leapt off her palfrey the very moment the abbess's man led their tiny party past her father's gate. The soft mist that was descending from a gentle gray sky had dampened the courtyard, and she slid on the slick surface as she landed. It was fear for her father that kept her upright.

Cloak flying, she tore across the short distance between gate and door, sprinting into the forebuilding. Her footsteps rang sharply against the stone steps, the sound of her panting, panicked breath echoing back to her from the cold walls. She raced across the landing and into the hall.

The day's serene stillness wafted through that big room's wide western window, filling the chamber with what seemed an unnatural quiet. Her heart rose into her throat. Despite that it was time for the meal, the tables were yet dismantled and stacked against the far wall. Even the fire burning beneath its round and protruding hood seemed to hold its breath. Choking on the fear she was too late, she flew from the hall to the bedchamber's door, where she came to an abrupt halt.

Borne on the day's warm, wet breeze, misty light flowed into the room through the open window. It muted the brightly painted clothing chests to dull shadows of themselves and grayed the vibrant green and reds of her father's bedcurtains. Master Colin, new white streaks in his black hair, stood at the bed's foot. His face was solemn, the set of his shoulders sad. Helewise sat on a stool at the bed's head.

The housekeeper shifted to look at her employer's daughter. Her eyes were red-rimmed, dark rings of exhaustion clinging beneath them. At Helewise's feet sat a basin of water and several leather flasks. Johanna drew a painful breath. Was she treating an invalid or bathing a dead man's body?

"Papa?" she cried softly, yet clinging to the doorway.

"Is that you, poppet?" Her father's voice was but a thready reflection of his usual deep growl.

Johanna's heart tore between the relief that her father was not dead and dread that he might soon be. Fifteen was too young to be left without a parent. Swinging the cloak from her shoulders, she threw it aside as she leapt to his bed, then caught her breath in horror as she looked upon her beloved sire.

Walter of Stanrudde's face was painfully thin, his skin seeming as fragile as that of an onion, its color just as sallow. Instead of wild red curls, his hair lay limp around his skull. The usual icy blue color of his eyes was now a dull gray, their life sapped by the terrible shadows that hung beneath them.

"Papa," she cried again, her voice tiny as she faced her father's death.

As he looked upon her, color returned to his cheeks and new life sparked in his eyes. He smiled, the movement of his mouth so familiar, yet so changed by his illness, it brought her to her knees. Lifting his hand, he clasped her fingers in a warm, tight grip.

Johanna's gaze caught and clung to his inner arm. One of the many moles that had ever dotted his skin had grown. Once the size of a pea, this one was now twice that and misshapen, the color a malevolent shade of black.

"Papa," she cried again as she pressed his hand against her cheek. Oh, but she could feel his bones through his flesh. Tears tumbled from her eyes as her heart broke, then broke again. How could he be so ill, so soon? True, at Eastertide, he'd complained of feeling unusually tired, barely managing to walk from the stables to the hall without needing to rest. He'd blamed his exhaustion on too much work and vowed to let Katel, Rob, and Arthur do more.

"Hey now, poppet," he crooned to her in that awful voice of his, "do not mourn me yet. I will be here for some time to come. How can I leave this world before I see you wed and dandle my firstborn grandchild upon my knee?" It was a falsehood. Although he wished what he said were true, he didn't believe it; she could see it in his eyes.

"Aye, Papa," she lied in return, wanting as desperately as he to believe.

"I am glad to have you home," he said, his eyelids drooping as he spoke, exhausted by even this much speech.

"You should have called for me sooner," she chided softly.

"What, to have you watch me lay abed? There's Helewise to do that," he retorted with a sigh. "You're too young to be trapped at an old man's bedside." His voice trailed off as his eyes closed and he drifted into slumber.

The silence that followed his words was awful and deep. Johanna loosed another tiny sob. She released his hand, gently laying his arm down atop his blanketed chest.

"He was holding himself awake in anticipation of your arrival," Master Colin said softly. "Take heart, lass. He is not always this tired. Although he can no longer rise, most days his mind is active and alert."

Johanna shifted on her knees to look up at Helewise, her gaze pleading for the woman to tell her what she saw with her own eyes was not true. Helewise only spread her arms in invitation. Already sobbing in grief, Johanna threw herself into the embrace.

"Hush, sweetling," the housekeeper bid her, rocking her gently in her arms. "You must not let him see you so distraught. Be strong for him as he passes from this vale into the next."

Her words tore through Johanna. "Nay," she cried out in anger, pushing free of the woman's arms. She stumbled to her feet. "He is not going to die. He cannot die; I will not let him go!" With that, she turned and raced from the house, not caring where she went.

Dressed in just his chausses and shoes, his tunic and shirt hanging off a peg in the warehouse's wall, Rob half-heartedly swept at the cobwebs that dotted the big building. It was busy work, meant to keep him away from the spice merchant's house for the day. He did not care to be there when Johanna returned.

In order to see what he did, he'd thrown open the warehouse's waterside door. As the day's muted light flowed into the building, it brought with it the gentle lap of the river against its bank. Just beyond the door, the willows rustled in the same breeze that brought him the sweet smell of a gentle, summer mist. The mill was still for the moment. Against its silence, he could hear the warble and cheep of the smaller birds, their calls cheery in the general dullness of the day.

As always, the sylvan sounds eased what ached in him. Rob sighed and forgave himself his cowardice. This cleaning wasn't all busy work. The warehouse did need to be prepared for what would soon be coming his way.

Both Katel, Master Katel now, and Arthur, accompanied by Aleric, had departed some weeks ago as two separate parties, each with a different route to travel. At their backs were whole pack trains, the baskets on their beasts filled with the spices and those blends for which Master Walter was now renowned. Although their ultimate purpose was to reach London to replenish Master Walter's stores from the wholesale spice merchants, they would take their time as they journeyed, moving from fair to fair, from manor house to abbey, trading all the way.

While some of what they took with them would be sold for coin, the remainder would be exchanged for goods. Of those goods, they kept what could be carried on a packhorse's back to the next stop, against the possibility of selling it there. What was too large, or was replaced by something more salable, they sent back to Stanrudde. Once it was here, it needed to be assessed for value and a buyer found.

It was in the doing of this that Rob had found his talent. He never forgot what it was that this merchant or that said he needed. Some of his trades grew to great complexity, as wood went to one, who gave wool in return, which went to another in trade for fulled cloth, and so on. Each man got what he wanted, while Master Walter took a profit off every trade.

Sadness hit in a slow-moving wave. This would be his last summer to turn trades for Master Walter. Yesterday, after two months of growing steadily weaker, his master had finally relented and called for his daughter to return from her convent school. This meant the spice merchant no longer believed he would recover.

Rob's sadness grew. Once again, he was losing both home and family. When Master Walter was gone, Katel would be the master here. Rob had no doubt he'd swiftly find himself upon the street, fortunate if Katel left him his shirt upon his back.

From beneath the sadness came a sharp thrust of

pain. Helewise had begun planning Johanna's wedding. Rob leaned heavily upon his broom, fighting the anger that followed pain. Johanna shouldn't have to marry that whoreson. Katel would never honor her the way a man should his wife.

Only then did he realize where his wayward thoughts were once again leading him. Even as he chided himself for the wrong he did, he could not stop himself. It wasn't just his body that had betrayed him with Johanna, it was his heart. Against all that was right and proper, he loved his master's daughter.

Nay, it was more than that. He needed her. From their earliest years, he'd found such joy in sharing his triumphs with Johanna. More than even Master Colin, Johanna took great pride in his accomplishments. It was her praise and excitement over his achievements that kept him strong against Katel's constant, secret belittling.

He squeezed his eyes shut as the pain outstripped his sadness. Johanna, and how she made him special in her life, was more precious to him than any riches he could imagine. If he would survive the loss of his trade and his master, the thought of losing her was tearing him in two.

From beyond the warehouse's wall, he caught the sound of someone running. Whoever it was stopped along the river's edge. Rob frowned. Any other day he wouldn't have minded sharing this place with another. Just now, he craved complete privacy in which to cherish his mournful thoughts.

Not bothering to don either shirt or tunic, he set the broom into the corner, then turned to the threshold of the water door. Here the river's bank was cut away to allow those barges bearing goods for Master Walter to dock before the opening. Water lapped at the warehouse's foundation, murky and swirling against the current.

He leapt from the threshold to the bank, landing

upon the same spot that Johanna had once named hers. Gone was the shallow hole that had served them as a private place in those earlier years. The willows now owned it, their roots having spread across the surface to pry at the warehouse's foundation.

The memory of the first time he and Johanna came here rolled over him. It had been to protect him that she'd kicked that regrater. This almost made him smile; then the sadness returned. She'd protect him no longer, nor he, her.

He kicked once at the twisted and woody ground, then eased around the gnarled trunks. Crossing the bank, his footsteps absorbed by its thick carpet of moss, he peered through the cascading willow branches at the river's edge. There was a flash of blue beyond the waterfall of green and gold.

"Whoever you are, be gone with you," he called out. "This stretch belongs to Master Walter, and you may not trespass."

Rather than depart, there was a rustling in the foliage. It was Johanna who pushed through the thick layer of branches. He stared at her in shock and not a little horror. For the first time in three years, she'd left her father's house without an escort. They were alone.

For months, ever since Mistress Katherine's funeral feast, he'd avoided being alone with Johanna. That did not mean he'd escaped her. Nay, not at all. She, and the wondrous feel of her in his arms, haunted his dreams. Mornings found his shaft hard and aching for her.

As she stepped into the inner reaches of the trees, she let the branches fall behind her, concealing them from the outer world. The persistent mist left dark spots on her pale blue gowns, the damp silk clinging here and there to the slender line of her body. Loosened by her run, careless tendrils of bright golden-red hair escaped her plait to curl around her face and shoulders.

"What are you doing here?" he cried out, taking a backward step as he considered the valor of racing back into the warehouse and barring the door on her.

"Oh, Rob," she cried, her voice tiny with pain.

Worry against his reaction to her died. Seven years had passed, but he still remembered the despair of finding himself orphaned. "You have seen your father," he said softly.

She took a step toward him. Rob caught his breath. Sorrow made the lines of her face seem all the more delicate. Her mouth softened as her lips trembled. Tears shimmered in her eyes, until they were bluer than blue.

"No one told me," she breathed, then bit her bottom lip to still its quiver. When she was successful, she continued. "Why did none of you tell me?" Anger's edge touched her voice.

"He would not let us," he said. "He was certain he would recover and did not wish to worry you."

If tears yet trembled in her eyes, bright pink spots took sudden life in her pale cheeks, making her freckles stand out in sharp relief. "I thought you were my friend," she shouted as her fists clenched. "You should have told me! How could you leave me in ignorance?"

"Johanna, he bid me to silence," he tried to explain, but she threw herself at him, slamming a fist against his bare chest.

Rob cried out, not so much hurt as surprised at her attack. He caught her by the wrist. "Johanna," he protested. Her retort was to send her other fist crashing into his shoulder. This time it did hurt.

"Cease I say," he snapped at her, grabbing her other wrist. Holding her hands captive, he glared down at her. "I told you he bid me say nothing. I will not defy your father, not even to please you."

She said nothing, only tried to wrench free of his

grasp. He tightened his grip, determined to hold her until she calmed. As they fought in silence, the sky above them opened. Not even thickly knit willow branches could stop what swiftly became a steady, soaking rain.

The moisture was cold against his skin. It filled her gowns, until they lay plastered to her body. Still, she fought him, writhing and pulling, not to escape him, but to lay yet more blows. Aye, she was strong, but he was by far the stronger. Once again, Rob tightened his grip on her wrists in the demand that she recognize this.

"Cease," he warned. "I will not let you go, not until you give me your word you'll strike me no longer."

At this, she drew a deep and ragged breath. And kicked him. Hard. He yelped against the bruising blow.

"The devil take you," he shouted, giving her a sharp shake. "You will cease!"

She chose that moment to strain back from him with all her might. In the next instant, she was falling, pulling him down with her. Thinking to catch himself, he released her arms, but not soon enough. Johanna gasped as she hit the mossy earth, then again as he fell atop her.

The rain beat down on his back. Digging his fingers into the vibrant green of the moss, Rob pushed himself up on his hands and knees over her. "Have you gone mad!" he shouted, angry at her for both hurting him and making him hurt her.

She made a small and helpless sound. Rob stared down at her. Hair, turning the color of honey as it dampened, trailed in wet strands across her face. Her mouth trembled. The expression in her eyes was so lost and alone, his anger died.

"Oh, Rob, I am so afraid," she breathed, her hands coming to rest on his bare chest.

Sobbing, she threw her arms around his neck and

pulled him close to her. Every muscle in Rob's body tensed to leap up from her, he swore it was so. Save that his legs slid against the wet moss.

As he settled atop her, his thighs parted, his hips coming to rest neatly against hers. With naught but thin, wet silk between her and him, he could feel her breasts against his chest. This woke his shaft, sending fire, hot beyond all toleration, raging through him.

Without thinking what he did, he relaxed until he lay full atop her, the way a man laid atop the woman he meant to love. As had happened before, she fit against him as if they were created one for the other. Desire went soaring beyond his ability to ever catch it back.

She shuddered beneath him, and her movement sent a matching thrill of passion through him. Her hold around his neck eased as she caught back a sob. Bracing his forearms at either side of her shoulders, he lifted himself slightly to look down into her face.

Tears yet filled her eyes, but the color in her cheeks held new heat. There was no fear in her eyes as she looked up at him, only wonder. She lifted a hand and pressed her fingertips to his lips.

The touch of her flesh to his made him catch his breath. As she echoed his quiet gasp, her breasts moved against his chest. The heat within his belly went to boiling.

She moved her fingers across his face, tracing the line of his cheek. Her lips parted as she did so, as if the very feel of his skin were making her melt. Catching a strand of his hair, she pressed it into a damp curl against his cheek, then let her finger follow the line of his jaw.

When he could bear her touch no longer, he lowered his head and rested his mouth on hers. Her lips yielded to his, then her whole body softened beneath him. In the next instant, she cradled him against her.

Feeling tumbled atop feeling. Rob forgot the rain

that chilled his skin. He forgot that this was the one woman he mustn't touch. All that mattered was that she was his.

Reaching down, he caught a fistful of her gowns and pulled. She lifted her hips to aid him. Not only did her gowns move upward, but her motion sent yet another wave of passion through him.

She tore her mouth free of his. "Wait," she breathed.

Rob growled in refusal, kissing at her neck, then her ear. He eased downward, lowering his head until he caught the tip of one breast in his mouth, sucking at it despite the wet silk that lay in his path. She cried out in pleasure and arched beneath him.

Again, he reached down for her gowns. This time, his hand met the bare flesh of her thigh. Her skin was smooth and soft beneath his palm. It was beyond his ability to stop himself. His hand slid upward along her leg toward her nether lips.

She trembled beneath him at this caress, breathing in sharp small gasps. When he rubbed his finger against the most private of her places, she cried out in wonder and lifted her hips. "Again," she begged softly. "Touch me again."

Her words made his shaft strain at the harsh wool that contained it. Easing back to kneel atop her thighs, he did as she commanded. She panted against the caress, her hips moving in glorious mimicry of lovemaking. Each motion sent the heat in him raging ever higher.

He slid his finger into her. She threw back her head and cried out in delight. In wonder, he caressed her in this way, letting her movements and cries drive his own need for her almost beyond bearing.

When he could tolerate it no longer, he eased to the side. Tearing at the waist string of his chausses, he shucked the garment, shoes and all. Ah, but it wasn't enough that he was bare. The need to see all of her made him strip off the belt that bound her garments to her waist. As he reached for her hems, meaning to remove her gowns, she sat up, lifting her arms to aid him.

It was in appreciation that Rob stared at her when she was bare, her forgotten garments slipping from his hands. The rain gleamed against her white skin, laying a glistening trail of moisture through the valley between her breasts. It caught in glittering droplets on the golden hair that curled over her nether lips. Reaching out, he cupped the fullness of her breasts in his palms, then moved his thumbs against their soft pink peaks.

Shivering, she shifted and leaned toward him, resting her forehead against his shoulder as she lay her hands against his chest. He caught his breath and closed his eyes when she turned her head to press her mouth against his throat. Her palms slid against his wet skin. As she drew her hands steadily lower, her mouth traced a heated line up his neck. When she nuzzled at a place just below his ear, her fingers dropped lower still, until she explored the hard length of his shaft.

It was Rob's turn to tremble. He was panting and nigh on blind with sensation when he finally caught her by the wrists to make her cease. She looked up at him in question.

Pressing his mouth to hers, he again straddled her hips, then eased her backward, her wrists yet held tightly in his hands. When she once more lay beneath him, he stretched out full-length atop her. Again, her body softened beneath him, their two forms melding in preparation for becoming one.

His mouth took hers, his kiss scalding in its demand that she release possession of herself to him. She moaned beneath his onslaught and yielded, her thighs parting. His shaft entered her and found the barrier of her maidenhead.

The shock of resistance, one with which he had no experience, made him tear his mouth from hers. Freeing her wrists, he began to push away from her. Johanna cried softly and caught her arms around his neck. Recapturing his mouth with her own, she moved against his shaft in invitation.

"Johanna," he breathed in protest against her lips. He could not take her. Whether he accepted it or not, she belonged to another.

Still, she moved against him. His heart broke. God and men had erred when they gave her to Katel. Within him grew the ferocious need to keep her as his own. If he was to do so, it was more than this they must share.

"Nay!" he insisted, threading his fingers through her hair to gain her attention. She made a tiny sound of protest and opened her eyes.

"I would make you my wife," he begged. "Say you will agree. Make your vow to God and me, telling me you will love me always."

Her smile was beautiful as she relaxed beneath him. "Aye, I will have you to husband." Her words were yet breathless with passion. "From this moment forward, I am your wife. My heart is yours, so I swear before God and all His saints."

He touched his mouth to hers. "And, you are my wife, mine to keep and hold safe. So, I swear this day, may God strike me dead if I break my word."

"Love me, Rob," she breathed against his mouth. "Love me as I love you."

This time, when she moved against him, there was no need to resist. She was his wife. His mouth slashed across hers. As he shifted forward, desperately needing entry, she thrust upward. What she should have given to Katel, she gave, instead, to him.

Passion raged in him as the warm tightness of her body closed around him. She cried out beneath him, lifting herself to accept him within her. He moved to thrust within her once again, then again.

With each and every stroke, he lay his mark upon her, making her his for all time. And, by the time he'd spilled his seed, she had made him hers.

Chapter Twenty

Stanrudde
the hour of Vespers
Ste. Agnes's Day, 1197

"Mistress, we can stay here no longer," Leatrice warned softly, her fear over a repeat of last night's violence deepening with the shadows. "Night will soon be upon us."

Johanna glanced at her, then back to Stanrudde's tiny keep tower atop its tall mound. Caught within the circle of the wooden wall around it, the keep's yellowish stones glowed a warm orange-gold in the setting sun, the dying day already casting the hall that sprang from its side into darkness. "Not yet."

"When, then?" Leatrice's words were a quiet moan.

Although they stood as far as they could get from the keep and see it, it was still too close to the crowd for her. For the whole of this afternoon, Leatrice's voice had barely lifted from a whisper, as if she thought a loud cry would spur folk to violence. Despite this, her terror of being alone was the greater; it kept her close to her former mistress.

"Soon," Johanna replied, her attention focused on the tower as if by will alone she'd keep her Rob safe. "Soon."

It was only as she repeated the word that she recognized its truth. Yesterday's lesson was yet fresh in her mind. It wasn't safe for a woman, or even two, to travel unescorted on the streets. They would have to make their retreat before full darkness.

Her heart clenching at the thought of leaving Rob alone in his imprisonment, Johanna lifted her gaze to the tower's roof. There were but two armed men atop the keep. Guarding the gate were only three more. How could their captain believe so few would be enough to protect Rob against so many?

As she had every quarter hour since she began her long vigil, she scanned the mob that filled the short stretch of frosty grass between her and Rob. No longer was this crowd made up of only the humble, hungry folk who had attacked her. Many of these here were drawn from the ranks of Stanrudde's middling merchants. They wore brightly colored gowns and tunics all in good repair, although their attire lacked the fur trim or golden bits their betters affected. Until yesterday, these unfortunates had believed they would survive the winter with life and limb intact, if somewhat leaner. Last even's riot had stolen from many of them trade, home, family, or supplies, shoving them into reach of death's cold grip.

Although their chanted calls for Rob's death had quieted, their need to repay the one they believed at the root of their own annihilation bound them here. With each passing moment, a new fire appeared on some makeshift hearth as folk set themselves to keep watch throughout the night. This they did against the possibility that the council they no longer trusted meant to spirit away the prisoner under cover of darkness.

"Mistress," Leatrice began again, her voice softening in a try at persuasion, "if he's to hang, it'll be done when all can see. He is safe enough until the morrow." Although Johanna had said nothing to Leatrice of Rob or her worry for him, the maid had drawn her own conclusions.

It was Leatrice's bid at comfort, along with the

worry that there was nothing she could do to stop what happened here, that set Johanna's tongue in motion. "Katel did this," she breathed in pain. "I do not know how or what he did, but somehow Katel has made this happen."

"The master did this?" It was a sharp question. Leatrice's gaze darted across the crowd as if assessing just what it was her mistress thought her master had done. "Do you mean he caused the riot?"

Johanna nodded in silence, rendered speechless by her need to see Rob. She ached to touch him, to prove to herself that he was yet whole and unharmed. To leave this place before she'd done so was unbearable.

Ah, but what she wanted was impossible. Twice, a cart had tried to approach the tower, no doubt containing supplies for the prisoner. Both times, the mob had refused to allow it to pass. Later, a group of councilmen, Katel not in their number, had tried to talk to the crowd, only to be sent running. How could she expect to accomplish what they could not?

"You are certain the master has done this?"

Johanna tore her gaze from the tower to look at Leatrice. The girl now wore Watt's mantle, while Johanna hid her own features beneath the shield of Leatrice's hooded cloak. The exchange of garments had occurred when the crowd began to call for the death of the councilmen and their families. No longer did the maid's pretty face reflect fear. In its place was an unusual depth of consideration.

"Leave it be," Johanna begged quietly, her words breaking against the pain in her heart.

Of this morn's hope and confidence, none was left. She was too late to stop Katel, her opportunity to save Rob having come and gone in yesterday's fit of pique. All she could now hope for was heavenly intervention. As much as Johanna wanted to believe that the Lord God would intercede on behalf of an innocent man, it was very difficult to hold onto that in the face of the crowd's determination to see him dead. What if the Almighty was as blind as she'd been to Rob's plight?

It was in the forlorn hope she might prod the heavens to move that she murmured, "Oh, Leatrice, I have a terrible need to pray."

"Do you love him so much then?" the maid replied, her expression filled with the shared understanding of a woman's heart. Although Johanna made her no response, Leatrice loosed a friendly sigh and, as equal to equal, tucked her hand into the bend of her former mistress's arm.

"Come then. Mayhap if we go together to St. Stephens, the father will let us stay the night." Turning, she led the taller woman down the lane.

They had nearly reached the church when they came upon the same cart that had twice tried to breach the crowd. This time there were a goodly fifteen men gathered at its head, with at least as many at its rear. If cloth was lifted on a frame over its bed to hide what the cart contained, it did nothing to conceal the three women who perched at its front edge. It was Mistress Alwyna, widow to Peter the Wool Merchant and mother of the crippled councilman, who sat there, two whimpering maids at her side.

"Be still," the widow snapped at one maid as she vented a terrified moan. "The crowd has thinned, and we have trebled our men. They'll neither stop us or do us any harm."

Johanna's need to see Rob soared. In its wake, all thought of discretion was forgotten. If that cart was going to the tower, she was going with it.

Tearing free of Leatrice, she darted toward the party. She was yet yards from her destination when one of those guarding the widow stepped out to stop her. One glance at her own gowns and humble cloak placed her with those in the field in his mind. He shifted to keep himself between the one he protected and a potential attacker. "Stand aside," he demanded brusquely.

Finding her path blocked only sent Johanna's need to reach Rob to greater heights. It was with more passion than sense that she called out, "Mistress Alwyna, I pray you for the sake of my son and for your husband who was his godfather, might I speak to you a moment?"

"Drive on," the man shouted to the one goading the oxen.

"Nay!" The widow's strong voice preempted the command as she leaned over the cart's edge. Peering through the gathering gloom, she tried to identify the one who'd called her. "Who is there? Come forward so I might see you."

"Have you taken leave of your senses?" Leatrice cried softly, having finally caught up to her. "When they try to force themselves through that crowd, they'll all be killed."

The maid's words rang in Johanna's ears, keeping her where she stood, but not for the reason Leatrice named. If she approached, the widow would surely call aloud her identity. Once that happened, all hope of seeing Rob died. Despite the number of its inhabitants, Stanrudde remained like unto a small town. Rumor moved faster than a fire through dry thatch. This attempt could do nothing but convict her when Katel loosed his accusation.

Still, her heart's hungering to see Rob was the stronger. If she died for it, so be it, but there was no sense in being foolish about it. Johanna yanked her cloak's hood even lower on her brow.

"Go to her," she quietly begged Leatrice. "Whisper to her who it is that pleads for her ear, bidding her not to reveal my identity. Do this for me, and I vow to you, I'll go from great house to great house until I find someone to give you and your child home and hearth."

Leatrice shot her a startled look, then her eyes came to life with gratitude. With a swift nod, she hied herself to the cart's side as quickly as the child within her would allow. Johanna watched Mistress Alwyna lean down as Leatrice stretched upward to the limits of her short height. In the next instant, the widow's head reared back.

"Who?" the old woman cried out, a strange tone to her astonishment. She swiveled to once again peer into the shadows, seeking out the features hidden beneath Johanna's hood. "Come forward, then," she commanded, but there was hard suspicion in her voice.

Hope faltered in Johanna at the woman's odd reaction to her name as she remembered Mistress Alwyna as friendly and kind. True, she and the wool merchant's family had had little dealings since her Peter had been apprenticed. A few years later, Peter the Wool Merchant had died, ending all contact. No matter. She'd come too far to retreat because of an odd tone of voice. Bowing her head, Johanna slipped past the men, not lifting her chin again until she'd stopped at the cart's side.

For a moment, Mistress Alwyna simply stared at her, the woman's eyes widening at finding the spice merchant's wife's hair uncovered, then narrowing again at the threadbare gowns. At last, she leaned back a little on her perch. "For what reason do you stop me?" she asked, her voice low, her tone yet wary.

"Please," Johanna said, keeping her words quiet, "you are for the tower. Take me with you. I must speak with the one held captive there."

The widow's brows drew down, her face the picture of distrust. "To what purpose?"

Confusion grew in Johanna at such hostility. Against it, she guessed she'd have but one chance to plead her case. She hesitated, carefully planning what she would say so it would satisfy the widow without revealing Katel's impending charge of adultery. Mistress Alwyna wouldn't wish to abet ones she believed to be illicit lovers.

"It is my husband," Johanna said, straining to make certain her words remained private between the two of them. "I fear he may have done something that has caused the Grossier of Lynn to be arrested and threatened with death. Help me to speak with Master Robert so I might do what I can to protect an innocent man. It is against the possibility my husband might have done no wrong that I beg you not to reveal what I do this night."

Johanna's spirits fell as she finished. This wasn't going to work. Katel had done too effective a job of convincing all of Stanrudde he was no threat to anyone. Who would believe their amiable spice merchant capable of such evil?

Mistress Alwyna's face softened. "Well now, this is an interesting turn," she said, more than content with Johanna's explanation. "There's room for no more. If you wish to come, you must take the place of my maid, doing for me what she would have done."

"So I will," Johanna breathed in relief and a gratitude so deep her knees weakened with it.

"Els," Mistress Alwyna said, glancing at the younger of the two maids beside her, "you have won yourself a reprieve. There's one who would take your place. You may hie yourself home."

"By myself?" the girl squeaked. Barely more than a child, her eyes widened in a new fear. Like Leatrice, the terror of what might happen to her when she was alone and unprotected was even greater than that of the crowd.

"I can take her, mistress," the other one offered, her voice lacking any belief her wish might be granted.

"Mistress, you may send them both away. I will take the place of the second one." Leatrice's voice was strong, her tone decisive. Johanna glanced at her former maid in surprise. If she'd known offering to find

Leatrice a place would end the girl's sniveling, she'd have made it hours ago, just as she had intended before the calls for Rob's death intruded.

"There's a woman after mine own heart," the wool merchant's widow replied, smiling in approval at Leatrice's stout offer. The movement of her mouth made the years slip from her face, banishing the old woman to reveal the shadow of the girl she'd once been. In her brown eyes lived a taste for life's spice, a need to dance upon a cliff's edge so as to better tolerate what was mundane. "Bow your head and cover your face," the widow hissed to Johanna.

When Johanna had done so, the old woman called, "Tom, come and help Els and Marta down. We have found us two braver souls who are willing to do what these cowards will not."

When the maids had dismounted, the man lifted Leatrice into the cart, then offered a hand to Johanna. She waved him off and climbed in on her own. In the next moment, the driver flicked his goad and the cart lurched into motion.

As it lumbered into the throng before the keep, hours of muttering reawoke its shouts. Leatrice yet held tight to her newborn courage, sitting straight and true on her seat. If Johanna kept her head bowed against the possibility of recognition, there was no room for fear in her heart, not when it was consumed with her hard-won opportunity to see Rob alive.

"I have had enough of this!" Drawn by the reemergence of rage from those besieging him, the captain of the guard's voice echoed down from the tower's top. "Cease! You have all heard my word that I will hold him until the sheriff's arrival. Go to your homes, trusting my words. Or, if you choose to stay here, thereby naming me liar, know you that I am familiar with each and every one of you. When the sheriff comes, I will tell him the names of those who tried to steal from our king his right to do justice!"

If it did not empty the field, the shouting died away at this threat, leaving the cart to pass unmolested to the gate. Those who escorted Mistress Alwyna spread themselves before the opening, weapons pointed outward against any possibility the malcontents behind them might think to charge. They did not.

In the next moment, the cart passed through the wall and came to a halt in a small courtyard. As it stopped, Johanna grabbed up her skirts and leapt from its bed. Mistress Alwyna handed her a tall, heavy basket to hold, so that her hands might be busy against any request for aid. It was an effective shield, being nigh on half again as tall as she.

Johanna clutched it to her, impatiently studying the weave of the basket, as the men set to unloading what lay inside the cart. A mattress was leaned against the cart's side within her view, then came the bedposts and pieces of a frame. Hope found fodder on which to feed. If a councilman's mother brought such comfort to a prisoner, it was a clear statement that those outside had good reason to fear the council might betray them in their blood lust.

"Mistress, what is this?" the captain cried out in complaint when he joined them in the tiny courtyard.

"My son has ordered me to see to Master Robert's needs, and so I shall do," the old woman retorted. "Take me to him."

Evidently the captain agreed, for Leatrice caught Johanna's arm, and they crossed to the stairs that rose from the small courtyard to the tiny hall. The maid was careful to lead her former mistress as if she were blind. Johanna might as well have been, being unable to raise her head to see where she went.

In the hall, she could hear the snap and pop of torches, but it remained almost as dim within this room as it was outside. Judging by the number of footsteps it took to cross it, this chamber was smaller than her father's hall. There were rushes on the floor, but they had long since been beaten into dust, while the air within reeked of smoke and unwashed men.

They halted at a stone wall, where the keep and the hall came together. The hope in Johanna doubled. In holding Rob in the tower's upper chamber, not the barren, windowless storeroom that lay below it, into which the common criminals were thrown, the council was again making a statement that they believed him innocent.

Despite all this, her heart was not satisfied. No matter what the council believed, it was the crowd outside that needed to be convinced. If she could not find a way to expose what Katel had done, Rob would die simply because Stanrudde's folk demanded it.

Iron grated on iron, the sound of a key scraping into its slot. "Why have you locked him in?" Mistress Alwyna cried in protest.

"I have given my word to both the council and the townsmen that Master Robert will remain within this keep until the sheriff's arrival. If he is locked in and I am the only one who holds the key, then here he shall stay, no matter who tells me what." Layered in the captain's voice was a day's worth of frustration and new resentment at having to explain himself to a woman.

The latch lifted with a rusty groan, then leather hinges squealed as the door opened. Following Leatrice, Johanna crossed the threshold into the room. It was Mistress Alwyna who pulled her aside to let the men carrying the bits of bed enter behind them.

As Johanna dared not lift her head until all possible witnesses were gone, she studied the glittering braid trimming the hem of the widow's green overgown. It sparked and gleamed, catching a light that should not have existed. Her gaze wandered beyond the braid to the golden glow that touched the wooden floor. There were candles lighting this room! Indeed, the council was sparing no expense to make their prisoner comfortable.

Johanna drew a swift breath in understanding. This could only mean the council was divided on the issue of Rob's guilt. The town fathers were playing both sides of the fence, unwilling to further antagonize Stanrudde's folk, but not wishing to expose themselves to any charge of slander, should Rob survive.

"How is it with you, Master Robert," Mistress Alwyna called to him as her men assembled the bed.

"I am as well as any man can be when he faces death for something he has not done." Johanna caught her breath at the hopelessness that filled Rob's tone. "Mistress, I know you mean well," he went on, his voice just soft enough to take the sting from his words, "but this night finds me lacking patience for sociable conversation. Hie and do what you must, then be gone with you."

Despite how his despair made Johanna's heart ache, the familiarity of his complaint shot through her. Aye, time had passed, but Rob had not changed. Just as he ever had done, he craved privacy in which to straighten his emotions.

At last, the bed was assembled. The men departed. When she heard the last footfall, Johanna began to lift her head. Mistress Alwyna pressed a hand on her arm in warning.

"Leave us to tend to Master Robert's needs in pri-*y*," the old woman commanded.

"If that is what you'd have me do," the captain replied, his voice filled with flat stubbornness, "then be aware that I must lock you within whilst you do it."

"You will not!" Mistress Alwyna's words were a shocked protest. "We are but women. We have no plots or tricks to play."

"Leave it be," Rob said. "He is commanded by the council to keep to the letter of the law and so he is doing."

"My pardon, Master Robert—" the captain started.

"I have had enough of your pardons," Rob replied, his voice as quiet as it was lifeless. "Be gone, locking the door as you must."

As the key once more grated in its slot, Mistress Alwyna claimed the basket. "Best you keep your voice low as you speak to him. Be swift at it, then come aid your maid, as I must speak to him, as well. Who knows but that officious prig isn't listening at the keyhole. He'll soon be demanding we leave, mark my words," she hissed, moving with Leatrice to the bed's side.

At last, Johanna raised her head. She stood beside three thick night candles, set atop their iron holders. The bed, yet bare of linens and blankets, those residing in the basket Leatrice now opened, had been placed along the wall before her. His back to them, Rob stood across the room at the narrow, slitted opening that had been carved from the stone wall.

Gone was the robe Johanna remembered from yesterday. Now he wore but his shirt, his dark hair curling lightly against its white collar. The garment clung to the powerful line of his shoulders, its hem reaching well past his hips to reveal brown chausses. Knee-length boots the color of rust were held in place by crisscrossing brown garters.

Between his pain and her relief at finding him unharmed, Johanna's eyes filled with tears. Forgetting that both Leatrice and Mistress Alwyna might witness what she did, she threw back her hood and crossed the short distance separating them. As she lay a hand on his shoulder, she whispered, "Rob?"

He whirled on her, his movement so swift, she stepped back, her heart falling. Yesterday's insults had destroyed all care for her in him. Now he would shout at her, revealing all as he damned them both against Katel's coming charges.

Instead of rage, it was amazement that filled his

gray eyes and softened the raw-boned line of his face. He looked at her uncovered hair, then to the green and brown gowns she wore beneath a maid's cloak. When his gaze again met hers, he shook his head slightly, as if he could not believe it was truly she who stood before him.

Johanna watched him in return, this time seeing him without hatred, bitterness, or even yesterday's terror to blind her. No longer did she seek the boy in him. Instead, she caught her breath in appreciation for the man he had become.

Dark brown hair clung to a clear brow, accentuating the high, harsh lines of his cheekbones. He wore his beard trimmed to a narrow line against his jaw, which only complimented its strength. Set over fine, pale gray eyes, his dark brows curved gently away from the narrow, straight line of his nose. Her gaze shifted to the scratches on his cheek, the ones he'd taken on her behalf. They were already fading.

Of a sudden, he smiled. As it had done yesterday, the motion of his mouth set those deep creases into his lean cheeks. Happiness brought warm lights to the cool gray of his eyes. He reached out to finger one of the wayward strands of bright hair that curled around her face.

"You came to me," he breathed in astonishment as the sounds of linen being stretched across a straw-filled mattress echoed in the room.

"How could I not?" she whispered, savoring the thrill that his touch sent through her. "Did you not come to me at the risk of your own life? I owe you nothing less than the same in return."

Happiness dimmed. He released her hair to gently caress a bruised spot on her face. "Is that all this is? A debt to be repaid?" As quiet as his words were, the pain that filled them was terrible, indeed.

The tears she'd thought to master spilled from her eyes. Against his need to hear what lay in her heart, she forgot they were not alone or that she was wed to another. Placing her hand against his heart, she stretched upward until she touched her mouth to his.

"Nay, I came because you are the man who holds my heart, the only man I will ever love, and my one, true husband," she murmured against his lips.

As Rob drew a sharp breath against her words, his mouth once more claimed hers. However brief the kiss, there was so doubting its message; he loved her still. Against the knowledge she had not destroyed what was most precious to her, yesterday's blazing heat returned. She clung to him for as long as she dared before retreating.

He watched her, joy dimming into confusion. "How can this be when you said—" he started.

She pressed her fingertips to his lips to still his words. "Forgive me. Yesterday I was a blind fool. If this day finds me yet a fool, at least I am no longer blind."

"You have my pardon without question or condition," he murmured as he caught her hand and pressed a kiss to her palm.

With a gasp at the shock of sensation this sent through her, Johanna tore free of him and stepped back. Only with distance did she realize what they'd done and what might have been revealed. She glanced over her shoulder to see if Mistress Alwyna had noted any of this. The woman's back was to them as she worked. Relief returned breath to her lungs and she turned back to Rob.

"You must tell me how I can help you," she said, keeping her voice low. "All I know is that Katel has contrived some way to prove I have committed adultery with you."

It was as these quiet words left her mouth that she understood what fate it was Katel planned for her and why the testimony of nuns did not matter.

She stared up at Rob in shock. "Mary save me," she cried, her voice at its normal level, "he will use his proofs to convince those who want your death that I am your lover. He intends that I should hang alongside you!"

Chapter Twenty-one

Stanrudde
an hour past Vespers
Ste. Agnes's Day, 1197

Rob stared down at Johanna, wanting desperately to disbelieve that Katel would do anything to harm his wife. Too late, he felt another of the spice merchant's traps close around him. It was not Johanna who was a blind fool, but himself. Katel meant his vengeance to be absolute. Not only would he destroy the man he hated, but the woman his nemesis loved. Still, Rob shook his head in refusal.

"What man makes himself into a cuckold when no wrong had been done?" he asked, his voice also lifting into the audible range. "Even if Katel wished to do so, he would have to fail. I haven't seen you in years."

"He is right, mistress," cried the petite, dark-haired maid. Drawn by Johanna's words, both she and Mistress Alwyna had turned from their task to look at them. "Am I not your witness that no adultery has been done? I have vowed to cry to all who ask that you have held tight to your virtue all the time I have known you."

Rob glanced at the one who offered this testimony, his gaze descending to the small bulge that indicated a child grew within her. There was no wimple to cover her head, meaning she was unwed. This was hardly a credible witness.

"Leatrice, you do not understand," Johanna cried. "No one will care what you say. They will not even care that I have been convent-bound these last months."

Convent-bound? Rob stared once more at Johanna, this time in the terrible fear that she had committed herself to God in order to escape Katel. If she had, she would remain forever beyond his reach, even after Katel's death, the dreaming of which had occupied much of his past few hours.

"Aye," Mistress Alwyna said, understanding sparking in her dark eyes, "I see how it could happen. Those beyond the walls care naught for what is true or false, only that they feel themselves avenged.

"Now," she went on, crossing her arms before her as a new edge sharpened her voice. "I think me I must ask what reason Master Katel has for making lovers of a virtuous wife, one whom he appears to adore, and the man who claims not to have seen her in years." There was enough steel in her words to say she'd do no more to aid them unless she was convinced by their reply that they did no sin.

"It is an old grudge, dating from my time in Master Walter's household," Rob replied, attempting a dodge to shield Johanna.

The old woman lifted her brows, that simple motion conveying she was not satisfied.

He glanced down at Johanna, only to have his heart take flight. Careless tendrils of red-gold hair lay gently against the delicate line of her cheeks. Beneath the wisps of gold that served as her brows, her eyes were very blue. This time it was no wish on his part that made him see affection for him in their depths. He smiled. If she had ever forgotten her love for him, it was forgotten no longer. With each and every look, she offered it to him once more.

As he watched, Johanna's gaze filled with the fierce refusal to name what they'd done as wrong. It was she, not he, who offered Mistress Alwyna her explanation. "Although I was promised to Katel, Rob and I, we . . . we traded vows, although we did so without witnesses."

She paused, leaving the woman to draw her own conclusions as to the consummation of those vows. "Since I have been wed to Katel, I have been naught but faithful."

"This is true," Leatrice added. "So I and any who have ever served Master Katel would say."

Rob barely heard the maid's supportive statement. Instead, the memory of sharing his oath with Johanna washed over him. There could have been no witnesses, not for them. Every bit of passion he'd known in that moment returned, bringing with it his need for her.

Johanna raised her gaze to meet his. New color stained her cheeks. It was not embarrassment's heat that seared her flesh. She, too, had lost herself in the shadows of the past. Need for him sparked in her eyes.

As had happened in the alley, the very essence of her wrapped itself around him. Without thought, he reached for her. She swayed toward him, her head lifting as her mouth softened, inviting his kiss.

Mistress Alwyna laughed, the sound low and warm. "Ach! You've just finished persuading me of your innocence. You'll ruin it all if you persist in what you are doing."

Her words startled Rob into a quick, backward step. His heels hit the wall behind him. Dismay flooded him. To what corner had control fled?

As long as the world believed Johanna was Katel's wife, touching her in the presence of others was disrespectful, not only to the witnesses, but to Johanna. Ready to spew an apology, Rob looked at the two women who had beheld his misbehavior. Amusement, not condemnation, touched their faces. He glanced to Johanna, with even stronger words at hand. Her face still glowed with desire for him, her gaze reflecting only disappointment at being interrupted.

Rob relaxed. How could he have ever believed time or circumstances might change their love or their need for each other? It was this that kept him from trading vows with any other woman. In his own mind, Johanna would always be his wife, his to touch and love whenever he willed it.

Need and determination forged themselves into one within him. She would become his wife, this time not in private, but in the eyes of the world; he would have no other woman, save she. Logic threw back its head and laughed in scorn. What chance had he of this? He was locked into a tower and facing death. Rob tried to ignore his inner voice as he looked at the old woman.

"If my heart is clean of sin, I will make no apologies for the affection I bear her," he said softly.

"Nor I, for what lies in my heart for him," Johanna added, this verbal confirmation of her affection sweet to Rob's ears.

"I did not expect it," Mistress Alwyna replied, then, with a decisive nod, her expression hardened and her voice lowered. "Now, I say we set our heads together and find a way to free you both from this morass. First, Master Robert, know you your man is already flying on his way to Lynn, having departed no later than an hour after you requested it. When he arrives there, he will meet the one I've called to protect him and your evidence on their return trip to Stanrudde."

"My thanks, mistress," Rob said, trying to let this good news encourage relief to grow in him.

The old woman shook her head. "I tell you, I yet reel at how Master Katel has fooled us all. Never would I have given him credit for such depth or such cruelty. How callously he hurts so many to wreak vengeance against two souls."

"Aye, so he does," Rob replied, his own heart burning with the willingness, if not the way, to see Katel pay for his crimes, "and he'd be swift to stir more violence in the populace, were he to learn we were plotting together against him. He'll not be content until I hang."

Johanna glanced up at him, sadness touching her face at the thought of his death. "Then no breath of this meeting dare escape, until a way to stop him has been found. Rob, tell me you know what it is he's done and how I can aid you." As she spoke, she stretched a hand toward him to punctuate her plea.

The desire to twine his fingers with hers was nigh on overpowering, so much so that he crossed his arms before him to stop himself. "This summer, Katel stole a goodly amount of grain from me. It was this that was released last even, done so in my name to make it seem as if I were dealing in outmarket wheat." Only as he spoke did the many threads of this plot finally begin to weave themselves into whole cloth.

"Dear God," he said, in begrudging admiration for the complexity of what Katel had wrought, "but only now do I see it all. This is why he welcomes the sheriff's investigation. You say he tells you he has contrived proof of your adultery?" he asked Johanna.

"Aye," she replied, yet trapped in confusion.

"Then, I am certain Katel yet has seed in store," he told them. "When the sheriff arrives to investigate, Katel will 'find' this proof of his. Whatever this is, whether parchment or token of some kind, it must not only connect Mistress Johanna to the grain, but reveal the location of his hidden stores. In all horror at what his wife and her lover have done, Katel will bear this proof to the sheriff, crying himself cuckolded. It is then that we both will hang."

"Pleading our innocence with our last breaths," Johanna mused.

With a glance at her, Rob again focused his attention on the wool merchant's dam. "Tell me, Mistress Alwyna, would the council consider allowing the poor cuckold the opportunity to sell what he has found on his own property?"

"Mother of God," the old woman breathed. "There's not a man among them, my son included, who wouldn't see that as just compensation for his shame and your sin. Do you think the sheriff would allow it?"

Rob shrugged. "If he does not claim it all for king and court, he will, taking a portion of the profit for himself. Not that this would overly trouble Katel. He must have already reaped himself a rich sum on what he sold last even. To add to that after our deaths would be the crowning bit of pleasure he accrues in having destroyed us."

"Nay, he cares naught that there is profit in the remaining *koren,*" Johanna said, her tone flat and hard. "It exists only to prove my adultery, for only if I am thusly shamed, do my father's properties fall into Katel's hands and not my son's."

Rage tore through Rob at the news that she'd borne Katel a child. With it came the image of Johanna lying beneath his enemy. He struggled to tame his jealousy, common sense reminding him that Katel was her husband in all eyes save his; Johanna had had no choice but to bed him.

Beside him, Johanna breathed out a long and almost anxious sigh. "I know now what I must do. The sooner I am returned home, the sooner I will find whatever it is he has hidden that ties me to that grain. Only in destroying it will Rob and I be safe." She turned as if she meant to depart that very minute.

Fear for her exploded in him, slaughtering his own selfish need to own her, body and soul, even during the years they'd been apart. He caught her by the arm to hold her in place. "You will not!"

"You must do better than that, Mistress Johanna," Mistress Alwyna said, speaking over his complaint. "Once you've discovered his hiding place, you must send to me, so my men can retrieve the wheat. If we leave Master Katel without that which he has stolen, one portion of his threat against you will be disabled. Meanwhile, Master Robert need only wait for his man and mine to return from Lynn with evidence of his innocence. Between us all, we will see this evil exposed."

"Are you mad?" Rob snarled at Mistress Alwyna. "You cannot expect Mistress Johanna to return to her husband, not when he seeks her death." He looked from one woman to the other, waiting for them to realize the impossibility of their intentions.

"Rob, if not me, then who?" Johanna freed herself from his grasp, her expression filled with her determination to protect him. "There is no one else to do what needs doing."

"Send yon maid," he demanded, pointing at the pregnant girl.

"Would that I could go in her stead, master," Leatrice replied, seeming not the least bit pleased at this reprieve. "However, I would get no farther than the gate. Because I dared to let Master Katel's seed take root in my womb, the master has dismissed me from his service, threatening me with violence should I attempt to return." If her fists clenched, Leatrice bowed her head in what might have been shame.

Only then did Rob recognize in her even features and dark coloring the sort of woman Katel had always favored. Her words eased his jealousy, reminding him that Katel had never found Johanna attractive, then filled him with a new rush of anger. While the spice merchant plotted to destroy his wife with a false charge of adultery, he indulged himself in that same sin, along the way making more of the bastards he so despised.

"That hypocrite!" Mistress Alwyna cried, her thoughts having followed his.

At this, the maid raised her head. It was not embarrassment that filled her, rather hatred's fire. She lowered her hand to caress her swollen abdomen. "Know you, Master Robert," she said, her voice harsh with promise, "I now offer you the same vow I gave my mistress. When the time is right, I will cry aloud your innocence for all the world to hear."

Although Leatrice might hope to have the opportunity to destroy the one who's used her, Rob doubted her ability to harm Katel. Nonetheless, it was hardly wise for a man in his particular state to refuse any offer of aid, no matter its likelihood. "My thanks for that, Leatrice. If you are without hearth, you will find a home at mine, that is, if you are willing to come to Lynn." He only hoped he lived long enough to fulfill the offer.

Against this kindness, the girl's need for vengeance dimmed and the fierce harridan transformed back into the child she was. Her lips trembled, her eyes filled. "My thanks, Master Robert. You are very kind. I beg pardon for earlier thinking you guilty of this crime."

"Given," he said with a small smile.

Mistress Alwyna set an arm around the girl's shoulder. "You need not go so far away to find a place, Leatrice. There is always room in my house for a stout-hearted servant like yourself."

"You do not mind that I have sinned?" Leatrice asked, her cheeks now bearing twin wet streaks.

"We are all sinners of one sort or another," the wool merchant's mother replied. "If Our Lord can forgive, so should we. I wager you've learned your lesson. Now, come," she said, turning the maid back toward the bed, "we have work to complete, and they have matters to discuss between them that are not for our ears.

"By the by, Master Robert," she called over her shoulder, "I've brought you your mantle and your pin, against the chill of this room. I'll leave it on the mattress, taking my son's with me as I depart."

"My thanks, mistress," he replied, waiting for the two of them to turn their backs. The moment they did, Rob dragged Johanna a step closer. "You cannot do this," he commanded, worry for her eating at his heart.

"You cannot stop me," she replied, her jaw set to its most stubborn angle. "Do not worry so. Katel dares do me no physical hurt, else he'll lose those properties he so desires. Besides, he has no reason to suspect that we have shared what we know and now plot against him. Nor will he ever know, not if revealing it places you in harm's way." She made these final words sound like a vow.

"You are mad if you think he'll stand idly by and let you destroy the vengeance he deems we both deserve." This was a fiery breath of rage.

Against his anger, Johanna's facade of bravado slipped to reveal the fear that lived beneath it. "Let me do as you know I must," she begged. "I pray you, do not send me away with only harshness between us, when I need you to bolster my courage. Let us not waste what little time we have left."

It was what she did not say—that she might fail and they would die—that killed Rob's remaining complaints. He tried to convince himself she was correct in thinking Katel would do nothing to hurt her. Just now, her husband was as trapped in his own plotting as were his victims. Unless the scheme played itself out to its finish, Katel would only reveal himself as the schemer.

Johanna lifted her chin to a cocky angle, once again hiding concern behind a bold expression. "No more complaints. If you had not wished to involve me, you would have reported the theft of your seed to your own sheriff and stayed in Lynn."

Rob forced himself to smile as he dropped his hand to finger the frayed edge of her green sleeve. It was odd to see her dressed in these worn gowns, dyed in the colors of her father's house. He could only assume she'd done so to avoid recognition as she sought him out.

Touching her sleeve was not enough. His hand rose, and he drew a fingertip down the elegant curve of her cheek. At his caress, pink again stained her skin. Catching a tendril of hair, he curled it around his finger. Her expression softened against his play.

"What," he chided, shaking his head, "do you think, I would let the world shun you because you have the misfortune to be tied to a thief? Nay, even after all these years, Katel rightly wagered I would do nothing to jeopardize you. I came to Stanrudde, hoping to find some way of resolving the issue so you would not be hurt."

"You came to protect me against the wrong my husband did," she murmured in pleased astonishment.

"Aye, so I did, only to drop blindly into his trap," he retorted, yet irate at himself for his idiocy.

A spark of amusement woke in her gaze. "And here I thought you brighter than that," she teased. "You, better than most, know what sort of man Katel is."

Pleased that he'd given her ease enough to laugh, even if her amusement was aimed at him, Rob's brows quirked up, his lips lifting. "It has been nigh on a score of years. In my dotage, I forgot the depths of rancor he bears me."

"Dotage, indeed," Johanna scoffed as she smiled at him. Her eyes sparkled, and the glow in her cheeks grew until the droplets that marked her skin seemed bright gold. "You are but two years my elder. Three and thirty is not old for a man."

"Think not?" With that, the joy of teasing her returned. His smile broadened. "Look you more closely," he bid her, his taunting tone urging her to remember their first kiss. "See you the gray that now streaks my beard?"

At his words, Johanna's eyes lightened to their

brightest blue. Her lips tightened, and her brows lowered into a mummer's overdrawn expression of skepticism. With her hands fisted on her hips, she leaned a little closer as if truly peering at his beard.

"Where?" Her voice was thick with disbelief. "I see not one thread of white amidst all that brown."

"Look closer, it is there," he insisted. "Here," he said, reaching for her hand, "let me show you where it is."

With a fine, rich laugh, Johanna stepped back from him. "I think not," she retorted, her face alive with pleasure at this game. "The last time you bid me look closer, the result was a brief period of heaven with naught but hell to pay after."

Once again, the key rasped in its slot. The latch groaned in complaint as it rose. Johanna gasped, yanking her cowl up over her head. "Rob," she cried softly, wanting more of a farewell than this.

Instead, Mistress Alwyna rushed to shove the basket into her arms. Leatrice pulled her back to the corner of the chamber. Rob dared no more than a final glance, praying she could read every bit of his care for her in that single look. Turning his back to the room, he stared out into the night.

"It is time you were done," Otto, son of Otfried, told the women.

"We were just finishing," Mistress Alwyna replied. "Come then, you two."

Rob listened to the sweep of skirts leaving the room. The door closed once more, the key turning, the latch moving to drop the bar in place. With Johanna gone, there was no further need for pretense. He leaned his forehead against the cold stones and closed his eyes in despair. The certainty that he would next see her standing beside him on the hangman's platform rose, then would not be dislodged.

Chapter Twenty-two

Stanrudde
Mid-August, 1180

It was to protect his fabulously expensive goods that Master Walter used the cellar in his home as his workroom. The only access was by a spiraling stairway set in the corner of the master's own bedchamber. Arched windows, so small not even a child could gain illicit entry, dotted the walls, and most days served as the only source of light.

If that meant it was always a little dim and cool in here, it wasn't vision that was most important to a spice merchant. Rob breathed deeply. The air was so thick with scents he could nigh on taste it.

His afternoon chores included, among other things, creating a bishop's special blend. It was the ingredients for this he now gathered. Once he'd combined the appropriate portions of *caneel,* ginger, and nutmeg, he would take it, and his other mixtures, to the apothecary's shop where they would be added to the herbs that finished them.

The riches around him were stored in myriad forms. Some had been left whole or in sticks, while others were powdered or ground, turned into chunks, cakes, or crystals. There were even flasks filled with spiced liquids. As he moved around the cellar, he ducked carefully beneath the stone arches that sprang from the line of pillars running down the center of the room. In attaining his present height, this low, curved ceiling had became a hazard. He'd hit his head more often than he wanted to remember.

When he had what he needed in his sectioned trough, he returned to the worktable. This was set in the southeastern corner of the cellar, where the kitchen abutted the house, leaving Rob far enough from Market Lane that he could barely hear the regraters. Here a pair of windows allowed a hot and humid August's day to tumble through thick, stone walls.

Caught in the sun's warm yellow glow, Rob's wooden funnel revealed a golden grain, the tool casting a shadow on the stack of small cloth sacks behind it. Reaching to the back of the table, he drew forward his scale. The day's honest light caught in its metal pan, the sudden glare blinding. As the tiny brass cup swung, Rob stared at the apparatus, the memory of how he'd come into his apprenticeship searing through him.

Guilt followed, so terrible and so deep it nigh on tore him in two. With every kiss he gave Johanna, with every touch, he betrayed the master he so loved, the same man who had given him his life and trade. The same man who lay dying overhead. As he did each time guilt struck at him, Rob fought it with the reminder that he and Johanna were well and truly wed.

It had taken several weeks of feigning interest in Church law before the abbot told him what he so dearly wanted to hear. Rob now believed that when a girl entered into a betrothal before her seventh year, as Johanna had done, she could later nullify it by informing her sire she no longer desired to wed her intended. This, Johanna assured Rob, she had done years ago.

When asked what constituted legitimate marriage, the abbot waxed eloquent, stressing that, although other churchmen protested to the contrary, it was the proper order of events that left the couple married. First came the expressed intent to wed. Once both had accepted the proposal of marriage, this must be followed by the exchange of vows. Only after these steps were completed did consummation sanctify the union. At the question of the number of witnesses needed to verify these proceedings, the abbot insisted none were necessary if all had been done as he'd stated.

As the war that raged in Rob once again retreated in uneasy truce, he leaned against the table in exhaustion. So went his days, his thoughts alternating between the two extremes, both truths refusing to be denied, each counteracting the other. Below it all lurked the certainty that, no matter what, he and Johanna would not be allowed to keep each other. The sunlight disappeared, dropping him into an abrupt darkness.

"Rob?"

At Johanna's soft call, Rob looked up from the table. As this cellar rose from ground level, rather than being recessed to a few feet below street level as many tradesmen's shops were, the window was of a height with her face and Johanna set her chin into the opening with ease.

This day she'd used a ribbon to loosely bind her hair at her nape before plaiting it. Strands escaped to curl, soft and golden-red, along the lift of her cheekbones and down the slender line of her neck. Her gowns were rose and cream, the colors complimenting her skin tone and making her eyes seem all the bluer.

Rob sighed at the love that filled her gaze. Doubt disappeared. Johanna and her care for him was all that mattered and all that held him limb to limb. Of a sudden, the thickness of a stone wall and the width of a table were more distance between them than he could bear.

And, equally as swiftly, it was entirely too little distance. Worry quirked into existence, guilt trying to creep back in upon its heels. They dared not be witnessed together.

"You shouldn't be here," he warned her, his voice low. She only looked at him, her expression still and sad.

Sudden panic shot through him. "Your father?" he demanded.

A shake of her head assured him that her father yet lived. "He is awake. Master Colin has been closeted with him for the past hour."

The corners of her mouth drooped. "Oh Rob, Papa has called for Katel to return. Helewise is taking me to the tailor's to fit my wedding attire," she breathed in agony. "What are we going to do?"

A wholly new panic rose in Rob. In his certainty that he was doomed to fail, he'd put off telling her sire of their private vows; he wanted to hold onto the dream of keeping Johanna as his own for as long as he could. Now the time for revelation had come.

He closed his eyes and swore himself to success. Johanna was his. How could he let anyone else, especially Katel, have her? As he opened his eyes once more, he freed a long, slow breath.

"What is there to do, save tell your sire we are already wed," he said softly.

"Mistress Johanna?" Helewise's impatient call rose from the courtyard.

She gave a single, frightened cry. "I am so afraid I will lose you."

"Never, save through death," Rob replied, his voice deepening with his promise.

He extended a hand, his fingers just reaching to the window's ledge. She stretched her hand within to catch his. At the touch of her fingers against his, the courage he needed filled him. His heart burned with the conviction that Master Walter could not part them.

"Take heart, knowing I love you. You are all in the world to me," he vowed to her.

"As you are to me," she breathed in return.

"Johanna!" In her irritation, Helewise forgot to use the appropriate title. "Where are you?"

Johanna tried to pull free of his grasp. Rob squeezed her hand to hold her in place. "I sleep in the warehouse this night as I did the last." It was an intense and hurried hiss. "Come to me."

The memory of their passion the night before brought a smile to her lips. "If I can." Then, she was gone.

As the sun again streamed in upon him, Rob stared at the scale. Johanna had said her father was awake just now. He turned and started for the nearby stairway. Although the thought of telling Master Walter how his generosity had been repaid terrified him, the need to keep Johanna as his bore Rob up the stairs and into Master Walter's bedchamber.

It was as bright in here as the cellar was dim. Day's light streamed in through the wide window, making the rich bedcurtains glow in jeweled tones of red and green, while the carving upon the spice merchant's bedposts stood out in sharp relief. Master Colin had set his stool close to the bed's side, his voice urgent and low as he conversed with the dying man.

Rob could not afford to hesitate, else his nerve would vanish. "Master Walter," he rudely interrupted, "I must speak to you about Johanna." The moment the words flew from his lips, his fingers chilled to the temperature of ice. His heart pounded in his chest as if he'd run a mile or more.

Master Colin turned sharply on the short seat to look at him. "I think that would be wise," the apothecary said, disappointment touching his gaze. "But, before you do, know that I have been to the abbey, albeit on my own business and not seeking after yours.

The abbot mentioned the odd questions you have asked him."

Rob's heart went from racing to a dead stop in his chest. Shame made his throat thicken. They knew, the two men he loved most in the world knew what he had done.

"Master Colin also tells me he thinks he saw Johanna last even, passing through his yard," Master Walter said from the bed. His voice was beyond tired and barely loud enough to be heard. "I suspect you'd best come and spill your tale, lad."

It was the sorrow in his mentor's tone that sent shame spiraling even higher in Rob, until it stung at his eyes. He crossed the room, coming to a stop at the bed's side, Master Colin rose from his stool and set a hand upon Rob's shoulder. His touch was neither comforting nor condemning.

"Come, then, and take my place," he said gently.

Rob settled his long frame on the stool as best he could, then glanced into the bed. Against his will, his gaze flew to the growth that clung to Master Walter's arm. He caught back his gorge. Now the size of a babe's fist, the suppurating thing was more than ugly. He forced himself to look into the spice merchant's face.

This was by far the worse. Master Walter's illness was eating him alive, making him a wraith before his passing. Rob swore he was so thin he could see through him. Ah, but if the man's eyes were sunk deeply into their sockets, enough life yet filled their icy depths to show Rob what he did not wish to see.

"Tell me what I am thinking is not true," his master gently pleaded.

Shame warred with Rob's desperation to own Johanna. The outcome was that the truth fell bluntly from his lips. "I love her. We are married, she and I."

Master Walter stared at him. The silence that followed was worse than any scream or threat or blow could have been. Rob sat still and cold upon his stool, waiting for whatever punishment God deemed his due for having so betrayed his master.

"After how I have loved you, how could you have done this to me?" The words left the spice merchant's lips in an aching, disbelieving breath.

Rob swallowed. All was lost, not only Johanna, but his master's love as well. His heart broke. There was no answer he could make to this question.

"Some of this lies upon my shoulders, Walter," Master Colin offered, his voice quiet as well. "Where you have been too often away, I was here and saw the affection develop between them. Thinking it naught but an innocent friendship, I did nothing to stop it."

The expression in Master Walter's eyes was as flat and dead as he would soon be. "Nay, Colin, there is no one to blame, save myself, for I know my daughter's nature better than any. I was wrong to keep her unmarried for so long, dallying in the vain hope Katel's sire would tire of my excuses and find another for his son." He turned his exhausted gaze on his youngest apprentice. "Rob, I think we must needs discuss your future."

It took all Rob's will to continue to face the man he'd so hurt. "What future can I have save death?"

"Would that it might be so easy for you," the dying man returned with but the slightest bitter edge to his voice. "Unfortunately, I am the only one for whom that escape is possible."

"But," Rob insisted in confusion, "I must die if Johanna is to wed Katel, else she is a bigamist. We are married, she and I."

Master Walter shook his head. "Nay, lad, you are not, and no churchman can make you so."

"But, we vowed, we . . . we laid as man and wife," he breathed in one last attempt at holding tight to the promise he'd made to Johanna.

Master Colin crouched down at his side. "Rob, you are listening with your heart. Listen with your head, and hear what your master is telling you. Only at great expense could you prove yourself wed to Johanna. She must marry Katel, no matter what the two of you have done."

Rob glanced from man to man in growing dismay and understanding. Both of them were worried that he and Johanna might truly be wed. Despite that, they meant to take her from him. Aye, and they would succeed because he was but ten and seven, lacking the family connections or the wealth to stop them. Fed by his helplessness, outrage woke. They were going to steal Johanna from him so they might give her to that cruel whoreson!

"Nay!" he shouted, slamming a fist into the mattress. "You will not do this."

For just that moment, the powerful Walter of Stanrudde reappeared behind the death mask. The spice merchant's eyes chilled to their coldest blue, and his jaw jutted out in rage. "Do you dare to shout at me when it is you who have sinned?" he flared back, only to cough in the effort it took to raise his voice.

This killed Rob's anger, leaving only despair behind it. It mattered naught what he did or said. Nothing would change what happened here. Guilt again settled on his shoulders, this time because of how he failed Johanna. In daring to trespass where he knew he should not go, he had not only destroyed her, he'd made certain that Katel would hate and hurt her. It was the need to find some way to shield her from the wrong he'd done that spurred him to speech.

"Nay, you must listen to me," he insisted, his voice hoarse with tears. "You cannot give her to Katel. He hates me. When he knows what she has done, he'll only hurt her."

"Do you think I do not know that?" Master Walter said in harsh retort.

"If you know, then how can you wed her to him?" Rob demanded.

Pain of the heart joined pain of the body in clinging to the gaunt angles of Master Walter's face. "Years ago, I put my name upon a contract, and there it stands to this day, mocking me even as it demands I do as I agreed. Every time I think on the man Katel has become, I am reminded of how I traded my daughter's life for something I might just as easily have earned by mine own efforts."

He paused to cough once more. "No matter what my will, Rob, I cannot change what I have done. She must marry Katel. Rather than resist me, aid me in shielding her from him."

That brought Rob upright on his stool. "How?"

Master Walter let his head sag against his bolsters. "Speak for me, Colin; my strength is gone."

Yet squatting at Rob's side, the apothecary did as his friend bid. "Knowing as he does that death is upon him and that Katel will not have you here, Master Walter has already arranged for you to go to Lynn, where you will be apprenticed to the grossiers' trade under Master Wymund."

Once again, shame ate at Rob as he glanced in guilty gratitude at his master. He should have trusted that Master Walter would not leave him homeless. So too, should he have understood the intent of the many questions the grossier had asked him when that man stopped in Stanrudde last month to bid a final farewell to an old friend.

"However, in the light of what is revealed this day, there are conditions you must accept before he will send you into this new apprenticeship." Master Colin paused, then laid a comforting hand upon Rob's shoulder as if he meant to soften what he would say. "The first is that you must leave within the hour, before Johanna returns. Johanna will be told that you were offered coins to leave her and that you accepted."

Horror tore through Rob. "Nay!" It was a raw-edge cry. Tears filled his eyes as he reared up off the stool, stumbling away from the bed in outraged refusal. They would not only take Johanna from him, but her love, as well. "Is this what you call protection? Nay, I will not do it! What you ask will only hurt her."

"Rob, once more you think with your heart," Master Colin chided. He came to his feet and reached out, his gesture a plea for understanding. "She must marry Katel, and she cannot go into that estate mourning you. If she hates you, it will help to satisfy Katel's wounded pride when he discovers she is maiden no longer."

Although this would, indeed, put a layer of protection between Johanna and the man they'd have her wed, Rob yet shook his head in refusal. To bear Johanna's hate was worse than dying, worse even than betraying his master. "You cannot ask this of me. I love her."

"For the moment," Master Walter said, his voice thready and weak. "You are young. The memories will fade, and you'll soon find another to hold your heart."

Rob only shook his head. Master Walter was wrong. His love for Johanna, and hers for him, would last beyond this awful plot of theirs.

"Finish, Colin," the spice merchant urged, "I must soon sleep."

"The second is more warning than condition. Should you ever return to Stanrudde, thinking to tempt Johanna from her vows to Katel, all the protections that Master Walter has created to shield her from him will be removed. In doing this, Master Walter will encourage Katel to treat her as many men treat their adultering spouses. Against this same fate, be you warned not to speak of what has occurred between you and her."

Whatever resistance remained in Rob now drained from him. He stared at his master in utter defeat. "You are saying that if I persist in claiming we are married, or make any attempt to change the way you would have matters, you will allow Katel to abuse her. Even kill her?"

"My daughter has betrayed me, just as you have," Johanna's father returned, although there was only sadness in his voice. "In doing so, she forfeits my protection. It is my love for her that causes me to extend it to her yet again. If she betrays her husband, thus me, a second time, then she must bear the consequences of her actions."

Hurt seethed in Rob as these conditions wrapped themselves around him, demanding he do as they say in order to protect Johanna. "What choice have I?" he asked flatly.

"No more than I," his master replied with equal resignation.

As the girl and life he so loved slipped from him, Rob reached out to hold one piece of it close. "Arthur must come with me," he said. "Katel has no more fondness for him than he does for me."

Walter gave an approving nod. "I thought you would not be separated. Wymund has already agreed to take him. Arthur will join you once he has returned from his travels."

The spice merchant drew a deep breath; the blankets barely rose with the motion. "Now, come and bid me your last farewell. Ach, lad, but I am going to miss you."

The hurt his master did him urged Rob to deny this request. But, where his heart might ache, logic would not let him shirk responsibility for what he'd done. In the end, Rob knelt at the bed's side.

The dying man reached out to draw a bony hand

along his apprentice's cheek. It was a brief, but gentle, caress. As his arm fell back to the bed, the corners of Master Walter's mouth lifted. "Do you know how often I have wished you were mine own son?"

It was a statement of love. It was a statement of forgiveness. It was more than Rob could bear. Despite the horrible wrong he'd done, his master loved him still.

Fisting his hands into the blankets, he buried his face into the bedclothes. He lay there, beyond tears or protest, and prayed that he might die. Hell would be easier to survive than this.

Master Walter threaded his fingers into Rob's hair, his touch a father's caress. "Remember always that I will be watching from heaven. Make me proud. Succeed, reaching the heights that I know you can."

Tears filled Rob's eyes. He raised his head and caught his master's hand to press the skeletal fingers to his lips. "Forgive me," he begged, tears scorching his cheeks as they fell. "I am so sorry. Pray God, you forgive me," he whispered.

"You know I already have," Master Walter replied, his heart's own moisture puddling in the deep hollows beneath his eyes. "Colin, go with him as he gathers his belongings. He can leave no sign for Johanna that might explain what happened here."

Chapter Twenty-three

Stanrudde
two hours after Vespers
Ste. Agnes's Day, 1197

Although Mistress Alwyna offered a man to escort her home, Johanna refused. The fewer who knew who she was and where she'd been, the better chance she and Rob had of holding onto their lives. Thus it was alone and unprotected that she left the cart at the church only a few lanes distant from her father's home. Memories of her attack the previous day set her fancy to conjuring up ruffians in every shadow. With fear nipping at her heels, she pulled her cowl low over her brow and hurried around the corner.

This night was just as dry and clear as the preceding day, the air so frigid it stung at her nose. Having risen hours ago, the moon already hung high overhead, a nearly complete silver disk adrift in a milky sea of stars. Beyond a dog's distant bark, there was no sound; darkness had only deepened the unnatural quiet that held Stanrudde in its grip.

Something moved, rustling at the side of the lane. Johanna shot a nervous glance toward the sound, then caught her breath. Fear forgotten, she stopped to stare. This was Katel's handiwork, done without care or concern for whom he hurt.

The moon's unearthly light poured into the front of a ruined shop, rendering plastered walls the pallid hue of a dead man's complexion. Like a sightless eye in a ravaged face, splintered shutters hung from a torn wall, no longer shielding the workshop's interior from the street.

Anger rose in her. He deserved to have his evil exposed to the world for such cruelty. Ah, but the moment she thought this, outrage dimmed into a mother's worry for her child.

If the world might shun her because she was tied to a thief, it would do far worse to her Peter once folk learned of his father's evil. Everyone would say her son's blood was tainted. How could she expose Katel, knowing it would hurt her son?

In the next moment, her eyes narrowed in scorn at herself. What a fool she was. They'd say the same of Peter were his dam to be hanged for adultery and grain speculation. Thoughts of the future were better left for later, after she'd done what she had to do.

There was another rustling, this time from behind her. A man's voice, barely louder than a whisper, carried in the still air. Johanna's heart took flight, spurring her legs to do the same and she sprinted down the lane.

Since she had no desire to go blindly into another confrontation with Katel, she avoided the gate. Far better that she first probed the servants, divining what she could of his temper and his plans. To hide her reentry, it was to the apothecary's shop she went, once more pushing past his bushes to trespass through that man's private yard.

Passing the distillery's hearth, she rounded the kitchen's corner. Light escaped from under the cooking chamber's door. With it came the muffled sounds of work being done; Wymar had reclaimed his domain.

Johanna reached for the latch. Wymar would also know what was what in the house; he always did. A jumble of smells greeted her as she opened the door, the eclectic mix somehow managing to work itself into a delicious whole. As Philip before him had done, it was ofttimes Wymar's skill that tempted men to part with coins for the goods Stanrudde's spice merchant sold. Her stomach rumbled in reaction to the aroma, reminding her she'd had only a bit of cheese and meat over the course of the day.

Pulling the door shut behind her, Johanna glanced around the small chamber. If most of the food stocks were still missing, the kitchen tools once again hung upon the walls, the pots and platters in their places. Small lamps sat in each corner of the table, no more than bowls filled with rendered fat in which a bit of burning wick floated. Still, their oily brightness added to the fire's cheery light, making it possible for Wymar to labor in these dark hours.

The cook stood at the table, a sieve, through which he'd been forcing meat and vegetables to create a sauce, dangling from his hand. Already a big man, a taste for his own dishes had made him bigger still, until it was a nine-month babe he looked to carry in his belly. His pale hair clinging to a steam-dampened forehead, he stared at her until she threw back her hood.

Relief woke in his blue eyes, followed by a welcoming smile. "Mistress! I did not hear the gate bell ring. Where have you been? We could hardly believe it when we returned to the kitchen to find you'd disappeared."

His cry brought his two young scullery lads, Elyas and Rauf, upright on their pallets. Together, they split no more than a baker's dozen worth of years between them. Their faces glowed in the fire's light, the grime that usually covered them washed back to a fine line at the edges of their cheeks. Having already retired for the night, their scrawny chests were bare beneath their mantles-turned-blankets, their shirts and tunics folded neatly aside for the morrow.

"I have been praying," Johanna lied with ease, then smiled to cover the coming falsehood. "You are working too hard if you missed that bell. I was so hungry I came here first without thinking to ask. Do you know if Master Katel is home this even?" She came forward to lean against his table's edge.

Wymar's pleased expression soured. "Aye, mistress. Or, rather, he was when I was last within."

Years of experience translated both his words and expression for Johanna. "Ale or wine?" she asked. Ale made Katel mean, wine made him sleep.

"Wine, mistress."

Johanna hid her sigh of relief. Katel would sleep then. Now, if only luck held, she might begin her prying this very moment. She hesitated, uncertain how to broach the subject of Theobald to the cook.

"Hungry, are you?" Wymar asked. Letting his sieve fall into the pot, he turned to cut a slice from the only ham hanging above the fire. This he set on the table, then took the smallest of his mixing bowls and ladled broth into it from the three-footed pot that stood amid the coals. When he was done, he placed both meat and bowl before her on the table. "Eat and enjoy, adding to your prayers the hope for better next year."

Johanna gratefully lifted the bowl to her lips. The rich aroma of the clear soup filled her senses and she didn't set it aside until she'd drunk the last of it. Picking up the slice of ham, she took a bite, yet trying to devise some clever way of asking over her husband's agent. There wasn't one. At last, she simply spewed the question.

"What of Theobald?"

So unexpected an inquiry brought Wymar's brows up high onto his forehead. "Well now, if it wasn't his departure that brought me back into the kitchen in the first place. I had to fix oatcakes for his packet. He and two others left here on the master's business.

They'll not be back before the morrow, if that's what you're asking."

Johanna smiled. This was a gift, indeed. She now owned both the time and freedom to search the house.

Wymar turned back to his sieve and sauce. "I'll tell you, I am more than thankful to be returning to my own hearth," he said in amiable conversation. "Cooking over that inner one is no easy feat. The hood ever gets in your way."

"So you are back in here to stay, are you?" However casual her probe, her need to hear the answer was urgent, indeed. Katel had once protected his own stores against the riot he meant to foment. If he'd given Wymar permission to return, it meant he planned no further unrest, and Rob was safe, at least, for the moment.

"Aye, thanks be! Those lads'll be toting the rest of my supplies back here come the morrow. The master says that with that foreigner in custody, the threat of violence is gone. I only pray they hang him, so we might return to living as best we can in these troubled times." The cook's voice descended into spite, which was the closest to vicious he ever came.

Confidence soared in Johanna. This was perfect! Content that Rob was trapped and his wife was ignorant, Katel had celebrated by drinking himself to sleep, while Theobald was gone.

Johanna turned to leave, eager to begin her search. The upended bathing tub stood just beyond the door's frame, tipped against the wall so it would dry. All of her gratitude over this morn's kindness returned. This was followed by shame at not having offered Wymar his due when she first stepped past the doorway. She turned back to him to right her wrong.

"Wymar, I think it is to you that I owe a thousand thanks for this morn and its many gifts."

The cook's gentle smile returned. "Do not give them all to me, as there's plenty of places to spread them. Why, if it weren't for young Elyas, over there, you'd have had naught to wear. That's the clever lad who found you those gowns, such as they are."

Johanna turned her gaze on the younger of the two boys, an unremarkable child with thin brown hair and wide eyes of the same color. "Was it you, then?"

When he shyly nodded, she smiled at him. "You are a miracle worker, child. I'd have sworn there wasn't a single garment in the house that would fit me. Wherever did you find them?"

"They were in the green chest, the one in which we keep the ewers," he said, his face solemn as he let this astonishing fact fall from his lips.

He'd found them in one of her dowry chests? Johanna stared at him in disbelief. "You must be mistaken," she said in automatic rejection of something so impossible.

"Now, lad," Wymar chided, "what sort of tale is this to be telling the mistress? You know the only things kept in those chests are serving pieces and table linens. My pardon, mistress, but he has a way of making the everyday into something a wee more dramatic."

Elyas's face took on the indignant expression common to all children whose elders refuse to believe what they know is the truth. "It is no tale! The chest is where I found them. I knew they were there because I saw the master put them there."

"What?" The words left Johanna in a soft breath of amazement. Katel had put these gowns into one of her dowry chests? Her misgivings about Elyas's claim dissolved in new interest. "When did you see the master do this?" her certainty that this had to do with Katel's plot making her voice sharp.

At this seeming rebuke, the lad's confidence dissolved into a start of guilt. His lips trembled. Tears came to cling to his thick fringe of eyelashes.

"It was before Christmastide and I did not mean to spy on the master," he wailed. "Rauf had taken the last platter, and I was supposed to tell the maids it was time to remove the table cloths, but the master's cat went beneath the table. I only meant to play with him for a moment."

Johanna crossed the room and knelt beside his pallet to stroke his cheek. "Do not cry, mannikin," she bid him. "I am not scolding, and you've done no wrong. Can you tell me exactly what it was you saw the master do?"

Still sniffling, the boy looked up at her, his eyes widening in fear, as if he wasn't certain he should reveal what he knew. Johanna ran her fingers through his mussed hair in a soothing caress. His face relaxed enough to let his mouth move.

"The master came into the hall with Theobald. They thought the room was empty, not knowing I was under the table. Theobald emptied the green chest, and the master looked at the gowns, saying he was certain they'd fit you. After that, they put the garments in the chest, then put it all back on top of them. So, when Wymar said there was nothing to fit you in all the house, I remembered—"

Tears slipped down Elyas's cheeks. He wiped them away with the back of his hand. "I shouldn't have watched, but I was afraid to tell them I was there."

"How can this be?" Wymar protested, coming to stand at the end of this lad's pallet. The way he set his hands onto the roll of fat that served for his hips said he yet doubted the boy's truthfulness. "If the gowns had been there, someone would have seen them."

"If no one did, then I think me I should have a look and see why not," Johanna said, working to keep the excitement from her voice. How strange, nay how fitting, it would be were Katel's exposure to come because a lad sought to do her a kindness. "Elyas, would you dress and come with me? I'd have you show me exactly where you found these."

The boy glanced to his direct superior. At Wymar's irritated nod, he reached out for his stack of clothing. "I have to come right back," he warned his mistress as he pulled on his shirt, "else I'll be too tired to work on the morrow."

Chapter Twenty-four

Stanrudde
the hour of Compline
Ste. Agnes's Day, 1197

Knowing just how dark it would be in the hall, Johanna borrowed one of Wymar's lamps. With no breeze to threaten the flame, she and Elyas crossed the courtyard, bathed in a steady circle of light. Johanna glanced up at the house her sire had built. Moonlight glowed bright white on its square corner blocks and turned the knobby gray rocks between them into pewter.

No longer did looking on this dwelling stir emotion in her. If her love and pride had been gone for years, her hatred and bitterness were more recent departures. Now, it was just a pretty house that belonged to someone other than herself.

The door in the forebuilding was already barred for the night. She tapped gently at the wooden panel. The one who answered, Dickon by name, was a manservant Johanna knew only a little, as he'd been employed but a few months prior to her departure for the convent.

The lamp threw sallow light onto the bold planes of his face, making his eyes into naught but harsh gleams set in pockets of darkness. He watched her for a long moment, then shook his head. "You should not come within, mistress. The master is in strange spirits this night."

"He is not sleeping?" she asked, her disappointment that Katel's overindulgence would fail her on this of all nights greater than her surprise at his warning.

"He is, but I cannot say he will stay so," the man replied. The air was so cold his breath clouded before him as he spoke. He drew his mantle more tightly around him. "Twice, we've laid him in his bed, only to have him return to the hall. Best you stay the night in the kitchen and come again on the morrow, when the wine has cleared from his brain." He began to close the door on her.

Johanna caught it with her hand. "I fear what I need from the hall cannot wait," she insisted.

He hesitated, then shrugged. "As you will, mistress."

As Dickon stood aside so they might pass, Johanna urged Elyas inside before her, then followed the boy, her lamp held high to illuminate the stone steps. As the door shut a gust of air rushed up the stairs, setting the lamp's flame into a wild dance, casting gyrating images upon the walls around them. Elyas cried out in fright, hastening up the stair as if the devil were on his heels. Johanna followed him in, entering the big room on the dying echo of his cry.

Save for the crackle and hiss of the fire on the hearth, the room was quiet. The unusual thickness in the darkness at the western wall said that was where the foodstuffs from the kitchen now sat. The firelight gleamed on the bare wood of the table before that wall, marking where Wymar had worked while trapped within the house.

Although the men within the room had laid out their pallets for the night, they were not yet abed. Instead, they'd drawn benches near to the fire to better enjoy its warmth. Elyas's cry had stirred them all into peering over their shoulders to see who it was that came.

With their faces caught half in darkness, half in light, there was no reading their expressions. As Dickon crossed the hall behind her to join his comrades, Johanna scanned their backs, one gray tunic after another, seeking Watt from among them. He was missing.

"You shouldn't have let her in." Syward, one of the older men and the longest employed, whispered harshly. The fire's light made his cropped and grizzled hair glow white and traced black along the deep creases marking his face. "You heard what the master said about her."

If Dickon only shrugged, Syward's words set Johanna's nerves to jumping. Did this mean Katel had already begun her denouncement? If so, then there was no time to waste.

"Come, Elyas," she said, keeping her voice low as the tense silence returned to the room, "show me where you found these gowns, but quietly so."

They crossed the hall to the corner where the dividing wall that split the room in twain met the outer stone wall. It was here that her mother's chests sat, just as they had from the first day they entered this house. Night cloaked the big wooden boxes. If it was too dark to see which one was green and which was brown and blue, the one bound in brass gave itself away, its metal trim catching the light from her lamp as she drew nearer.

As she passed it, Johanna glanced at the bedchamber door. It was ajar. Once she'd set her bowl upon the brass-bound chest, she returned to carefully pull it a little more tightly into its frame.

"They were on the very bottom, mistress," Elyas whispered to her when she rejoined him. He was already kneeling before the green chest.

As he lifted the lid, Johanna lowered herself beside

him to stare past the bowls and ewers the chest contained. She shook her head in disappointment. "Elyas, I can see the chest's bottom through these pieces. No one could have missed seeing that there were gowns in here."

"Nay, mistress," he insisted, "they were on the bottom that is under this bottom."

Johanna frowned at him. She knew this chest as well as she knew herself. "This chest has no false bottom."

The boy loosed a martyred sigh at discovering she was yet another disbeliever, then reached in to lift out a bowl. "I will show you."

Not willing to risk that he knew what she did not, Johanna helped him empty the chest, taking care to see that she made no noise in setting aside the dishware. Curiosity brought the men to stand a respectful distance behind them. When all the crockery was out, Elyas reached in and caught his small fingers around a tiny lip in the wood. The bottom of the chest shifted, then came free.

As he brought up the thin sheet of wood, Johanna leaned over the box's edge. The lamp's light speared into its murky depths, finding something smooth and almost white at the newly revealed base. Parchment.

Both excitement and terror filled her as she reached in and lifted out the small stack of sheepskins. Setting them in her lap, she raised the first one into the light to see what lay upon it. A strong, even script, one she did not recognize, filled the page. "To my dearest love, Johanna," she murmured as she read aloud the starting line, but what followed it made her continue in silence.

Sickness grew, and she gave thanks that none of those behind her could read. This was supposed to be a love note from Rob to her, describing a recent tryst as one yet caught in the throes of adoration might do to his lady love. However, instead of scribing words of love, Katel had indulged himself in re-creating every obscene and sinful act he could imagine.

The signature at its end was Robert of Lynn, proving Katel had known where Rob was, even if she hadn't. There was no seal, but then, what fool would affix a seal to a note that went to his married lover? The date set beneath Rob's forged name was ten years past.

Setting this one aside, she looked at the next missive. It was dated six months later, and the next was six months after that. All of these were periods of time when Katel was away on his fair circuit.

She skimmed them, one grotesque missive after the other, then sighed in disappointment. Nowhere was the stolen wheat directly mentioned. Instead, the last note, dated just before she'd retired to the convent, talked about how the sale of something she held for Rob would generate great wealth. Since Rob was a grossier, and grain had been illegally sold in Stanrudde, the sheriff would not need to make a great leap in putting the two together.

Nor was there any mention of where the seed was located, only that she held something in store for Rob. As it was she who leased and collected the rents of the properties that would be her son's inheritance, it was an easy assumption that she had access to any and all of the buildings. Once again, the broad implication connected her to the stolen seed, even if the shire's lawman might need to make a long search before he found it.

Once again, Johanna stared at the filthy letters that lay in her lap. Her skin crawled. She looked to the hearth. If she still had no idea as to where the wheat was, she would see these things destroyed. Once they were gone, she'd restore the chest and the crockery, with Katel none the wiser.

Coming to her feet, she went to the hearth and shoved the whole mass of them onto the burning logs.

For a moment, the flames spread away from their edges, as if even the fire was disgusted at having to consume such obscenities. The need to wash her hands grew. She rubbed them against her skirt, but her fingers still felt stained by the wickedness that had filled those parchments.

If Elyas thought nothing of joining her at the hearth, the menservants were not so bold. They stopped at the outer edge of the fire's light, curious, but not willing to intrude. Slowly, the flames caught hold of the parchments' edges and the reek of burning skin filled the air.

As Johanna watched the skin sear, a set of lines leapt out at her from the topmost one: "*. . . rigid with passion as I remember how pure your skin is, your breasts are as white as milk against the green moss that carpets our riverbank. As the willow branches close about us, I see again how you spread your thighs to me . . .*" As it browned, those horrible words were scorched out of existence. Only when they were gone did the meaning behind the description penetrate past her horror.

In each missive there had been talk of a riverbank, one where willows stood and moss carpeted the ground. The image of the bank she and Rob had once called their own woke, complete with willows and moss. She frowned in thought. Was it possible Katel meant that same place? How? He could know nothing of their affection for it.

From deep in her memory came the recall of Katel and a maid coming to tryst upon that same stretch. Triumph rose with this inner picture. Katel had no idea of what she and Rob had done there, he was but placing the description of the bank in the missive to draw those he wished to lead in the right direction.

With a quick breath, Johanna turned to stare in the general direction of Stanrudde's watergate. In that instant she knew where the seed was stored. Katel had put it in her father's first warehouse, the same building that now stood derelict and broken, so badly in need of work that she'd let it stand empty, thinking it too old to be worth repairing. She nigh on laughed out loud in her excitement. Now all she needed was a trustworthy messenger to bear the information to Mistress Alwyna.

She turned to look at the men behind her, only to again curse the hatred that had kept her blind for so long. As they were connected to Katel and Theobald, she'd had nothing to do with them. The only one she trusted wasn't here.

"Where is Watt this night?" she asked in the forlorn hope he would soon be returning. She kept her voice low against the possibility Katel was not as settled into slumber as she hoped.

It was Syward who answered her. "Gone, mistress, with Theobald to Lynn."

"To Lynn?" she retorted with a start of fear. Her words echoed back to her in the quiet room. "Why do they go to Lynn?"

The man shrugged. "It has to do with that Lynnsman they have over in the tower. Theobald is off to retrieve the man's ledgers for the council."

Johanna stared at him. That wasn't at all what Theobald did. He went to make certain that Rob's man never retrieved the evidence Rob needed to prove his innocence.

Triumph dissolved into new and desperate urgency. If that evidence did not come, then all that stood between Rob and the gallows was if Mistress Alwyna removed that wheat from the warehouse. That was, if it truly was there.

Panic grew. If not Watt, then who? Again she scanned the men and, again, she rejected them. Even if they did not like their employer, they still served their bellies. She'd not trust them to do something for her when it might mean they'd jeopardize their position here.

She looked down at the boy beside her. Elyas was watching the flames gnaw at the skins, his nose pinched shut against the smell. Nay, not him, he was too young. Ah, but Wymar was not.

As she identified her messenger, she needed to go to the kitchen that very moment. Johanna glanced to where the skins now writhed upon the flames. Not one scrap of these parchments could remain unconsumed for Katel to find. Her gaze darted to the emptied chest. She couldn't leave the chest open and unpacked. But restoring it would take too long! Once again, she looked at the child.

To ease her panic, she would send him first, then follow in a few moments. She squatted down next to the lad. "Elyas," she said, keeping her voice low and catching his thin shoulders in her hands to give emphasis to what she would tell him. "Run you to Wymar, saying to him that I need his aid in a little boon."

He blinked at her, returning her gaze with his own solemn look. "What should he do for you?" he asked. With his fingers yet tight on his nose, his voice was stuffy.

"It is simple, but it must be done this very night. Wymar should go to Jehan the Wool Merchant's house and ask for that man's mother. He should say that he comes on my behalf, then he must tell Mistress Alwyna that what she seeks she may find in the broken warehouse near the watergate. Can you remember that?"

He nodded and released his hold on his nose. " 'What she seeks she may find in the broken warehouse near the watergate,' " he repeated.

"Good lad," she said, turning him toward the door. She gave him a gentle shove to set him on his way. "Now run you and tell him what I said."

Elyas stopped and turned back to look at her, his hands now twisting in his tunic. "It is very dark, mistress. Wymar would be afraid." His own fear echoed in his words. "Must he go this night and by himself?"

It took every ounce of her will not to scream at him that he must run from the hall for her this instant. "Aye, this is most important," she told him, keeping her voice calm. Once again, she turned him toward the door, but instead of walking, he pressed back against her hands.

With each breath the need to run grew in Johanna. Once again, she looked from hearth to chest. Panic soared ever higher. She was trapped here. He had to go.

"Go, Elyas," she urged him, her voice rising against her now frantic need to see this message on its way. "Go now, and swiftly so."

Shoe leather squeaked on wood as Syward turned, then strode for the hall's exit. The sound brought Johanna leaping to her feet, her heart in her throat. Although she could hardly believe that he might have overheard her, worry blossomed into rank fear. What if he had and now meant to betray her? Mary save her, but all of these men were witnesses to what she'd discovered about their employer.

It was terror that made her call out, "Where do you go?" to Syward.

"To the privy, mistress," the man snapped back in irritation.

Elyas raced after him. "I'll walk across the courtyard with you," he cried. "I do not like to be alone in the dark."

The bedchamber door crashed against the wall behind it, the sound reverberating throughout the room. "Well now, if it isn't my loving wife," Katel called out. However slurred his words, they were edged in steel. "Wherever have you been this day? How callous of you to keep me waiting."

Chapter Twenty-five

Stanrudde
Mid-August, 1180

As the day was too hot for a brisk walk, Johanna and Helewise took their time returning from the tailor's shop. There was naught but silence between them. This was fine with Johanna, as her thoughts were on the riverbank and last night's meeting with Rob.

She again congratulated herself at her cleverness in managing to slip away undetected. This time, it had only cost her a handful of ribbons to convince the maid who tended Papa throughout the night to say nothing of her absence. Since the girl was just dense and romantic enough to believe her mistress had, indeed, gone to pray for her betrothed's health, there was little chance she'd spill what she knew.

The question was, would the twit accept the lie twice? Mother of God, but she must. Only the promise of meeting Rob later this evening had made the tailor's poking and prodding endurable.

As the thought of marrying Katel filled Johanna, so did the prospect of having to lay beneath him as a wife did with her husband. When she did this with Rob, it brought her great joy, but the very concept that she might have to do the same with Katel made her skin crawl. She narrowed her eyes in determination. There had to be a way to slip out this night; she and Rob had plans to make if she was to escape the fate her father willed on her. Aye, and after they made their plans, Rob would hold her.

It was this Johanna needed even more than his passion. Only when Rob's arms were around her did she feel as if she'd survive. With every passing moment, her life crumbled around her, all that was familiar and precious slipping beyond her reach.

If it was not bad enough that her father was dying, Tom the Lackwit had passed last week, departing gently for the afterlife as he slept. Against his son's death, Philip announced that he would retire, going to end his days with a married daughter. Considering his age, this was to be expected, but Helewise's abandonment was not. Of late, the housekeeper had spoken often of her village, where she and Aleric had been raised. Even if she didn't say as much, Johanna knew that both the housekeeper and her brother meant to leave when Katel became the master.

Loneliness thrust through her, followed by a touch of anger. Everyone so disliked Katel they would not stay, but no one seemed to appreciate how, in their departures, they abandoned her to face him alone. Traitors, all of them!

As they entered the gate, Johanna saw Master Colin standing in the forebuilding's shadow. Her heart rose to her throat at the deep lines that scored into his face. It was sadness that was eating through his skin as if to lay its mark upon his bones. He hadn't looked like this since his wife's death. With a wordless cry, she hurried across the courtyard to stop before him.

"How is Papa?" she demanded.

"Resting," he replied, his voice husky as if tears filled his chest.

"What is it, Master Colin?" Helewise asked as she came to a halt beside them.

"I fear I am mourning the ending of my life in this world," he replied and tried to smile. There was no answering light in his dark eyes. "This surprises me, as I had not expected to do so."

"You've decided then?" Helewise's voice was unusually gentle. "The abbot has agreed to take you?"

"Aye. Once Walter passes, there is no one left to hold me on this side of the abbey's walls." This time when he smiled, it was in wry amusement. "The tonsure will be a blessing in disguise, I think me, as it means I'll have that much less hair to comb."

Johanna caught her breath as she understood Master Colin meant to take his vows. Here was another precious person who was abandoning her when she most needed him. Her loneliness grew larger than any anger. If not for Rob's vow to never leave, she would have wept. There'd soon be no one left within these walls who cared for her.

"Helewise," Master Colin said as he caught the woman's arm, "will you come aid me? It's time I sorted through my Kat's belongings."

"I should see to the master first," the housekeeper protested, but Master Colin was already leading her away from the forebuilding and back toward the gate. "He was fine a few moments ago. Johanna can tend to him by herself for the little while I'll keep you away. You will, won't you, lass?" he called over his shoulder to her, but gave her no time to protest or agree as he bore the housekeeper ever nearer the gate. "Come, I pray you. There's not much to look at, but touching what is hers makes me ache all over again."

Johanna watched them leave the courtyard, then turned to stare at the door in the forebuilding. Although she never shirked sitting at Papa's bedside, her heart quailed at the thought of approaching her sire. It frightened her to look upon him, each time she did so a reminder that he was leaving her. Although the adult she wished she was tried to accept this, the child within her ever cried out angrily refusing to let him go.

With a sigh, she squared her shoulders and entered

the door, climbing the stairs to the hall. It was blessedly cool inside, easing her overheated skin. As she reached the wooden dividing wall that cleaved the one long room into hall and bedchamber, she stopped to look at her mother's chests and smiled. With Helewise preoccupied by both Papa's health and plans for a wedding that must not happen, the maids were letting their chores slide. All three coffers wore a light coat of dust.

Once, these chests, along with the linens and serving items they contained, had been her only wealth. Even if that were no longer true, Johanna yet thought of them as her property—hers, and hers alone. It was against her pride of ownership that she used her finger to trace the letters "Joh" atop the green one, "anna's" on the brown-and-blue one, then squeezed "dowry" between the brass bands on the rusty-colored one. Brushing her hands one against the other in satisfaction, she passed from hall to bedchamber.

Master Colin had closed the shutters before he left the room, rendering the sleeping chamber dim and stuffy. She strode to her sire's bedside. Papa lay very still. A start of fear hit her, and she checked to see if his chest was rising and falling. Only when she was certain he yet lived did she breathe again, then quietly pulled the bed's draperies shut around him.

With naught to do until he awakened, she went to the window and threw open the shutters. Leaning into the opening, she sought to absorb the sounds and smells of the far more normal life that went on around this deathwatch. Overhead, the sky was yet a bright blue, but clouds built, promising rain this night. She hoped it held off until after she'd seen Rob. There'd be no explaining wet gowns to Helewise, come the morn.

The air was so heavy it made the smoke from the kitchen puddle around the peaked vent on its roof. Shimmering with heat, the thick stuff snaked its way along the thatch until it reached out to mingle with what rose from beneath the roof that shielded the distillery's hearth. Enjoying the shade that length of thatching provided them, the maids who tended whatever potions stewed there were chatting and laughing as they worked. Next door, Master Herebert's wife was taking her husband to task over some misdemeanor, her voice piercing as she scolded.

All of this was so familiar and right, it offered her at least a momentary ease from what so frightened her. This was her home. As long as she had Rob beside her, she could survive, even if everyone else left her. Turning her back to the window, she returned to her father's bed. The stool that had long since become a feature here was set too close to the wall. Johanna drew it toward her, but her grip on the seat was not as tight as she thought. It slipped from her hands and fell to its side, clattering loudly on the wooden floor.

The noise sparked a rustling within the curtains. "Who is there?" Papa's call was so very weak. Johanna was glad the drapes were shut so he couldn't see how this made her grimace.

"It is me, Papa. My pardon, I did not mean to wake you."

Setting the stool upright beside the bed, she pushed back the draperies to look in at him. It took all her strength not to flinch as she did so. He, too, was slipping away, going to a place far beyond her reach and from which he would never return. Loneliness once again pulsed through her.

"Ah, but I am glad you did," he said to her, an odd tenseness to his voice.

She settled onto the stool, frowning in concern for him. "Are you hurting again, Papa?" A glance at the wall confirmed that the concoction Master Colin had created to deaden the pain that now ever gnawed at her father still sat where they left it.

"Aye, but it is nothing that brew will ease," he said. "Rob has spoken with me."

The breath left Johanna's lungs in a rush, only to be replaced by guilt. Despite that she was certain what she and Rob did was not wrong, in the doing of it she had betrayed her father's trust in her. Johanna slammed her heel down upon that thought. It was not she who was doing the betraying, but Papa. He meant to force her to wed Katel, who was a hateful, evil man.

Lifting her chin to a proud angle, she said, "Then you know that I can no longer marry Katel. Rob loves me, and we are wed."

Rather than comment on what she said, he asked, "Are you with child, sweetling?"

Johanna froze. Never in all her life had she thought her father might ask her such a question. Shame woke, so deep she bowed her head against it. "Nay, Papa."

"Are you certain? When was your last woman's flow?"

Her shame worsened as he mentioned this most private of subjects. It squeezed at her heart, trying to obliterate her love for Rob. Why had it never occurred to her that what she and Rob did together might get her with child? Instead, all she'd thought about was his love for her and the pleasure she found in his arms.

"Two weeks past," she returned, her voice tiny.

"Have you known him since then?"

Tears trickled from her eyes at this horrible, horrible question. Of a sudden, she no longer felt like a virtuous wife, but rather some immoral maid who laid with any lad. She could only nod.

Her father sighed. "Then, Master Colin will fix you a brew to make certain naught lives in your womb. It is bad enough that he's left you. It would be doubly so were he to leave a bastard behind to ruin you."

"What?" It was a breathless cry that sprang from her lips. Shocked from her tears, Johanna raised her head to stare at her father. Even as she heard what he had said, she refused it. The thought of Rob gone was more than she could tolerate.

A terrible sadness filled the receding planes of her father's thin face. "Ach, poppet, I cannot think how to tell you this. Rob has pulled the hood over all of our eyes. He's lied to you, sweetling. His tale about the abbot and proof of marriage was naught but a falsehood."

These words were like knife blows to her heart, made all the more painful because they followed her father's mortifying interview. Doubts appeared from some hidden coffer in her mind. Everyone knew that marriages were made before the church door. It took a priest's words to make the bond true. Shame's befouling light tried to turn what she and Rob had done into a sin. Still, her faith persisted.

"Nay, Rob would not lie to me. He asked the abbot."

Her father only shook his head. "Would you like me to call the abbot here to confirm what I tell you? I can do that if you will it."

"Nay," Johanna moaned softly, shaking her head against the confusion that whirled within her. Her father was wrong; he had to be. Rob never lied to her, but then, neither had her sire. "When Rob returns, he'll prove to you he did not lie," she cried out.

"Poppet, do not fool yourself into thinking he will be back. He is gone for all time," her sire said with yet another deep sigh.

"Where did he go?" It was an aching plea, begging her father to deny what he'd just said. Once again, tears filled Johanna's eyes, a single droplet trickling down her cheek. When it reached her jaw, her father lifted a hand and used his thumb to brush it away.

"I know naught, save that he has coins enough to take him anywhere he wills."

Johanna jerked upright on the stool and tore away from her father's touch as she understood what he'd done. Papa meant her to wed Katel, will she, nill she. To achieve this, he'd deprived her of the only one willing to stay with her. "You sent him away!"

However fiery her accusal, a terrible emptiness yawned within her. Her protest came too late. It did not matter what had happened or why; Rob was gone, and Papa would see to it he stayed far beyond her reach. There was nothing she could do to bring him back to her.

Never had Johanna known such pain. It was a moment before she realized her heart was breaking. Against her helplessness, faith disappeared. How could Rob have allowed Papa to send him away from her when she needed him so?

"Love, I did not," her sire crooned to her. However strange his voice, it was a soothing tone. "All I did was test him. I wanted to be sure of his affection for you before I broke your betrothal to Katel and placed you in his care. I told him he could have you, but you'd come to him with only your shift to your name."

His words shattered her. "You have disinherited me?" A little voice within her scolded that this was no more than she deserved for how she had sinned against God and her sire.

"Ach, my little love, it was but a ruse." He claimed her hand, holding it tight in his hot, dry palm. "I only wanted to know that his heart was true."

Johanna drew herself up to her tallest. However hopeless the battle, she'd fight it to the end. "Now I know you lie. Rob's heart is true. Whether I had wealth or not, he would have accepted your offer and made me his wife in the eyes of the world."

"Nay, child, you have mistaken him." Her father's hand tightened on hers in an attempt to convince her that his lie was true. "He raged! Praise God that there was no one within the house to overhear him, else the tale of your debauching would soon be spread to every corner of Stanrudde. It was to protect you and your name that I offered him a goodly sum to still his tongue. He took this, lass, then demanded more. I had to vow to give it to him, but said he would not receive it until after you were well and truly wed to Katel."

"You are lying," she whispered, her love for Rob clinging to her heart by its fingernails alone.

"Would that I were." Her father eased back into the mattress, worn from this much conversation. "The proof of my tale lies in his departure, does it not?"

Although everything within her protested that Rob would never have traded coins for her, her ability to resist was failing beneath her sire's pounding onslaught. Depression came creeping over her. Whether he loved her or not, Rob was now leagues beyond her reach.

Johanna stared at her sire. There was nothing left to stand between her and marriage to Katel. In her desperation to avoid a fate she could not tolerate, she sought within her to find some remaining defense. It was a shoddy barrier that she devised.

"No matter what you've done, Rob will return for me," she told him, even while the hopelessness within her said he never would. "Rob will not allow another to wed me. He loves me."

Papa only shook his head, his eyes filled with sadness. "Believe as you must, child. I tell you what, let us make a bargain, we two. You say he'll come. I vow to you now, if he arrives before you are wed to Katel, I will see the betrothal broken and marry the two of you, instead. If he does not, then you must wed Katel as has been so long planned."

With that, her father released his breath. His eyes closed, and he drifted back into sleep. Johanna stared at him, battered and bereft. So deep was her hopelessness, not even anger's spark could find fodder in it.

His promise hung before her. She grabbed for it, clutching it tightly into her heart, despite that she knew he only offered it because he was certain Rob would not return. It was all that kept her from drowning in her fear and loneliness.

"He will come," she told her sleeping sire. "No matter what you've done to drive him away, Rob will come for me. He must," she sobbed quietly, "else I will surely die."

Chapter Twenty-six

Stanrudde
the hour of Compline
Ste. Agnes's Day, 1197

Johanna turned to stare at her husband. Caught in the yellowish light of the lamp she'd left atop the trunk, Katel's fleshy features seemed made of wax. His white shirt took on the color of the parchment she'd just burnt, while the deep red of his chausses browned. Spiked from sleep, his pale hair stood out about his head, but his gaze was alert. If he'd been drinking, he'd not had enough to make him drunk.

Her gaze slipped from him to her mother's green chest. With each breath, she tasted the stink of the skins. The time for hiding what she'd done had come and passed. All was lost.

Katel blinked, then frowned as he stared at the skirts flowing through the edges of her cloak. There was a flash of surprise in his eyes as he recognized the gowns he'd hidden. With that, fear for herself and Rob tightened its grip on Johanna. Their fates had been sealed from the moment Elyas removed these garments from their hiding place. One glimpse of them told Katel he was exposed.

"What is this?" her husband hissed as he turned to look toward the corner. Betrayer that it was, the lamp's merry flame cheerfully scattered its light onto the dishware strewn along the wall.

Staggering over to the emptied chest, he stared into its barren depths. A swat of his hand sent the false bottom tumbling to the floor. The clatter of wood against wood was loud in the room's intense silence.

Johanna flinched at the sound. Her survival, and Rob's, now rested in the hands of a child, one given to fanciful tales. What if Wymar did not believe him, as he hadn't about the chest? The certainty that the cook would not sent her heart spiraling downward into despair.

Katel turned, swaying slightly as he did so. As he strode toward the fireplace, he regained a little more control over himself with each step. He was steady on his feet by the time he stopped before the hearth.

Coughing against the thickened air, he leaned down to snatch the smoldering remains of a forged missive from the hot coals. It was as Johanna watched him stare at the blackened thing that this morn's angry need to outlast Katel's threat returned. She'd only just reclaimed her life from the hatred that had consumed her; she couldn't give it up so soon.

When Katel raised his head from the charred skin, it was to aim his gaze beyond her. "What do you think this is?" he barked at the menservants who yet clung to the edges of the light. "Some public show to entertain you?"

Shoes scuffed, men cleared their throats. The sounds died away in the next instant as they disappeared into the eclipsing blackness that held the hall in its clutches. When they were out of earshot, Katel turned a wicked glare on her.

"Think yourself saved, do you?" His words were a heated breath. "I can replace them in two hours' time. Now that you've seen them, I suppose I must move a little faster than I'd planned. Just as well, I'd say." A brief and savage grin darted across his mouth. "It would be rude to keep you waiting overly long for your death."

Johanna stared at him in dread. Two hours? Did he mean to set the folk to rioting once more? Ach, but it would take longer than two hours for Mistress Alwyna to receive her message, reach the warehouse, and cart away the wheat.

If it was even there. That was, if she knew to go. Johanna refused to give way to these negative thoughts. It was hope that set her to seeking some way to stall her husband long enough for salvation to occur. One night's time was all she needed.

First things first. Katel would remember how her hatred of Rob had yesterday driven her to race into a maddened crowd. If she didn't now react angrily to having her name tied to his, Katel might suspect all was not as it had been.

Screwing her face into a mask of outrage, she spat out, "How dare you so foully tie my name with that betraying bastard." Inwardly, she begged Rob's forgiveness.

"Tut," her husband replied, his smile glorious for having so tweaked her. "Why worry so over something we both know isn't true? I think me you should be glad I chose him as your lover. Better to stand at the gallows next to someone familiar than beside a stranger."

He reached out to open her cloak. Mock dismay creased his brow. "Why, Johanna, wherever have you been, all dressed up like some poor and unmarried maid? One might think you were trying to disguise yourself so you could go a-trysting with your lover," he whispered to her. "What other reason would a woman who usually dresses in finery have for such attire, save sin, eh? Ah, but you were frustrated this night. Your lover is locked out of your reach."

There was an odd vindictive pleasure in knowing how wrong he was. Ah, but since he was fishing for another reaction, she gave it to him. "The sooner they hang that bastard, the better for this town and me," she snapped, adding yet more mental apologies, then tried a jab of her own. "How can you do this to Peter?" This she made into a soft plea, a mother's prayer for her child.

Katel's eyes hardened. "What care I for him or his inheritance? I should give him the same as I got from your sire," he whispered, his ancient rage over the terms of her father's will getting the better of him. "Let him try to trade on the glory of Walter of Stanrudde's name with no coins to aid him, just as was done to me."

His words rang in the quiet room, then echoed back to him. Katel started, sudden guilt appearing in the depths of his eyes as he frowned in confusion. Then he shook his head. "Nay, I have once succumbed to your manipulations; I'll do so no more. The fate I intend for you can only improve life for Peter. Once I am avenged, all will be as it should have been those many years ago. When I finally own the wealth your sire denied me, I will be able to rebuild my trade, creating wealth aplenty for Peter to inherit."

He turned his gaze on her once more, his eyes dark with recrimination at the doubt she'd caused in him. "Mayhap, I have been too hasty in plotting your death, forgetting that my son might be injured by your passing. It was a mistake to remove you from that convent of yours. I think I shall return you."

A satisfied smile touched his mouth. He stepped away from the hearth and called out to the hiding men. "My wife and I are leaving. One of you fetch us mounts."

Johanna stared at his back in bewilderment, not quite certain what had happened. Had speaking of their son convinced him not to kill her? Or, did he simply mean to confine her so she could not interfere while he played out the last of his plot? A quirk of triumph followed this. Praise God! *My wife and I* he'd said. He was not sending her, he was riding with her!

She calculated the time it would take: three hours there at a gentle pace, since Katel could do no better than that, then another three hours back. If the prioress was generous, she'd offer him a pallet in the stable so he might sleep out the remainder of the night. Ah, but even if he refused and rode directly back to Stanrudde, Katel wouldn't see the city's gates again until well after first light. She had done it!

No one appeared out of the shadows in answer to Katel's command. "What is this?" His voice rose in irritation. "Have you all gone suddenly deaf? Or are you too dense to decide among you who's to go?"

There was a shuffling in the darkness. As one, the group of them reappeared. They stood, shoulder to shoulder, just within reach of the fire's light. It was Dickon who spoke on their behalf. "Master, you have not been yourself this night. We've agreed among us that we'll not let you do your wife any harm, no matter how you command us." His was a hesitant proclamation.

Johanna shot them a startled look at this offer of protection, then willed them to withdraw it. She and Katel must ride out of Stanrudde. A flash of rage shot across Katel's fleshy features at so unexpected a challenge. This was followed by a mummer's mask of consternation.

"My pardon to you all," he replied, then sighed. "I know I have behaved oddly this even. It's these threats the populace make against me and my family, but fie on you for thinking I would hurt my wife. When have I ever struck her?"

He paused, bending a wounded gaze on each man. They all shifted as they acknowledged their master had never once abused their mistress, at least not with his fists. Only then did Katel continue. "Nay, the only reason I call for mounts is that I would return her to her convent. There will she be safe, far from the reach of this town's madmen."

Johanna watched the menservants relax at this. In their minds, the convent was a sensible place to put her, whether they thought they were protecting her from the rioters or from her husband.

Katel waited a moment, then delivered to them their punishment for daring to confront him. "Since you men are so concerned for my wife's safety, you'd best come with us. I know how upset you'd be were some rogue knight or daring thief to attack us on the road."

There were tired sighs and quiet groans at the thought of a night spent in the saddle. "Master," one of them said in an attempt at rescuing himself, "you spoke earlier as if Stanrudde's troubles were ended. There may be no need to cloister your wife."

"Would that this were true," Katel replied with a wistful sigh. The barest hint of cruelty gleamed in his eyes. "However, as long as the council as a whole refuses to hang that man, I fear there will be no controlling the crowd."

Johanna heard the promise in his words. Once he was returned from her convent, he meant to see the missives replaced, then rouse the mob. If Mistress Alwyna had not received word, Rob would die on the morrow.

This set her heart to aching all over again. She wanted more than just a single kiss between them, before they were forever parted in this life. Would that she and Rob could, indeed, escape to some faroff place to live as man and wife.

Johanna nigh on jerked, so hard did the realization strike her. If Elyas succeeded, if Wymar went, if Mistress Alwyna found the grain, it would be Katel who hanged. She'd be a widow!

The worry in her ebbed beneath the rising tide of joy. Once Katel was dead, Rob would come to fetch her home. She knew to the depths of her soul, he'd ask her to wed him. This time, there'd be no one to say them nay.

"Master," tried another, "it is full dark outside. Should we not wait until morn's light?"

"God will guide us, His moon giving us the light we need," came Katel's sanctimonious reply. "Enough complaining. Ready yourselves. Against the possibility of attack, we'll go as a group to the stables as soon as I am dressed." He glanced across their number. "Where's Syward?"

"The privy, master," Dickon humbly replied.

"Then he'll be the one to stay behind and guard our door."

Katel caught Johanna by the arm. As he started for the bedchamber, he pulled her along beside him. Wanting nothing to dissuade her husband from his current path, she walked happily at his side, her thoughts on a far more pleasant future.

As her husband stopped to claim her lamp from atop the brass-bound coffer, he shot her a harsh glance. "They babble like babes, but you make no protest?"

Johanna shrugged. "What is there to protest. You are only taking me to where I wish to be."

Only when Katel continued to stare at her, did she realize her mistake. Yesterday's woman would have spit and hissed, simply because her husband was forcing her to do what she did not wish to do. It was too late now to do anything save to raise her chin and stare down at the shorter man.

Katel's brows rose, his smile beautiful as he devised some awful trick to use against her. "I am so glad you feel that way," he said, "for you will be there a very long time."

"What do you mean?" Johanna retorted, trying for some of her old harshness.

"When the prioress sees you with your hair uncovered and wearing these worn gowns, she will be convinced of your sin. I will tell her that only this very night did I discover that you had been committing adultery each time I departed Stanrudde for the fairs," her husband said, his voice sweet as he spun his plot aloud for her. "I shall cry in fear for you, telling her how your lover demanded that you leave me to live with him in sin. When you refused, he did you this damage." He raised a hand and touched a finger to one of the bruises on her face. "He is a violent man, your paramour. A great brute."

"What nonsense," Johanna retorted in scorn. "The lady prioress is no fool. Do you think I will remain silent over my attack? While you might be able to convince her that I have sinned in the past, she'll not believe that any lover beat me."

"You're right," Katel agreed all too quickly, "but then, that isn't my true intent. I need her to offer you sanctuary, not as a retiree, but as a sister. Thus, by subtle means, I will reveal to her that were I to ever hit you, those properties of yours go to Stanrudde's abbey. At the end of the interview, she will think it is I who have beaten you and that you concoct the tale of an attack in order to keep your child from losing his inheritance."

"What?" Johanna cried out. "I have no calling and so I will say."

"While this may be true," Katel said, shaking his head, "it does not really matter. On the morrow, the world will believe you a heinous criminal. If the prioress has offered you sanctuary, you will have the choice between the hangman's noose and taking your vows. I suggest for our dear Peter's sake that you choose sisterhood. You can, then, dedicate the remainder of your days to praying for your son. He'll be needing all the heavenly aid he can muster, for who knows what I will leave him."

With that, Katel shoved her into their private chamber ahead of him, then released her. "Up, one of you," he called to the maidservants who were pretending sleep on the floor. "I want my finest traveling gown, the orange and blue, my boots, and my warmest cloak. Bring also the thickest of my chains and my rings, along with my better gloves. I have a prioress to bend to my will!"

Johanna waited until he turned his back to her, then closed her eyes. It wasn't clemency she'd bought by mentioning their son, it was a stay of execution, followed by a lifetime's imprisonment.

Nay, she refused to believe it. Katel would be exposed, and when he had been, Rob would come for her. Rob loved her. He would not leave her trapped and alone, not a second time.

Chapter Twenty-seven

Stanrudde
an hour past Prime
Ste. Blesilla's Day, 1197

Rob sat in the bed, his back braced against its head. His fur-lined mantle was drawn tightly about him, his legs were covered by the blankets. So, too, were the yellow woolen draperies tightly shut around the mattress. Despite all this the interior of the bed was only endurable, not truly warm. Then again, it was summer in here compared to the frigid, hearthless room beyond this fabric shield.

With a yawn, he rubbed at his burning eyes. It had been a long night. Plagued as he was by his fear for Johanna, sleep had been impossible. Instead, his mind busied itself in playing out every possible scenario that could lead to her death at Katel's hands.

"Turn back! You'll not enter here! Hie all of you, keep them from coming!" The single shout rose from beyond the keep's wooden perimeter walls to float through the narrow slit of this chamber's wall. "Go back!"

In the next moment, every one of the souls who kept vigil before the tower took up the chant, and it rose to a thundering roar. Rob sighed as their venom reminded him of the fate that he wasn't convinced he could escape. To distract himself from his morbid thoughts, he tried to deduce who it was that came.

It couldn't be the sheriff; the crowd wouldn't have bid him away. It wasn't a council member, for there were no calls for his or her family's death. Who, then?

Staring up at the yellow cloth stretched from pole to pole overhead to make a ceiling, he waited to see just how brave this visitor of his was. The chanting erupted into screams of fear. This was followed by a wary quiet, punctuated by a few moans.

"What sorts of idiots stand unarmed between bowmen and where they wish to be? You'll let me and mine pass or, by God, I'll command them to aim at you rather than over your heads the next time." Given in English, there was no doubting that this man meant to fulfill his threat, were the crowd to offer further resistance.

Rob's brows raised at this. Not brave, then, but strong. Who came to see him with enough bowmen to frighten the mob? Again, he considered the sheriff, only to reject him once more. The shire's lawman wasn't English, and the one who'd issued that warning used the tongue like a native speaker.

Outside, the gates opened and shut. Sailing up to Rob's tower room on the day's chilly breath came the rattling of harness rings, the stomp and blow of tired horses along with snippets of conversation from men even more tired than their beasts. His confusion deepened. This had the sound of an army, not just a few bowmen. Ah well, there was not much longer to wait before his curiosity was satisfied.

Bad enough that he had to meet men in his shirt and chausses, but he'd not do it so whilst lying abed like some invalid, or a king. Pushing aside the bed curtains, Rob sat at the edge of the mattress and donned his boots. When they were again cross-gartered to his legs, he stood and straightened his mantle around his shoulders. It was native vanity that made him use his fingers to comb his hair as best he could. Earlier this day, Otto, son of Otfried, had brought him water and cloth for washing, no knife for shaving of course, but a comb was another matter. That was a private possession, rarely shared.

It was a few moments before the key squealed into its slot. When the door opened, Otto entered, followed by Mistress Alwyna. Beneath her mantle, the old woman yet wore yesterday's green gowns, now sadly rumpled. Framed in a sturdier wimple than what she'd earlier worn, her face was drawn in exhaustion. Dark rings that matched his own hung beneath her brown eyes

Rob's surprise at seeing her here died beneath his overwhelming need for news of Johanna. Ah, but with Otto in the room, he dared speak no word of her. The best he could do was to eye a silent plea to the old woman, begging for some sign to put him at his ease. Mistress Alwyna offered him a nod and a reassuring smile. If it wasn't enough to satisfy him, it did allow him to draw a deep breath, the first one he'd taken since parting from Johanna last night.

On Mistress Alwyna's heels came a knight. Beneath a brown, fur-lined cloak, the man wore both tunic and chausses of knitted metal rings. Atop his armor there was a brown surcoat trimmed in golden embroidery. Like the needlework, the jeweled hilt of the sword belted to his side proclaimed that he was no simple bachelor knight, but a man of some consequence.

Not a handsome man, this stranger's visage was raw-boned, his nose slightly crooked, saying he'd once broken it. His hair, flattened from wearing his head gear, was brown as were his eyes. In facial hair, he affected the same fashion Rob did, wearing his beard trimmed closely to the line of his bold jaw.

As Rob watched him in some bemusement, wondering who he was and what brought him to this tower, the knight came to an abrupt halt. His gaze locked onto Rob's face, his eyes widening. "Jesu Christus!" It was a cry of astonishment.

Mistress Alwyna gave a tired laugh, then clutched her hand into the crook of the warrior's metal clad arm. Rob's brows shot up when she nigh on leaned against the knight's shoulder. To see a merchant's mother behave so familiarly with one who was obviously classes above her was strange, indeed.

"Did I not tell you?" the old woman said, speaking in fluid French. The knight made her no response; he but rudely stared.

Fed by his tiredness and the stress of contemplating a seriously shortened lifespan, Rob's irritation rose from simmering to claim a new and potent life. Caged he might be, but he was no animal to be ogled. He narrowed his eyes to glare at his better.

"I beg your pardon, but what business have you with me?" he asked in French. "If you came only to stare, I suggest you leave."

The knight caught his breath, then looked at Mistress Alwyna. "Even his voice is the same, Mama. I did not believe what you wrote, but here he stands!"

Mama? Startled, Rob looked to the old woman, then back to the knight. "What is this?" he asked, his voice lowering in confusion.

His visitor stripped off his gloves. As Mistress Alwyna released him, he stepped forward to offer his hand in greeting. "My pardon, but I have forgotten all courtesy in my shock. I am Richard, Lord Meynell." He paused, a small smile bringing golden lights to the brown of his eyes. "And, you, Robert of Lynn, are my brother, son to Henry, Lord Graistan, just as I am."

Rob drew an outraged breath, spurning this nobleman's hand as his chin jerked upward in arrogant refusal of that estate. No man, despite his station, had the right to call him bastard. Once again, the insult this did his mother's memory rushed through him, anger tumbling along behind it. It was the hurt child in him who screamed that she had been no rich man's whore.

"Richard, have a care," Mistress Alwyna said gently, "he has no more liking for being called bastard than do you."

That shocked the arrogance right out of Rob. He stared at the smaller man, only now seeing the knight's subtle resemblance to Mistress Alwyna. Yet, he'd called himself Lord Meynell. That could not be. What sort of Norman would offer his common by-blow lands and title?

This Lord Meynell again smiled at the one he had named his kin. "I see you wondering," he said in English. Having learned it at his mother's knee, it was without accent. "To date, all of our father's family, save one, remains as mystified as you that Henry of Graistan should have so loved his bastard son. Did you ever meet your sire?"

Rob's mouth opened to protest that his father had been Ralph Attegreen, but the adult in him would not let the words pass his lips. It was time to acknowledge that his sire had been Lord Graistan, just as the villagers had proclaimed all those years ago, just as his mother had insisted on her deathbed. Just as he'd always known. He sighed in acceptance.

"Nay," he said with a breath of resignation. "My mother never told him she bore his child. She felt he had compensated her well enough by providing her a rich dowry."

"A pity that," Lord Richard replied. "Our sire was a good man, and he would have liked to have known of you. Did Mama tell you that you are his image? She says she thought it was his shade she saw when she first met you." He stopped himself with a shake of his head. "Enough of that. There will be time for conversation later. Just now, we must attend to the matter at hand."

Turning, the nobleman looked back into the tiny

hall, then glanced at Otto. "Go see what is taking that Lynnsman so long." It was a command, to which Otto responded with a brisk nod. The soldier turned on his heel, leaving the room without either shutting or locking the door behind him.

Already amazed at finding family where before he'd had none, Rob's astonishment grew as he understood. "You are the one Mistress Alwyna called to see that my evidence came unmolested from Lynn to Stanrudde?"

Only as the words left his mouth did he comprehend what this meant. His heart took flight. With his book here, Katel was finished!

Lord Richard offered him a wry, if tired smile. "I am an obedient son, who always does as his sweet mama requests. I live to ride like a madman from Upwood to Lynn to Stanrudde, all in less than a day's, or rather, a night's time." His dam swatted at his shoulder for his cheekiness, and her son laughed.

"If this is what you did, then I cannot offer you thanks enough," Rob said, marveling that a lord, albeit only half Norman, would have so inconvenienced himself to assist a commoner and a man unknown to him.

"It was my pleasure," his brother replied. "We who are baseborn must aid each other, no? Glad I am I was nearby, so I could do so."

Still stunned by all this, Rob looked at Mistress Alwyna. She, too, had been a Norman's leman, but she'd done right well for her son, then wed herself a rich merchant afterward. He wondered what his mother would have won had she also pressed Henry of Graistan to acknowledge her child as his. Rob's lips twisted in refusal. Nay, he liked his life and what he did, wanting nothing more from it, save Johanna.

As her name rang in him, he realized that Otto was gone, leaving him free to ask the question that ached in him. "Tell me," he demanded of the knight's mother, "what do you know of Mistress Johanna?"

A tiny frown settled between Mistress Alwyna's brows. "Her servant came to me last even with directions on where the wheat was laid—"

"You've found it, then?" Rob interrupted in a rush of hope. Better and better!

"Aye. We carted it to the abbey for safekeeping. You did not tell me he had taken so much. We were the whole night moving it." However stern her words, her tone made it a toothless rebuke.

"What of Johanna?" So deep was his need to know she was safe, he forgot to use her title.

The old woman's face softened, pity filling her gaze. "She is gone, Master Robert. The night gatekeeper says that Master Katel departed with her and his household guard late last even. I fear that he discovered what she'd done and has run to avoid being here when we expose him."

As his heart tore in his chest, Rob turned his back on those who watched him. Bowing his head, he pressed his palm to his forehead and closed his eyes. For a second time in his life, Katel stole from him the woman he loved, the one who was by all rights his own wife.

"Does the gatekeeper know where they have gone?" he asked without turning. His words were hoarse with the unfairness of this fate.

"Nay, he stated no destination," she said sadly.

Rob drew a deep breath, trying to restore his control. Instead despair ate at him. No matter Johanna's assurances, he could not believe Katel would leave her unharmed if he knew what she'd done. The thought of her hurt or dead because she'd protected him turned his heart to stone. If she was gone, then he had no further wish to live.

His newfound half brother came to stand silently at his side. Too deep in grief, Rob did not look up. There was not even strength enough in him to tell the man to leave him be.

"I think me our sire gave you more than just his image when he made you, Lord Meynell said after a moment. His voice was soft. "It is a terrible thing to be plagued with a constant heart." He stopped and sighed. "Or, to find that one loves another man's wife."

In his fellow bastard's voice rang an intimate knowledge of Rob's own estate. Against it, Rob's shoulders relaxed, and he managed a shallow breath. Raising his head, he looked toward his new kin. Lord Richard had his gaze focused on the bed.

"Take heart and tell yourself that there is nowhere they can go where they cannot be discovered. All it takes is time." He paused to glance at Rob. There was an odd gleam in his eyes, as if saying these words reminded him of something else. When he saw that Rob watched him, he offered a small smile. "But before you can begin your searching, you must first be cleared of these charges."

His calm tone and sensible words were just what Rob needed to help him draw the shattered pieces of himself back into a whole. As the grief receded, hope returned, bringing with it the strength to continue. He knew good men from one end of this world to the other. There was nowhere Katel could take Johanna where Rob could not ferret him out. And, once he had found them, Rob vowed to himself he'd see Katel's marriage to Johanna annulled for bigamy. This time, he did have the money and connections to challenge their joining.

"My thanks," he offered the shorter man, meaning it wholeheartedly.

"Do not be so quick to thank me." A spark of amusement came to life in Lord Meynell's eyes. "Mama tells me you have made yourself into a wealthy man. You may one day find me knocking on your door, complaining against the money lenders' high rates and asking you to return my many favors."

Rob gave the breath of a laugh. While he knew his new kinsman was yet working to steady him, there was something in the man's voice to suggest he truly meant to pursue that sort of private business arrangement. If this should come to pass, Rob would eagerly offer what he could. No matter how much it was, it would not be enough to repay Richard of Meynell for what he'd just done.

"By God, Rob," the panted words echoed into the room from the hall beyond it, "what has happened to Stanrudde that its folks should so threaten one raised in its bosom?"

Rob turned, dumbfounded, as Master Arthur, Cordwainer of Lynn, staggered into the room, huffing as if the box in his arms weighed four stone instead of less than one. If Rob's dearest friend was not as tall as he, Arthur was yet by far the broader. Just now, his face was reddened from the cold where his golden hair and beard did not cover it. Both the shoemaker's capuchin and the gown beneath his brown mantle were bright green, which made Arthur's eyes seem all the greener.

"Pardon, my lord," he said as he passed the nobleman on his way toward the bed. Dropping the coffer on the mattress, he fell to sit beside it, groaning as if his back were broken. "I am done in, I tell you!"

"What are you doing here?" Rob demanded, staring at the small, yet locked chest in which he kept his personal notes and books. Why had they brought the whole box, instead of just the book he'd requested?

Lord Meynell cocked his head, one side of his mouth rising in suppressed amusement. "I only hope you do not mind that I deliver both a coffer and a man, but the one would not be separated from the other."

"Where is Hamalin?" It was a worried question.

The nobleman shook his head. "Your servant never

came. Because my mother's note said your need for what lies within that box was urgent, I waited only an hour past the time he should have reached Lynn before deciding we could tarry no longer. That was when your housekeeper sent for this merchant, saying you trusted him like no other. Master Arthur rode with the box, against the possibility I was not who I appeared to be." There was no rancor in his voice at what had surely done him insult.

As a wholly new fear rose in Rob, this one for Hamalin's welfare, he again damned himself as a blind fool. No man sits idly by waiting for his enemy's servant to fetch evidence to prove his innocence. Katel's men would have been watching the gate, waiting to see that Hamalin never reached his destination.

With Katel's final blow, every bit of Rob's anger and arrogance returned. The need to see the spice merchant dead became like a living thing within him. It was better to bankrupt himself than to let this whoreson continue to walk the face of the earth.

Rob looked to the small box. This was the first step in Katel's exposure. The sooner he was adjudged innocent, the sooner he would be free to find Johanna and make her a widow.

Ah, but what he'd considered the answer to his troubles was that no longer. If what lay within this coffer would satisfy the eleven who remained on the council, they weren't the only ones to whom he needed to prove his innocence. It was the folk who besieged this tower, the men who'd been hurt by Katel's evil, that he needed to convince. To them, Rob was a Lynnsman, a foreigner, therefore suspect simply because he did not hail from Stanrudde. Now that their trust in their council was broken, he doubted they would believe anything their leaders told them. Still, nothing was achieved by standing here.

He looked toward Mistress Alwyna. "The key for

this box is with my belongings at the abbey." His voice was flat against what now raged in him.

"Just as well," she replied, "since that is where we will be taking you. The council met early this morn so I could reveal to them your tale and the stolen wheat, as well as what my son has brought from Lynn. As they fear the townsmen will no longer heed them they've asked the abbot to plead your case before the populace. Are you ready to pass through their ranks as we make our way to the abbey? We will walk you in the open, seeking to draw as many of them to the market field as we can. The more that witness, the better."

If it meant a chance to do Katel hurt, Rob would have ridden through hell on the devil's back with his eyes opened. "Aye, I would see this matter finished, once and for all."

Chapter Twenty-eight

Stanrudde
two hours past Prime
Ste. Blesilla's Day, 1197

Rob strode from the room ahead of his newly discovered half brother and that man's dam. Yet again groaning at the burden of the coffer, Arthur hurried to join him. "It is Katel who's done this." The shoemaker's voice was harsh with hatred. "May God damn that worm to hell!"

"I intend to do worse than that to him," Rob snapped back, his voice low.

As they crossed the hall toward the door at its far end, Rob's need for vengeance congealed into strategy. Of a sudden, he was grateful he didn't wear his gown. To appear in so magnificent a garment before the townsmen would condemn him before he even had a chance to speak. He raised a hand to the expensive pin that closed his mantle around his shoulders. Even this was too much wealth to display before his accusers. He glanced at Arthur's plainer mantle and simple pin.

"Hold a moment," he said, catching his friend by the arm, bringing him to a halt. "Trade me your mantle for mine."

"As you will," the shoemaker replied without question. Setting down the coffer, Arthur eyed Rob in curiosity as he freed his overgarment from his shoulders.

"Is this a permanent trade? If so, I'm getting the better bargain."

"If I live past this day, I'll tell you that you are wrong," Rob retorted as he pinned Arthur's simple woolen sheet around his shoulders. As his friend donned the warmer, richer mantle, Rob leaned down and lifted his own coffer. It would be better if it seemed no man waited on him.

"What are you doing?" Mistress Alwyna asked as she and her son came to a halt beside them.

"Katel forever relies on appearances, making himself seem to be what he is not," Rob said. "I think me, it is time that I did the same. If I appear to be a simple tradesman, rather than a wealthy merchant, will the folk not be more apt to hear me out?"

The old woman's brows rose in appreciation of this ruse. "Aye, so they might."

Once again, Rob started across the hall. When he stepped out to the wooden platform that hung a full story over the bailey below them, he blinked against the day's almost blinding light. Bright it might be, but there was no warmth to be had in all this day's sun; the icy air nipped at his ungloved fingertips.

With no forebuilding to shield the landing or the stairs from the elements and the tower set so high above the city, he could see past Stanrudde's walls. A great sheet of gray filled the sky in the near distance, moving steadily toward them. He wagered there'd be sleet again before None this day.

His gaze moved to that which was closer at hand: the jumble of houses set every which way between the city walls and this tower. The charred and broken timbers left by the fire lay like an untended wound on the body of the town. Still, where yesterday the lanes had been locked in the silence of death and destruction, the new day brought with it rebirth. The sounds of hammers filled the air. Workmen called to one another, seeking another peg or nail or a bit of wood or reed to stop a hole. Flashes of color appeared against the frigid gray-brown of the lanes; although they were not many, folk again moved along the streets, out doing those everyday chores that gave life its normalcy. There was even a brave regrater out and about, calling aloud the quality of his roasted chestnuts.

Rob descended into the bailey, only to stop in surprise when he reached the ground. His estimation of an army had not been wrong. Dozens of armed men filled the tiny space squatting near hastily lit fires, their mantles caught tightly around them against the cold. These were battle-hardened soldiers all, wearing boiled leather hauberks sewn with steel bits beneath their plain cloaks and metal caps upon their heads. If the swords buckled to their sides were without jewels, they were just as lethal as their lord's.

"Up, you surly brutes," Lord Meynell shouted to them, his voice filled with affection. "We'll be taking this man to the abbey. On foot," he added.

There were sneers of disgust at this, but not a man groaned aloud. Instead, they grabbed their shields and came to surround the four who made up their lord's party. The town guard opened the gates and Otto, son of Otfried, preceded them out beyond the wooden walls.

"Make way," the captain of the town guard shouted. "Make way for Master Robert, Grossier of Lynn, who goes to the abbey to present his case."

Noise exploded from the crowd at this news, every man there screaming for Rob's death. The more foolhardy among them exhorted the others to attack the soldiers so they might instantly wreak upon Rob the punishment they deemed he deserved. They were in the minority. The greater number had taken heed of what sort of damage trained soldiers could offer, and they shouted down these hotheads. With no choice left to them, the shouts fell away into grumbling. The group closed ranks behind the armed men, not willing to let their sacrificial lamb out of their sight.

They made a strange procession, soldiers in their brown and gray, followed by those dressed in colors far more gay. As the throng slowly made its way around sharp corners and down narrow lanes, more townsfolk came. Whether vengeance or entertainment brought them, none could know. Rob glanced behind him as they approached the abbey's market field and smiled in satisfaction, his need for retribution gratified by their numbers. The more who heard him denounce Katel and believed, the more certain the spice merchant's destruction became, no matter to what corner of the world that whoreson had run.

The holy brothers were prepared for their arrival. Forewarned by the council, the monks had erected a dais near the gate, placing it against the outside of the abbey's stone perimeter wall. Their father abbot's grand chair sat at its middle, Abbot Eustace already seated in it.

Once again, the churchman wore his jeweled miter on his head, while the ermine that trimmed his mantle shone against his black robes. His gilded staff glinted in the sunlight, held forward to remind all that he was Stanrudde's rightful leader of souls. Behind his chair stood the higher ranking of the brothers; they made a solid wall of black through which there were but glimpses of the glittering samites and rich damasks that the hiding councilmen wore.

"Come forward Master Robert," the abbot called, his powerful voice booming against the walls around him. His English was fluent, if heavily accented. "Come display to me the evidence of your innocence."

This proclamation sent the mob's muttering to a higher pitch. Fed by their dissatisfaction with the council's handling of this issue, man after man called aloud the uselessness of this. In their shouts lived the fear that now the Church would join the council in trying to deny them what they saw as justice.

His coffer yet tucked under his arm, Rob lengthened his stride to step up onto the dais, Arthur, Mistress Alwyna, and Lord Meynell on his heels. As he did so, the shouting in the field grew until every soul chanted out that Rob should hang. Against their fury, Lord Meynell's soldiers spread themselves out before the platform, forming a wall of men, shields at the ready, swords in hand. The only opening was the space before the abbot's chair.

Abbot Eustace rose to his feet. Again and again, the churchman slammed the base of his staff on the wooden planks beneath his feet in a demand for quiet. This only spurred on the chanting. Anger at their disrespect burned bright red in the churchman's narrow face. His eyes took fire at the insult the townsfolk did him.

"Hear me!" he bellowed to them, but his words made no dent in the mob's outrage.

Lord Meynell leaned forward to speak to one of the men before the dais. That man began to beat his sword against his shield. As the rest of the soldiers did the same, the din grew deafening as each side tried to outdo the other.

There was a touch on Rob's sleeve. It was Colin, his face solemn. The former tradesman's mouth moved, but his words were beyond hearing. Rob leaned down.

"Knowing that we have a long acquaintance, the council has asked me to be ready to testify to your character if called to do so," Colin shouted to him. "So, too, did the council command that the key to your private coffer be located. As there was not room upon this platform for so many, your servants bid me bear this to you"—he tried to offer Rob his scrip—"saying the key lay within it. Rob, what goes forward here?" the monk asked, the outsized purse yet in his hands.

Rob looked from the former tradesman to the scrip. He smiled. This couldn't be better. "Nay, hold it for me until I call for it," he said, his voice barely audible over the furor. "As for what happens here, I'll explain all to you later, over another sip of that wine."

Colin's eyes widened, and his mouth turned down in disgust. "If you can jest over that now, this cannot be as bad as it seems." With that, he receded to his brothers.

Once again, Lord Meynell leaned down to speak to his men. Two of the soldiers shouldered their shields, then drew crossbows out of their back scabbards. As the men strung the cords in their bows as if preparing to fire them, the chanting died a sudden death, leaving only an intense and distrustful silence.

"What sort of sinners are you," Abbot Eustace bellowed at them, venting his ire. "How will you face your Maker if it is discovered the man for whom you demand death is not guilty of the crime? This morn, your council did come to me, begging me to be their intermediary. Master Robert says he has evidence of his innocence. Let me look upon what he brings. If it is not enough to convince me, know you I will command he be held for the sheriff and executed, just as you request!"

As folk acknowledged that they must allow for at least the pretense of a trial, they stirred in uneasy acceptance. The sound of so many moving in so small a space was loud, indeed.

"Much better," the abbot told them as he reseated himself and looked up at Rob. "Master Robert, where is this proof you say you have."

Rob held out the coffer that he carried. "It lies within this box, my lord abbot, which has come to me from Lynn only this morn. Before I open it, I would have those within the crowd know that the box has not been in my hands since I departed my home, now two weeks past, long before this false charge was levied against me."

"Aye, it is no surprise you call the charge false as it's your neck we'd see stretched," a heckler threw back. "This is naught but mummery, meant to baffle us when we all know it was his man who went about our town offering outmarket grain to regraters."

"Who says it was my agent?" Rob retorted. Many were the calls that attested to this. Rob shook his head. "I'll call you all mistaken. My man never left the abbey walls that day, save for a few moments to aid in quelling the tumult that took place before this house's gates. So the whole monastery will swear."

It was Brother William, the porter, who stepped forward in response to this. "Aye," he called to the crowd. "Hamalin of Lynn passed by gateway but twice that day, once in and once out, all within a quarter hour's time, then not again."

This sent a wave of shock crashing through those who watched, but there was no easing in the animosity that touched their faces. Not enough had been said to change what they held as true. Again, Rob held up the coffer.

"I will repeat, what's stored in here has not been seen by me since my arrival in Stanrudde."

When another murmur of disbelief rumbled through those who watched, Lord Meynell stepped forward. "To this fact, I will swear," he called to the crowd in their own tongue, "for it was I who brought the coffer here from Lynn. Master Robert has not opened it since it came into his possession."

From the field's far end, a man raised his voice. "That is Temric Alwynason who speaks. I know him as a good man. If he says that this is true, it is."

This testimony from one of their own caused a subtle relaxation in the throng's hostility. Rob shot the nobleman a quick aside at the odd identification, but this was not the time for curiosity. "Brother Herbalist, will you bring me the key?"

Colin came forward, Rob's scrip extended before him. Where before there had been concern in his face, his eyes now gleamed in understanding and appreciation for the show that Rob was staging. It was one tradesman's appreciation for another's ability to sell.

Once Rob took the leather sack from him and knelt before the coffee with its key in his hand, Colin turned to face the townsfolk. "You know me, one and all, just as I know you, having given you posset and potion to ease your ills over all my years as apothecary of Stanrudde."

He waited as the crowd shouted out his name. Some among them threw thanks and greetings in his direction. To this, Colin nodded and smiled. "Now, I would have you heed my word when I affirm that Master Robert has had no access to his key. It has dwelt within these walls"—he pointed to the abbey's gate behind him—"whilst the grossier was locked safely in yon tower. Moreover, I would testify to this man's character, telling you that he is an honest man. This I know, for I raised him at my knee."

Again, a wave of sound flowed over the marketplace. The need for blood atonement was rapidly being replaced by frustrated confusion. If they could not blame Rob for what had happened, who, then, would pay for the damages that had been done to them?

In full view of all who watched, Rob threw open his chest and pulled his personal book from its depths. This was naught but a stack of sheepskin with holes punched along one side so a cord might be woven through them. Coming to his feet, he handed the thing to the abbot. "My lord abbot, will you tell them what it is you now hold?"

The seated churchman turned leaf after leaf, skimming the many entries scribed upon the skin. In the ensuing moments, the silence in the field grew. Rob could hear the sparrows chittering to each other in the abbey's garden. A man coughed, another cleared his throat. A raven flew overhead, its harsh cry echoing raucously against the abbey's tall stone walls. From a few lanes distant, a woman's voice was raised in song as she did her daily chores.

"I see a man's weekly notes," the abbot said at last, "marking sales he's made, names of men he's met and what business he has done with them. He marks how long his journeys are as he moves about pursuing his own endeavors. This cannot be a concocted piece. There are times when the hand that writes it is strong and clear, while in others exhaustion shows in the forming of the letters."

"Thank you, my lord." Rob reclaimed his book and opened it to the appropriate leaf. "Read aloud this entry," he said, pointing to where he wished the churchman to begin.

The abbot nodded. " 'On this day, the feast of our Blessed Virgin's assumption into heaven, my agent does report to me that wheat which I last year contracted to buy has, instead, been sold to another. For this the folk in that hamlet are not to be blamed, as the one who purchased it didst pass himself off as mine own man, the thief holding in his possession a facsimile of mine own seal.' "

Rob turned the leaf and pointed to another entry.

" 'On this the day of Saint John the Baptist, I have made another sorry discovery,' " the abbot read. " 'Upon arriving at the hamlet where Emond Sparewe is headman, I was informed that the one calling himself my new man had arrived before me, purchasing from them what I should have had. This is the second time the wily thief has struck, if it is indeed the same man, since these two events are separated by a great distance.' "

The quiet in the marketplace was absolute. Once

again, Rob turned a leaf and, once again, the abbot read. " 'On this St. Lazarus's day I have at last made the discovery for which I have so long awaited and am mortified at what I have found. Who would have—' by the Virgin!" the abbot cried out, leaving off his reading when he saw the name that Rob had scribed upon the skin.

"Say no more, for first I must explain," Rob told him, careful to keep his voice loud enough so that all within the marketplace would hear him.

He stepped forward to the dais's edge and spread his arms. "The grain that was stolen from me is the same seed that was sold illegally the evening before last, the same wheat that caused others to rampage. I tell you now, it was not I who sold this grain." His pronouncement was followed by the growing demand that he name the thief. As Rob held his hands up to beg for quiet, a new call pierced the air.

"Make way, make way for Katel le Espicer! Make way!"

Rob's vision blurred, so great was his astonishment. The abbot looked at him. Amazement lived in every line of the churchman's narrow face, but in Abbot Eustace's eyes there was the certainty of a divine Hand at work.

Katel, four men at his back, urged an almost staggering mount into the crowd. His progress was achingly slow as each person had to shift four others to make room for his horse to pass. The spice merchant wore a thick, fur-lined mantle atop a heavily embroidered traveling tunic done in shades of orange and blue. A thick gold chain lay atop his mantle, and rings gleamed atop his gloved hands. His gaze was caught on Rob, an expression somewhere between triumph and confusion settling onto his thick features.

"Master Robert." This was but a hiss, coming from the forefront of the crowd. Rob glanced down; Leatrice looked up at him. "I would testify as well," she begged him.

Her whispered words were drowned out by Katel's louder call. "What happens here?" It was the befuddled cry of one who has no other thought in the world than minding his own business.

Rob raised a hand to point at Katel. "There is the one who stole my grain. It is Katel le Espicer who released illegal *koren* onto your marketplace and caused the destruction of your town." Gasps rose from the crowd at this surprising accusation.

Katel threw back his head, his eyes wide in outrage. "Are you mad!" His voice carried to every corner of the field.

Despite his protest, those nearest to him closed around his horse. One man dared to reach up and take hold of the tired mount's bridle. "Leave go," Katel commanded him. "How can you give credence to such a charge? I am a spice merchant. What would I have to do with grain?" The man did not comply.

"What, indeed," Rob retorted. "What Master Katel did, he did for hatred of me. Years ago, he swore to see me hurt for a wrong he'd deemed I'd done him."

"So I would confirm," Arthur called, coming forward to join Rob. "Master Katel made Master Robert's apprenticeship like until hell with his torments."

Colin stepped to the edge of the dais. "I, too, would avow that Master Katel meant Master Robert only harm. Had not Master Walter already betrothed his daughter to you, Katel"—the monk eyed his friend's former protégé—"he would have seen your apprenticeship with him ended."

Katel sighed and looked around him, displaying naught but contrition for his observers. "I beg your pardons, Arthur, Master Colin, and, you, as well, Rob, for the sins of my youth. Would that I could return to the past and change what I did, but a misspent youth does not render a man a thief."

"Nay, why lower yourself to steal, when you have Theobald of Peterborough to do it for you," Rob retorted. "Here upon these parchments did I scribe the saga of your agent's deeds. Those at the hamlets where he struck described him well enough." He took his book from the abbot and turned to the appropriate entry. "Emond Sparewe says that the one who came was small of stature, delicate of feature, looking childlike despite his grizzled beard and hair. Today, I have learned that Katel le Espicer employs such a man."

As some in the crowed called out in confirmation of this description, Rob spoke on. "When I realized it was you who'd done this, I saw that the hamlets where your agent went were no farther than a day's ride from the fair you were attending at the time.

"Once you had what was mine, you waited for me to discover it was you who'd taken it, knowing I would come to confront you. And, when I came, you released the wheat in my name, knowing that folk would riot. You did not care that lives and homes would be destroyed by what you did."

A low thrum of hostility returned to the throng. Every man who stood upon the grassy stretch turned his head to see how their wealthy spice merchant would respond. Katel did not disappoint.

"This is an outrage!" he shouted. "I cannot believe that you think these good folk fools enough to believe what must certainly be crass forgeries. How long did it take some clerk to make those things for you? You are a wealthy man. How much did it cost you to create evidence against me?"

"I think me you are the wealthier," Rob retorted, touching Arthur's borrowed mantle and pin. "You gleam where I am drab."

"They are not forgeries," someone in the crowd shouted out. "We have all heard Father Abbot attest that what he looked upon was genuine enough. Do we not all accept that those skins of Master Robert's came this morn, brought here in a locked box from Lynn by one we all trust to speak the truth?" Rob's new supporter cried out to his fellow townsmen.

A flash of shock danced across Katel's bloated features. The spice merchant had been certain he'd succeeded in ending any threat from Lynn. If worry for Hamalin grew with Katel's reaction, it was in that instant that Rob forgave his mother for making him a bastard. He would not have had his proof to confront Katel if not for his father's other bastard, Lord Meynell.

"From Lynn?" one of Katel's servants cried out in surprise. "Master, I thought you said the council named Theobald to retrieve those ledgers." There was more than confusion in the man's voice; a touch of vindictive triumph lurked in his tone.

From behind the monks, Jehan the Wool Merchant limped out. He stood before the crowd, braced on his crutch. "The council set no such mandate," he cried out. "We sent no man anywhere, being content to wait for the sheriff's arrival."

This sent the noise level to a new and far more hostile tone. Folk began to call out that the spice merchant was guilty. One man cried out for hanging, but this time it was Katel he meant to see dangling.

"Papa!" The call pierced the thrum. "You must tell them none of this is true."

Rob scanned the crowd. A tall lad in his early teens, his hair a bright golden red, thrust his way through the throng toward the knot of folk around the spice merchant. He breathed in surprise. Johanna's son was Master Walter's image. With recognition came sudden pity and a strange sort of comradeship. Just as Rob's life had been destroyed when Ralph Attegreen refused to claim him, this boy was witnessing the end of the world he knew.

"He cannot, lad," Rob called to Johanna's son, then turned to look at the abbot. "My lord, someone should take that boy away from here. He should not have to witness this."

Even before the churchman turned to him, Lord Meynell sent a few of his men into the crowd. Folk parted to let them pass. When the soldiers took Katel's son by the arms, the boy thrashed against them. His resistance was futile; he was steadily borne toward the dais.

"Nay," the boy screamed, "you have no right to deny me. I will stand with my sire."

"He does not need you to sacrifice yourself for the wrong he has done," the abbot told the lad.

"I have done no wrong," Katel moaned, then continued with exaggerated drama. "Woe be it that a man is forced to reveal his wife's shame before his son!"

As Katel buried his face in his hands, his shoulders shaking as if he sobbed, the crowd grew quiet. It was quite the show Stanrudde's folk were getting this day, and they were enjoying it immensely. Rob glanced at Johanna's son. The boy had gone still between his captors. His face was so pale his freckles stood out as bright, tawny marks against his white skin. "Nay, Papa," he said, almost to himself. "Do not do this."

When Katel raised his head, there were tears in his eyes. "It is very difficult for a man to admit that his wife has made him a cuckold, but she has. I accuse the Grossier of Lynn of adultery with my wife. Years ago, they succumbed to their lust for each other. It is they who plot against me, not me against them."

Leatrice did not wait for an invitation. The pregnant maid stepped boldly past the soldiers and clambered onto the platform. "He lies!" she screamed to all those in the field. "His wife is no adulteress. Two years have I served in that household, and not once has Mistress Johanna strayed from her vows to her husband."

Katel wiped away the tears that touched his heavy cheeks. "Leatrice, lass," he said kindly, "I know you love your mistress well, but you can no longer shield her from the wrong she's done."

"She has done no wrong," the maid sneered. "It is you who stole the wheat and you, again, who hid it in the mistress's warehouse." She looked around her. "I vow to you all that this is true, may God strike me dead if it is not." She paused to draw breath and allow the Almighty to do as she dared Him.

More than a few who heard her glanced overhead for their Lord's reaction. When she continued to live, the muttering for Katel's death reawoke, gaining new vigor. A touch of worry appeared on the spice merchant's flaccid face.

"Leatrice," he said, new steel beneath his silken tones, "you know none of this is true. If the council believed any of it, they would be accusing me, while the captain of the guard stood by waiting to arrest me."

"What have I to fear?" the pretty maid retorted, holding her hands out. "Every soul here knows that the council has not yet had the chance to arrest you, as they are only now hearing the evidence, along with the rest of us."

That said, she scanned the crowd, throwing open her mantle to reveal the bulge Katel's child made within her. "If any man out there asks why or how I should know what I do, I will tell you all it is because I am the one who has shared Master Katel's bed these past two years. I know all his secrets, because he speaks in his sleep!"

"You lie!" Katel roared.

"Master, I can tolerate the sin no longer," called one of Katel's servants from behind him. "The lass speaks the truth about your plot. My pardon to all of you, neighbors," he called to those around him, "but I only discovered what he was about last even. Let me pass. I am for the spice merchant's house where I will gather my belongings and quit his employ."

The muttering folk parted to let him pass, then closed around the spice merchant once more. Katel could do no more than wrench himself around in his saddle to stare at the departing servant. Honest shock flowed over his face.

"Nor can we," shouted another manservant. "Better to starve than live in the house of the man who meant for Stanrudde to burn. So do we all feel." Once again, the throng made way for the remainder of Katel's household to pass.

"How can you lie like this?" he shouted at the man's back. "You know nothing of what I do."

Rob shook his head, suspecting these were the first truthful words Katel had spoken since entering the field. Ah, but they did him no good. Once more, simple men congealed into a mob, their threats rumbling from them, the volume rising swiftly upward until it became a muted roar.

Lord Meynell leaned down to speak to his men. "Take the boy into the abbey." It was a brusque command.

As the muted roar became a bellow of rage, horror turned to terror on Katel's face. "Nay!" he pleaded to those around him. "She lies! They all lie, having no evidence to support their words. They know nothing of which they speak!"

Truthful words, every one. They were also Katel's last coherent words. He squealed in terror as those around him grabbed him down from his horse.

"Nay!" his son howled in pain and tore free of those who held him. The lad flew into the crowd as Stanrudde's folk did to his sire what Katel had planned for them to do to Rob.

Panic exploded in Rob as the mob turned on the lad, intent on ending Katel's line. He could not let Johanna's son, Master Walter's grandson, die. He did not give himself time to reconsider before he leapt into the fray to save the boy.

Chapter Twenty-nine

The Priory of Ste. Anne
one hour past Sext
Ste. Blesilla's Day, 1197

Outside the prioress's office, sleet battered at the wooden walls. The wind howled at the door, demanding entry as it thrust icy fingers into the room. In response, the single branch of candles in the center of this bleak room cast swords of light toward that portal. The light made the floor tiles gleam, all green, rust-red, and white, then threw new brightness onto the priory's chair of state.

That piece was a homely item, untouched by paint or carvings, its tall back dwarfing its aged occupant. Rob watched the prioress, struggling to rein in his impatience. Now that Katel was dead, she had no choice but to release Johanna.

The churchwoman, dressed in the black habit and white wimple of her order, leaned out of the chair's depths toward him. Caught in the frame of her headdress, the old woman's skin was soft and loose, seemingly held to her bones by the web of wrinkles that crisscrossed her face. "You may not see her." This was a steely proclamation.

Rob stared at her, shocked by the harshness of her reply. The joy that had buoyed him against exhaustion slipped as his thoughts turned, trying to find some reason for so absolute a refusal. Certain she'd misunderstood his message, he tried once more. "My lady prioress, I have come to fetch Mistress Johanna back to Stanrudde. Her husband has died, and her son has been sorely injured. She must return to settle his estate."

The old woman's faded green eyes narrowed to slits as her mouth tensed. "She cannot leave the priory."

Rob's shock descended into anger. Johanna must be desperate for news of him and the outcome of their defense. Although her son, Peter, was being well tended by Colin and his master's wife, Rob knew the boy had a soul-deep need for his mother just now.

It had already taken him too long to get here as it was. First, all the councilmen had all wished to offer their apologies. Although he'd shrugged these off as swiftly as possible, the abbot had caught him next, wanting to speak to him about the stolen wheat. No matter how dearly Rob needed to find Johanna, he could not refuse the churchman, not after all the good the abbot had done for him. An hour had been eaten simply in polite refusals of the offer to join the churchman at his meat.

After that, he'd gone to Master Walter's house, seeking the servants who would know where Johanna was. They had been reluctant to open the gate to him, fearing he meant them harm for what their master had done to him. If more precious time had been wasted in soothing them, at long last one of them, Syward by name, had agreed to lead him here.

Now that he was here, this churchwoman was going to refuse to let him see Johanna? Nay, she would not. "I am telling you, I must see her," Rob demanded, his voice rising to a threatening tone.

The old woman didn't even flinch. "Have you trouble with your hearing?" she snapped back. "Listen again as I tell you: You may not see her."

Rob's fists clenched. Once again, someone was putting a barrier between him and the woman he named his. His emotions swelled past all his ability to control them. "You cannot deny me!" he roared.

"In that you are wrong," she retorted, her own anger making her words cool, rather than hot. "You are no one I know. If she were truly widowed or her son injured, the city council would send a messenger with whom I was acquainted to inform me of this. As you are neither her husband nor her kin, you have no right to demand anything in regard to her."

Rob caught his breath against the urge to cry aloud that he was, indeed, Johanna's husband. Were he to do this, the prioress would only call him liar. To her, and all the world, it was Katel who owned that title. Now that the churchwoman was set against him, he had no choice but to retreat and find another way to pry Johanna free of this place.

"That would be true were she a nun, but she is only a visitor." His voice softened. "Please, let her be the one to choose whether she will see me or nay."

"How dare you argue with me." The prioress rose from her chair, her face twisting in dislike of him. Once, she'd been a tall woman, now she almost bent in half. Grasping the walking stick from beside her chair, she used it to brace her on her feet.

"Once again, you are wrong," she spat out. "Johanna has chosen to retire from the world, seeking to find a closer relationship to her God, as well as forgiveness for her many sins. As a novice, she can have no visitors. Now, begone with you, granting me the courtesy of never returning. In case you have not that willpower, know that my gates will ever be barred to you." It was a cold dismissal.

These words tore through Rob, leaving him breathless with hurt. Last even, Johanna had mentioned she was convent bound. Had she had so little faith in their future that she'd given herself to God to escape Katel's plot? All the joy he'd known in anticipation of this reunion departed, leaving him drained and empty.

Heartsore, Rob stared after the churchwoman as she hobbled through the office's inner doorway. When she had stepped into the cloistered reaches of her domain, she pulled the door tightly shut behind her. It was but another statement of her intention to keep Johanna from him.

Depression tried to consume him. Of a sudden, Master Colin's ancient words rose in him. Doomed was the man who lacked the courage to ask after what was his heart's desire. Aye, and second chances were a rare thing, never to be refused. This advice was as good in affairs of the heart as it was in business matters.

Hope roared to life in him. If a married woman wished to enter a convent, it took her husband's permission to do so. Rob had never given his permission for Johanna to enter this convent; thus any vows she'd spoken were worthless. Ach, but that might take years to prove they were wed. What he needed was to twist Abbot Eustace into declaring them well and truly wed.

Hope doubled in strength. He had cartloads of wheat in the abbey's courtyard. Surely, if offered in trade, the churchman would find it in his best interest to move at all speed on this issue.

"Master?" Syward asked. "What will you do now?"

"Do?" The word left Rob in a gust of blazing determination. He turned on his heel and strode for the door. "I think me, I shall return to Stanrudde and speak to the abbot. This woman cannot stand between me and my wife."

The Priory of Ste. Anne
two hours past Terce
The feast of the Conversion of St. Paul, 1197

The storm that had arrived three days ago had finally exhausted itself, leaving in its wake naught but a still and icy cold. In an effort to trap what heat they could within the cloister, the nuns hadn't removed the shutters that shielded the walkway from the elements. Thus, what was usually an open-air passageway became a long, dim corridor, lit only by the tallow lamps.

This afternoon found Johanna sitting on one of the wooden benches that lined the wall. The majority of the sisters bore her company. It was their time for laboring, the nuns doing what women everywhere else did: plying their needles. In this case, the sisters worked on behalf of Stanrudde's abbey. Some of them produced grand embroideries; others sewed the simple garments given to those laborers who worked for that house.

Guided by the same rules as their brother house, labor was done in silence, or what passed for silence during the winter. From up and down the cloister's narrow length, women sniffed and coughed against the cold. It was in the hopes of restoring suppleness that they raised their fingers to their mouths, blowing the warmth of their bodies onto them. Behind it all, the rustle of fabric could be heard, along with the squeaking draw of thread passing through it.

Johanna's hands were cold as well, but her heart was by far the colder. She stared at the lengths of linen that lay across her lap: the unassembled body of a shirt. A threaded needle pricked its weave.

Why she'd been given sewing to do she did not know, nor did she care. Her tasks during her last stay at the priory had been to tutor the girls who came to learn the same lessons she had, so long ago. It mattered naught what she was asked to do, since she was beyond doing anything.

From the passageway's end came the steady tapping of Mother Sybil's walking stick. One by one, the nuns raised their heads to acknowledge their prioress's presence, all, that was, save Johanna. It would have taken more strength than she owned to do so.

Three days had passed since Katel brought her here. The morn after her arrival, that being Saint Blesilla's Day, Johanna's heart had burned with the certainty that she'd succeeded in saving Rob from Katel's plot. She'd been certain Rob, or someone, would come before day's end to fetch her back to Stanrudde.

By the dawning of the second day, her faith strained against doubts. Still, she assured herself that Rob's absence did not mean he was dead. Many were the circumstances that might have kept him from finding her here. By yesterday's dawning, depression had set its claws in her heart. Evil doubts tried to rise in her, whispering to her that he had abandoned her once again.

Johanna tried to slay them. Had she not failed him once by disbelieving when she should have kept her faith? She couldn't allow herself to make the same mistake twice.

Instead, she kept telling herself that, years ago, Rob had vowed to love her always and he had kept his vow. If he had promised that only death would keep them apart, then Katel must have won.

The tapping stopped before Johanna, and the hems of Prioress Sybil's black habit flowed into soft heaps onto the stone floor. Slowly, Johanna raised her head. The prioress stood as erect as possible, her nostrils flared, her mouth tense and harsh, as she looked on one who had been a former student.

How easily Katel had poisoned one who had known Johanna so well for so long. Three days ago, Johanna would have sworn the prioress would never have been taken in by Katel's lies. Now, in every word Mother Sybil uttered over how Johanna must find succor from her sin in prayer, Johanna heard herself convicted of adultery.

With a hurried glance over her shoulder, the old woman thrust out a hand, as if Johanna were once more a child, not a woman of one and thirty. "Come with me to the lady's chapel," the prioress commanded. There was a raw urgency to her words. "We must speak."

Johanna's heart sank. These lectures were unendurable in her present state of mind. Once Mother Sybil had her cornered, she'd ramble on and on about how Johanna must commit herself to God. Yesterday's rhetoric had been so intense, Johanna had finally agreed to don a novice's habit simply to win free of the old woman.

Ah, but on the issue of taking her vows, Johanna would not budge. She had no desire to be a nun. If Rob was dead, then she happily waited for the sheriff to find the grain and come to fetch her back to Stanrudde. It would be with joy, not fear, that she faced the hangman; Rob would be waiting for her in the hereafter. If Rob was not dead, but had abandoned her once more . . . Johanna stopped herself, not even wishing to think of this.

"Mother Sybil, could we speak another time?" she asked quietly.

From the courtyard beyond the dorter, came the sound of the gate bar being dropped. There was a subtle murmuring among the sewing nuns as they all aimed their gazes in that direction. The gates were opening, rather than the smaller, inset door through which most folk walked. This meant a substantial party was arriving.

"Nay, we must talk now, and you must go to the lady's chapel." This was a frantic demand.

"My lady prioress!"

Johanna looked in the direction of the man's quiet call. Their chaplain, a man almost as old as Mother Sybil, stood at the end of the hall. Beside him were two of the farm laborers that the priory supported.

In the courtyard, metal jangled. Horses whinnied as men called out for their mounts to halt. Female murmurs rose into a quiet trill of fear. Every one of the sisters stared at the woman they hoped could protect them from attack.

All save Johanna. She smiled. It was the sheriff, come at last. Forgetting that the prioress knew nothing of what Katel had plotted, she said, "Do not fear for me, my lady, I will go with him."

"You cannot!" the prioress shrieked as Johanna rose to her feet. This set all the other women to squawking and crying as well. "You cannot go with him. I will not allow it!"

"I know you mean well," Johanna told her, "but it is better this way."

It was with a light step that she started for the office. The churchwoman hobbled after her. "Your life and your soul will be the forfeit, Johanna. Do not do this!"

"Nay," she assured Mother Sybil, "it is not I who have sinned. No matter what my husband said, you must believe that I have done no wrong."

"No wrong!" The prioress caught her by the arm. However gnarled and twisted her fingers, the old woman's grip did not lack for strength. She pulled Johanna to a stop, then grabbed her by the other arm and shook her. "Did you not come here in unfit gowns and with your hair unbound and uncovered? How can you even contemplate this? Mother of God, but you were bruised!"

Johanna stared at the prioress, unable to make sense of her protest.

"Mother Sybil!" Sister Porter came streaking down the corridor, her black skirts and mantle flying out behind her. Usually harsh in temperament and stern in attitude, her plain face was twisted in terror. "Forgive me, but they threatened to batter down the door if I did not open it to them. There are so many of them!"

At fright in one usually so bold, panic erupted in the hallway. Women screamed and leapt to their feet. Needlework flew in all directions. Some turned toward the chapel in the hopes of sanctuary, while others went toward the dorter to hide under their blankets. In the chaos two tallow lamps fell, their crockery bowls shattering on the stone floor. Rendered fat oozed across the hard, cold surface.

The scattering women thrust past their prioress. Mother Sybil released Johanna to steady herself. With her mind yet fixed on the sheriff and death, Johanna once again started for the office.

"Catch her, Father," the prioress screamed to the chaplain and his aides at the head of the corridor. "Bring her to the chapel. We will bar the door and hold her there against them."

Chapter Thirty

Stanrudde
Late August, 1180

Johanna sat on the cot in her bedchamber. She hadn't moved since Helewise had placed her there, once she was fully dressed. With her head bowed, her hair flowed freely down around her, a curling red-gold curtain. She stared at her hands in her lap. Her fingers seemed a deathly white against the blue-gray of her wedding gown.

"Rob will come for me," she whispered to herself, her voice as pale and wan as she felt.

Today was *Dies Mala,* a day for bad luck. Even the priest at St. Stephen's had suggested the wedding date be changed. Ah, but Katel was in a great hurry to say his vows to her. Until he'd done so, Papa's will could not be read, or so the abbot had told him.

"Rob will come for me," she repeated to herself. Only these words stood between her and what she could not bear.

Papa had died three days ago. She tried to find tears to shed at that thought, but she'd cried so much of late, there was no moisture left within her body. With a shaken sigh, she forced her head to lift. This took every ounce of energy she owned.

Her father's bed still stood in its corner, just where it always had, but it no longer belonged to her sire. Katel ordered it be stripped, its linens, draperies, and mattress, burned. So, too, had her husband-to-be demanded that the woodwork be washed with the harshest of soaps, against the possibility that what felled Papa might be contagious.

Katel's new curtains were blue and gold. For vanity's sake, so were the blankets. It was a finer, softer mattress that filled the bed's box.

Where her father had been frugal and simple in his tastes, Katel was already spending her inheritance, even before he had it. In the last days, he'd bought himself three robes, all of them made of the finest fabrics, and sent the goldsmith into bliss by ordering four heavy chains for himself. He was sating his anger, repaying himself for having to take a bride who was no virgin. Still, if Katel continued at this rate, what her father had accrued over his lifetime would be gone within the year, leaving her impoverished as well.

Once again, desperation nipped at Johanna's heart. "Rob will come for me."

In her mind's eye she conjured Rob. He would appear out of the crowd at the moment the priest demanded any objections to her joining to Katel. Rob would call out that they were already wed, then take Katel's place before the church door. Together, they would share new, public vows to replace the private ones they'd traded.

"Rob will come," she assured herself. He had to come, else she would be trapped in a horrible place from which she would never escape. Beneath her depression there was the tiniest spark of anger at this thought.

"I think that he will not, little mistress," Helewise responded from the doorway. There was a quiet sadness in her voice.

Johanna stared up at her. It was time. She could see it in Helewise's eyes.

The need to run from Stanrudde, as far and as fast as she could, woke. It would do no good. No matter where she went, Katel would find her. Even if Katel no longer wanted her, he still meant to wed her. Only if they were married could he spend what Papa had earned.

Johanna tried to stand; she swore she did. "I cannot rise," she breathed. "You must help me."

The housekeeper came to sit beside her on the cot. Wrapping an arm around Johanna's waist, she pressed her former charge's head into her shoulder. For just a moment, Helewise rocked her, crooning just as she'd done when Johanna was a babe.

"Helewise!" Katel's impatient call rose from the courtyard floor. "Hie you and bring her down. It is time."

Glancing at the window, Helewise huffed in deep dislike. "How he slavers to get his hands upon what was once your sire's. God be praised he had sense enough to keep this a private affair, given that your father is barely cold." Johanna loosed a dry sob at this reminder.

Helewise pressed a kiss to her forehead. "You will survive this," she said softly. "You are my strong and fiery girl, who is always brave, where I feel weak and powerless. Vow to me that no matter what he does to you, you'll not let him take your spirit from you."

For some reason Johanna could not fathom, Helewise's words made that spark of anger in her grow. In its heat, she found, if not strength, then comfort. Even Helewise knew that this marriage to Katel was an awful, evil thing. How could her father have demanded that they wed, when Rob loved her?

Guilt shot through her at this thought. Her father was dead. It was wrong to think ill of him.

Her thoughts slipped to Rob. Better than any other on this earth, Rob knew the sort of man Katel was. How could he have left her to this fate?

Anger grew yet again. This time, its heat sent the illusion of power through her. Rob had better come. If he did not, she would never forgive him.

"God be damned," Katel sneered from the doorway. His new tunic was a maroon samite over which he wore a summer mantle of gray. A braided chain, loaned to him by the goldsmith until his own were finished, lay across his chest. Atop its clasp sat a great, round piece of amber to match his new tunic's golden trim. "Here you sit, Helewise, when I have called that it is time to leave. I will not tolerate such insubordination in my servants. You are dismissed. Be gone by week's end."

Johanna's back stiffened in surprise at this. Who did he think he was, telling *her* housekeeper that she must go? The anger in her expanded, eating up all that ached in her. By God, it felt good to hate. Her eyes narrowed as she plotted some way to see he paid for this.

"Such was my intention, Katel," Helewise replied. There was nothing of her usual show of meekness in her voice. "I will not be in a house over which you are the head."

Shock dashed across his features, then died. He shrugged. "We are in agreement, then. Now, bring her, or you'll not stay the night to witness her bedding." He turned on his heel and left the bedchamber.

Johanna stared at Helewise. "I hate him," she breathed with every ounce of passion that lived in her.

"That's my fiery girl," the housekeeper replied in proud approval. "Come, then." Together, they rose and descended to the courtyard.

The Priory of Ste. Anne
two hours past Terce
The feast of the Conversion of St. Paul, 1197

"Johanna!" The shout echoed from the prioress's office. "Where are you?"

New fire took life in Johanna's cold, dead heart. "Rob?" she breathed. "Rob!" she shouted.

As joy exploded within her, she lifted her heels. The priest and the farm laborers were holding the inner office door shut against Rob. She heard the crash of his shoulder against the panel.

"Let me by!" she screamed at them. "It's Rob!"

"You cannot go with him, child," the priest told her, yet straining to hold the door shut. "To do so is sin."

There was a brief pause in the battering. Footsteps tapped on the office's tile floor, receding away from the inner door. "Take her now," the chaplain cried. The two serfs released the door, then grabbed her by the arms.

"Rob," Johanna shouted as she writhed between them. "They are forcing me away!"

Although she fought them, the two men steadily dragged her down the corridor toward the chapel. She peered hopelessly over her shoulder. The office door was yet closed, with no sign of Rob. Ahead of her, the prioress was waiting at the chapel's door. Sister Porter had the bar in hand. "Do not let them keep me here!" she screamed to Rob.

One of them slipped in the spilled fat. As he stumbled, his grip loosened. Johanna wrenched her arm free and turned on the other. With every ounce of strength she owned, she kicked him. The man barked in pain and released her to grab his damaged leg.

Once again, there was a crash, and the old priest stumbled aside as the door flew open. Rob stepped into the corridor. He wore a thick brown tunic with a soft leather vest atop it. Despite his hooded cloak, traveling had left his hair badly in need of combing. His face was reddened with the cold, and he looked not to have slept for several days.

Never had he looked more beautiful to her. Johanna threw herself against him, latching herself tightly to him so no man could part them. He laughed and wrapped his arms around her, his embrace no less tight.

"I thought you were dead," she cried into the curve of his neck. His skin was warm against her lips. "When you did not come two days ago, I was certain I had failed."

"I was here," he said, lowering his head to press his lips against her cheek. "She would not let me see you."

Of a sudden, a touch of his lips on her cheek wasn't enough for her. Johanna turned her head and pressed her mouth to his. With her lips, she begged Rob to prove to her this was no dream, that he was, indeed, alive and that he had come for her.

Rob's arms tightened in response to her request. His kiss deepened until Johanna gasped against the heat he made in her. The joy of loving him, of desiring him, tumbled through her, feeding her starving senses and making her hungry for more. She rose slightly, letting her body flow into his in that wondrous unity. Rob drew a sharp breath at this, then his mouth slashed across hers. Johanna's knees weakened with desire.

"Do not!" the prioress screamed from the corridor's opposite end. "Stop, I say," the churchwoman shouted, the angry tapping of her stick growing louder with each breath. "Adulterers! Sinners!"

"Stop, sinners!" the priest echoed.

This only made Johanna hold Rob tighter. Adultery or not, she would let no one separate them. Not today, or ever.

Rob lifted his mouth from hers. "It is not adultery to kiss one's own wife," he replied calmly.

"Wife?" Johanna breathed. Astonishment was followed by spiraling pleasure. "It was true, then? What we did was no lie?"

"It was no lie," Rob told her, the gray of his eyes so soft with love for her that it took away her breath. "You, love, were a bigamist, but no longer. The one who pretended to be your husband has suffered the fate he planned for us."

Tears filled Johanna's eyes. This was no fantasy. She had succeeded, and Rob had not abandoned her.

"Deceiver! Her husband is Katel le Espicer." The prioress came to a halt alongside them. Behind her stood her chaplain. The menservants had thought the better of this whole matter and remained at the far end of the cloister corridor. "It was Master Katel who brought her here demanding that I give her sanctuary against you, who had beaten her. To do so, she committed herself to Christ."

"I did not!" Johanna retorted, shocked that the prioress would lie about such a thing.

"I did not think you had," Rob replied, his mouth lifting into a smile.

He stepped back far enough from her to retrieve a fold of parchment from his vest. This he handed to Mother Sybil. "You'll pardon me, my lady prioress, if I do not tarry to explain my rights to you. The abbot has done a much better job than I ever could."

As the prioress stared at the great disk of wax that hung from the skin by a thread, Rob placed his arm around Johanna and turned her toward the office door. His hand at the small of her back urged her to haste. They hurried through the small chamber into the courtyard.

Johanna stared in surprise at the dozens of mounted, armed men who filled the space between the priory's simple wooden walls. At the troop's head rode a knight, astride a tall brown warhorse. The nobleman wore full mail, the helmet and mail coif on his head obscuring almost the whole of his face.

"Are you so wealthy that you can afford to hire an army?" she asked in awe as Rob swept her toward the only riderless horse in the courtyard. A pretty chestnut color, it was as tall as the knight's destrier, but lacked the heaviness of muscle—a merchant's mount, not a warrior's.

Rob shook his head and laughed. "Nay, not at all, at least I wasn't yesterday. When we combine our estates, the matter may be different. Come love, I'd be gone from here before the prioress finishes reading what lies in that missive."

He grabbed her by the waist and lifted her into a sideways seat on the saddle, then mounted behind her. Johanna caught her arms around his waist. Pulling herself into the shelter of his arms, she rested her head against his shoulder.

When the nobleman saw they were mounted, he gave a call that set his men into motion. Saddle leather creaked, harnesses jangled. Horses danced as they turned. As each man exited the priory's gate, he spurred his horse to its fastest speed. Rob turned his horse and followed the other men out of reach of the Church.

The quick pace they kept made all conversation impossible. When they neared the crossroads, the party slowed to a walk. Johanna looked up at Rob. "We are not married, then?"

If there was disappointment in her at this, so, too, was there a touch of relief. Had her marriage with Katel been a lie, then her son was now a bastard. She did not want that title for her child when neither she nor Peter had any choice in his creation.

"Abbot Eustace believes we are," Rob replied. "However, it may well take a hundred pounds and years of bickering among churchmen to verify it.

Against the possibility he was wrong, the abbot could not command the prioress to release you, had you, indeed, offered yourself to God. But I could not tolerate the thought of being separated from you for another day."

"Ah," she breathed in pained understanding. Her thoughts turned, seeking a way to shield her son from the sting of bastardy. "Why spend the coin on proving us married? If Katel is dead, then I am a widow in the eyes of the world. Let us stand before the church door and repeat what we said so long ago."

Aye, this would shield Peter from the world, but only until her death. If she and Rob had children between them, they, not Peter, would inherit what her father and Rob left them. That was, unless Rob adopted Peter as his own.

Johanna sighed. As much as she loved Rob, she couldn't imagine him doing so, not after all the hatred Katel had shown him. Nor could she blame Rob for it. What man didn't want to put his own children first?

"Love," Rob said, glancing down at her, "if that is your will, then I bow to it, but we are already wed. I have waited sixteen years to be with you. I crave the simple joys of marriage. I would eat at a table with you sitting beside me as a wife does her husband. I would retire at night with you, sleep beside you, then wake in the morn to find you yet there. Will you bid me wait until the day we again trade vows before you grant me this?"

His words shot through her, reminding her of the pleasures she'd known both in his arms and in their few joinings. Her heart took to racing in excitement while searing heat filled the core of her being. Wait another day? She did not wish to wait another hour. A deep shiver shot through her.

Thinking her chilled, he shifted to pull her closer so he might tuck his fur-lined mantle around them both, cocooning them against the day's snapping cold. Their nearness only fed her longing for him. Johanna turned her head on his shoulder, needing to feel his skin against hers. Ever so lightly, she pressed her lips to his throat, drawing her mouth upward until she kissed the spot just below his ear.

Rob drew a swift breath in reaction. "May I take that as a sign that you'll not deny me?" His voice deepened with the passion she made in him.

"You may, indeed," she breathed into his ear.

"Dear God, but we still have hours to go. I vow I will die if you intend to do this all the way home. God be praised. My brother has come to rescue me."

Johanna straightened, shocked from her lust by his words. The knight who headed the troop now rode alongside them. She looked from the nobleman to Rob, then frowned in confusion. "You have no brother. You were Ralph Attegreen's only son."

The smile Rob offered her was chagrined. "Nay, love, I am bastard born."

"You are not a bastard!" she retorted in old habit.

He shook his head. "Aye, I am and so I have known since my mother's death. That I did not wish to acknowledge it does not make it untrue."

"Apparently, this is a common experience among bastards," the knight commented with some humor. His English was without accent.

Rob laughed. "Johanna, this is my half brother, Richard, Lord Meynell, as kind and caring a man as I will ever know."

"Or, lend money to," Lord Meynell replied. There wasn't much to see of the man's face beneath the concealment of his metal coif and his helm, but Johanna caught the glint of gold in his brown eyes. Then, he smiled at her, setting deep creases to either side of his mouth.

"He has your smile!" Johanna cried in startled recognition.

"Nay," the nobleman said with a quiet laugh, "we

share our father's smile, as do all the rest of our half brothers. I am glad to meet you, Johanna of Stanrudde." His gaze shifted to Rob. "Now that we are at the crossroads, I have come to bid you fare-thee-well, not to see you again until the summer months."

Rob nodded to him. "I will offer you another round of thanks for all you've done and bid you God speed and good journey," he replied. "Have you decided yet?"

"On whether I will tell the others of your existence?" The nobleman cocked his head to the side to peer at his half brother around the helmet's nose piece. "Mayhap, I will keep you to myself for a time. Were Rannulf to get wind that he was connected to a man of substance, he'd be in a flurry to drain your coffers dry, borrowing against the building he's doing at Upwood."

Lord Meynell laughed at this private jest, then turned his gaze on Johanna, once more. "Again, Mistress Johanna, I am glad to have made your acquaintance."

"And, I yours," she replied, awed at discovering Rob's noble connections.

The nobleman set his spurs to his brown steed to join his men, who were already filing to the left at the crossroads. In a few moments, they were gone from sight. Stanrudde lay directly ahead, but yet a long ride distant.

As Johanna settled herself more comfortably in the saddle before Rob, he began to talk of his life since their parting. She tried to concentrate, but her thoughts kept drifting to her son. How could there be happiness for her when it meant shame and heartbreak for her child?

Chapter Thirty-one

Stanrudde
an hour past Sext
The feast of the conversion of St. Paul, January, 1197

There was no one waiting before the abbey when Johanna and Rob rode past its gate. Teased into it by Rob's tale of Katel's death at the hands of the crowd, she glanced around the market field. As she shuddered at so horrible a fate, she reminded herself of how far reaching the evil of Katel's plot had been. Theobald now occupied the lower level of Stanrudde's tower, charged with the murder of Rob's agent, Hamalin. Hamalin had fought to keep his life, injuring Theobald and killing Watt.

She sighed and stared at the houses as they made their way up the coopers' lane toward the chandlers' enclave. This morning, the workshop windows were open. Tradesmen and their apprentices were hard at work turning wood and metal into barrels. Stanrudde's folk once again safely trod their lanes. Children shouted and raced down the alleyways, dodging the slop thrown by maids from the upper windows of houses.

Johanna stared at her father's tall house as Rob turned his mount into the courtyard. This day, the split stones that made up its walls sparked a glassy black in the fierce and frigid winter sun. The worry and sorrow in her deepened. Too much of the past was bound to this house, and she wanted no more to do with it.

Ah, but there were things to be attended to before she could bid this part of her life adieu, not the least of which was finding some way to resolve Peter's future. Together, she and Rob had decided to sell the house and the spice trade, as one. Given the right man, its vitality could return. So, too, did she need to hire an agent to look after her sire's properties, as the majority of them lay within Stanrudde's walls.

Rob dismounted. Johanna slipped off the saddle into his embrace, her arms clasped about his neck. As she settled against him, her hunger returned, bringing with it the need to renew her acquaintance with his body. The fire that woke in her helped to ease her worries a little.

Rob caught her mouth with his. Johanna did not deny him. As his kiss deepened, sending those wondrous waves of heat through her once again, his fingers worked to remove the nun's wimple that covered her head.

"Blasphemer!" The man's deep and outraged cry echoed around the enclosed courtyard. "Do you dare to kiss that holy sister?"

Johanna tore away from Rob and whirled in his arms to face this new challenge. "I am no nun," she protested even before she knew who it was that would now accuse them of wrongdoing.

At the corner of the forebuilding stood a small monk, face wizened and hair as white as snow. She stared for a moment as the years peeled from the man's face. "Master Colin," she cried in recognition.

"Why is it none of you can remember that I am now a brother?" the former tradesman complained with a quick laugh. "Arthur, I can understand, for he has never had the best of memories. But, you, Johanna, you are sharper than that."

Johanna smiled at his jesting chide. "My pardon,

Brother Colin. What are you doing here?" she demanded of him.

"Among other things, I have been waiting for you," he replied, taking a few steps toward her, then stopping. Beneath thick white brows, concern flickered to life in his dark eyes. "I would speak to you if you will allow it."

"Why would I not?" she asked, surprised.

"I had the notion you were not so fond of me."

The corner of Johanna's mouth lifted slightly. "Mayhap, I was not for a time." It was a hesitant admission of the hate she'd borne for him. "Things changed recently."

The old monk closed the space between them to catch her hand. Holding her fingers tight in his dry, hard palm, he looked up into her face. Reflected in his gaze she saw the knowledge of the wrong he and his sire had done her. But, where it had ceased to ache in her, it yet rankled deeply in him.

"It was to protect you that Walter did what he did," he said, the words tumbling past his lips. "He feared for what would happen, were he to allow your marriage to Rob stand. You must understand, Rob was but ten and seven and did not yet own the mastery of his trade. Even if you'd been married before the church door as is mete, Ketal's sire would have fought it. If your union held, he would have set himself to destroying the trade, thinking to revenge himself for this betrayal. You, Rob, all Walter had built would have been gone." The words were a plea for forgiveness and understanding. "He was dying. There was time for nothing else."

She freed her hand from his, then caught the old man's face in her palms and pressed a kiss onto his creased brow. "How can I not forgive you, when you and Papa meant only my good?" This she offered him, even though by forcing her marriage to Katel, her father made Peter a bastard.

Brother Colin's eyes glistened as a tiny smile touched his mouth. "You cannot know how we hurt over what we did that day. Thank you, lass, for my sake and your sire's. You have taken a great burden from my shoulders." With a small smile, he freed her hand and stepped away. "Now, I must return to my pots and stills. Go you within. Your son has been impatiently awaiting your arrival."

Johanna blinked in surprise at this. "Peter? What is he doing here?"

Rob reached out to embrace her from behind, drawing her a step backward until she leaned against his chest. "He was hurt trying to defend Katel from the crowd, love."

With a gasp, Johanna turned in his arms. "You didn't tell me," she cried out, pushing away from him. A touch of anger woke in her. "How could you not tell me!"

Rob shrugged and shook his head. "I saw no need to worry you, when he is so greatly improved."

"He is fine, Johanna," the monk said, laying a calming hand upon her shoulder.

Johanna did not stay to be consoled. Rushing to the forebuilding, she flew up the stairs. A child's laughter echoed to her from the hall, followed by Peter's distinct hoarse tones of amusement. Worry and anger warred with relief. If her son could laugh, all could not be as bad as she was imagining.

She stopped in the hall door. A goodly number of the household servants were within the room, presently at loose ends because of their master's demise. Among them were others she did not know. No doubt these were Rob's servants. There was something familiar about the tall, golden-haired man who stood at the hooded fireplace with his back to the room.

At the hall's center a lad of ten or so with curling brown hair was turning a slow circle. A length of yarn trailed from the child's hand. Leaping and pouncing,

Katel's cat was following the trailing string through the rushes.

Peter was seated on a stool to one side of this arena of activity. A great purple bruise marked one of his eyes, another one, this more yellowish than purple, lay along his neck. His left arm hung across his chest, supported by a sling. He was smiling as he watched the cat play.

"Peter," she called as she strode across the room to kneel before him. Lifting a hand, she ran her fingers through his curling hair and tried to smile. Words failed her. Not only had her son been attacked along with his father, he'd witnessed his sire's death.

The previous moment's laughter died from his brown eyes, leaving only deep sadness in its place. "Mama," he cried softly, "Papa is dead."

"I know," she replied, reaching out to embrace him.

He laid his head against her shoulder. "I tried to stop them, but I couldn't." There was such helplessness in his voice.

Tears touched Johanna's eyes. "Ah, sweetling, you mustn't blame yourself. Even if you had succeeded in preventing the folk from what they meant to do, you could not have saved your father from his fate. He did a terrible thing."

"I know," he managed to get out in a choked voice. Peter's shoulders shook as he fought back a sob. "Mama, I hate it here in Stanrudde."

"I've been telling him he should come to Lynn, mistress," the lad with the string said as he came to squat beside Peter's stool. "Folk are friendly in Lynn," the child assured them both, his green eyes solemn.

"I want to go," her son said, his bitter tone only partially hiding the pain in his voice.

Johanna leaned away from her son. "But what of your apprenticeship?"

Peter threw back his head in aching defiance. "My

master no longer wishes to keep me. He says it will be bad for business."

The blond stranger came to crouch down at Johanna's opposite side. "There will be plenty of masters willing to take you in Lynn," he said, "especially when they learn you are from Master Robert's household."

Johanna glanced at the man, then caught her breath and looked again. "Arthur?" she cried in surprise.

Arthur's green eyes sparked with pleasure. His lips bent within the confines of his thick blond beard. "It is good to see you again, Johanna. I would have you meet my son, William." He nodded to the boy at her other side. "He is Rob's apprentice." With a groan, he lifted himself back to his feet. "I am not the man I once was," he complained, shaking the cramps from his legs.

Johanna stared up at him. "You are married?" She wasn't certain why this should startle her so. For a second time, she glanced from Arthur to his son. There was very little to name them father and son, save for the color of their eyes. Will offered her a shy smile, then rose to again play with the cat.

"Did I not tell you he was well?" Rob called from the hall door. "It is a malaise of the heart that is plaguing your son just now." His voice gentled as he took the space Arthur had vacated to Johanna's right. "And, so he should feel. I have told Peter how deeply it hurt me to lose the man I believed was my father when I was naught but Will's age. So, too, have I told him the tale of his grandsire's generosity and love for that orphaned lad."

Peter sat back on his stool and rubbed at his eyes, then wiped his nose on his sleeve. "I have thought over your offer, Master Robert." Even as he spoke, the corners of his mouth were pulled downward by the same weight that tugged on his heart. "If my mother chooses to go to Lynn with you, then I will, as well. I have not yet decided on the other."

"What offer is this?" Johanna glanced from Peter to Rob.

"Were you worried over your Peter's state?" A tiny smile touched his mouth as his gray eyes warmed to nearly blue. "Fie on you, love," he chided. "Was not your father like unto mine own? If Peter wills it, I will make him my son, and so I have vowed to him." His expression sobered as he reiterated his promise.

Johanna shifted to sit on the floor as she looked in astonishment at the two men she most loved. "You would do this for Katel's son?" Her words were but a soft breath.

Rob shook his head, the rawboned lines of his face filled with gentle chastisement. "Nay, I do this for your son and for Walter of Stanrudde's grandchild."

So great was her love for Rob that Johanna thought her heart might burst. Beyond speech, she reached out to embrace him. This was the man to whom she was married. This was her husband, who owned in his heart the same generosity of spirit her father had known.

With that thought, the wrong that had been done all those years ago was made right. The last of the bonds that had so long trapped Johanna in her misery broke. She gave thanks to God that she had survived to know this moment, for all that came after would be happiness.

Chapter Thirty-two

Stanrudde
two hours past Vespers
The feast of the conversion of St. Paul, 1197

As Rob closed the door on the servants in the hall, the bedchamber fell into an instant dimness. Still, the teasing and the laughter penetrated the thick wooden panel. It was against the possibility that they meant to take their jests to a more physical level that Rob set the bar.

Carrying a tallow lamp, Johanna crossed to the room's far end, where a fresh night candle had been left on its iron stand. Once the candle took light, she set the lamp on one of the two clothing chests that sat behind it. Between the two there was enough light to chase the thicker of the gray shadows into the corners. As she turned back into the room, she laughed again.

"I am overwhelmed. I vow my head reels against such a fabulous tale," she cried aloud.

Once Peter had gone to seek his rest in the kitchen, she'd heard the story of these last days from every participant and all possible angles. It had stunned her to learn it hadn't been Wymar who'd carried her message, but Syward, who'd done it as a boon for Watt.

But the strangest of all was Leatrice's bold lie. "Speaks in his sleep, indeed! In all his life, I doubt Katel once uttered a coherent word whilst he was at his rest. That cheeky lass was but repeating what she'd heard us say in the tower."

"Then, it is fortunate we told the truth," Rob said, standing before the bed as he removed his mantle and his vest. These he hung over the clothes pole at the bed's head, then worked at loosening his brown tunic.

"This is different." He touched the blue and gold curtains that draped the bed. "I remember the curtains as being red and yellow."

"Katel bought new before our—" She stopped herself, not willing to say "marriage." She was wed to Rob and only Rob. "—after my father died."

"Ah." He pulled off his tunic. Dressed only in his shirt and chausses, he sat upon the mattress to loosen the cross-garters that held his knee-high boots to his calves. Once he'd set aside his boots, he smiled at her, then patted the mattress at his side. "Come and sit with me."

New shyness took root in Johanna. Of a sudden, she saw herself for what she was: a woman of one and thirty, old enough to be grandam. Yet, despite her many years, she had little experience in bedding. What if Rob laid with her, then was sorry he had committed himself to her?

"Nonetheless, Johanna did as he bid, easing into place beside him. He caught her hand, lacing his fingers between hers. "This is how married folk do upon retiring," he said, an almost awed tone to his voice.

Johanna looked at him, then sighed at herself and her silly fears. This was her Rob, the same boy she had loved and the man she did love. She raised a hand to catch a strand of his hair. When she pressed it into a dark curl upon his cheek, he smiled at her. She traced her fingertips downward from the high lift of his cheekbone until she smoothed the narrow line of his beard, then raised her hand to trace the outline of his lips.

Fiery lights came to life in the cool gray color of

his eyes. "I will sit here all this night, if you but promise never to stop touching me," he said softly.

Once again, the shyness struck. She drew a sharp breath against it. With what-ifs tangling in her brain, she let her hand fall from his face, then chewed nervously on her lower lip.

Rob's brow creased in concern. "Did I say something amiss?"

"Nay," Johanna said, her worry growing. "Nay, I am just now realizing how much time has passed between us. Rob, I am no longer the girl you remember."

Concern eased from his face to be replaced by a mummer's expression of skepticism. "Old, are you? Show me the gray that streaks your locks."

His teasing eased a tiny bit of her worry, and Johanna laughed, just a little. She freed the nun's wimple from her head, then tossed aside the plain head covering. "Do you find any?" she asked, tilting her head toward him so he might view her braids.

"How can I tell when your hair is plaited so tightly?" he retorted.

Her smile grew as she loosened her hair until it flowed freely around her. Once again, she tilted her head toward him. "Now, do you find any?"

"Nay, not yet, but I am not finished searching." Rob brushed her hair over one shoulder, thus baring her nape.

"What are you doing?" she asked as he turned her head away from him.

"I am looking on the underside of your hair for the gray you say you own." He touched his lips to the sensitive skin of her nape.

Johanna shivered against this caress. Heat returned to life in her belly. "Do you find any?" she asked, her words breathless in what he did to her.

"Not yet," he replied, his breath warm against her skin as he kissed his way down to the collar of her white undergown. Johanna melted at his play. Her hand fisted into the blankets against what was both torment and pleasure.

"Perhaps, if I saw your hair displayed against a white gown, instead of this gray one, I could better see the truth," he said between gentle nips along the curve of her neck.

"But, of course," she managed in a trembling voice. The heat within her was moving rapidly upward, nearing boiling. "How sensible."

Her fingers tore at her cord belt. Where it went, she didn't care. Rob ceased his torment to loosen the tie at the back of her gray novice's overgown. Johanna came to her feet and pulled the garment over her head, then tossed it onto the ground. Her undergown, which lacked any tie or lacing to give it shape, was unbleached linen, not truly white.

"Nay, that will not do," Rob said, shucking his shirt. "I need something whiter still, else I might mistake gold for gray."

Johanna stared at him in admiration. His shoulders were broad, his arms well muscled against an active way of life. The night candle's golden glow outlined the strong planes of his chest.

"How white?" she asked, her voice choked against her growing need to touch him.

Heat darkened the skin along his cheekbones. He held out a hand to her. "I remember that your skin is very white," he said. His voice roughened with the same passion for her that she felt for him.

Johanna swallowed as what burned in her destroyed all reluctance. Age and inexperience were forgotten as she tore off the loose undergown, taking her chemise with it. It was without shyness or shame that she stood before him.

The cool gray of his eyes warmed as he looked at her. Reaching out, he lay a fingertip to her shoulder, then traced a line downward to draw a circle around the peak of her breast. Johanna's knees shook, her eyes closed. Down his finger went, past her waist. She loosed a soft cry and braced her hands upon his shoulders to keep herself upright. As he followed the curve of her abdomen, she leaned forward, resting her brow against his head as she enclosed them in the red-gold curtain of her hair.

His finger stopped at the place where her leg met her hip. He leaned forward just far enough to catch the tip of her breast in his mouth. Crying out, Johanna threaded her fingers into his hair, urging him to do more.

At her response, he moved his hand along the curve of her thigh until he brushed his palm against the most private of her places. A new and deeper trembling started in the core of her being, then shot through her, until she feared she'd fall. With a gasp, she pulled away from him.

"Do I displease?" he asked. The amusement in his tone said he knew he did not. So did what strained at his chausses.

"No more teasing," she begged softly. "Love me, Rob."

"Always," he promised, rising to discard his final garment.

Once more, her heart took flight as she gazed on him. How had the boy she'd loved turned into such a beautiful man? There was no flaw on him. If his frame was large and powerful, it was only gentleness that radiated from him. She knew she would find comfort and protection in the shield of his arms. What a fool she was to worry. He was hers, and they had sixteen years of wrong to redress.

Reaching out, she clasped her hands behind his neck, then pulled herself against him. He made a sound deep in his chest as he embraced her. The feel of his skin against hers was wondrous. His shaft lay between them, hard and more than willing to do as she bid.

She rubbed herself against him, gasping as she teased them both. This time, the noise he made sounded more like a moan. He caught her face in his hands, tilting her head up to his. His mouth took hers, his lips slashing across hers.

Johanna let the passion in his kiss feed the aching emptiness in her, then begged him for more. She stroked her hands down his back to his hips, holding him tightly to her as she moved in tiny motions against him. He gasped against her mouth.

It happened so swiftly, she wasn't certain how he'd done it. In the next instant, she lay beneath him atop the bedclothes. His mouth was scorching a path down her throat, then lower still, until he suckled at her breast. With a sharp cry, she arched beneath him.

Once again, his fingers came to rest atop her nether lips, stroking at this secret place of hers. Of their own volition, her hips lifted, and she could not catch her breath. Between what he did with his mouth and the great stabs of pleasure his fingers were sending through her, Johanna was certain she would die. She cried out, again and again.

He shifted atop her. In fierce joy, she softened beneath him, opening her thighs to urge him to make himself one with her. The heat of his shaft seared her, but when he lay his mouth atop hers, his kiss was gentle, even placid.

Johanna frowned. It was his passion for her she wanted now. She caught his face in her hands and took his mouth with hers, as he had done to her.

He groaned at this. With that, she lifted her hips and demanded that he give her what she so needed. He thrust forward. Johanna cried out as they were joined, in pleasure mingled with just a little pain.

Lifting his mouth from hers, he kissed her brow,

then rubbed his thumb across the fullness of her cheek. "Have I hurt you?"

"Nay," she growled, "but I will hurt you if you persist on dallying when we have other matters at hand."

This made him laugh, and he began to move slowly within her. What pain there'd been was soon destroyed by the wondrous sensations his slow and careful motions were waking in her. The intensity of it grew into a burning urgency. She lifted her hips, begging him to move faster.

When he ignored her, she did it again, thrusting herself down on his shaft. This sent so strong a thrill through her that she did it again. And again.

The next time she moved, Rob met her thrust with his own. She cried out against the great bubble of feeling that was trapped within her. Her legs clutched around Rob's hips, her arms wrapped around his back.

Rob's breathing grew ragged and hoarse as the force of his thrusts increased. Pressing his mouth to her ear, he told her how no one save she could please him. Then, he told her how much he loved her.

What filled her burst with his words, until it flooded her with sensations so glorious Johanna cried out in the wonder of it. Still, he moved within her, each thrust more urgent than the last. Pleasure grew. At the very instant she thought she could bear it no longer, Rob cried out. Johanna swore she felt his seed as it entered her.

Yet gasping against his exertions, Rob relaxed atop her to kiss her lips, her cheeks, her brow, until he finally nuzzled at her ear. Adrift on a hazy sea of spent passion, Johanna shifted to better accommodate the weight of his body atop her. Oh, but there was glory to be had in lying so with him. She could feel his heart beating against hers, as if they shared but one.

Johanna awakened, deep in the night. Her head was pillowed on the bulk of Rob's shoulder; his arms were around her as he held her close to him. She listened to the deep, even rhythm of his breathing.

Her arm was atop the blankets. The interior of the bed was now breathlessly cold. Tucking the bedclothes over her, she shivered. They lay so close that this involuntary movement sent the wondrous sensation of her skin against Rob's shooting through her all over again. Johanna smiled. Rob was right. There was great joy to be had in sleeping with the one you loved.

Awe filled her. To think, this would be hers to own for all the days of her life. Turning her head slightly, she pressed a kiss to his arm.

Rob drew a sudden breath at her caress, then shifted and stretched. Bending his head, he kissed her shoulder, then stroked his hand down her arm until he could lace his fingers between hers. "I knew it would be marvelous to wake next to you. Dear God, but I love you. How have I existed for all these years without you at my side?"

Johanna smiled. "You mean in your bed." It was a soft taunt.

Rob raised himself on an elbow to look over her shoulder at her. His face was all shades of gray, the lift of his cheekbone lighter than the line of his beard. She could feel more than see the frown that touched his brow. "I want you for deeper reasons than to warm my bed."

She rolled onto her back to look up at him. "I know that." Raising a hand, she smoothed her palm down the strong line of his chest. "It's just that at this very moment, I cannot think of any better reason for wanting you. Touch me again," she begged him quietly, "and let me touch you until I am sated with the feel of you."

Rob's smile was a gleam of white. "How long do you think that might take?"

"No longer than three days," she replied.

"Three days? Why so short a time?"

"Because," she replied, running her fingertip down the length of his torso to where his shaft already thickened in response to her play, "that is how long it will take the tailor to make me a new gown."

She closed her hand around that part of him that was most male. As he caught his breath at what she did, she spoke on. "I have no clothing here save that novice's gown. Somehow, I cannot think you want the world to watch as you debauch a poor defenseless nun."

His laugh was low and deep. "Three days? Without a stitch of clothing to your name?" he asked again, easing back down alongside her. His fingers came to trap the peak of her breast.

It was her turn to gasp. "Unless you would buy me something from the old clothes seller." It was a weak retort.

"My wife does not wear another's castoffs." He lowered his head to nuzzle her ear. "Do you think if I pay the tailor more than he asks, he'll stretch it to four?"